GW00733386

THE LANES

David Van Otter

To Jasper Binns

David Van Otter.

dopLin

First published in July 2017 by
Doplin Books, Brighton

Find us on Facebook

Production Editor: Xanna Eve Chown

Copyright: David Van Otter © 2017
Cover photograph by the author

The right of David Van Otter to be identified as the author of this Work has been
asserted by him in accordance with the Copyright, Designs and Patents Act 1988.

All rights reserved.

The moral right of the author has been asserted. All characters in this publication
are fictitious and any resemblance to any persons, living or dead, is purely
coincidental. No part of this publication may be reproduced or transmitted in any
form or by any means, electronic or mechanical, including photocopying, recording
or any information retrieval system, without prior permission, in writing, from the
publisher. This book is sold subject to the condition that it shall not, by way of
trade or otherwise, be lent, resold, hired out, or otherwise circulated without the
publisher's prior consent in any form of binding or cover other than that in which it
is published and without a similar condition including this condition being imposed
on the subsequent purchaser.

ISBN-13: 978-1544049229
ISBN-10:1544049226

For Xanna

'It were a piece of vain flattery to pretend that this work (…) entirely contents us; that it is not, like all works of genius, like the very Sun, which, though the highest published creation, or work of genius, has nevertheless black spots and troubled nebulosities amid its effulgence, – a mixture of insight, inspiration, with dulness, double-vision, and even utter blindness.'

Thomas Carlyle

'Cast forth thy Act, thy Word, into the ever-living, ever-working Universe: it is a seed-grain that cannot die; unnoticed today it will be found flourishing as a Banyan grove (...) after a thousand years.'

Thomas Carlyle

CHAPTER ONE

He came into a flat land of deserted lanes. Some of these lanes, especially the turnings, were rather peculiar, but in indefinable ways – you might say a certain wistfulness lurked about them, or that they were waiting for something rather than leading anywhere. Walls stood, and sometimes crumbled a little, on obsolete boundaries, curving round the corners, grey faced and nondescript except that they stood dumb witness to their passers by and were quietly insistent in teasing each traveller with all the veiled possibilities of quaint histories. Histories from which arose always a silent and secret sadness. Though the sun shone, a thin veil of suspicion was never entirely relinquished in this place, which in the end always revealed less than it hinted at, and kept its puddles in dark ditches whatever the weather. The questioning bellow of a hidden cow might be listened to attentively by leaf hoppers and lace wings and horse flies, in their private green places, and the smell of distant manure might be just appreciable on the cool air, but agriculture, though present and frequently visible, was somewhat at odds with the true spirit of the place.

Johnson was brought to a halt on the middle arch of the stone bridge by the sight of a crow picking an unwary minnow from the sluggish stream. He watched the whisking up of the fish's last moments. Wriggling in the beak, a tiny silver life flapped off with. Most ordinary people would perhaps have been thrilled and dismayed at the sight and moved to ponder on the doom each may suddenly be heir to, and to think perhaps that which we seek and expect might not come to pass after all. It was impossible to know, however, what Johnson felt, for Johnson was not an ordinary fellow and did not have an expression which could be read.

A mile further on where three ways met, a house rose white with little pointed windows behind its brick wall upon a bank. The gate said 'The Laurels' and hollyhocks jostled poppies cornflowers and delphiniums along the soft slabbed path to the door. He stepped up the bank and looked over the wall at what he could see in the garden: trees, a little lawn, bay and box, an outhouse, more and lower hedges, a dovecote, distant beanpoles the glint of a greenhouse. The place was perfectly still, no dog lurked or slept here. There were beehives however – whose denizens noisily patrolled the effulgent flora – and unseen hens clucked and scratched somewhere near. Johnson entered through the gate and made a furtive and wary progress behind things, slipping round apple trees and the wood pile, digressing as if he sought to smell out a scent, but with ever a weasel eye upon the windows.

It could be here. Yes, it might be very well in such a place that he would find her. For he was as certain as he could be that he would find her. There could be no doubt, either of her existence or of his powers of discovery – as long as he was not interfered with. Or plucked from this life by some black predatory thing. He came to rest beside a tool-shed and sniffed its creosote. Taking off his bowler hat he crouched here beside a water butt where he could see most of the garden and all of the rear and side of the house as well as the end of the path and the gate. His teeth clenched on the cigar holder which resided almost permanently in the corner of his grinding bite and so wrenched the musculature of his face that the dirty white sphere of the eye on the other side was enlarged to a glare whilst its fellow appeared half closed. The day progressed. A breeze got up and died down again. Leaves rustled and wavered. Poultry clucked, a small cloud passed over and swept a dimness swiftly over the slates of the house, as if wiping them clean, birds settled and called and launched themselves away. The sun slid from the zenith and rolled gently toward evening. No one came or went from the house, nor was there any face in a window.

He raked the stiff brush of his severe short hair with his stubby fingers and wondered whether he should stay or go. Go and come back. Darkness found him still there; like a weed sprouted and assuming its place he was accustomed now to the nettles beside him and the staves of the barrel and the gravel under the shed. Intermittently he closed his eyes for a few minutes where he crouched, but otherwise his wariness and watchfulness continued through the night. The cigar holder now pocketed, both of his eyes were like little off-white moons peeking above the water butt.

The dawn brought a thin grey mist to ease the light into being.

The walls of the house slowly brightened through the dissolution of the dark and the cobweb grey to resume their firmness and their refulgent whiteness. Johnson's faith in what lay silently behind the little gothic windows kept him staring. He was cold and damp with dew. Droplets stood out upon the nap of the bowler as he reassumed it.

A door opened. A figure – not by any stretch of the imagination the right one – emerged from the rear of the house and made its way between the vegetables with a bucket. This woman, middle aged, heavy built, domestically horizoned, pinafored, thick stockinged, fat legged, was going to feed the chickens whose preoccupations she probably shared, thought Johnson. He settled back down on his haunches and watched her broadcasting grain and kitchen scraps from her fat palms whilst making sleepy, conversational, encouraging sounds. Afterwards her bucket clanked and squeaked towards the shed. Johnson very quietly retreated behind the woodpile as the woman opened the door, fumbled with unseen things and banged about on the booming wooden floor within and then made her way back to the house after kicking the door shut. He scanned all the little windows and actually saw as well as heard half of an upstairs casement open with a whine and a creak. This must have been done by a hand and an arm but he glimpsed neither. Then smoke began to rise from a chimney and he quickly removed himself from the woodpile, making his way along past the bean rows towards the far end of the garden where he settled amongst piles of old flowerpots, a broken wheelbarrow and the compost heap. He was beyond the greenhouse now and the house showed a different and more distant aspect; a new silence settled over it, embroidered at the periphery by busy birds and unseen sheep as well as cattle. Johnson retrieved the empty cigar holder and clamped it in position, determined that his instinct would be vindicated by the sight of what he so earnestly wanted to see but could not quite imagine.

Hours came and ticked and slid off into wherever they go, (was it the same place flames go when you blow them out? he wondered) and the practical woman came again and lifted carrots and came again and filled a log basket and came again and hung out washing on a line which she propped with a tall prop and came again and wound water from the well and delicately hefted the full bucket to dribble considerately on infant lettuces. No one else came. There was no man. This at least kept Johnson here and attentive. He was sure she was there. He inspected the washing line for youthful female things, the bright pretty pastel things of his imagination but there were only flapping sheets which sailed across his view and annoyed him into creeping to another position behind gooseberry bushes. Then he heard voices.

A door had been opened, but it was not this back door it was the one at the front which he could no longer see. He jammed the bowler on his head and scampered carefully on all fours between the bushes and along the foot of the wall round the other side of the house until he could see, through gaps in the screen of shrubs and flowers beside the mossy path, the sage green door and hear the voices, one or other of which was surely about to emerge. He could see the hall stand with hats sticks and umbrellas. He strained to see whether there were any brutish heavy masculine articles amongst the acceptably fashionable parasols but the door was only half ajar and he could draw no conclusions. He saw also the corner of a mauve rug and a glimpse of what was probably a watercolour landscape on the wall. He could not see the long case clock which displayed phases of the moon.

'Your letters, Mademoiselle.'

There was the soft swish of skirts then a girl stepped out onto the path. Oh yes, very much a girl, here she was, he was right, he knew he was right, she must be the most perfect candidate. She was tall, slim, with almost blonde hair and everything about her poised and delicate. She wore a cotton dress of lilac with a white collar, a straw hat and the most elegant and dainty boots he had ever seen. On her arm was a wicker basket. She walked quickly and with a careless and unaffected rhythm which nonetheless showed off her figure as one as near perfectly proportioned as any Johnson could imagine or could ever remember seeing. The gate swung closed after her with a click and she made her way down the lane, quite as beautiful as any flower or any garden or any immaculate thing in creation. Most importantly she exuded a disarming innocence, she was, you could see, even in the distant look of her, blessed with an indefinable pure quality that would always have all who came across her opening their hearts and dedicating themselves to her noble whim.

He cautiously raised his eyes above the hollyhocks, looked all around and then suddenly shot through the garden like a gust of wind and vaulted over the wall, landing back down into the lane as if it were minutes since he had left it rather than a night and a day. He set off at a very smart pace in the opposite direction both to the girl and the way he had come, the bowler hat alone visible from the fields, bouncing importantly along above the hedge.

CHAPTER TWO

The pungent and exotic aroma of elephant dung hung heavily about the avenue, instilling awe and a measure of dread in many of the more innocent passers by. The road directly abutted the high walls of the menagerie and whoops and shrieking calls as well as the occasional rumbling thunderous growl often had people scurrying nervously past wondering whether anything could ever get out; some avoided the route entirely. Johnson passed ruminatively along past the exotic cries and scents toward the folly on a little eminence above the river where today the others of his degree were foregathered. Half a dozen figures were visible as he approached, some lounged about the stone seats and balustrades of the open rotunda, others, the assistants, were wary of the imminence of an authority much higher and more remote than their familiar masters and slouched expectantly but respectfully behind the pillars.

Johnson grunted at the assembly of colleagues, some of whom looked askance at his grubby moleskin suit and wondered how he got away with it. They were each in the trim livery of their cast – bottle green jackets, jodphurs and top boots. Their presence was at the royal command – the monthly progress reports were due and in varying states of nervousness they awaited the appointed hour and the arrival of the court. There was Simpson, leaning against a wall fiddling with a huge butterfly net, he had in fact been a celebrated entomologist prior to concentrating on birds. He was good looking in a slightly old fashioned sort of way – he probably had not changed his hair style since his mother had first given instructions to the barber on his behalf, though he remained well groomed and, especially on these rotunda days, smartly turned out. He was quietly intelligent, and friendly without being more sociable than was necessary. He was respected without being particularly admired; no one disliked him. Perhaps he could have been a little more commanding with his underlings – some thought him too easy going.

And here was Willoughby, a very different character, who

wafted an immense monogrammed silk handkerchief over a marble banquette before sitting rather primly upon it and greeting Johnson with a snort and some sarcasm, 'Oh good morning Mr Johnson, we've missed you, where on Earth have you been?' He neither expected nor received any reply beyond a darting glance. Willoughby had a whole platoon of undernourished and dispirited youths who did all the work but he would never allow any of them to attend gatherings like this. He himself had never been known to dig a trap, carry a crate, collect forage or attend to anything that involved any physical effort on an expedition beyond the casual perusal of a map or perhaps the idle stirring of a camp fire. He was however, a clever and cunning fellow, much travelled and fluent in at least half a dozen languages who had many triumphs to his name and commanded considerable respect at court. He made no secret of the indisputable fact that he was a cut above the rest of them. He cultivated the attitudes and mien of the gentleman amateur and would have everyone believe animal collecting was a hobby of his which he indulged in as a favour to the King rather than as a paid officer carrying out his duties. This was true to the extent that he certainly did not need the money, for he was 'The Honourable Sir Jolyon Willoughby Bart' on his note paper, and lived in a large manor house in some style, with servants.

Jemima, who was still relatively new, had not yet recognised that the solid man in the bowler hat was never going to be conversational. She would find more small talk in a limpet. But she smiled and proffered her hand and said something she immediately regretted which might have been, 'Nice day for it.' Jemima, being new and young, had yet to be recognised as the powerful force she was. People were in for a surprise.

Johnson worked alone – always. The others had servants and minions and helpers of varying intelligence and education and usefulness. Simpson for instance had two, one of whom was the strange and unnerving Culvert Grimes. Nobody could ever remember the name of the other one. They had considerable experience in Simpson's specialism which was birds with a particular inclination toward the huge and flightless. They leaned on either side of a pillar and from a distance seemed to be whispering conspiratorially, however Grimes' words were stoically ignored by the other – who hated him.

Not far away, her great tweed rump firmly settled on the edge of a plinth where it looked as if she was about to dislodge the unfortunate faun that stood there with a casual flick of her substantial left buttock was Maudie, as she insisted on being called, a middle aged woman with a very loud voice who suffered no nonsense, had been at it longer than any of them, had forgotten more about animals than any of them would ever know, would brook no argument and knew where absolutely everything was to be found, what it ate and how it might be come upon unawares and subsequently trained to do her bidding. She was much given to pointing and finger wagging and it was sometimes with difficulty that she managed to restrain her forthright tongue in the royal presence. She had no real official position but had been around for too long for anyone to get rid of her and had lately, she thought, taken the unfortunate Jemima rather under her wing. However Jemima, though fresh faced, would soon prove herself more capable than any of her colleagues, and in due course would make it clear that she needed no help from the likes of Maudie. She had as her seconds-in-command two girls, called Pippa and Willis, both also young and very keen (but rather shy, they whispered now to one another behind a statue of Artemis).

There was a Wilson and a Turner, both averagely talented animal men, who shared a passion for honeybadgers, armadillos, pangolins and such; they were capable but went about their work rather quietly and, except on the occasion when they revealed a giant aardvark, did not attract much attention, which neither of them minded very much.

Mr Kelp was a funny looking man who some thought wore a wig. He accumulated tortoises of various sorts and sizes (some immense) as well as an assortment of nature's more peculiar manifestations: rare crabs, sea urchins and the like (which were kept in very large bubbling glass aquariums) also chameleons, and a small and very sluggish alligator. Mr Kelp was old fashioned and short sighted and sported pince-nez on a ribbon; he was very friendly, smiled continually and would chortle at the drop of a hat. The things he lately brought back from his little expeditions, however, were often too small greatly to excite the royal imagination.

Then there was Murgatroyd, a round, almost spherical, bald man who had never done anything much apart from provide the zoo with its only water buffalo, a huge and unpredictable beast from which he was inseparable. He had a sort of grudging respect for the musk ox too, but beyond these beasts – both of which shared a disdain for their immediate surroundings – his interest in zoology seemed largely to have petered out. Consequently nobody paid him much attention. Anything he presented at the monthly audience was always the work of his assistant, a very tall youngish man called Proctor who by occasionally producing things like an albino raccoon – rather like a rabbit out of a hat – saved his superior from having the continuance of his employment questioned.

In the interests of completeness mention should probably also be made of Burroughs. Burroughs had gone off quite some considerable time ago – was it five years? – clutching a Sanskrit manuscript and balancing a gargantuan kit-bag on his shoulder in search of the Yeti. Administratively he was untidy and officials were itching to erase him from the payroll, but he had not yet faded entirely from the memory of his erstwhile colleagues, and there were some at court who liked sometimes to nod sagely whilst rolling the delicate stem of a claret glass in their fingers and to declare softly with an abstracted expression and raised eyebrows that 'Burroughs may yet surprise us all.'

Such were the King's animal collectors: some clowns, some who had sunk into a rut of their own gouging, but mostly they were intelligent and dedicated; some bright and clever. Most remained ever anxious for the acclaim and royal recognition that would be attracted by some zoological coup and the coup most aspired to was the presentation of some infinitely rare specimen.

Suddenly there was an awareness of footsteps and everyone stood up and assembled in the middle of the well of the rotunda as Vangrannicus, the Chamberlain accompanied by two footmen blustered in self importantly, inspecting everyone and marshalling them into a proper line. Then there was a short squeaky blast on a bugle which made Jemima jump and all of a sudden there he was – the King.

'The Royal Specimen Hunters, Your Majesty,' announced Vangrannicus formally with a little bow, although everyone knew perfectly well who everyone else was. A portable throne received the descending royal rump, which was always lowered with the divine certainty that there would never be nothing there to receive it, the kingly cloak was gathered about the majestic knees and the sparkling eyes of this most important of men glanced over those before him.

Although he was designated King Dagobert IV, the name in use amongst those who were allowed to call him by name – and there were surprisingly many, he did not stand on ceremony overmuch and had some quite democratic inclinations – was Frederick. For day to day wear he favoured a deerstalker over a crown and was much in favour of comfortable footwear, often, as today, taking the form of sandals which rather surprised people when they noticed them peeping beneath the crimson cloak. He was thought to be somewhat eccentric. Whenever there might be something for him to read or inspect – as today – he wore half-moon gold-rimmed spectacles. He was educated to an exalted but rather rarefied degree which often led him to places not many of his subjects could follow but it had given him an open and receptive cast of mind so that unless he was constantly reminded by officious masters of ritual and protocol as to what was seemly he would happily chat with anybody, no matter what their genealogy or social standing as long as they knew what they were talking about and were interesting. His library was immense, he loved music and paintings, kept an astronomer, ran his own printing press and took a great interest in milling and baking. Visitors to his kingdom often said they could not understand what he wanted with all those windmills scattered all over the downland, white and whirling, near and far. But his greatest passion, which dominated everything else in his life, was his menagerie. This was a collection of living fauna larger than any other in his or any other kingdom and what gave him the deepest joy was to introduce some rare antelope into its enclosure, or some previously unknown beetle into its glass box. He was destined to go down in history as 'The Zoo King' and his obsession was such that he regarded these periodic audiences with his collectors of rare animals as much more important and interesting than treasury matters, or all those red faced generals or all those tedious archbishops. The chance that they might have come with something, and that he would be surprised by an addition to his collection imbued these meetings with all the excitement that a small boy might feel looking for the postman on his birthday. Something new to enter into the great zoological register, something to tick off the list, or best of all something previously unknown to present to the world, these things made his heart beat faster.

Not that he was really expecting anything today, there had been no rumours and he could see no signs of any surprise crate, no dung shovel, no strange whimperings or barking.

'Good morning ladies and gentlemen,' said Frederick. 'What news? Reports please. Mr Simpson?' The royal eyebrows invited his statement.

'Er, yes, Your Majesty, thank you, Your Majesty. We've been active following up reports of a previously unknown horse-fly, and plans for an expedition to acquire a pair of maleo are well advanced –'

'Maleo? I don't remember anything about this, what are maleo?'

'It was an appendix to the last written report, Your Majesty, but then we weren't sure where it lived. Now we know it lives on an Indonesian island called Sulawesi.'

'And it is precisely what kind of a thing, this maleo?'

'Chicken-sized bird, Your Majesty, but most interesting looking, it has a huge sort of black helmet on its forehead. One complication might be that it has some odd breeding requirements, er... What was it please, Grimes?'

'Volcanic soil, sir. It has to have volcanic soil in which to incubate its eggs, sir.'

'Oh yes, that was it.'

'Could it be got, volcanic soil? Does it need to be fresh and hot?'

'Oh no, not hot, Sire, I don't think so, but yes, I don't see why we could not get some.'

'Very well, continue.'

'The new enclosure for the bustards is almost ready, Your Majesty, and there's a report from the vet about the cassowary, very favourable, the plaster comes off on Tuesday. Er that's all, Your Majesty.'

He bowed. Behind him, Grimes and the other one bowed.

'Very good, good work, Simpson. Keep me in touch about the maleo – could I have a paper on it? Excellent.'

The King turned now to Jemima, as a stab of old-fashioned gallantry reminded him that he should have done first. He flicked a forefinger at Vangrannicus who knew immediately what was required and advanced to whisper in the royal ear, 'Ms Cake, Your Majesty.'

'Ms Cake?' Frederick raised invitational eyebrows again and smiled at the newcomer – this was only her second appearance at the Specimen Hunters' audience.

Jemima won the battle to vanquish the nervousness that, to begin with, uncharacteristically fluttered in her voice, and soon found herself confidently reporting the claims of some freelancers to have captured a hairy nosed wombat. She was investigating but thought it unlikely to be true. She and the vet were still inspecting the bat that she had brought from her last expedition, and hopes were high that it was indeed a separate and previously unrecognised species.

'If substantiated it will have to be named I suppose?' cut in the King.

'Yes, Majesty, Frederick's Bat we thought, er, with your permission of course.'

The King smiled and nodded his approval.

'Thank you, Your Majesty. And we are still getting accounts from the north of a mermaid, or mermaid-like creature. I can't believe it's really some sort of homo-aquaticus,' (a nervous laugh) 'but I would propose going up there to find out what exactly is at the bottom of it all.'

'So to speak,' said the King, and everyone laughed, including the Chamberlain who looked quickly around to see if anyone was not laughing.

'A mermaid,' mused Frederick, more seriously, and those present could see the lure of myth elbowing science aside in the royal mind. 'Goodness me. I wonder what it is. What do you think it could be, Ms Cake?'

'Hard to be sure without some first hand evidence, Sire, but it seems to be a marine mammal of some considerable size with a number of sightings both in the sea and estuarine waters.'

'Goodness. Yes, yes, Ms Cake, I think you should make this a priority. And if there are any particularly interesting signs or sightings you will send a messenger immediately and we shall join you ourselves.'

'Of course, Your Majesty.'

'Anything else?'

'Some of the Madagascan toads seem to be changing colour, Sire, I've made a written report. Whether it's in response to their surroundings or there's something wrong with them, we're not sure.'

'From what to what?'

'Orange to purple, Your Majesty.'

'Hmm,' the King reflected on this for a moment in silence and then moved on. One by one, the zoo people were called upon to report, but mostly it was routine stuff with no new species. Then the King turned to the ostentatiously patient but rather supercilious figure now leaning on a statue. 'Mr Willoughby?'

Willoughby stepped forward with a gait that was, the Chamberlain thought, rather too relaxed to be quite respectful, and in making a joke of his opening remark further irritated that official.

'Well, I regret once again – no dodo.'

Nobody laughed, but it was plain he did not care.

'However, once out of quarantine, Your Majesty's collection will be the more complete for a pair of Owston's Civets – charming little beasts and of course very rare, Your Majesty.'

The King stirred, 'Any unusual attributes, the Owston's civet? And who exactly was Owston?' It was obvious he would have been much happier with King Dagobert's Civet.

Willoughby had to extemporise, he had never clapped eyes on these animals, the entire mission to bring them back from their distant corner of the planet had been conducted by his hard pressed band of underlings.

'Quite unusual Your Majesty, they nest in trees but live chiefly on fish, interesting markings and a very distinctive scent. They are named for a Professor Owston, no longer with us, I believe.'

A stifled whimper from Jemima told Simpson and Johnson and the others that this was wrong and another little wedge of resentment was driven between Mr Willoughby and his fellow specimen hunters.

He knew no one would denounce him in the King's presence and smiled to himself as he took another leisurely pace forward and said, 'Your Majesty there is, however, a more exciting development to report.'

The King leant forward and looked eagerly over his spectacles. 'What, what, what is it Willoughby?'

'Your Majesty, I have the honour to report that even as we speak, my men are with all speed bringing from the most far-flung and inaccessible corner of the globe, from the most inhospitable and dangerous jungles infested with cannibals where it chooses to make its home, a magnificent and sturdy example of...' (he could not resist the pause for effect, the whole assembly froze in expectation) 'the legendary singing dog of New Guinea!'

They were dumbfounded. Those who knew what he was talking about and those who had never heard of such a beast were all equally lost for words. Could it be true? Could it possibly be true? Had he really pulled off such a spectacular coup?

Willoughby bowed from the waist with an exaggerated flourish of his arm. Excitement rippled through the assembly and the Chamberlain had to call for silence.

'This is excellent work, Mr Willoughby, we are delighted. Does it really sing?'

'Oh yes, Your Majesty, sweet as any nightingale, it is truly a wonder.'

The King stood up, became quite agitated, asked questions about when exactly it was due to arrive, called for his secretaries and his Chamberlain and gabbled a dozen convoluted orders which were to be transmitted at once to his minister of works, (building was to begin forthwith on an entirely new enclosure in the menagerie) the master of the King's music (who was to be ready to write down in musical notation the songs of the royal dog) the captain of the guard (sentries to be permanently stationed at appropriate points when the thing arrived) and then having just remembered to congratulate Willoughby and his invisible men on sterling work he was on the point of sweeping out of the rotunda when Vangrannicus reminded him that there was yet one hunter to be heard. Impatiently, Frederick resumed his throne, which had already been folded away and was only just replaced beneath him in time, and demanded with undisguised dismay when he saw the scruffy moleskin suit step forward.

'Oh heavens, yes, Johnson! Come on then, what have you got?'

Before he could answer, Vangrannicus leant over to speak in the royal ear. The King listened, sighed and nodded, whereupon the Chamberlain himself addressed Johnson, 'Mr Johnson, why are you not wearing the livery of your position?'

Johnson scratched an armpit – not nervously, just because it itched, there was nothing nervous about Johnson – and said, 'At the cleaners, but it don't fit anyway... Sir.'

Vangrannicus's inclination to pursue this potentially disciplinary line of interrogation was reined in somewhat by a yawn from Frederick who just wanted to get back to the North Tower, drink some sherry and think about his singing dog. However, the Chamberlain made bold to assume his most officious demeanour and, in tones so forthright that they reclaimed the attention of the assembly, which was bored and anxious to be dismissed, barked, 'Mr Johnson you have failed to attend the last three audiences and have offered no apology or explanation to His Majesty, this is the most appalling and disrespectful, not to say treasonable behaviour, what do you have to say for yourself?'

'Been on a mission.'

'What? What mission? For three months? Do you not have deputies? Where have you been exactly?' A glance at the notebook. 'You haven't put in any expense claims.'

The King looked up from his reverie and over his half moon spectacles to ask, 'Brought anything back?'

'No, Your Majesty.'

The audience was at an end, the King stood up, there was shuffling about and the beginnings of preparation for the procession back to the castle. It seemed Vangrannicus's desire to give the scruffy recalcitrant specimen hunter a public dressing down was not to be fulfilled, and then Johnson, who had fixed the King in a very rude stare and was giving the other armpit some attention, addressed his sovereign in a hoarse and urgent whisper, 'Unicorn, Sire.'

'What? What did he say?'

Johnson approached Frederick to the extent of a couple of impertinent and conspiratorial steps which would have outraged Vangrannicus but for the stunning effect of the word 'unicorn' which he had heard clearly and which stopped him in his tracks. So had the King heard it, though he could not believe his ears.

Johnson said it again, his coarse breath activating his hoarse gravelling larynx which in turn drew a deep echoing bass resonance from the thick ribbed chest below, and created with it a strange and fascinating harmonic rumble of a voice. Staring his divinely appointed ruler in the face from his new position barely three feet from the royal person he buzzed and gurgle-growled, 'Unicorn, Your Majesty, I been workin' on the unicorn,' and he left his mouth half open, showing some teeth, in what might have been an attempt at a grin, and was silent.

Willoughby and some others had made out the word and it was whispered around the room which quickly seethed with murmuring and barely suppressed laughter. Willoughby did in fact splutter and bend over with his hand over his mouth in a theatrical gesture which encouraged many of the assistants and some of the guard until open laughter broke out.

'Silence!' shouted Vangrannicus.

The King peered closely at the sunburnt bullet head, the frayed collar, the distressed moleskin jacket with the bulging pockets, the gnarled thick fingered hands, the smell of cigars, for a long time before saying, 'Look here, Johnson, you must know, there is no such thing as the unicorn, you of all people as a royal specimen hunter must know, that sad as it is, there is no unicorn.' He shook his head sympathetically at this honest, but deluded, retainer and sat back in his portable throne, interlocking his fingers and rapidly twiddling his thumbs. 'Not now, probably never has been.'

'Beg pardon, Majesty, but believe there is unicorn.'

This set the assembly off again, Maud was braying like an ass, Simpson's men were openly sniggering and some of the courtiers who had nothing to do with the menagerie and had been lounging at the entrance to the rotunda playing cup and ball or reading letters during the reporting now had their attention taken by this new sensation and were crowding the doorway trying to get a glimpse of Johnson.

The King adjusted his spectacles and sat forward again, signing with flapping fingers for Vangrannicus's help but simultaneously saying, 'What on Earth makes you believe the unicorn exists? You are an experienced zooman, are you not? Your face is very familiar, you have been with us a long time I think? You uncovered some spectacular insects, if I remember rightly and yes...yes the mole rat, was it not you that founded the mole-rat colony? How can you believe in a fairy tale animal?'

Vangrannicus bent over and spoke rapidly into Frederick's ear: 'Always been a bit of an odd bod, but a very good worker until these recent absences. Written reports very poor or non-existent and he doesn't say much but, as Your Majesty rightly remembers he did get the mole-rat things and some lizards and some huge beetles, poisonous I think.' He closed the notebook he'd been referring to and straightened up to glare around at the unacceptable behaviour amongst the courtiers.

Johnson said, 'Difficult to catch, looking for bait, takes time,' and looked down hoping to be dismissed. He did not like these audiences, he did not like being looked at, he did not like being spoken to. He wanted to be left alone to get on with it.

Willoughby's stage whisper, 'Johnson has finally lost it, poor fellow,' was clearly audible; Maud looked to the heavens and said, 'Idiot'; Simpson had folded his arms and was looking at Johnson with deep puzzlement; whilst Jemima Cake tried to remember what she knew of the myths and legends of the unicorn.

'Look here, Johnson, this can't be right you know. How on Earth did you get this idea? The unicorn is a myth, a legend, an old story, it does not exist. Now don't you think you'd be better off looking for something that you might actually find? After all, that's what we keep you for you know.' Frederick was by nature an indulgent and sympathetic person, and unbelievably so for a King. He would have put an arm round the unfortunate retainer if they'd been in a more private place. Johnson, however, would not respond to chumminess, cajolery, jollying or the like. He had set off down this particular path and nothing would bring him back. He was capable of watching a hole in a river bank for days at a time without sleep or nourishment, the rain and the cold wore him down less than stone, he was steadfast, perpetual, purposeful. And the possibility of the unicorn having come to Johnson's attention, that animal would have no choice in the end; it would have to reveal itself. It might very well be, indeed, that Johnson's obstinacy was a faith so powerful it could probably itself conjure the thing into being.

The King was increasingly aware of the restlessness around him. The court wanted to be off, the cocktail hour was approaching, there was to be a dinner for the Venetian ambassador that night, important as they might be in this kingdom, rare animals could not stop the schedule of government, petitions, diplomacy, taxes and politics. He rose and beckoned Vangrannicus. 'Have him brought to me tonight.'

'But the Venetian –'

'After the dinner obviously. I want to find out what he's really been doing. And if he's not up to it anymore he will have to be replaced.'

'But, Majesty, I could speak –'

'No, no, leave it to me. There now come on.' He wrapped his cloak about him and turned to go, the bugle squeaked, the specimen hunters, bar one, stood belatedly to attention and the royal entourage, arranging itself into the proper order as it went, began to shuffle back toward the castle.

Johnson jammed his bowler back on his head, turned and marched rapidly out of the rotunda and away down the other causeway, whence he had come, back toward the animal smells. His colleagues looked after him and then at one another in silence for a moment.

Willoughby slowly shook his head and said, 'It would appear that the strange Mr Johnson has finally lost his marbles. He was always somewhat peculiar of course, but with this we now know he has gone round the bend. Very sad.' He assumed the expression of a man who took no pleasure in the fall of a colleague, which was easy to do since none of them were, even when not off their heads, remotely of the calibre to challenge his supremacy. However, surprisingly there was about Willoughby, just apparent to a very careful observer, a distinct hint of a slight uneasiness.

Maud folded her arms and said, 'Mad as a hatter. I've seen it coming. Spends far to much time on his own.'

Simpson looked at his feet and wondered, 'You don't think he's actually on the trail of something, some sort of goat or rhinoceros or something and is playing a joke on us by calling it a unicorn?' Which was precisely the origin of Willoughby's unease.

Jemima laughed and said, 'Oh, do you think so, wouldn't that be marvellous. Actually when you think about it that's probably where the old unicorn stories came from isn't it? Rhinos and mutations and narwhals and things.'

'So it is said,' muttered Willoughby quietly to himself, and then to the others, 'I think we should keep an eye on him, don't you. We wouldn't want him coming to grief in some way, if he's got these strange ideas there's no knowing what he might be capable of.'

Everyone agreed with this, though none of them knew exactly what he meant. Proctor would have liked to have stayed to hear more, but Murgatroyd was anxious to get back to his water buffalo and insisted he come away.

It was Willoughby's habit to remain aloof from his fellow raree finders but today the Johnson incident had made him linger and he actually found himself descending unusually into a measure of hob nobbing with his colleagues – he must keep close tabs on anything out of the ordinary that might be going on, he now decided, otherwise his position might be undermined. If anything needed doing he must be sufficiently well informed to take the lead. But it was not too painful, Simpson was perhaps not such a boring chap really, it seemed, and allowances could be made for Ms Cake, she was after all very young, and a woman. And rather good looking. The Maud creature remained impossible of course – he found her massive freckled flesh where it bulged within the rough wool of her clothes and burst out into her bull-like neck, or erupted from the cuffs in podgy wrists, utterly repulsive. The wiry grey hair stuck up and out wherever it would and was liable to lash one in the face if one got too close, or worst of all, shed bits of itself into your tea-cup.

'Poor Mr Johnson, do you think though that he could really believe in the unicorn?' asked Jemima, who had been joined by Pippa and Willis now that the intimidating formality of the court had withdrawn. (Their relationship with their boss was obviously much more chummy than that enjoyed by Simpson's men.)

'He's rather strange altogether isn't he,' said Pippa tentatively. 'Weird even, I don't know how he dares stand before His Majesty looking so scruffy, he looks a bit like a tramp'.

'Off his head! Always has been,' reiterated Maud unswervingly.

'He's an oddbod for sure,' said Simpson. 'But I wouldn't write him off just yet you know. I wouldn't be surprised if he hasn't got something up his sleeve. Remember the mole rats – none of us believed in them until he brought them back –'

'By god, yes,' said Kelp. 'Ugly as sin!' And laughed.

'So what do you mean exactly?' asked Willoughby. 'Have you heard anything? Have you anything to base your suspicions on?'

'Well, no. It's just a feeling I have,' said Simpson. 'Let's wait and see.'

'Well I suppose I would like to think you were right,' said Willoughby – this did not ring true and even Jemima who hardly knew him at all looked up in disbelief – 'But I'm afraid I think it's more likely he's just gone a bit mad. I think he's spent so much time looking for weird animals and considering different combinations of body parts that he really believes in the story-book unicorn. I think he's persuaded himself he can actually go and find it. Did you see that look in his eyes?' He waved the handkerchief again preparatory to dabbing his forehead, 'He's doolally tap.'

'Quite right!' said Maud, who perhaps coveted the role of chief eccentric character in this fraternity, and it may have been in an effort to emphasise her candidacy that she was now trimming the beak of a budgerigar she seemed to have brought out from a pocket in her jacket.

Kelp who was busy inspecting his portable aquarium for leaks muttered 'There are more things in heaven and Earth, Horatio...' and would have gone on to make some remark concerning the ocean depths and mermaid sightings but something in the corner of his glass box bit his probing finger eliciting a cry of pain and the necessity of sticking the wounded digit immediately into his mouth, shut him up.

Jemima only knew that Johnson never said anything, didn't seem to like anyone and frequently stank worse than his quarry. She asked what they thought the King would do about him.

'Ah, who knows,' said Simpson, looking about to make sure the group was not overheard.

'Whatever he does is right of course, because he's the King. But he can be very unpredictable.'

'His Majesty will not leap to any conclusions,' said Willoughby, 'He may seek advice.'

'Zoological or psychological?' asked Jemima.

'Both probably,' said Willoughby, 'And very likely mythological.'

'What are you implying? asked Maud, replacing the green feathered lump into its secret compartment. 'Do you believe King Dagobert IV capable of believing in monsters?'

'Our beloved sovereign is capable of a great many things which are no doubt beyond our grasp,' said an emboldened Culvert Grimes, who thought this was a most risqué satirical witticism and looked about for appreciation but was ignored.

Then Jemima said, 'What was the unicorn anyway? Where did the idea of it come from? There must be, or have been some beast which gave rise to the legend.'

CHAPTER THREE

The King strode along the causeway which lay across the river's flood plain back toward the old fortified parts of the town and the castle. He walked as vigorously as he thought, and was therefore difficult to keep up with if you were an overweight, out of condition courtier, fond of good food and vintage wines, as many were. Why on Earth they weren't allowed to come by carriage or donkey or any sort of animal or conveyance, they did not understand for the life of them. After all it was a good mile and three quarters from the little island with the rotunda, which made over three miles there and back, and they weren't all as young as they used to be. But Frederick was adamant, walking was good for the body, the soul and the mental faculties, and it was one of his rules that this particular little fixture in the court calendar must always be attended on foot. It wasn't so far that it would kill any of them and yet far enough to remind them how unfit they were getting. After all, the audience with the specimen hunters was held only once a month. Those that muttered, 'Why could it not be held in the castle?' were always told that it had historically been held in the little rotunda due to its proximity to the menagerie and hence was convenient should any beast need to be brought out, or the King attend his zoo to be shown something. Some of them privately baulked at the convenience of a three-toed thingummyjig taking precedence over their own. It did not occur to them that they might like even less the regular parading of unclean creatures along the tapestried corridors of their own courtly preening grounds.

Frederick set off at a deliberately smart four-miles-an-hour, but as the mist began to roll up from the river and the marshes, and then sneak over the parapet and curl about the feet of the stone statues that stood at regular intervals on high plinths all along both sides of the way, he slowed somewhat as his thoughts of matters of state and mental preparation for the forthcoming diplomatic dinner receded to give way to more mysterious topics. All matter was becoming obscure as the fog got thicker, obliterating the distant sight of the ends of the causeway and drifting about the heroes and heraldic stone beasts which rose up on either side and appeared even more huge as more and more parts of them disappeared in the shifting cobweb of grey droplets. There were knights and saints and kings but the ancient builders had also loosed their imaginings freely upon the stylised animals of arms and mythology. The usually swift royal passage along this road was slowed by the fog and Frederick found that the marble claws and beaks and talons looming above him, their presence enhanced by the creeping cloud which kept the rest of them secret, took him over with thoughts and visions he could not dismiss. Thoughts into which the interloping unicorn must make its way.

The same statues were here every time he came along this road but today they seemed to be more intensely present than usual. Frederick stopped and stared at the leonine lower portions of a gryphon, its huge and powerful paws becoming more alive in the fading light, its great feathered head and cruel beak veiled by the atmospheric gauze, but looming above and threatening to reappear at any moment. It might have stepped up from a different palaeontological realm or down from a distant star sign and only just this second have come to rest.

There could never have been a gryphon of course, it was a pure feat of dreams and fables. It was said to hate horses. Why should it hate horses? Maybe they had meant it ate horses. But my, what a wonderful thing it was and what a marvel it would be if one were found alive and snorting and stamping amongst all his fat courtiers. And then the unlikely anatomy of the gryphon reminded him of the platypus (he had two in his collection, courtesy of Willoughby's crew). What more unlikely mixture of parts and attributes could anyone possibly dream up? And yet it was real. He could do an about turn and go and look at his pair of them if he wished – though they always looked a bit shabby and rather disconsolate – so it would be a mistake perhaps to rule out the possibility of the existence of things just because they might seem unusual. There could surely be nothing as unlikely as *ornithorhyncus anatinus*, the most outrageous brainstorming amongst bibulous biologists at some Christmas party could not invent something as bizarre and rule breaking as the duck-billed, egg-laying, beaver-tailed, otter-footed venomous mammal which defied classification and obstinately occupied its own category entirely separate from other living things. If such a thing as that could exist, why was it so laughable that Johnson seemed to believe there was a slightly unusual ungulate monoceros galloping about somewhere which had become sufficiently rare that it had not been commonly seen since pre-enlightenment days? After all, what had they sent Burroughs out after?

He had come to a complete stop, deep in thought staring at the gryphon's paw, and the entourage were bumping in to one another behind him in the fog, wondering what was going on. This agglomeration of officials and petitioners and hangers-on itself assumed the nature of some monstrous beast, a higgledy-piggledy caterpillar, the muttering and murmuring coalescing into a sort of groan. The distracted imagination of the King, as he turned back towards this befogged beast which seemed to follow him everywhere, for a moment indeed saw it, in the midst of his musings, as one monster, some sort of ungainly questing beast, and stared for a moment with the intensification of the realisation there were far more things in heaven and Earth than were yet represented in his menagerie. And this gave rise to a sudden stab of anxiety – perhaps there were rival collectors already on the trail of creatures his advisers scorned so openly as childish figments. A wave of anguish flooded over him as his heart foretold the derision of the world that would be heaped upon his kingdom when it became apparent that he had been the ruler who had failed to open his mind to the possibility of the unicorn. When the magical beast was conjured from a wooden horsebox to clatter on the real cobbles of some neighbouring royal courtyard, triumphantly before the heaving crowds, how cringing cowed and stupid would Dagobert the Fourth become before his ancestors, his people and posterity. He was the Zoo King. He was looked upon as the chief of all animal collectors. No one lavished more money and hospitality on beasts and fowls and fish and creeping things since Noah. If there might be even the remotest, slightest chance that there could possibly be even the tiniest billion to one that Johnson was actually on the scent of something, Frederick must give him every bit of support that he could. Though perhaps at first – the caterpillar was getting louder and more restless, and the Chamberlain was saying something to him – perhaps at first, with a modicum of discretion.

'Sire, it's past tea time. It would be unwise perhaps to bottleneck the schedule when we have so much to get through.'

Frederick nodded, turned on his heel and marched off, disappearing at once and completely into the thickening mist.

Resuming his smart pace he found himself marching alone – his followers would take a minute or two, once they realised the delay was at an end, to lumber their centipede limbs into forward motion and for the moment were left, out of touch and out of sight.

Frederick continued to review the stone figures as they loomed and were gone while he went steadily along. The wyvern, weird and somewhat forlorn he thought; the basilisk, fierce and upright on its coils, displaying nothing of its fear of the weasel (a fatal indisposition which Frederick would only become aware of once he was free to linger later amongst the medieval bestiaries in his library) and topped with a diminutive crown which somehow accentuated his poisonous unpredictability since it was worn with no suggestion of the weight or trammellings of duty other than that of bringing death to whomever fell into its path. Like a little token judicial black cap.

Gradually the beastly figures became more ordinary, like leopards and lions, rampant and passant, and almost domestic like boars and harts. But still the partial sight of a clawed foot or a floating disembodied head or snout or beak or antler gave new wonder to the passer-by and gave rise to possibilities unimagined in conventional veterinary circles. And then it was just people. At first a preponderance of the other-worldly, the beatific and sainted, demi-gods radiating angelic and heavenly powers and assumptions, and then, beyond these, as Frederick progressed ever closer to the castle walls, followed mythological heroes with clubs and spears and shields and then the merely illustrious, generals and the like, often depicted in the guise of mythological heroes but most known by now to have feet of clay. But even with the human figures, when they came and went in the furling of the fog they were at first one thing and then evanesced and reappeared in the cloak of another, stranger character, and each could be the other and who could certainly distinguish a holy toe from a pagan one? And then, as the fog cleared over the running waters where the marshy flood plains gave way to the real river below, the truly mundane though extravagantly apparelled figures of Frederick's own regal ancestors, and last of all, his grandfather, Hubert (King Ferdinand the Third) whose life had been dedicated, Frederick knew, not to the imperial ambitions the sculptor had striven to depict but to his extensive model railway.

Thus, thought Frederick, doth that great causeway unwittingly stretch out the panoply of human aspirations and imaginings. Usually he just stormed along it without looking much but he was glad today for the fog which by half obscuring them gave these figures a life which the mind leapt to fill with flesh and malice. The stone bodies were heavy and immortal but today seemed to move upon their pedestals, restless perhaps at last to flex their god-like capabilities. Frederick was glad to have been awakened to possibilities which had been in danger of being overlooked. The Chamberlain was sprinting to catch up and would soon drag his Majesty back into the exigencies of the ritual of the day, but not before Frederick had impressed upon him, 'Don't forget, bring Johnson to me tonight, in the library, I will see him in private, let no one see him.'

'Very well, Your Majesty.'

CHAPTER FOUR

Daphne – strictly speaking Her Royal Highness, the Princess Daphne, but she would sigh with exasperation if anyone ever tried to call her that – was painting her nails in the boudoir she chiefly inhabited in one of the round towers. The room was very large but so littered with ricks of clothing and a cultivated non-tidiness, so imposed upon by a scruffy chic which its occupant thought perfectly pitched to announce a studied contempt for anything as bourgeois as rebelliousness and yet hinting at preoccupations above and beyond normal considerations like the look of things altogether that it appeared small and uninviting. Which latter it definitely was. No one was allowed in here except Belinda, Daphne's maid and she only when specifically called for.

There was a bed of course, high with four posts though it was hardly noticeable amongst the bales of material, discarded gowns, cloaks, mannequins and tottering pillars of hat boxes. There was a mirror, large and practically prominent. And there was one picture, over the fireplace. It was a picture of an empty horse. That's what she called it, the Empty Horse. It depicted some noble but exhausted and disheartened steed caparisoned in the accoutrements of war but with a poignantly empty saddle, being led off under a tree by a grim-faced young squire. Daphne liked this painting. She liked it in many different ways. Sometimes she liked it because it presented the misery and pointlessness of war and the idiot sacrifice of gullible young men. Sometimes she liked it because the poor and put-upon horse at least had survived and though it might mourn its rider, it should never have been taken into battle in the first place. Sometimes – most often in fact – it was a horse whose empty saddle invited her to leap into the frame of this differently imagined reality, this more real world beneath the lovingly painted oak tree, into which she would plunge and prance and gallop right away from this ridiculous little realm with its stupid little monarchy and the embarrassing decorum and protocols foisted upon her like a rigid little cage that held her fast and crippled her desperate soul.

This was a powerful dream of fulfilment wherein the world beyond would recognise her true worth, where the originality of her mind would enrich the lives of others, and she would be appreciated for her true self, not because she was a princess.

But sometimes the saddle stood for another very particular sort of emptiness. There were times when it represented a vacancy, not only on the horse but in her amorous heart. The dark leather and stiff pommel awaited one worthy of the place, the place upon the strong and loyal animal, the place in the frame above her hearth, the place in the huge and yearning hole in her heart. Sometimes indeed this horse waited to be mounted as Excalibur waited in its stone, for the once and future and forever prince who would meet all the demanding criteria of this most acute and discerning and careful girl. Ordinarily and in company this was a girl who laughed at love and characterised it as an immature preoccupation which she had the power to side-step; she herself preferring books and her piano and the arts, of which she was such a precocious and mighty patron, but there were these 'sometimes' when she could look at the decorated yellow reins and yearn with all the rack and rigour of one in the grip of nature's tumult for one sufficiently handsome and wise and valorous to ride into her boudoir and sweep her out of it.

Tonight, however, Daphne was to be subject to one of the tortures reserved for the royal persona which had been riveted upon her at birth, rather like an iron mask which she could never take off. As Princess Daphne she must attend one of those dreadful dinners where your clothes hurt, the food was cold and not at all what you wanted and the conversation stilted, where everyone was awkward and just wanted to get home and tell everyone all about the marvellous time they'd had and whose hand they had shaken and what so-and-so – who regularly had his picture in the newspapers – had actually said to them. Everyone would be nervous, except for her father, who was too interested in everything ever to be nervous, and herself, who was more likely to be overtaken by boredom and embarrassment. Sometimes she simply wanted to scream at the walls of rigid smiles that surrounded her from beginning to end.

'Belinda!' She had reached the last toe.

The door opened.

'Remind me, who is it tonight?'

'Venetians, Miss.' (She was not allowed to call her Ma'am or Your Royal Highness or anything.)

'What colour is their flag? I have to know what to wear.'

'I really wouldn't know Miss, you'll probably be safe with purple.'

The finishing touches were put to the foot, which rested on a volume of Byron's works which itself was piled upon the three volumes of Burton's *The Anatomy of Melancholy*. In due course the foot was introduced rather glumly into a shoe of the requisite elegance and the Princess surrendered herself once more to what a Princess had to do.

Daphne's progress from the relative sanctity of her apartments toward the Great Hall of the castle was a process of the gradual but inexorable erosion of her privacy and accretion of the multitudinous barnacles of state. At the first landing she was joined by her ladies in waiting who formed a giggling gaggle behind her (some of them were very immature – the appointments were made on the basis of their parents' efforts in the field of this or that royal cause – it was one of the ways the royal purse could run to the upkeep of such an extensive menagerie) further along the corridor her secretary joined her with a big book which contained the names of all the people who would be at the dinner, those who would be presented to her, what they had done and appropriate remarks for her to make should she be in the mood to be prompted which she often was – none of this was remotely natural – then someone from the kitchens showed her a menu and was ready to answer any questions or orders she might have about the food, ditto a butler regarding the wine since following her mother's death she was supposed to be in charge of this sort of thing though she took no interest in it whatsoever, left the whole thing to those paid to do it and never interfered or gave any orders or asked any questions. On the next landing there was a great coming together as two flood tides of officials, pages, squires, minor nobility, those serving the Princess on the one side and those serving his Majesty on the other, met and miraculously failed to collide, forming one jumbled phalanx of regal pomp which marched into the anteroom where the principals greeted the visiting Italians, took a drink of some fiery spirit and threw their glass into the fireplace (actually only the men did this, nobody had been able to explain to Daphne to her satisfaction why this should be so, and remembering one of her more memorable tantrums the waiters were on strict orders to keep the trays well away from her Royal Highness) and then shambled into the huge room set with the most immense dining table imaginable.

Amongst the Venetian legation there was a dark young man of rather haughty mien who seemed not to be able to keep his eyes off the Princess Daphne. She was outraged. Who was this oaf? Who did he think he was indeed? How did it come about that someone with no manners at all should be invited to a state dinner? She sought out her secretary. It transpired that he was the Italian prince, the guest of honour, no less. So it seemed the bottom pinching mentality was not confined to the lower orders but ran through the whole race of them. It would have been her inclination to snub and ignore him as bluntly and as rudely as she could had he not been who he was. Even she drew the line at inciting diplomatic incidents.

Of course he was to sit next to her at dinner. She could not help passing some remarks and appearing at least to listen to what he said – for all she loathed the whole affair, it was her job and she'd been doing it for years, especially since her mother had died. And then it was revealed: he, at least, had been made to believe that they two were regarded as a potential match. Ugh, Christ, oh the horror and embarrassment. She did not know where to put herself and would have run from the room but for the fact that she was too practised a princess and knew she had to bear it for the hours of the dinner at least. But it was purgatory. Especially since he was not afraid of letting it be known that he thought it rather a good pairing.

He was handsome certainly, but no extent of physical comeliness could render him acceptable since the role for which he believed himself ear-marked was simply not vacant. That empty horse would be filled only and entirely by Daphne's imagination. Not by this preening and pushy, altogether too tall, altogether too flesh and blood personage passing the potatoes.

He spoke English immaculately of course but inevitably teasing latin lilts lifted the words and some vowels could not help but betray their origin, all of which, combined with the naturally opulent baritone timbre, produced a most pleasing and mellifluous voice, which indeed, for those susceptible to that sort of thing would have the listener succumbing to the pheromones that swam from his every breath. Princess Daphne however was determinably resistant to the charms of anyone making assumptions, and his very presence was a monstrous affront to her autonomy, an outrage, yet another despicable antediluvian attempt to ignore her as an individual and manipulate the fate of the unfortunate personage she was continually obliged to appear to be.

How dare they allot her a husband! Without ever even asking! Without ever even raising the subject. Parading her before this chap as if she were a horse for sale or something!

After the fish, however, which Daphne waved away (all those bones and such sad eyes) she had calmed down somewhat and resolved to visit her indignation upon those that really deserved it, which was not this young Italian prince, however annoying his apparent acceptance of the matchmaking might be. She would have to stifle her rage until she could corner her father. In the meantime she turned her attention to dissipating the rather embarrassing youthful egoism of this scion of whatever he was scion of, and uncovering the person within. A thing she was generally good at. Disquietingly so, some thought.

He played a lot of tennis, he had a lot of horses, though he did not ride much; he had been taught the piano (but Daphne knew without hearing him that he couldn't play; she really hoped he was one of those that knew they could not play) he wrote a lot of poetry (god help us, quick change the subject) he could stand on his head (why would anyone want to?) but that was enough about him he wanted to talk about her (what?). By the time they'd reached dessert she had to admit he was not so bad. And she could not deny that he had an original and sort of sideways sense of humour, as well as very nice eyes, lovely smooth slightly shiny skin, the most expressive dark eyebrows and knew almost as much as she did about Praxiteles.

He laughed uncontrollably when she very deliberately inserted her ear plugs for the speeches. 'Why should I listen? It's always the most dreadful predictable drivel – even Daddy, he doesn't

write his own any more he got bored with it too.' He laughed with
her at the applause and table thumping when she pointed out how
the most enthusiastic were always those with the most medals.
All in all she survived the dinner quite well, even though it was
the occasion of the revelation of this most appalling affront to her
individuality and her future happiness. As soon as she was able
she shook Alfonso's hand and absented herself from the hall. Once
back in the sanctuary of her lair she began once more to seethe,
coming quickly back to the boil like a previously-heated kettle
being returned to the hob. She shed the disguise of her formal dress
as quickly as she could, donned trousers and a man's flannel shirt
and looked meaningfully at the Empty Horse – someone would
have to suffer for the ignominy she had endured this night. In due
course when the rattle of carriages on cobbles had finally ceased,
when the great chandeliers were lowered and the myriad candles
laboriously snuffed, when footmen and pages and kitchen boys had
withdrawn below, sucking with them all the clatter and detritus of
regal ritual and silver service, she rose from her chaise, pulled a
little black felt hat shaped rather like a helmet onto her head and
slipped out into the long corridors and winding stairs which, if you
knew the way, interlocked like a puzzle and could be made to bring
you to the King's private apartments.

CHAPTER FIVE

The link-man that Vangrannicus had sent to seek out Johnson cursed the labyrinth of narrow muddy lanes as he made his way uncertainly into the dingy quarter where the oldest part of the old town cascaded beyond the medieval walls into a shabby shanty town which occupied the foetid landward side of the citadel between a stagnant pond and a dark and sluggish minor tributary of the true river. He was nervous of asking directions; the few people he saw slumped outside mumbling shebeens or creeping round the horse shit did not look as if they would be in any particular awe of the fleurs de lis on his tabard, and some of the few that looked up when he passed looked distinctly as if they might be sizing him up for a cudgelling. Eventually he found the road which had been described to him, one which led out of the town and across a vast meadow whose grasses susurrated in a light breeze and made their own waves like a little sea. Difficult to make out in the dark until he had traipsed a further mile or so, there was, looking back at the town and castle with a detached air solidly unimpressed by either the grandeur or the squalor which were squashed together opposite to it, a substantial stone cottage with its door open and a light burning.

Stepping at last over the threshold, the King's messenger did not even manage the first word of, 'His Majesty King Dagobert requests and demands the immediate presence of zoo-keeper Johnson in his private apartments,' before the figure seated on a hard chair facing the meagre fire stood up, turned round, grabbed a bowler hat from the hat stand and marched past him on the way out. The link-man's dignity was dented. He shouted at Johnson, 'I say, will you, Stop! Where are you going?' but he had to gallop to catch up in order to say it and the terse, 'I know,' which Johnson emitted in a cloud of hoarse cigar smoke upset him considerably.

'Stop, what do you mean you know? How can you know before I've told you? Do you realise that failure to comply with a King's man in the execution of his duty is a serious crime.'

'I'm not,' said Johnson and walked on.

There was a noise behind them and the door of Johnson's house was shut by a small person whom the link man had caught no glimpse of. Very many more people than he had never seen her. But it was a fact that the door was closed and it had not closed on its own.

'You must hear the official summons, you can't just walk out.'

Johnson passed silently on. The messenger could hardly keep up with his relentless pace, they were already half way across the great flat expanse of the ghostly grassland.

The dim, fluttering, feverish lights of the hovels and taverns beyond the clean sweep of the fresh meadow beckoned the traveller to emerge from the purity of night into human civilization, which could not but think itself irresistibly desirable. The shambles of smelly and ramshackle nidification spread before the castle walls in reality glowed with dull pain and hummed with desperation. The closer it came, the more the wanderer feared the half light of the dull hearths whose underglow made demons of those huddled over them; the more he recoiled from the screams and coarse laughter which punctuated the low babble of human chatter; the more he wanted to free the enslaved beasts, their lives fettered to the sad botched clutter of collective human aspirations.

Johnson looked beyond the tumble of cottages to the stern magnificence of the citadel and fortress which rose up behind it with brighter and steadier lights, ensigns flapping dimly from their poles, almost lost in the cloudy height of the night. Humanity was there subdued by the thickness of the walls and the enforced decorum of the royal establishment, yet it had little more allure for Johnson whose experience of the world had taught him a measure of detachment from his own species as much as from ant and hornet, wildebeeste and toad. He took each creature and its tribe on its merits but rarely placed any faith in people or wild pigs.

This frontier land between people and wild nature which he and the messenger now trod was a familiar one to Johnson. Equally familiar as a hinterland in both directions. Often misty, dark or blurred by the shaking of the wind, this end and beginning of different realms, where strange creatures lurk and eyes strain to see them for what they might be. Where men imagine things they cannot quite see and beasts see men they cannot at all understand. Johnson had patrolled it for a long long time, flitting into the hive of men when necessary and roaming back into the wild as the spirit and the season moved him.

Reaching the other side, he and the linkman now passed amongst the skewed and fragile dwellings of the town's frontier, and made their way through the mud and rubbish, the untidy jumble of poverty which fed with its labour and its taxes the great fortress, like roots providing for some huge tree. At the drawbridge, the messenger called, 'Ho! The King's messenger!', was recognised, or ignored, by anyone present or awake in the porter's lodge, and the pair were soon through the gate, across the vast parade ground and disappearing through a door and into a tangle of stairs and corridors that delivered them into a vestibule, lit by a calm and steady candelabrum before a polished door upon which the escort knocked most deliberately, and most respectfully.

The door was opened and the messenger turned and disappeared without a word. Johnson entered the dark library and looked about him at walls of books until he found a balustrade and stairs and, at the bottom of the stairs in a pool of light, Frederick sitting at a desk reading and talking to himself. He commented on what he read and it was not always obvious which was the text and which his observation.

'Ctesias, hmm – who perhaps should have discovered the gnu – gave us one of the earliest written descriptions of the unicorn in his *Indica* (c400 BCE). He was followed eventually by a number of Romans – including one Julius Caesar, hum, that man crops up where you'd never expect him.

'I see, so, before he was followed by a number of Romans, however, this Ctesias was preceded by whoever wrote the bits of the Old Testament that mention the unicorn.

'Interesting...

'Except that they don't. In the original, what they mention is something called the Re'em, which the translators of the Septuagint with cavalier inventiveness chose to render as "unicorn" but was no such thing. (More likely it was the aurochs, of blessed memory but no remainder trace.) Oh for an aurochs, those oxen we have aren't the real thing, I've always known that.

'These Roman post-Ctesians can easily be painted mad or credulous by we scientific moderns, but for the most part they were neither – though a case can be made for "confused". Yes, I agree its damnable confusing...

'Their waters were muddied by the interfering rhinoceros. Which would keep sticking its horn in.' (He snorted softly at his own joke.) 'It seems in fact... that... yes, about the rhinoceros there is no doubt, and there never has been. Pliny, Aelian, Appolonius of Tyana, they had all almost certainly seen rhinoceroses in the amphitheatre where they (the rhinos) would have been teased and tortured along with a multiplicity of exotic fauna for the diversion of the Imperial throng. What a cruel rabble they could be. They each also wrote about the unicorn... but their familiarity with one creature did not stop it nosing its attributes into their descriptions of the other, infinitely rarer one. So that we are told frequently that the unicorn has feet very like an elephant, a black horn and a tale like a boar. Whereas... where was it?' (He was reading from and referring back to at least half a dozen books propped, piled and opened on the huge desk.) 'Ctesias and others, especially in the East, (goodness, Genghis Khan, in due course, amongst them) spoke unambiguously of a wild ass type. There is no doubt... however... that classical zoology was aware of two monoceri, even though... sloppiness often crept into which had what type of feet and where, precisely, that single horn protruded, brow or snout.'

He leaned back in his chair and Johnson, who had by now quietly approached from behind, was about to make his presence known when the King started up again.

'What there was never any confusion about was that these animals, and especially their horns, were medicinally marvellous. For hundreds of years, if not millennia, all animal horns were deemed beneficial and the rhino's was worth its weight in gold. Prized even beyond this, however, was the horn of the unicorn, the "alicorn", rarer than hen's teeth and worth a King's ransom. Just think of it, even a small fragment could set you up for life, a whole horn could only be aspired to by a handful of the super-rich, royalty, emperors, potentates and popes. Not something we would want here, by jove. Only whole animals in my collection thank you very much. Stuff and nonsense. Stuff.' He turned to the marker in another volume. 'This was so in the West and in India, but not, surprisingly perhaps, in the Far East. The unicorn has been as much a Chinese beast as a European or Indian one. There it is known, principally, as Ki Lin but, though equally solitary, elusive, invulnerable to capture, magical and pure, in China the beast seems to be much gentler than its western cousin... and not so much... not treated as a walking chemist's shop.

'The Chinese... would appear to be... in fact much less muddled about the rhinoceros and the unicorn, they are quite clear not only in their differentiation between the two identities, but also in keeping the characteristics of each creature distinct from those of the other. So that the Chinese unicorn shares... many of the physical attributes of Ctesias's animal but has none of the grosser distinguishing features of the rhino or... where was it?... Kartazoan.'

'Ahem.'

'What? Ah, aha, Johnson, there you are, come here, come here, please sit down.'

Johnson proved to be more inclined to soften towards the conventional mores in this bookish night-time assignation, and deigned to settle on a chair opposite his sovereign, and even relinquished the stern bowler to the care of an occasional table nearby. He remained stiff-necked however and the dark eyes stared steadily without blinking.

'I've been reading up a bit, you know, about the...the, er, this unicorn phenomenon, phenomena. You seem to have prompted me to do a bit of digging – dashed interesting this whole business you know – your mentioning it this afternoon seems to have set me off.'

Johnson was not going to say anything much until the King asked him a direct question, that was obvious. He never really entered into conversations, preferring to gaze about him, wary but invulnerable, like an ox suddenly beset by goats. Though respectful he looked as if he could easily become annoyed. He darted glances up and sideways from time to time but mostly he fixed his would-be interlocutor with a steady gaze which, even for the monarch in his own library instilled a measure of unease. 'Yes,' he said.

The King had forgotten his question. Had he asked a question? 'Well, so Johnson, pray tell us, are you on the trail... have you seen something, something that might be...?'

He was silent for a long pause and then said, 'There is unicorn, King, I will get it.'

Vangrannicus would very likely have struck him if he'd heard such an insolent, impertinent form of address. Dagobert the Fourth was himself somewhat taken aback but was coming to realise that the man before him was in many ways beyond the scope of human custom. He was like a farm dog who would come to the door but no further; he would not yap with pugs and poodles.

'So where is it? Where might it be found? Have you seen it? What does it look like? Are you actually sure it is an authentic unicorn?'

Johnson's enigmatic and oblique response was, 'Need virgin. Looking for the right sort of virgin.'

The King was nonplussed for a moment and shook his head, scrabbling amongst the books on his desk. Then, staring and frowning at Johnson he walked across to the bookshelves, climbed a ladder and came down blowing dust off a large old volume. 'You don't mean to say... Do you actually believe this old story?'

He was somewhere between annoyance, pity and amusement. The book was a medieval bestiary and contained, as he remembered it, an account of the legend that unicorns are to be successfully caught in only one way. A strong and mighty beast, there was only one subterfuge to which it would succumb. The unicorn could only be tamed by a virgin maid.

He found the place and recited, translating from the Latin, 'It can be caught in this way: a girl who is a true virgin must be taken to the place in the woods where it dwells and is left there alone. When the unicorn sees her he jumps into her lap and embraces her and there goes to sleep. The hunters come and capture it and carry it off to the King.'

He stared at Johnson, returning, for once, his steady gaze. 'Johnson, are you telling me that not only do you believe the unicorn exists but you actually believe this medieval codswallop? Oh come on, what are you really on about? Do you think the story stands for something? What do you mean, what is all this about?'

*

Like a frayed and delitescent silhouette made indistinct and questionable as to its exact shape by a smooth but unpredictable motion through the gloom, stopping to disappear for moments at a time and then emerging again as the suddenly moving shadow of some item of furniture, a figure made its way along the corridors of the royal ants' nest in search of its father. Daphne's caution was in this instance unnecessary since the palace snored and no one was aware of her wanderings, but she knew well that though she was perfectly entitled to go where she would, in reality her presence anywhere troubled and excited and embarrassed such a multitude of servants, guards and lackeys that she found it much the most expedient plan to go about on such missions as this stealthily and in disguise. She had over the years twice been taken for an interloper and caused an alarm, but there was never any real danger of arrest – the guards were amiable chaps and entirely useless – and on the whole she preferred that risk to the continual irritation of persons questioning with their eyes where she was going or what she was doing here at this time of day, or at this time of night as it might be. Incognito was a habit she had got into in childhood and never given up.

Where the devil was he? Not in his chamber, which had been her first port of call; he would not be in that damned zoo place surely at this time of night would he? On the occasion of the arrival of some weird beast that would only show itself at night, he had been known to have an armchair, blankets and cocoa all carried down the causeway. But she did not believe that was where he was tonight, there was no zoo news as far as she knew. He was not a carousing King, and would not have lingered over liqueurs with either visiting Italians or any of the resident courtiers (quite a few of the latter would have liked nothing better but had long since given up any hope of turning their sovereign in that direction). Then the obvious dawned on her – of course, if he couldn't sleep he was probably in the library. Fifteen minutes later she was outside the door. The little door, that is the one to the library gallery. Consequently as she entered and emerged from between bookshelves and peered over the railing she saw far below the little cocoon of yellow light from the King's lectern that illuminated both her father and a strange man who looked as if he ought not to be in a library. Or in the castle at all really. Who could he be? Had her father been alone she would have swooped down and accosted him angrily but she was somewhat thwarted by the presence of this other, and not knowing quite whether he was someone who could be ignored.

She heard her father speaking but couldn't make out any words, the cathedral space of the library and the way the acres of leather bindings seemed to squash and absorb most of the sound, leaving only a residue of the slightest whispering echo to bounce about the books, had the effect of reducing his utterances to a distant mutter.

Then she did hear something. Very clearly indeed. It was not her father but the other one, the bullet-head protruding from the dirty black coat that suddenly said, very loud, 'Virgin! Must be virgin, King!' and she shied backwards like a startled horse, shocked, confused and then outraged. (Johnson's broadside of a voice, when fully charged, would shatter any venerable acoustic.) He must be one of them. He was some sort of Mr Fixit for the Venetians, he was some scumbag Mafioso doing a deal, it was her marriage they were talking about and these dreadful people were demanding assurances about the Princess Daphne's intactness. It was unbelievable, it was horrible. How could her father even entertain such a man, how could he even allow such a topic of conversation? She found she was sitting on the floor, looked down upon by the stern and disinterested spines of scientific journals, each full of incontravertibilities no doubt, but all blind to her sudden trauma.

When she had collected herself and crept back to the balustrade she was partly relieved and partly frustrated to see that there was no one there. The lamp still burned on the lectern at the desk where her father had been sitting but he was not there, and no more was the mysterious stranger. The Princess had been angry on her way to he library, now she was on the verge of apoplexy and it made her eyes water and brought a tingling sensation to the tips of her toes and fingers. Had she gone down into the nave of the library she would have come upon the King who was up a ladder returning books to a high shelf in an alcove. But she did not. She ran out in a state of great agitation, her thoughts mixed up, not really knowing at first where she was going but then realising that she was running after the Italian pig who spoke of her as if she was herself an item of livestock. And her father had not demurred! At least she had not heard him say anything. Was it credible? Would Frederick really deal with such people in these terms? He was less than perfect, she had very good reason to know that, oh yes, indeed, but this? His own daughter? He had suddenly turned into a different person. Perhaps she had never really known him as she thought she had. The flaw which had already caused one terrible tragedy had all the time perhaps been hiding others, equally important and horrific, from her. Blindly she negotiated without thinking the network of stairs and corridors, she would overhaul this Hymeneal gangster and give him what for. It did not occur to her at the time but she afterwards realised that she went after the foreigner rather than her father because having to face up to the King's apparent behaviour was much more complicated than simply chasing after a villain and a stranger.

Descending a spiral staircase she glimpsed the dark figure through an arrow slit making his was across the courtyard. She tripled the drumming of her feet and was down and into the short-cut corridor and would surely confront him before he reached the gate, but though he seemed to move in a sort of loping shamble he was a lot quicker than you would imagine, and indeed he was already though the gate and heading into the town – she saw his shadow flitting along as she almost broke into a jog past the snoring sentries. But then she lost him. She found herself in the dark medieval jumble of the old streets, looking this way and that and straining to hear his footsteps. She gambled on the straightest lane, which actually led out of the town toward the open country, and hurried down it. She was rewarded with the relief and excitement of the sight of a now very distant black figure crossing the huge flat meadow. She stopped. Why is he here, where on Earth is he going? The Venetian delegation would be in the guest rooms of the castle, why was he not going back to his apartment? Though she felt a strong inclination to rush along on the trail of this mysterious shabby character, her impetus was somewhat held back by the darkness, the rather forbidding blankness of the meadow, a cold breeze that had sprung up, and the realisation that out here her disguise might become more trouble than, in the castle, it saved her from – equality and anonymity were all very well but wandering the wilderness in the garb of an ordinary youth she was laying herself open to fates that the most hardened footpads would think twice about before inflicting on a daughter of Dagobert. It wasn't that she was scared, for she did in fact frequently venture forth in disguise – she was a resourceful and adventurous princess – but experience had taught her that she needed to be better prepared. She would go back and think what to do.

But in all the trouble and confusion and notwithstanding the menace that was wont to creep amongst unruly nature out here, she found as she stood now beyond the great walls, she was again reminded of the allure of freedom. On every illicit extra-mural escapade she had never failed to feel that something beckoned. She felt on this occasion that there could be no doubt that she would be able to see things more clearly if she were only alone and away from everything and free of the rammel of ritual and expectation and dressing up and small talk and using the right fork and all that pondweed of castle life that just tangled her up and would not let her breathe, only then would she be better company for herself. She could no longer live all the time with an unexploded scream corked up inside her.

CHAPTER SIX

Willoughby was crunching toast, his slice held in the air away from the book which commanded all his attention. Ordinarily he would not have dreamt of wafting marmalade anywhere near anything from his own library but breakfast had caught him in the middle of a sort of trance which the words he read had inflicted on him and he had wandered in and sat down at table able only to apply the most mechanical motions of an automaton to the business of pouring, lifting, sipping, spreading and munching. What he read was truly a revelation to him and opened up one hugely unlikely but utterly compelling possibility. Could it really be? Could there actually be some remote survival from this weird antediluvian species? Extant. Not extinct. And hidden all these years. All these millennia?

The trail he had followed which had lead to this page weaved its specific path through the kingdom of Animalia: via the phylum Chordata, into the Class Mammalia, taking the byway of Infraclass Eutheria, forking into the Order Perssodactyla, on through the Suborder of the Ceratomorpha which delivered him amongst the Family of the Rhinocerotidae, and then was finally revealed to him the strange and fantastic and long extinct elasmotherium. The elasmotherium, just look at it – there was a detailed drawing – imagine that, what a peculiar beast. What a truly remarkable feature it had had. A huge long horn right bang in the centre of its forehead. What other creature could it possibly be? This surely was the actual unicorn. It must have been some prehistoric memory of this very beast which had languished in the human consciousness for thousands of years and become the white horse with the prong. This must be it. He dropped the toast with a plink onto his plate and pulled the volume up close to peer at the artist's impression of a reconstruction from the fossil evidence.

The more he looked at it the more ordinary it became. The fabulousness faded and it was with hardly any stretch of the imagination that the animal became not only possible but eminently likely. Was it not indeed just the sort of thing that might easily snort and whinny in a small herd meandering across steppes or veldt or prairie, causing barely a glance from passing Tartar, Gaucho or bushman? Then he thought of Johnson and his obstinate thick-headedness and the imagination living in that lumpen cranium being capable of making this whole thing up was laughable. He could not have made it up. Of course, he did not make it up. A very uncharacteristic nervousness swept over him with the realisation that he, Willoughby, believed in the unicorn. There was one, and Johnson had seen it. During that breakfast Johnson's status in the fine mind of Willoughby moved from annoying grubby idiot who demeaned the profession to serious rival who had had the effrontery to steal a march on him. This was serious. That mono-syllabic peasant had actually come across a chance survival of the lost species, a quadrupedic sasquatch, a monocerautic yeti. Something must be done. This was the greatest thing ever; new species of spiders and the like could not hold a candle to this. His mind raced.

What? What must be done? Well, first of all Johnson must be watched, his every movement must be monitored. Willoughby rang the bell with a single urgent exaggerated tug and remembered as the butler opened the door that all his men were still far away crating up the singing dog – damn. But, probably for the best, something as big as this and as secret as this should not be entrusted to the hired help. He stood up and began to pace up and down before the marble fireplace. His slippers stepped in and out of the shaft of sunlight which beamed down onto the Turkish rug, and Newsome, the ancient butler who had waited upon the Hon. Willoughby during the latter's entire life so far, stood patiently by the door trying vaguely and vainly to anticipate what might be required of him. Willoughby was wrenched to and fro, as he looked back at the book on the table – dangerously close to the marmalade – the wonder of the thing the amazing, bizarre miraculous possibility of the survival of the thing knocked him sideways and the calm command he usually exerted over everything gave way to a sort of frantic anxiety when the dread thought that the discovery, the revelation to the world, the unveiling of living mythology to a bemused population, that all this should fall to someone who was not him. Someone who was Johnson for god's sake! He suddenly guffawed at the irony

The butler stood and waited. But no instructions were forthcoming (he must have rung for something) instead the abstracted face which had continued to ignore Newsome was suddenly swept past him and through the door without a second glance. Newsome might have tutted and looked heavenward had he not been so used to his employer's ways.

His master strode up the stairs and ransacked his wardrobe for clothes scruffy enough to constitute a disguise – a search which bore no fruit of course and then he had a brain wave. Returning to the breakfast room where Newsome was clearing the table he explained that for purposes that need not be gone into now he needed some old clothes and after looking up and down the very large bulk of the butler to confirm there could be no help in that direction he whispered a suggestion which plunged that good man into an inexpressible consternation. His outrage was strangled by the proprieties in which he daily trussed himself but Willoughby got the message, the speechlessness and the bulging eyes told him just how improper it would be for him, the master of the house, to insinuate himself into the servants quarters and plunder their most intimate and private possessions. Willoughby had been all for plunging through the green baize door into what had been since the beginning of the feudal system the only no-go area for self-respecting members of the upper class, and just helping himself.

Newsome said he would see what he could do. Knowing that if he did not do something Willoughby would just wait until his back was turned and would soon be clawing his way into the drawers and tiny wardrobes of unconsidered retainers, scattering underwear and secret billets doux. A little later as his master, back in the study, was once more running a magnifying glass over the image of Elasmotherium there was a cough and he looked up to find Newsome standing with a bundle in his arms which was a chunky pullover belonging to the chauffeur and some corduroy trousers which usually warmed the no-doubt hairy legs of the gardener.

Willoughby whooped with delight, declared the butler a 'Good man!' and muttered conciliatory stuff such as: after all, he paid their wages so it was with his money they had bought these things, so they were sort of his, and any way he was only borrowing them wasn't he, he wasn't going to keep them for god's sake. Anyway if he had had time to explain his need to them they would surely have queued up to donate items in the furtherance of his urgent mission. Look here, just chuck them some of my stuff, would you? We could just do a swap.

Newsome presumed on their very long acquaintance to give him one of his grandest sniffs and most ironic bows before making a very stately exit.

Willoughby repaired swiftly to his own quarters and after some fiddling and trying and rejecting accessories of one sort and another presented to his full length dressing mirror a raffish, decidedly un-aristocratic figure in a shapeless black felt hat that would not attract a second glance in the Lanes of the town. Or so he thought. In fact though he might fool himself in the mirror, there was something which no amount of moth-holes and odd boot laces could quite hide completely from the casual observer, and that was a natural curl of the lip, a characteristic and unfortunately permanent semi-sneer of distaste which Willoughby's face would always naturally relax into and which would always betray him to anyone looking closely. It would take surgery or perhaps a set of false teeth with an exaggerated overbite to complete the job – to make him look sufficiently odd that people would be embarrassed to stare at him for long enough to see him for who he was. But first it would take an awareness on his part of the problem of this sneer, and his time before the glass had concentrated only on the shabby clothing (and the assumption of a rather comic slouch which Willoughby took to be characteristic of the unfortunate classes); he had not looked hard at his own face.

Willoughby was cursed with an arrogance which repelled people as much as his wealth attracted them and demanded their respect; his background and circumstances created in this way a tension of positive and negative magnetism that effectively created a force-field about him, either frightening people and tongue-tying them or enraging them and making them want to spit on his brogues, a force-field which separated him from many of the pleasures of normal social intercourse, and in as much as this gulch had divorced him from much of the fun and relaxation of ordinary life he was to be pitied.

But he was difficult – his self-centredness ran very deep within him and even Newsome, who loved him and who had held his hand whilst they had fed the ducks together and taught him to bowl a hoop and ride a bicycle, knew in his heart of hearts that Willoughby, as a grown up, was not really much liked and was in many ways not very likeable. And he was used to Willoughby's childish attitude toward rules, which was that none of them were intended to apply to him, and if his exemption had not been made explicit it was merely an oversight.

However, Newsome and some few other intimates of long standing saw other things. They saw that not infrequently was Willoughby blessed with little epiphanies which allowed him tantalising and unsettling visions of the things that most people already knew about. Like the value of little kindnesses, and the intelligence and hidden accomplishments of the unqualified and also that people could often reveal themselves to be articulate in ways alien to the orthodox.

The good butler was now asked to unearth any sort of cheap duffle bag that the house might harbour and pack it with smalls and socks, a toothbrush, a razor – er, no on second thoughts forget the razor – some sandwiches and a bottle of something and to have it ready when he came back. Willoughby, dressed like the butler didn't know what, then scurried from the house and entered the lane via the kitchen garden wall with an athletic leap that surprised the housemaid who happened to be looking out of an upper window and recognised her husband's trousers, but not the style or direction of their travel, and was most dumbfounded.

Willoughby knew little about Johnson, nothing more in fact than his name, what he looked like and his wilful obtuseness, so there was only one place he could begin – the zoo. If he wasn't himself present there they must know where he was or where he lived.

He must make sure that no one else was on the trail. As he made his way he began to wonder about the other animal collectors and whether any of them could also have cottoned on to the possibility of a survival from the fossil era. Would any of them have done the research he had? There was the King himself of course – he might have done so. He had a huge library, and the right sort of enquiring mind. But then… he had been dismissive of the idea in the rotunda, and more concerned with Johnson's mental health. Still, the possibility presented itself of triumphantly unveiling something to a man who by then already knew all about it. That would be unspeakably deflating. He could imagine the cackling of the courtiers, many of whom hated him, and were most adept at scoring points in the 'oh of course we always knew all about that' type of condescension. It would probably be prudent to make enquiries of the King's librarian, try to find out what books he'd been opening recently. But what about Wilson and Turner and Simpson and Jemima Cake, and that disgusting woman with the budgie up her jumper?

The latter was beyond the pale, but the others had been surprisingly bearable on that last occasion… but, no, they were none of them anywhere near his sort of people. And suddenly to cultivate their friendship with overtures about Johnson's unicorn would have given rise to suspicion; there was the danger that he might actually be creating rivals by planting ideas in their heads.

Oh god, it was all getting complicated. First, thing was to find Johnson. When Willoughby knew exactly where he was and exactly what he was up to everything would become clearer.

The boots Willoughby wore were actually his own, but they were very old and no longer fitted properly so that the shambling locomotion which had first been affected was now increasingly real and his equilibrium was further undermined by a distinct and disquieting itchiness deriving from the pullover, whose grubbiness he had originally welcomed as a feature adding authenticity, but which he was becoming convinced was probably exuding anthrax, or some other creeping plague. So the figure that approached the menagerie office was not quite as at ease with itself as it usually was.

But, as he looked up and around at the zoo buildings, at the bricks and the moss and the lichen, bright red and green and gold, and heard the whooping of gibbons which so excited the children queuing at the turnstile of the main gate and watched those green leaves of the great sweet chestnut tree which were visible above the wall wafting in the slight breeze and the sunshine, Willoughby, though troubled, was yet oddly enlivened. He was beginning to feel an excitement – he felt he had a new purpose and for the first time in ages he was not bored. He was anxious because he wasn't entirely sure quite what he was going to do, but he was not bored. Usually things to be done resolved themselves into instructions to be handed down; he was suddenly at the centre of things rather than sitting aloof at the top pulling strings. In this new situation he was aware that floundering and flustering and dithering lapped about him and might well sweep him into their lake of confusion and failure, he must be decisive and determined if he wanted to succeed.

If Johnson led him to the mythical beast how exactly would he wrest attention from that man, the mere accidental instrument of the discovery, and manoeuvre the spotlight to shine on the animal catcher whose researches had predicted its discovery (Willoughby already believed this) and was able expertly to classify and describe its origins. With any luck Johnson's role might be elbowed into oblivion with a little judicious management of the press, his colleagues and the court. Facts could be manipulated, everyone had their price. Memories were short and played tricks. If all else came to nought he could at least let it be known that it was he who had perhaps, for selfless reasons of his own, laid out the clues for Johnson to follow.

But first – where was he? Where the devil did the mysterious Johnson slink and snort through his allotted hours?

When he entered the zoo office Willoughby was immediately reminded that in concocting his disguise he had thought only in terms of not being himself, he had not given any thought to creating a plausible identity – he was just 'scruffy bloke' and 'scruffy bloke' was about to find that the world reacted to him rather differently than it did to Jolyon Ffinch-Hesketh Willoughby, Bart.

'No help wanted! Sorry nothing today – come back in a week there might be a bit of mucking out, thank you!' She barely raised her eyes from her ledger, the severe-looking, uniformed girl at the desk.

CHAPTER SEVEN

Culvert Grimes was feeding grain to a gaggle of assorted exotic fowl and their chicks clucking and whistling around him in an old enclosure beside the river. His mind was elsewhere and he almost crushed a tiny downy infant pecking too close to his Wellington boot before he flung the dregs from the bucket in an arc across the ground and leaned against the wall with folded arms, looking at the birds and contemplating the world and the very many things in it which he could put right if only he had the chance.

Culvert Grimes, though he was physically at ease in this pensive posture, nonetheless looked not quite balanced, ungainly in some indefinable way. His body never looked entirely at rest even when the eye detected no motion. He always had about himself a certain awkwardness, and awkwardnesses seemed to be thrown up around him; flung up by the friction of his earnest, unpredictable toing and froing, bristling and bustling, by his constant and energetic endeavours to be noticed. Experience had taught him that people were likely to shy away from the churning energy of his runaway brain – he had restrained the outward spectacle of himself, he had learned not to speak out all his thoughts, and even sometimes to hold his tongue entirely. Whereas, as a boy, people could see from a great distance that this child was peculiar and barely in command of himself, now they were likely, at first, to take him for nothing more than awkward looking. And then to find themselves ambushed by a disturbing character. Some thought he needed 'looking at' and were not averse to saying so.

He had no small talk, but the sheer and unexpected directness of his rigid smile, goggle eyes and bold bludgeoning comments and questions, as they were brought to bear on whomever he had cornered, made the weather and other pleasantries irrelevant. You might have thought people would have been repulsed by him, and many were, but a surprising number failed to back away. After the initial double take at his effrontery some people indeed became fascinated and a little amused by this uppity, forthright, angular, broken nosed but rather arresting character with apparently no sensitivity and the clumsy manners of one for whom the norms of social intercourse were as foreign as a language he understood nothing of. The unconventionality and naïve inventiveness of his ideas held their attention, occasionally to a jaw-dropping extent. Some even became a little afraid of him. And he was clever, in an odd way, wasn't he?

Anyone he thought important or popular ran the risk of being buttonholed, for he loved to be the one to announce things to people, to tell them things that he knew but they did not. He wanted people to notice him and to remember him. And thence he would proceed to build a history of their mutual encounters which he would refer to and embroider a little more on each subsequent meeting until his victim came to believe that he really did know this persistent but admittedly sometimes useful fellow (his information was always punctiliously accurate); and he was convinced that it was indeed working, slowly his face was becoming familiar to many of those who strutted about the court or beetled along the castle corridors was it not? He thought himself the bosom friend of some of them. What he appeared not to see were the increasing numbers who scuttled round corners or through the nearest available door on his approach.

There was no malice in him. He never meant to do anyone any harm – he was always bent on his own aggrandisement rather than the doing down of others – but at the same time he seemed to have no conventional concept of morality and it was true that he was observed to take pleasure in the discomfort his presence often caused in people. He believed in status: he had to believe that there were people less important than him. He believed in being recognised by people that mattered, only in that way would he himself matter.

'Good morning Herr Schmidt!' (an attaché at the Fitzrovian embassy) 'The charcuterie on Thimble Street has genuine Fitzrovian sausages today, my regards to your family!' And yet he managed to bring off this sort of thing without any impression of impertinence – it was too out of the blue to be conventionally impertinent – nor was his manner in the least ingratiating. It was matter of fact and in a baritone that was arresting, egalitarian and not to be ignored. However the eyes always stared in such an off-putting way. Though his information often seemed to have been deliberately sought out to please the recipient, Willoughby believed it sounded lofty and oracular, as if it were one of the million things he had at his fingertips and which overflowed from him to the particular benefit of whomever he encountered.

'Good morning Sir John!' (Master of the King's Music) 'At the concert last Thursday they performed your second quartet in G minor without the repeats in the third movement. I noticed. Not many others did. Did you say they could play it that way? Did you give them permission?' This accompanied by some superfluous mime of violin playing.

But he rarely stopped to enter into conversation, even if the other signalled his or her readiness for it, he would merely nod a little bow and move on. This puzzlingly mis-integrated man did not really understand conversation. Beyond eavesdropping (he did a lot of that, he liked that) he'd never learnt to listen to people in the normal ball-batting tennis of a normal dialogue. Talk was for information. And he who demonstrated that he had information perforce demonstrated his superiority.

The animal collecting was for him, to begin with at least, a means to an end. When he learnt that there might be a job going with Simpson, one of the Royal Menagerie Men, he had immediately assumed a lifelong interest in zoology, read up on the subject intensely and hung around the zoo continually. His persistence paid off, it was too hard to get rid of him sometimes without saying yes – and he was given an interview; at which, due to its focus on zoology rather than personality, Grimes impressed sufficiently that a month or so later he had become a familiar figure in the bottle green uniform. Grimes would have taken up anything that commanded such a high place on the royal agenda – had the King's obsession been the theatre or fishing or carpentry or ping pong he would have launched himself equally enthusiastically into any of those activities and made a reasonable fist of them, for he was intelligent and adaptable. But somewhat to his surprise he had found he had a natural inclination toward zoology, and quickly became very involved with the animal world. He was already something of an expert on some of the birds which were the chief province of Simpson's group. He was very good at detail and there was a lot of detail in animal biology if you were prepared to look into it. And Grimes, who had never been squeamish, was prepared to look into anything. Relished it.

Today he was feeding corn to fowls in an obscure corner of the zoo and mentally running through the changes he would make when, as was inevitable, he eventually succeeded to Simpson's position. A shuffling noise behind him and he turned round to see a stooping figure in a black hat pulled down over his eyes peering through the wire.

''Scuse, Johnson, looking for Johnson, do you know where he lives?'

Probably best to draw a veil over Willoughby's encounter with the officious woman in the office which redounded to the credit of neither of them, suffice to say he had given her the slip and wandered about looking for any other of the staff to ask his question.

Grimes gave him a quick glance of appraisal, concluded that he was not anyone who merited any particular consideration, and held him at arm's length with a, 'What?'

'Johnson, Mr Johnson, looking for him, would you have his address I wonder? Please.' It has not yet been mentioned but Grimes suffered from a great reluctance ever to admit that he did not know something.

'Why are you looking for Johnson?' Grimes had turned fully round and advanced on Willoughby and brought his staring eyes to within a very uncomfortable proximity.

Willoughby was immediately wary of discovery and backed away looking at the ground. He said the first thing that came into his head, 'Got a message for him.'

'I'll give it to him. Who are you? Where have you come from? You want to be careful, there's tigers round the corner.'

'No, I'm supposed to give it only to him.'

'Don't you trust me, fellow? I'm in charge here. Who are you? Have you got a pass? Did you come through the turnstiles?'

This was all but intolerable for Willoughby. To be treated like this by some glorified farmhand made him shake within and it was with great difficulty that he reined himself in and stopped himself from assuming his natural posture, hurling away the felt hat and reinstating the natural order of things. Then he recognised the man. It was one of Simpson's damned birdmen – he'd been there at the rotunda. 'If he recognises me he'll know what I'm about for sure,' he thought. 'Oh hell.'

The lurid wattle and great horny casque of a huge cassowary slowly and slyly introduced itself from behind a brick pillar. It must have escaped from its adjoining cage and now peered circumspectly this way and that. It was huge, nearly five feet tall and, with its razor sharp clawed toes, more than capable of inflicting death or horrific injuries, for all its bemused look. It began to approach Grimes behind his back and Willoughby saw its legs from beneath the brim of his black hat.

'You are not a Herald or a Royal Messenger, my friend, you have not the tabard, you must show me some credentials before I can go giving out the whereabouts of Menagerie Men.' Grimes was taking the upper hand and beginning to enjoy himself. Other beaks, some stiletto, some huge and curved like chunky wooden scimitars moved about the rear of the enclosure and hopped from perch to perch and calls and cries and whoops and roars began to be heard from all around the zoo as the two strange men faced one another through the wire. Neither of them knew how unappealing they were – but there's nothing unusual in that. One was pretending to be what he wasn't without understanding that he ought to be less like he really was. The other never gave a thought to what he was, only to what he wanted to appear to be – which was not really a person but a station, a rank – he would have been happy to be totally hollow as long as people respected him for what he knew.

Willoughby wanted to look up and determine once and for all whether he had been recognised, but knew he must not. He muttered incoherently some stuff about a mysterious person who needed urgently to get in touch with Johnson, but was beginning to back away, preparatory to beating a full retreat, when Grimes suddenly said, 'Cottage out of town, across the marsh they say, he don't like visitors though.' And Willoughby couldn't help looking up in surprise and seeing such a twinkle in Grimes's eye that convinced him his cover was blown. Then there was a growl which sounded very close – the tigers were being fed. 'I'll come with you if you like, just let me finish up here and get my coat and we'll find the place together.' Willoughby was given the full staring eyes up close, and the deep voice which would brook no dissent. 'Just you wait right here and I'll help you... whoever you are,' and he laughed and the tiger growled again.

Willoughby did indeed stand there, rooted to the spot, cursing himself for an idiot. He had chanced upon probably the only complete nutcase in the zoo and it looked very much as if this nutcase had seen through his disguise. If he had, disappearing would leave this character free to tell tales around the zoo about himself looking for Johnson and pretty soon after that, the whole unicorn thing would no doubt attract far too much attention and Willoughby's plan would be at nought. He may even draw down upon himself the same ridicule Johnson had been subjected to. Should he go along with this man, which would at least delay his talking? But not for ever. And it looked as if he did not even know where Johnson actually lived. *We'll find the place together.* He was still in his quandary when Grimes came back, his eyes like headlights beaming above his rigid grin. He was wearing a huge great coat which all but obscured his boots and carrying a fur logging cap with ear flaps. 'Come on then, Mr Messenger.' (an encouraging clap on the back for Willoughby had him inwardly determining the most excruciating fate for this man when all of this was over) 'We must get going if we are to cross the marsh and get back before sundown.'

Even now, Willoughby was on the point of throwing off his felt hat, turning on his heel and making his escape, but he didn't. He probably should have done but he didn't. Perhaps he should simply have revealed himself and asserted his authority to wrest command of this little expedition from this numbskull, but he dithered, and then reluctantly fell silently into step with him.

CHAPTER EIGHT

There were many things Simpson wasn't very good at and croquet was one of them. But he didn't care – just standing here on the perfect lawn watching Jemima was a situation which for the moment eclipsed most of life's little difficulties. All his attention was taken by Ms Cake, who was a naturally gifted croquettiste and even in some of the rather gauche attitudes demanded by the exigencies of the game, cut a more attractive figure than anyone Simpson could ever remember watching doing anything. There were those who declared Ms Cake attractive in an unassuming next door style, though nothing special in the Helen of Troy way, but for Simpson the lightly bronzed, unblemished skin of her bare arms and legs, the honey blonde hair bouncing about the long, strong but vulnerable neck, and the dazzling white shirt – was it a man's shirt? – with the collar turned up, the gentle smile of her full red lips and white teeth, and the eyes, oh the eyes, those beautiful brown eyes... all transported Simpson into a world of dangerous make-believe.

In recent months he had acquired a reputation for being something of a frustratingly imperturbable character, and this not in the heroically stoic mould but more in the lumpen, reluctant to get on with it, mould. He was almost forty years old. Forty. He would be forty in a very short time. He was fiddling with something in his trouser pocket; he'd forgotten what it was. (It was a grenadier guard with no head which he'd promised to fix.) He had not seen his wife or his two children since Monday morning and here it was Tuesday afternoon. ('Got a lot on, we're incubating some very rare eggs and there are meetings about the maleo... the maleo, I told you! I'll get a couple of hours on the couch in the office, see you tomorrow, bye!')

Zoo people and civil servants were playing in the tournament and there were two spectators. Well, one really, because Mr Kelp who was sitting on a barrel on the other side of the wall was deep in a book. The donkey who was occasionally exhorted to apply himself to the heavy roller on the cricket pitch was standing behind him, rooted to the spot and giving every appearance of reading over Kelp's shoulder. Maude was watching the game, her bulk supported by a creaking bench beside the lawn from which perspective she kept her eye on she whom she believed to be her protégée. Acute observers, however, might have detected a momentary shadow eclipse Jemima's happy smile when the game oriented her towards the large lady and her bellicose and embarrassing words of encouragement. As the days and weeks passed Ms Cake was beginning to get the lie of the land. Increasingly she avoided the eye of the large and hearty lady.

Jemima was also coming to suspect that her colleagues in specimen collection might not be as well qualified as she. Certainly some did not share her dedication. Simpson may be an educated man, but he seemed to lack any sense of urgency about anything. One of his men knew a lot but unfortunately appeared to be some species of idiot, with whom it was impossible to talk sensibly. The other one never seemed to say anything much and though he may not be an idiot he did not make the best of a lively personality if he had one. Mr Kelp was an amiable bumbler these days however illustrious his past career; Wilson and Turner were capable and had a lot of experience but they needed more go, they weren't fired with enthusiasm. Willoughby might well have relevant qualifications and credentials, he had certainly attended some college which had clubs and common rooms and ties and rowing eights and May balls which had quite likely given him a degree of some sort, but what he was mostly was an absolutely unbearable and ridiculous snob. She had quickly concluded he was to be avoided if she was to keep her temper.

Thank god for Pippa and Willis, her bright little helpmeets. Together they were a jolly trio and had such fun that at times it was in danger of spilling over and then Jemima had to assume the role of stern parent and restrain their giggling to keep them focussed on the job.

Jemima had always been top of the class. At the infants school it was all gold stars and ten out of ten, at the King Ethelred Grammar School, her petite form tripping neatly up the steps to the stage at prize giving was a familiar sight every year, and then the first class honours degree. She had learnt at an early age that the natural rift between her intellect and the more sluggish versions allocated to most other people could cause deep resentment, so it was fortunate that her cleverness was adorned with modesty and friendliness. She did not have to dissemble, she was by nature an amiable and very sociable creature. The other side of the coin was that people were at times likely to take her for simply pleasant and pretty without ever discerning the keen mind within. Such people were likely to be taken aback when she asserted herself, which she was more than capable of doing when the time was right and the situation demanded it, and her easy-going persona did not preclude her from subtly undermining and out manoeuvring those who were deliberately obstructive and deserved it. The people at the zoo hadn't yet seen much of this side of her, but it was now on view, if they paid attention to the way she played the game of croquet, which was skilfully and ruthlessly.

Simpson was about to be roqued by the girl in question and it was with a sigh of inexpressible admiration rather than sporting chagrin that he saw his ball expertly cracked away to a far corner of the lawn.

As Mr Kelp reached the end of the chapter and closed his book, the donkey let go with a loud *ee-aw*. This just as Maud was bellowing, 'Go on my girl! That's it whack 'em off! Hurrah!' and the garden began to fill up with a sauntering throng of people suddenly disgorged from some nearby entertainment so that bellow and hubbub suddenly replaced the relative peace of this corner of the castle grounds. And a lot of this hubbub was in Italian, for there had been a lunch attended by the visiting Venetians, and amongst them and the others was the immaculately dressed Prince Antonio, ambling casually along the flagged paths, glorious and sure of himself as a most handsome lion with a full mane might walk the unfamiliar path with only minimal interest in his surroundings, as yet disdaining to eat those he encountered, just as Antonio disdained to listen to those about him. Then he stepped up from the terrace below and through the little hedge and was suddenly amongst the flannel trousers and pleated white skirts and huge wooden mallets of the croquet tournament and he stopped and he looked about him and he was pleased and he smiled even though a long and dainty cheroot lodged between his lips, and he saw Willis and he saw Pippa and he smiled and then he saw Ms Cake, and he smiled very much and he clapped his hands even though he held his white gloves in one of them and there was a danger that he might dislodge the superfluous raincoat which was draped precariously across his shoulders.

For obvious reasons, not a lot of croquet is played in Venice, and therefore Antonio's curiosity about the game appeared perfectly natural. His questions were welcomed by Ms Cake and her girls, as were his dark eyes and his high cheek bones and his floppy forelock. Nothing about him however was welcomed by Simpson, who was considerably irritated by this brutal interruption to his daydream on the theme of Jemima, which had been on the point of flowing into some risqué territory but which now was put to flight by the sudden appearance of the forces of reality. Which were also in this instance the forces of youth and exotica and wealth and beauty, in the person of this cursed perfect prince.

'You must be very strong, that hammer is very heavy, I think.'

'Oh no, not really, strength doesn't really come into it, its technique and precision that counts, a bit like billiards you know.'

'Billiards I know, oh yes, may I feel your hammer? Thank you, oooh very nice, how do I do it, like this?'

Jemima found herself in very close proximity to the prince as she adjusted his crouching posture – the instructional role more usually the prerogative of the male was assumed by Ms Cake, and a delighted prince succumbed, clearly relishing the situation and subtly inviting by studied ineptitude more and closer attentions.

Simpson was treated to a perspective on Jemima's knee and flexed calf which he had not seen before and he marvelled at creation. Then he seethed and could not completely restrain himself. 'I say, we are supposed to be actually having a game here, you know!' – but he only whispered it.

He was of late become somewhat otiose, it was true, but he was far from stupid and retained sufficient self awareness to realise he ought to get a grip on himself. He knew that these little fantasies about JC could be no more than that, and he knew that this was the visiting Venetian prince of whom he had heard, and that he must not appear to treat him with any discourtesy, therefore he fought to restrain his childish umbrage and he succeeded, sighing quietly at the inevitability of his retreat as he leant on his mallet and contemplated an evil looking black beetle, commonly called the devil's coach horse, as it scuttled and wriggled through the turf. Watching its progress he found himself reflecting on his own. Why did he suddenly seem to be up a cul-de-sac and unable to see any bright horizon? What was it exactly that did not seem to be right any more? Something, certainly was awry, going adrift, or stuck in the mud, but he didn't know quite what. He just felt, well, sort of dull all the time. He had lost his sparkle. That was what people said wasn't it? 'He's lost his sparkle.' How had he got here? He enjoyed life, yes he still enjoyed life, of course he did. He was truly excited about the maleo, of course he was. But there had been many birds and this was perhaps just another one. And he loved Millicent, and the kids were lovely, if noisy and very tiring. But wasn't there something else that he was missing, something that was creeping behind the gooseberry bushes deliberately avoiding him and running away to gladden other people's lives? He turned back to look at Jemima. She and the prince and Willis were laughing at something. He thrust his hand into his pocket and winced with pain as the jagged neck of the grenadier pricked him and drew blood.

Involuntarily he turned round and bent over to suck his thumb and found himself gazing over the hedge and the terrace and down the long wide flight of steps that lead the eye to a glimpse of a portion of the distant menagerie. It was his portion, the aviaries and large enclosures with their flightless occupants. He saw, tiny from here, the cassowary and an emu.

'Phoenix,' he thought, 'that's what's missing, that's what I want, that's what I want to be, that's what I need to be, a bloody phoenix, rising from the ashes,' and he smiled as ruefully as he could with a mouth full of thumb. Then he looked again and thought, 'Culvert Grimes is supposed to be on duty down there, I wonder where he is.'

The others had stopped laughing and were staring at him. 'Your shot, Mr Simpson,' smiled Jemima.

The Prince was moving reluctantly away along the path with his entourage, sneaking several looks back over his shoulder from beneath his quiff whilst a short, very animated man spoke briskly both with hands and voice aiming his comments urgently up at the Prince's ear. As they disappeared behind the trunk of an *araucaria*, Jemima looked up briefly at the backs of Italian suits before frowning over her ball and propelling it firmly through the middle of an impossibly distant hoop. Willis, who was not actually playing in the game wandered away and sat on the wide flight of stone stairs gazing at the distant cassowary but not seeing it. The interminable banter that had previously accompanied each strategic croquet shot was briefly silenced and Pippa for a minute or two seemed as pre-occupied as Simpson. Until a particularly useless clogging shot on the part of the fourth player, Simpson's partner, a novice who had been continually asking about the rules, brought about stifled giggles, apologies, and reassurances and then a resumption of the earnest merriment which characterised any game Ms Cake participated in.

The game was soon over – the result was never in doubt – and Simpson shook hands; even her hand her very hand he also shook and it was warm without being hot, smooth and the nails polished and manicured to a nicety. But he must not hold on to it, one quick sportive flick and then relinquish. And then he had to take his leave, being out of the tournament, and he had to be alone, being out of sorts, so he automatically wandered off to that huge wide imperial stone staircase that led down to the menagerie. He passed the seated form of Willis on the top step and then went on down the huge wide imperial stone staircase with the stone urns at intervals disappearing down the hill as if it connected two different worlds, which it did in a way. He had more than once seen the thick river mist below hiding all of the menagerie in its grey folds apart from perhaps the top of a giraffe, or the intermittent up-swung trunk of an elephant. He had some strange thoughts as he steadily descended. The animals down there often seemed morally better than the people up here, or at least their lives were less complicated. There were two different realms of being and no possibility of swapping one existence for the other. Instinctive, uncomplicated on the one hand, and then on the other hand devious, self deluding, ever prone to despair and weary with the burden of self consciousness and abstract thought and it's continual posing of intellectual problems.

Surely it was easier to be a beast? All the animals had to contend with were the practicalities of continuing to be, whereas men and women had to wonder who they should be and why they should be and whether they were being in the right way.

Then Simpson looked away down to the distant cassowary and wondered whether it had perhaps laid out Culvert Grimes with one whack of its vicious clawed foot. Was he perhaps bleeding to death just out of sight, amongst upturned seed buckets? It was an upsetting image and he began to hurry down the steps. But no, don't panic, he was probably just in the office, or sorting out the feed shed. All the doors were shut though. Of course it was a good half mile away, he could be in the loo or in any one of several places hidden from view, but Simpson began to get a feeling. It was a long, long way down however and he found his mind wandering again before he was even half way down. Just in the way he'd been remembering, some mist was actually now creeping in from the river which skirted the zoo, and with it philosophical cotton wool began to fur up his train of thought. People commonly liked to think of the animals as behaving like people – the much disparaged anthropomorphism – but the animals never want to be like people. They couldn't of course, because they can't understand what people are, how they can think all the time, think about things that aren't there...

Why was he in this strange mood? Why was he scurrying (he wasn't actually, he had slowed now to a plod) down to the zoo on his day off? 'Get real' that's what he needed to do, snap out of this pre-occupation with middle-age. That's what people said wasn't it? They spoke about 'the real world.' But usually what they meant by that was a mythical place where everybody agreed with them. Animals are always real though, they are always real aren't they? They don't have any choice. Because it is assumed they are incapable of imagining anything that's not real. They cannot go off into 'a world of their own.' They could not imagine an animal which does not exist, like the phoenix, say. Phwoooaaar, smell that, that's real alright – this as he descended into the level of the pungent atmosphere which often hung over the place if there was no wind.

The fog thickened as he disappeared into it. A cassowary that had lately kicked someone to death would wear exactly the same expression as a cassowary that had not, wouldn't it? He could imagine a cassowary kicking someone to death, but a cassowary could not imagine it, it could only do it. Then he started wondering what he could imagine and what he could not. He could imagine a dodo. But he had seen pictures of dodos. He could not imagine a roc. He tried but it always came out as a sort of an eagle which he did not believe was right. And what about the aepyornis? What on Earth was that like? Huge they said. Wouldn't it have been marvellous to see an aepyornis – the elephant bird. Ten feet tall. Like a giant ostrich. Long extinct.

At the bottom of the grey stone staircase, the grey fog reluctantly revealed the dark red bricks of the menagerie wall and he stepped along to the little side door, fumbling for his key (feeling a pang of guilt about the grenadier guard in his other pocket). The noise of the lock seemed very loud and the green door more austere than usual but for all the grimness that the thick damp air gave to the walls and flagstones he was glad to be here. He smelt the animals and the river and the muddy river bank and he saw a clump of nettles in a neglected corner and it was familiar, but it was also, just for a fleeting moment, as if he had never been here before. And he suddenly had the strange feeling that although he knew all the birds here and could list and describe every one without hesitation, he might be about to encounter one he had never seen before, some bizarre interloper mysteriously introduced in his absence.

Compared with the sunlit green and white of the croquet lawn this was a darker and a different place, it was as if he had descended from some sort of Olympus to a place of different beings, where indeed, being felt different and was done differently. The walls and iron bars had something of the dungeon about them and the gloom of imprisonment darkened the corners of many a cage, but he knew that the perspective that the visitor brought from above was not shared by those who dwelt here. There was a Miltonian profundity about certain of the denizens of this strange hotel, not all of whom wished for brightness and the open plain. Simpson himself felt so much more at ease to be back where conversation was refined to a look and a growl. He stopped to lean over and scratch vigorously the back of a tapir before proceeding past snuffling armadillos, a dreaming wombat and a sloth or two (challenging all philosophy with their vacant looks which saw everything but made nothing of it) toward his office which was in an old fashioned one storey outhouse and had small windows looking across to where the cassowary should have been.

He called out, 'Hello!' but he could feel Culvert Grimes' absence, which was confirmed when he found the door was locked. There was no corpse on the ground, but the cassowary was not where it should have been. It had got next door, somehow, amongst the emus. Simpson could not help looking it in the eye for a minute or two, but it gave nothing away. Then he went and sat down at the ancient wooden table which served as a desk, took a pencil from the drawer and sharpened it absentmindedly with a penknife from the other drawer. He leant back in the chair and tapped the blunt end of the pencil on the table top making little pouting movements with his mouth whilst he thought and wondered where Culvert Grimes had gone. And why. And then he put down the pencil and took out the grenadier, staring at its empty neck.

After a minute or two he got up, took up the little kettle and went to fill it from the standing tap in the yard, looking round to see if any other exhibits had got themselves where they didn't ought to be. All seemed well and he withdrew to the cabin and lit the gas ring in the corner. By the time the kettle whistled he had whittled a tiny piece of the end of the pencil into a lump which with some dabs of paint would pass for a guardsman's head in a bearskin and jammed it successfully into the metal neck. Admiring his work he took a sip of tea and then he yawned, stretched, eyed the old fashioned telephone on the wall resolving to ring Millicent in a little while, and lay his head on his arms on the desk for five minutes rest.

The light slowly changed and darkened about him as he slumped there in his cage like an ape in its pile of straw. When he woke up it was with a start, and his mind being a little slow to catch up with his eyes he found himself for a few seconds in that in-between place which isn't anywhere, that place into which we were all born where nothing has a name, and he looked up at the window and saw a huge red eye, burning like coal, big as a dinner plate looking sideways steadily at him. There was a little time, an eternal instant, before the shock and the fear were understood for what they were, and when the realisation came his brain caught up with the waking process and his head jerked up and the eye was not there anymore and he knew that he was in his zoo office and that it was getting dark, and then he remembered coming down here and who he was and all the realities he inhabited. But it had been there. He had seen it, that terrible red eye. He got up and looked out of the window and then opened the door and went through it and looked all around and many large birds quietly ignored him and the fog had gone but he saw that the setting sun was peeking round the hill and glancing off a lamppost and it was certainly this, proceeding to glint and refract through the imperfect glass of the little office window which had imitated the eye of the aepyornis. That must have been it, mustn't it? Yes that must have been it.

He went back inside, drank cold tea, fingered his soldier's head and then wondered with alarm, what time is it? He must have slept for hours. The watch with the square black face was not on his wrist. It was standing sentinel to his absence on the bedside table. Then he remembered why he had come down here. Where the devil was Culvert Grimes? He obviously had not been back all afternoon. This was very strange.

Would this be sufficient grounds for dismissing him? Taking him on had been a mistake, he now felt. The fellow was extremely knowledgeable, could name the parts of a flamingo or a corncrake at the drop of a hat but there was something wrong with him. He himself had not been put together quite right. And that grinning face really got on your nerves. How would Grimes react if he were to be dismissed? Not like anyone else for sure. Not in any predictable way. He probably wouldn't mind at all. He was not the sort of person you would feel particularly sorry for because you could not imagine him feeling sorry for anyone or indeed for himself.

Simpson hurriedly slurped some more tea, carefully pocketed the little soldier then went out – having forgotten to ring Millicent – locked the door behind him with his own key and made his way along the paths and between the cages and sheds and outhouses to the main gate and the zoo's administration office.

They were just closing up, the last visitors had been ushered out though the turnstile and old Joe was putting on his mackintosh.

With one arm in and fumbling and flapping for the other sleeve he looked over his shoulder at Simpson and pre-empted his questions with, 'Gone off. This morning with some scruffy stranger in a black 'at. Didn't say where,' and shuffled off, buttoning up. But then as he held the main gate open for Simpson and dangled the key, there was a postscript, 'Johnson. They mentioned Johnson, I think they've gone off to find him. G'night.'

Simpson frowned and fiddled with the grenadier. It was thoroughly dark now and beginning to drizzle. The croquet tournament was like a distant dream.

CHAPTER NINE

As far as disguise was concerned, Daphne had had some considerable practice in anonymising herself for her various jaunts, her little escapades, her midnight rambles, her afternoon awols, her delicious and sweetly therapeutic outings 'on the lam'. She had concluded that what was most important was not *not* looking like Princess Daphne but rather, not looking like anyone in particular, or, more precisely, looking like everyone in general. Concocting a figure whose apparel, demeanour, deportment, voice, posture, look, attitude were all so entirely unremarkable that no one would give her a second glance was something upon which she had unleashed her not inconsiderable talents, intelligence, and powers of observation many times. She knew, or experience had taught her by now, that drawing any attention to yourself was the thing to be avoided. Any attention at all. There must be nothing whatsoever to attract the eye. The background must always be more interesting than oneself, whatever it might be. It was not sufficient merely not to look royal or rich, true expertise in being incognito was rendering oneself boring, banal, utterly uninteresting to anybody. She had at first concentrated on disguising her sex, thinking going about as a lone woman would make her vulnerable, but she had discovered that just cutting your hair short and climbing into blokey boots and a donkey jacket were far from all there was to replicating a credible masculine persona. It might be a simple matter in Shakespeare but in this kingdom she had found that people were quite canny when it came to knowing who their Rosalind was, or anyone else's Rosalind come to that, and besides it was not inconceivable that the cross-dressing thing might lead to unwonted complications which might be worse than being recognised for who she was. So nowadays she avoided actually playing a boy as such and simply opted for a sort of androgynous look that would not challenge too strongly the assumptions of either those who took her for this, or those who took her for that. Instead of acting the part of a man, she let those who thought her male continue to do so by having nothing about her which starkly challenged that opinion. This was quite easy to do *en passant*, but in any sort of close contact or conversation she had to guess quite quickly which gender her interlocutor thought she was and adapt her character accordingly; she had found she was usually able to do this quite easily. Often, in brief interviews, all that was needed was choosing, 'Thanks, mate,' instead of, 'Oh thank you so much, you're very kind,' and it was hardly necessary to put on a baritone or accentuate the soprano – if people were given no need to wonder about you they did not wonder about you, they had other things to think about. And another reason for the gender-ambivalent look was that if people could not quite decide whether you were a girl or a boy they were unlikely to find you desirable in either of those directions, at least not on casual acquaintance. It was also in this mid-gender territory that weirdness often resided, or was perceived to reside, and a bit weird was good. Nobody wanted to sit next you if you were a bit weird. It had to be very finely judged though – the optimum amount of weirdness, she had found, was about two or three out of ten. If you scored any higher than that you were in danger of becoming a spectacle, and you spilled over into being sufficiently weird to actually attract the attention of thrill seekers, freak fetishists and other perverts. The golden rules, she thought, were: never look vulnerable, never look like easy prey for the sexually predatory, never look like you've got any money, and if you could look like you might be just sufficiently weird that people could imagine wishing they had never got into conversation with you, that was the best thing. She was not entirely right in this. Thought astute in some things, Daphne could sometimes make serious mistakes. There was no surer way to rivet people's attention than to be neither one thing nor the other. Such a figure constituted a puzzle that passers-by needed to solve. Nonetheless, so far, she had got away with it.

She squelched happily through the long boggy grass, her rubber boots demonstrating how well equipped she now was for her adventure. She had in her bag a raincoat, gloves and a pullover, also a torch, enough money for eventualities – as well as a few small bribes – and a map. This last she had yet to consult, since she was beginning on the intuitive principal – this had been the direction of travel of the mysterious man who had been talking to her father last night and this must therefore be her direction. She had resolved that she would focus on him, this dark, dirty unpleasant man. She was not sure who he actually was, though she was fairly certain, as she reflected on his speedy and deliberate disappearance through the town last night, that he was far too familiar with the place to be a visiting Italian. But he was probably in the pay of the Italians. He was probably some grubby local Mr Fixit, employed to uncover secrets and the eligibility of princesses. She hoped his nefarious commissions did not include the more unthinkable types of procurement and trafficking, but from the glimpses she had had of him there was something about his back, his short fat neck and that blunderbuss of a bowler that made him look as if he was capable of setting all considerations of morality neatly on one side, with a deft and very firm but apparently insignificant movement of his elbow. Be that as it may, she would not be frightened off, the important thing was that he was a target, something visible she could pursue which gave purpose to her escapade. It was getting out of there, away from that damned castle that was the important thing, and even if she did not know his name, Johnson was as good a hare to follow as anything else, especially since he moved fast and very secretively, and looked like whatever circles he mixed in – if he mixed in circles – they would not be courtly circles. It was, she thought, ironic that this slimy satyric go-between, as she thought him to be, would never lead her to the civilised excesses of the Venetian court, as his employers no doubt hoped, but was now re-cast by her as a light to guide her eager rebellious heart outside the whole flawed and crumbling edifice of nuptial power broking and into the rough, honest purity of dew-soaked nature.

In the castle she spent most of her time on her own, if she could. She had a lady's maid and ladies-in-waiting (what a stupid old fashioned title) some of whom were perfectly nice and even quite good fun on occasion, and there were some chaps about the palace whom she'd grown up with, some of them the sons of courtiers, some of palace officials so she was not and had never been short of friends. But there had always been something missing for her in their company. It was a something she yearned for without being able to define. It was a something she could not quite characterise, but something which she was sure none of her friends felt the lack of at all – none of them. And so she had come to think of herself as, well she did not like to use the word 'special' that sounded so arrogant, and she did not feel arrogant, but apart at least. Therefore she had often yearned to be alone to reflect on the missing thing, which was a sad thing, or perhaps just its absence was sad. So solitariness felt like her natural state.

But here, out here amongst the wind, the dark, the boggy meadow, the approaching forest with its ghostly silver trees, a long way from the castle she was very much truly alone. There was little chance of encountering any of the people she did not want to see. Being alone in the castle simply meant being away from other people, but if there weren't any people to be away from, 'alone' slid into isolation, which was another feeling altogether, since it was more difficult to think of herself as the person who was different from everyone else if there wasn't anyone else to be different from. That special something, that something which defined her did its defining in relation to other people and could only exist in a social setting. Perhaps it followed that she, whoever she was, did not really exist out here. Perhaps she would turn into something else. Did she hope so? Well… yes, and no.

What she wanted was a sort of obscurity – the ability to look without being continually looked upon. Or, more particularly, what she actually wanted was a sort of noticed obscurity. She wanted to be looked upon in her isolation and respected for her uniqueness, but she did not want people to get too close all the time. She would like to be talked about but left alone. To be totally alone and separate but disregarded would perhaps be unbearable.

She tried to imagine Helena Butterworth wondering where she was, pondering her disappearance, surely Helena at least would miss her. They had been friends since childhood, shared toys, holidayed together, and gone to the same school. Daphne looked at thistles and bindweed and wild madder moving in the grim little breeze and thought about Helena thinking about her. Would she have the slightest clue where she was or why she was here? No, of course not. She longed to tell her. Or perhaps she longed to be in her presence and hint at things without actually really saying anything, enhancing the mystery that enhanced the sense of the secretly tortured soul that no one could truly fathom for all sorts of arcane and indescribable reasons. She wanted to be both pitied and respected.

But then she told herself not to be stupid, it was idiotic to go about wishing other people were thinking about her, that was immature, childish, even, and whatever you thought about yourself it was never what other people were thinking, she knew that at least. But still...

Could she really confide in no one? Her uniqueness was not unusual, she ought not to fall into the trap of thinking it was. Oh god, it would be alright, probably, if it wasn't for the sodding *princess* nonsense. It was that that twisted everything up, made people talk stiltedly to her, be afraid of her. How could she possibly get to grips with being her ordinary self if everybody was made to bow and curtsey before her, if they had to ask her what everybody should be served at dinner, if every little school child was made to wave a little paper flag every time she had to go out and launch a bloody boat, if on each and every one of the official engagements she couldn't get out of, three or four people preceded her and half a dozen followed her to carry the presents and make sure she wasn't assassinated? She prayed nightly that her father would soon see sense, abdicate and declare a republic. He had been on the verge of it a few times but had always been dissuaded (forcefully she suspected) by the courtly mafia who would have a lot to lose. Maybe they just threatened him with taking his zoo away – that would do it. His precious bloody animals – thought more of them than he did of her, that was for sure – oh yes, she certainly knew that to her cost. It was also obvious that Dagobert liked the perks – the library, the royal apartments, the servants, the influence he exerted, foreign travel, meeting people... He would never give it up, even if he himself sometimes thought he might.

She would wait until everyone thought she was dead and then come back as somebody else.

The black heads of the primeval thistles, like the elaborate masks of voodoo dancers, moved and swayed and nodded as if in angry conversation with the wind, or perhaps they were warning her of something, or perhaps merely wafting her with their indifference and showing in their dance the untamed forces that held sway out here in the wilds. Daphne drank it all in and tried to feel herself shedding lumps of the irksome carapace of civilization. Helena Butterworth would never be able, in the firelight of her boudoir, to imagine what it was truly like out here – getting dark and chilly and the rustling and the whooshing of the leaves and the branches and the thrashing and whipping to and fro of the grasses, and the path barely discernible now, fading to a grey thread which would soon disappear altogether. She caught herself imagining describing the scene, a long time hence, when she had returned after innumerable adventures (there was a moon in the scene she described but none in reality) and then admonished herself severely – stop it now, stop being outside the idea of yourself, just get on with being here, just look at what you can see. Its people going about like that dreaming about things who get set upon, or who step upon things with big teeth that are liable to up and bite back.

At that moment, even as she passed out of the meadow in the gathering dusk and passed between the first trees of the forest, there was a sort of strangled animal noise and what sounded like a little high-pitched human laugh curtailed with a snort – but it was not close so it was by no means certain what it was – away in the gloaming coming from the birch trees at the distant edge of the meadow. She stood quite still for a minute or two and listened hard. The noise wasn't repeated and she moved on.

She picked up her pace – as much as she could in this light, the ground was uneven and the path itself overgrown – and found herself after a little while in a tunnel of low overhanging trees, which was sombre if not frightening, but the way forward here was easy to make out. And then she thought she saw a darker, man-sized shape faintly moving in the distance, and then a very little pinprick of yellow light. She watched the light intently to see if it would move, was it a fixed lamp or someone's lantern? She stopped, shifted the weight of her bag on her shoulder, stared into what was now the thorough going gloom of the night and hoped the tiny yellow would grow into a larger, warmer light and that it might signify comfort of some sort. She would have to get her torch out soon, but held off for a while longer, hoping to get an idea of what was ahead before revealing her presence. The wind was broken up and hushed into sighing gusts as she got further into the trees, walking stealthily now and listening for voices or any unnatural noise amongst the creaking of branches and soughing of leaves.

Some time later the strange animal noise was heard again, further away perhaps, although it was difficult to tell, and then the very faintest sparkle of light, shining for an instant up into the trees, momentarily lightening the undersides of the leaves, before suddenly dying out. It would never have occurred to her to think the noise might be a donkey. The bray of a donkey was a noise you heard around farmyards during the day, not in forests at night. She could not think what it might be. It had sounded primeval, half threatening and half terrified, a strange blend of killer and prey coiled round one another. She listened hard and then shrugged and moved on. Eventually she found a likely clearing with her torch, and was beginning to collect fallen branches to make a fire – she did not care if those with the light and the animal became aware of her presence, she just felt it would be alright. Though she was thoroughly aware of likelihoods and eventualities, sometimes she just didn't care. You could wear yourself out with worrying about everything – might as well be back in the castle if you weren't prepared to take a few risks. How did she know they might not be frightened of her? But then, when she was beginning to realise how reluctant damp green branches were to burn, and that perhaps, though she was perfectly capable and could do it if she really needed to, this outdoor pioneer stuff was just a bit tedious for someone with other things to think about, she heard a voice singing, and advancing through the trees toward the sound she was just in time to see the feeble twinkle of a bicycle light fly by to the sound of the Anvil Chorus from *Il Travatore* rendered uncertainly by a wavering tenor and she found herself looking at a metalled road undulating through the wood. Immediately she abandoned all thoughts of a smokey bivouac and decided to follow where the road would lead. Going in the direction taken by the bicycle. She marched along with her torch on full beam and thought about breaking into song herself but could not remember the words to anything. Not all through, anyway. Only snatches. There was no further sign of the strange light nor any more strange animal noises and in a couple of miles she was pleased to find that the road delivered her to a small village. It had an inn opposite the church – like they all do – and she walked boldly in to put up at it.

The locals were all intent on a darts match in the public bar and no one subjected her to the stranger-stare. She told the girl who sorted out the room that she was on an entomological field trip, cleverly giving a glimpse of a magnifying glass which happened to be amongst her things in her bag as she rummaged for something. It was quite likely that the girl neither knew nor cared greatly what entomology was, she did not seem at all inquisitive and was anxious to return to the hubbub round the back. ('With you in a minute, Frank!')

It was a large room at the front overlooking the village green which she was shown to. There was a dusty picture of her grandfather in full regalia as an admiral of the fleet hanging at a slight angle over the chest of drawers. Another girl came in with a bucket of coals and firelighters and started drawing the curtains with her free hand.

'Eve'nin', you'll be comfy in 'ere won't you, our best room is this, that wind's getting up a bit again, will you want a mornin' call, tea in the mornin' or coffee?'

She was kneeling down now and starting to lay the fire but Daphne forgot herself, caught off her guard she was suddenly the Princess again and spoke sharply, 'Oh don't fuss, there's no need for a fire, please leave it alone.'

They were both taken aback.

'Alright, as you like, I'm sure,' said the girl, picking up the bucket and making for the door.

'Oh sorry, I'm a bit tired I think – long journey – not really cold enough for a fire is it, not in here anyway…' but she was gone, and Daphne kicked herself for such a lapse in concentration. She lay on the bed and listened to the muted hubbub below which was punctuated by roars and shouts, no doubt occasioned by a winning throw or something. There was a time when she would have loved such an occasion, would have mingled with the crowd and revelled in what she would have persuaded herself was the re-discovery of her peasant roots, would have relished the oaths and the dialect and the crude jokes and the total and universal lack of etiquette, and felt that here was the real, the nitty gritty, here were the people, the salt of the Earth, the rough diamonds, the vigorous life close to the realities of toil and soil and hard times and always looking death in the face. But tonight, on this particular expedition, she found herself just wishing they'd all shut up and go to bed. She fished in her capacious bag and pulled out a photograph of the Prince Antonio.

She dozed for a bit on top of the bed and then got up and walked to the bay window, pulling back a little of the heavy curtain to look across the green toward the squat little church with its square tower. She wondered where this place was. Was she amongst the Lanes, she wondered? There was an area on the map which was a bit of a mystery, it had never been accurately surveyed – no one seemed to know quite why – and beyond being relatively flat and criss-crossed by a maze of little narrow lanes not much was known about it. Her quarry – the horrible man – had been heading towards this place when last seen. She'd imagined the people living amongst the Lanes to be peculiar in some unspecified way, inbred or something perhaps, and she tried to think whether the girls here – the only people she'd seen – had seemed odd in any way. Not really, but then she had paid them almost no attention.

She went and sat on the chair by the dressing table and unfolded the old map she had ferreted out from the back of a drawer in her own room in the castle and sought out that wilderness which she thought she must be at least on the borders of. It was indeed as she remembered: whereas the rest of the country was full of neatly depicted forests and contour lines and towns and villages and railways, this area was simply an extensive knot of jumbly little roads that could not possibly be an accurate rendition of the territory – it looked as if the map maker, having no information, had just made it up, doodled it in fact. The whole area was printed in a faint blue wash that indicated to the reader that this was the peculiar and un-mapped territory which, for whatever reason, had come to be just... disregarded; the heavy hint was that this was a place to be avoided, not because 'here be dragons' or anything horrible to be avoided, rather, simply that it was inconceivable that anyone would want to go there. At any rate it had failed to attract any conscientious cartographers.

Princess Daphne then espied, in a corner of this territory, drawn in wobbly but meticulous blue ballpoint pen, a tiny elephant. Yes, it had been she herself that had drawn that little elephant, she could not remember the actual act, but she remembered the beast so very clearly now, even though she had not thought of it for many years. It wasn't bad, she had always been proud of her draughtsmanship and this was a good example of her style. She also remembered that as a little girl she had thought that this strange light blue part of the map must be where all father's animals came from.

In the middle of the night she rose from the bed and felt drawn again to look through the window. The night was still, the wind had dropped and all was silent, but there were people, all dressed in white, lots of them, filing slowly across the road and climbing one after another over the low wall that surrounded the churchyard, walking across to lift the stone slabs of their graves and climbing back in, as if they had been allowed out briefly for the darts match. And yet they none of them looked as if they would be remotely interested in darts, they all looked like honest and holy artisans, who, wherever they had been were more than ready to go home. It was a dream of course, but it stayed with her when she woke and the sun streamed in through the crack she had left in the curtain.

Her early morning tea was set down unceremoniously on the bedside table, just out of reach – obviously her impatience over the firelighting had not been forgotten – and a new day dawned for Princess Daphne.

She sat on the side of the bed sipping the lukewarm infusion and thinking about Prince Antonio again. Would he yet have been made aware that she was not to be found? Would he have asked after her? Did he care where she was or what she was doing? He had seemed genuinely interested when they had been at the dinner, but perhaps that was just his way, perhaps he had been told to make himself pleasant to her. Had it just been a diplomatic flirt? Perhaps he was like that with all the girls. He was certainly very good looking. Why was she running away from him? Or was she running away from her father? Oh god, why was life so complicated? That was it really. That's what she was doing, she was running towards simplicity, that's what there must be in this unmapped wilderness of nothing out of the ordinary, surely everything would be simple and somewhere out here she would find truth and beauty and fulfilment and a straightforward life with straightforward people and an end to her constant anxiety.

If Prince Antonio wanted her, he would have to come out and find her. She got up, and still brushing her hair with her head on one side, she opened the window which squeaked and looked about. It was a lovely quiet morning, the wind had dropped completely, the trees on the green stood upright and unmolested and the great inn sign hung straight down heavy in its gravity wavering neither left nor right. The Black Widow. Urgh, what an unpleasant name! How would that have come about, she wondered? Perhaps it was the spider that was meant, though the very faded image was definitely a woman in weeds. Nothing stirred amongst the tombstones opposite, they were all peacefully dreaming this morning of their surreptious mass somnambulations, but there was a bicycle propped against the lych gate and she heard the Anvil Chorus again in her head.

With her hair safely stowed under her big hat, Daphne took up the tea – which was, as she expected, pretty disgusting – and still staring across the green, drifted off into another reverie. Birds were singing – blackbirds, sparrows, a robin, and then the raucous grating screech of a jay high in one of the tallest beech trees. The sun came out and warmed up the graveyard. And then… a great, and this time unmistakeable, bray of a donkey, which sounded as if it must be straining the sinews and rattling the sinuses to make a noise that was too big and very much the wrong shape ever to have been contained within such a diminutive quadruped in the first place. Whether it expressed pain, alarm, disgust or all three she could not tell. Somewhere the other side of the church, she thought. Was it the one she had heard last night in the forest? If that had indeed been a donkey and not something else, some strange hybrid creature of the night. She sipped again and grimaced.

'Bloody animals' she whispered to herself.

The tea had been made with a tea bag and the saucer was not quite clean. There was an empty beer bottle under the bench on the green She began to feel, with dismay, an all too familiar despair. That old black memory was seeping up and gathering again, and thickening, even though she was looking out on sunlight glinting on bright green leaves and collared doves were whirring amongst the branches of a lovely great old and twisted sweet chestnut tree, she was being crept up on by a particular night of terror which was always with her. One of the longest nights there had ever been. A night which had first fallen many years ago but which would never pass entirely away it seemed; a night which had never fully retreated from the tarnished dawn which followed it, which returned as a personal tide of time which would not leave her alone and insisted on lapping back to swirl about her troubled mind, to grip in its muddy clutches the life which should have grown up and floated away on other streams long ago but which was lurched back by the knots in this tether of time.

She knew in her heart of hearts that this adventure was nothing to do with uncovering some gaberlunzie who had been commissioned to delve her purity, nor was it really about escaping the stifling tedium of court life. It was really about her father. The fact that she could believe he would negotiate her as some sort of political chattel, that good old easy going Dagobert, everyone's favourite eccentric monarch, could happily sit in his library discussing with a stranger his only daughter's virginity as if she was some animal in his zoo with breeding potential. But there was something deeper and darker even than this. She was running away from her father, whom she loved too much to confront, because he was slowly driving her mad. She could not understand how he could be woolly and soft and absent minded and caring and conscientious and yet have done what he had done. All those years ago and yet it was still and would be forever true. He had invited a monster into the very bosom of the royal family. And now there was this Venetian business. And this could really be the last nail in the coffin of their friendship.

Was it any wonder she was not at one with herself, that she felt so different from ordinary people? That she intermittently craved a more ordinary celebrity persona, to be adored but to have no history, to be outrageous but to have no position, to be acknowledged for her personality and her artistry not for her sad and lunatic family. Was it any wonder that she wandered, almost insane, through this wilderness, in a whirl of self-doubt and facing – she barely stifled a guffaw at the phrase that presented itself – the imminent disintegration, yes that was it, the disintegration, of the ill-connected haphazard elements of her personality? That was it – she was cracking into pieces, pieces that leaned desperately on one another in a vain attempt to stay upright. She thrust the teaspoon into her mouth as if that would stop her from speaking and therefore from thinking. Or as if it would hold her together like some Frankensteinian bolt. Her eyes were wide open and she looked for a moment as mad as she feared she might become.

What was it that had suddenly sent her spiralling back into the familiar sadness? She ought to be away from it here, she ought to find freedom out here on the sky-blue roads. She looked around making an effort to see only what was before her, to stifle her imagination. The tea cup was at a perilous angle in its saucer as she gazed through the open window at the lovely gothic arches, at the maroon bicycle, she even smiled at her dream-vision of the people climbing back into their tombs, and she looked into the distance beyond the church and saw cattle and heard a distant tractor, but in spite of her efforts she continued to be besieged by things that she did not want to remember, but which she would never, it seemed, be able entirely to escape.

She did not hear the door open.

'Will you have the full English, Miss?'

She was infinitely grateful for the interruption and turned to the girl (a different one from last night) removing the spoon from her mouth, and almost dropping the tea cup which she juggled to safety, to give a hearty and relieved heavy sigh of, 'Just eggs and coffee, if you please, where is it, downstairs?'

There was one other guest. A man fiddling with something in his small rucksack on the floor. His plate was thinly smeared with the grease and streaks of brown sauce left by the plate-cleaning bread-wipe of a healthy appetite, which had been made, however, by the very deliberate circular movements indicative of a preoccupied mind.

CHAPTER TEN

Vangrannicus progressed along the corridor with the majestic inevitability of a planet in its motion (though with just a little more urgency) his richly embroidered cloak swishing and wafting with the rhythm of the striding stately steps which could never be seen to falter whilst the personage they conveyed was himself, the very Lord Chamberlain of the kingdom. He paraded like this even though there was no crowd to witness his progress away from the public areas of the castle toward his own private offices. He had become the act. It was second nature now after all these years – he was so very conscientious in letting no standard slide and keeping up the traditions, which included due reverence at all times for the dignity of his office.

Whilst the personage of the Chamberlain was ostensibly imperturbable, the man who inhabited the office was in fact troubled by unforeseen annoyances. These took the form of not one but two reports of missing persons. He was wondering whether they could be connected and whether they might have anything to do with the fire in the bakery last night, which had nearly caused a riot. Was there something going on? Oh yes, and *she* was not back yet. Her Royal Highness Princess Daphne was up to her tricks again.

The Chamberlain's spies had come one by one, and told him their tales as usual, but no one was aware of any actual rebellion or conspiracy in the offing. It remained a possibility however that the absence of Her Royal Highness (which was of course the most important absence of all the absences) might be a much more important absence than it usually was. Vangrannicus was used to the Princess Daphne going on one of her walkabouts. He usually knew where she was and more or less what she was doing – she had no idea of the extent of the ramifications of his network of agents and irregular watchers. She was a pain in the arse, but she was usually a fairly predictable pain in the arse. This time however he had lost track of her. This was worrying. Her escapades usually lasted only a day or two – a bit of soul searching amongst the proletariat and then, soon after she had run out of money, she could be relied upon to trail back to the cushioned luxury of reality. She had never been away for as long as a week. And with two other people apparently spirited away and half the bakery demolished and the disturbing possibility of food riots ensuing, he had to worry whether these individual symptoms might not add up to some huge outrage or scandal being on hand. Dread words like 'kidnap' and 'coup' rose up in his thoughts to remind him that it was only through his vigilance and the tightest of grips that the state was kept from destroying itself.

He did not like at all for there to be even a suspicion that he was losing control, that there was anything going on in this kingdom which he did not know about or indeed had not planned and instigated himself. It made him agitated and sparked the tic in his left eyebrow. The King must be informed of course of his daughter's being lost to view, but he'd been putting it off because he was still hoping for some positive information, for some clue as to what was behind this particular truancy so that he could enter the presence at least clothed in a mantle of some sort of authority, however skimpy. But that was another problem – the King had hidden himself away in his library for the last two days and given instructions that no one was to be admitted.

The ever-present minion who was carrying a sheaf of papers under his arm ran from behind to open the large oak door and, as Vangrannicus marched into the enormous oak panelled saloon which served as his office, scurried to put the papers onto the great table before rushing over to stoke the fire whilst his master did a bit of pacing up and down with his hands behind his back. This he did before the fireplace and therefore under the huge oil painting which hung above the carved mantelpiece and dominated the room. It was a strange and rather disturbing picture, its theme presumably drawn from the classics though most who saw it, however well educated, were hard put to it to come up with the reference. Central to the composition was a huge shaggy mother goat nursing a child sitting beneath her, with fat cherubic legs one outstretched, the other folded beneath him, holding his hands up to clutch the thick tufts of hair hanging down, his pink-cheeked face upturned to suck on a caprine dug which was held out for him by a nymph who with her other hand held one of the mother's feet. The goat's head was turned back to look at what was going on, and such a strange expression which mixed motherly love with a frowning malevolence had been created in that face by the artist's wizardry, and such a sly benevolence inhabited the eyes of the nymph and such a knowing and adult visage lurked behind the chubby folds of the infant dimples that all who saw the work were captivated, mystified and disturbed by it. The Chamberlain hated it, he said. But this was a royal apartment, not his own, and he could not get rid of it, however dearly he would have liked to replace it with a more conventional classical nude, or a battle, or better still a ship in a storm – yes that's what he'd like best, a good old man o' war, breasting azure waves with flags and foam and clouds flying. Not this damned goat. But for someone who would tell you he did not like it he seemed to spend a lot of time looking at it.

Vangrannicus prided himself on being a practical man and holding the reins of the kingdom in his firm and loyal grasp. Other people could not be trusted with important things, they were lax, lazy and slack, and did not see the far reaching implications and dire possibilities which may loom if even a small detail was not properly attended to, if even a little piece in the jigsaw of rite and ritual were allowed to lapse and be forgotten. He ran everything himself – he and his amanuensis, the faithful Ruscum, ran an extensive but very irregular web of assistants of one sort and another – there were two or three burly chaps who would do anything and say nothing if the price was right, plus runners, spies, accountants and the like, but there were very few fellow officials or deputies. Vangrannicus certainly delegated nothing of policy or decision making at all. Nothing twitched without he knew it. He could sail pretty close to the wind and he was not entirely averse to giving and getting the odd favour – it would be contrary to the great historical traditions of the office not to do a bit of bribery, to dabble in some minor corruption, and he was a great one for tradition – but generally, and certainly outwardly he was a stickler for the rules and regulations and the law of the land. He strove to do his best for the kingdom and his best for the King. Unfortunately the King sometimes, and especially so lately, seemed to have some of his own strange ideas about what was best for him, ideas which were at odds with history and therefore at odds with reason. He was in fact drifting into dubious territory, both morally and politically, and this was a cause for concern. He must be steered back on course. He must be winkled out of that library. Something should be done about that bloody menagerie.

He looked up and the mother goat's strange tender frown met his gaze as he lit a cigar and then slowly and abstractedly wafted the match to extinguish it. Should he really tell the King that no one knew where his daughter was? The telephone rang.

Ruscum darted across to answer it. 'The Lady Vangrannicus, sir,' he said, proffering the candlestick apparatus.

The Chamberlain spoke, breathing blue smoke into the black Bakelite. 'Hello dear... yes... oh, I don't think so... Will you? That's very kind of him... no, no, that's not his job, please, you should not ask him... most improper... I'll see to it tonight... Oh, not late, I'll be in for dinner, I should think. Goodbye.' Then he took off his great cloak and made his way over to his immense desk and settled himself behind it in the large high backed chair.

First there was a tray full of sheets with figures in columns and Vangrannicus took a sharp pencil and used it as a pointer quickly moving down the numbers, occasionally halting momentarily but then moving on to the bottom of the page which was then signed in ink and passed to Ruscum who blotted it and took it into custody waiting for the next which was not long in coming. This went on without a break for ten minutes until the tray was empty and Ruscum struggled with his sagging sheaf, taking it to the outer office where he did the next thing in the ritual procedure – put it all away somewhere probably. He was soon back however as Vangrannicus tackled the next tray which was full of memos. This time it was Ruscum who had a pencil and he marked each sheet with a cross or a tick according to the 'Yes' or 'No' muttered by his boss as it was thrust at him. They had almost fifteen minutes at this with only one, almost imperceptible, break in the rhythm when Vangrannicus stubbed out his cigar and happened to look up and saw the nymph looking at him, and was again unsettled by her expression.

Later Ruscum went and settled to scribbling busily in the outer office, a secretary was called to take the Chamberlain's dictation and soon there was a steady stream of paper on its way to be typed carried by the boy messengers Ruscum whistled up, and soon a contrary flow spread back along the corridor which consisted of paper for him to check and file one copy and send out the other by the hand of yet another brass-buttoned lad whose mother was so proud that he worked in the castle, and the place quietly hummed with determined important work notwithstanding the hints of incredulity and disdain which appeared to glint from the eye of the nymph if anyone looked at her from the wrong angle.

It was a little known fact that Vangrannicus himself had started out as a little brass-buttoned boy, many many years ago. He leaned back in his chair and was gratified by the coming and going of messengers (each one a little image of his own boyhood trooping before him), the distant steady clatter of typewriters and the tidiness of his desk which now contained no piles of papers. The cloak of the Chamberlain's office now hanging from the hat-stand was a darker blue than the messengers' tunic jackets and it was embroidered with gold stars. He thought of another cigar but restrained himself and patted together steepled fingers instead. The interlude of distracted self satisfaction was to be brief, however. The telephone rang in the outer office and shortly after Ruscum's head appeared round the door.

'The guard on the main gate says there's a woman desperate to see you – no appointment but she's in a bit of a state they say, I think its something to do with a missing person.'

'Name?'

'Oh yes, er, Simpson, I think he said.'

'Simpson? There is a case of that name isn't there?'

'Yes sir, same one, constables have it in hand, but insists on seeing you.'

The Chamberlain frowned and then said, 'Show her into the anteroom. Leave her there for half an hour. Then tell her to come back tomorrow. We should not have the authority of the police undermined like this.'

'Very well.'

Mrs Millicent Simpson, in her coat with the astrakhan collar, sat in the chair she was shown to, dignified, erect and frowning. Once alone, however she soon slid her handbag to the floor and slumped to rest her head in the palm of her left hand and allow the corners of her beautiful mouth to droop. She was thinking, of course of her missing husband.

Before he had capped everything by suddenly disappearing, Trevor had been observed to be deteriorating. He had always previously been the very predictable steady and responsible Chief Bird Keeper; he could be relied upon as husband, father, toy-buyer, bicycle repairer, lawn-mower, washer-up and utterer of laboured and clumsy puns after his third glass of wine. He had ever been the amiable, intelligent but slightly unexceptional chap that Millicent had known as spouse, friend and partner for many years. But he was now become, in the space of just a few weeks a silent, moody, preoccupied, unresponsive character who went through the motions of his domestic duties with none of the erstwhile cheery complaining, shirked his bedtime stories and spent longer and longer hours at the zoo. Something seemed to have happened to him. Something seemed to have got at him. Into Millicent's increasingly agitated ruminations about what might have brought about his physical disappearance, alarming words like 'kidnap' and 'blackmail' started to insinuate themselves. 'Adultery,' disappointingly was the first one that popped into the minds of those of her friends that she tried unburdening herself to.

Looking at some portrait sketches she had done of him soon after they met she was faced with the personality she had seen then, the personality that her very much younger self had detected and admired and interpreted (and of course, inevitably, to some extent invented.) Inconceivable that there should not have been changes, along with the physical ones, both in him and in her. Perhaps she had not been keeping up with the changes in him. When you're too close to something the perspective goes, doesn't it? Had she been keeping up with herself? Had she indeed – she thought as she leafed through the old drawings – left *herself* behind? What was that thing about 'ontogeny mirroring phylogeny' or something? Individuals evolving in the same pattern as the species? She did not know what it meant. She knew his skin was different, his eyes were sadder and duller, his hair was thinner, but she realised that she did not know what might have happened to his mind. What had time and Trevor's daily routines been doing to him over the years, what had the slow hammering away of life made of that original merry and amiable brain?

The very large clock on the wall trudged solemnly on, tick by tock, through Millicent's waiting time, and her weary mind continued the struggle to make sense of things. Faced with the silence of the lawnmower, the half-built tree house, the stoppered scotch bottle, she was even, in a curious way almost grateful for what appeared now to have become something that could not be ignored – the actual spiriting away of Trevor – for it gave her the excuse, the opportunity, to bring her plight to the attention of important people, to bring authority to bear on her predicament. Now that Trevor's absence had matured into a mystery of true disappearance, and there was even the possibility of abduction and murder or amnesia, friends who had abandoned her were drifting back, their prurience revived in a different and more excited guise.

A few days after officially reporting Trevor as a missing person she had taken the children to their grandmother for the afternoon and boldly strode up to the castle gate. As a member of the royal household (he might not ever go into the actual castle but it was a royal zoo and officially part of the King's demesne) he was entitled to certain privileges and one of them was a personal audience with the Chamberlain, and being his wife, the Chamberlain must see her, she knew that – even if the soldiers on the gate had to be loudly reminded of it. This room she had been asked to wait in, once she'd got past the louts in red tunics – where do they get them from these days? – was very nice and old fashioned.

It was as if someone had put a spell on him and he was turning into another animal. Slowly turning into a toad. She allowed herself an ironic smile. Or perhaps constant exposure to rare flightless birds had exposed him to some unidentified creeping brain fever.

There was a picture on the wall. There were few walls in the castle which did not boast something or other of this or that school, mostly courtesy of King Gustav IV, the current monarch's grandfather whose sobriquet had been 'Gallery Gus,' a fanatical art collector. This room had been assigned an odd little work depicting maidens in classical chitons dancing round something in a wood overshadowed by a rosy dawn.

The minutes ticked on and Millicent's chair became

uncomfortable. She got up and walked across the room to have a closer look at the picture. My, look at that, who'd have thought it? Millicent might look today like the *vrai bourgoise*, in the coat with the astrakhan collar which she never wore (except for rare formalities) but in her youth she had been to art college, oh yes, even she, the little housewife. And she had actually had herself a short career as a painter. 'Full of promise' was one review she would never forget. Her early works had been strange semi-abstract things, on huge canvasses when she could afford them. She thought her work of little worth if it failed to shock, not just the viewer but the painter herself – she sought to shake herself into a dramatic understanding of the horrors of the world. Jagged with fire and slapped with intestines and the frustration and insanity of the squashed dimensions of the death-wriggle of the intolerable human predicament. She had roared and blitzed her massive pictures with the coloured screams of lightning bolts and the retching maw of cannibalism spewing half-cooked infants into a vast gas-holder of sewage and vermin and writhing disease. And a great deal of burnt umber and crimson lake had found its way onto her dungarees and duffle coat.

But then she had met Trevor and soon afterward entered her sage green period. Which was self consciously mature and subtle and somewhat domestic but dotted with occasional flights of vigorously physical nudes pulsating with primitive rhythmic passions amongst neat gardens and flapping laundry. This work had been rather less well received even though she had thought it her best, and within a couple of years she was married, nursing little Oscar and art-teaching part time at the local secondary school. Then there was little Belinda and time had passed – the idea of the family was ever at odds with the arts wasn't it? – great art anyway, right back to the days when illumination had been a lonely and celibate vocation – and all of a sudden, as she looked at the brushstrokes and technique of the painting in this waiting room, she realised she had not even picked up a piece of charcoal for years. And she looked again at the unexpected thing you could just see hiding amongst the trees in the background of the picture and it made her smile.

Ruscum came in and nervously explained that she could not be seen today after all, could she please come back tomorrow?

Millicent looked him in the eye and sniffed cigar smoke on his clothes. She knew he was lying and Ruscum knew she knew he was lying and the more embarrassed he felt the more rigid he became for he did not like lying but would never disobey an order. In an effort to prevent himself from splitting in two, a sort of catatonia overcame him and all expression was banished from his face.

Millicent sized him up and said, 'You don't understand, my husband has disappeared, we have no idea what's become of him, his children are asking for him, he may have been murdered for all we know, the King must want to know what's happened to him, he's in charge of all the cassowaries and ostriches and things, if you don't do anything to help us I shall petition His Majesty with a formal complaint, his royal zoo will suffer without my husband who is a scientist and an expert, I'm sure His Majesty will be most displeased to know how I'm being treated here, surely there cannot be more pressing business than someone's life, and the royal aviaries.' She was doing well (she'd never uttered so many consecutive 'His Majesty's in her life), in spite of her somewhat frumpy coat with the astrakhan collar, Milly Simpson was a very attractive woman with a Gallic intensity lurking beneath the surface and in this forceful pleading mood she was even more attractive, she was a bundle of pheromones and big dark eyes and silky black hair and strong red lips and urgent yet very graceful and expressive appealing gestures which few men could remain unaffected by. Ruscum was flustered and began to back away. He knocked into an occasional table and its photograph of the Princess Daphne on a white horse.

The forthright one-sided conversation was heard by Vangrannicus in his lair just along the corridor and he was moved to investigate. By the time he was behind the slightly open door Millicent was inches from Ruscum's face as he retreated toward the wall and she was pressing home her advantage, reiterating the royal zoo connection, rattling off all sorts of things about the wellbeing of the cassowary, the quest for the maleo and her husband's unique knowledge, his intrepidity, his years of loyalty and service and spicing her case with an unspoken but ill-disguised contempt for lackeys in offices who did little more than drink tea and show people the door.

And all this about the zoo made the Chamberlain prick up his ears. He had been about to telephone for a couple of footmen to remove the noisy woman but he hesitated now – the other missing man, a much more important case than this one he had originally thought, the honourable Willoughby, was a man of some standing in the court, he was distantly related to the royal house. The police were aware of course that the disappearance of a man who had his own country estate and a butler was a significant event. But suddenly Vangrannicus – who was not naturally inclined toward zoology and who regarded the King's obsession with it as extremely irksome – remembered something that anyone else might have realised from the first: as well as being a wealthy and well connected man, Willoughby was a gentleman amateur, he was in fact one of the King's specimen hunters was he not? And this Simpson, it now seemed, was also a zooman of some sort. This was potentially worrying. Was it coincidence? Or was something going on? Something untoward in that damned menagerie?

A frown descended on Vangrannicus and he cupped an elbow in one hand and stroked his chin with the thumb and forefinger of the other, pursing his lips in a gravely pensive attitude. Two people connected with the zoo had gone missing. The King was locked away in his library and would see no one. The bakery had burnt down. No, no, forget the bakery, the bakery was a red herring he felt sure. Then a horrific thought flashed into his mind. Was the King actually in his library? Had he in fact been spirited away and all the do not disturb signs were merely the abductors' work? What to do?

He was, as ever, decisive. He burst into the anteroom. 'Ruscum, go and get two footmen and a locksmith, meet me outside the library main doors, pronto! You come here, follow me, Simpson, are you? Tell me quickly all about your husband – when and where exactly did you last see him?' And he was off, dragging her in his wake at a great pace down the corridor, only slowing as he passed an open door to shout instructions which instantly halted the noises of laughter and a typewriter. 'Get the chief of police, the reports on the missing persons, Willoughby and Simpson, and meet me in the library corridor, chop chop.'

A measure of consternation began to trickle through the ant-heap.

A little tremor threatened the routine of the day as Vangrannicus's swooping progress along the stairs and corridors left a little wash of urgency lapping into rooms which rarely heard zoological talk. At first there was not even sufficient substance for a rumour, just the vague sense in the air that suspicion and uncertainties were being generated abroad. It took no more than Vangrannicus's pace along the passageways and the unlikely composition of his entourage (unknown woman, police inspector, constable, locksmith, two people from the Chamberlain's own secretariat clutching sheets of paper and looking worried) to unsettle the equilibrium of the castle. No one imagined that the ruffling of the calm of the day could have anything to do with an animal that lived in children's picture books.

The locksmith was not required, the door was open. Vangrannicus motioned them all to keep back and rapped softly but urgently on the light oak door. There was no reply, he knocked again and listened for a minute before slowly turning the polished brass knob and slipping through the crack he pulled open. The King had not been abducted. He was snoring gently at a desk where he had slumped over an assortment of zoological and mythological works; he would be mortified to discover later that he had dribbled on a priceless medieval bestiary. The Chamberlain woke him gently and carefully, subtly planting the idea in the reviving royal consciousness that it was the King himself that had rung for attention.

The end of the desk was littered with crumbs, he had obviously not been entirely unattended during these days of 'Do Not Disturb'. The Chamberlain was, of course, hugely relieved to find the King present and unharmed, but took the opportunity, whilst his Majesty yawned and rubbed his eyes, to cast searching glances around the room and the desk and adjacent tables. Most of the book titles meant nothing to him unfortunately, for they were mostly in Latin and though he'd earnestly worked on his deficiencies throughout his career, Vangrannicus was a brass-buttoned boy at heart and had never fathomed the need for dead languages.

Millicent was thrilled by her tour of the private royal apartments which added a relish of excitement to the drama she was currently living through and she could not resist a peek round the open door.

Before she was rather rudely wrenched back by the police constable she had managed to snatch a view of His Majesty King Dagobert IV which she thought would fuel many reminiscences in her old age – she was delighted and shocked and amused by the rare privilege of being witness to such an informal and undignified pose. As well as the warm glow of the prospect of a little gossip-fodder, she found the revolutionary tendencies of her youth received a little spark of life and she smiled as the embarrassed policeman, who had caught a glimpse of the same sight and continued roughly to elbow her out of the way.

The door was firmly closed from within and the extempore collection of persons that Vangrannicus had marched down here were left to look blankly at one another, shrug their shoulders, raise their eyebrows, wonder where the nearest loo was and generally feel confused and inconvenienced. After a while the policemen started to mutter to one another and eventually took some papers from the officials and read and discussed them in low tones whilst everyone else was motioned to withdraw a little way from the door. Then the door opened, the chief policeman approached it, and was beckoned in, grabbing the papers his constable held as he went, the soft click of the mortise leaving everyone else in silence.

Millicent boldly crossed the corridor and sat on one of the elegant antique chairs that they had all so far been too deferential to use. She crossed her legs and for the first time in many years wished she had a cigarette. It must have been the smell of the Chamberlain's cigars. Oh, how she would love a cigar – she had smoked them habitually as an art student, but had not thought of smoking one since she had been overtaken by motherhood. She could smell it again, yes she really could, he must have lit one up in the royal library, you would never have imagined it being allowed. Out here a most ornate and rococo gold-enamelled French clock ticked lightly on its exquisitely rosewood inlaid whatnot. No one was moved to speak. There was shuffling of feet, stretching, then one of the officials also sat down, and another leaned against the oak panelling fanning herself with a sheet of paper. Millicent wondered whether the paper was about her husband and was about to ask, when the door opened, Vangrannicus thrust his head out and waved at her to come in. She was a little disconcerted, she had not known what to expect when they had all been peremptorily gathered and marched down here, but she definitely had not anticipated being in the same room as the King – whether he was asleep or awake. And her taking precedence over these other people did not seem quite right either, even though it was her husband that was missing.

It was not, of course, the same sort of semi-religious experience that a true dyed-in-the-wool divine-right monarchist would have felt, but even for an ex-revolutionary like Millicent, there was still that odd feeling one gets when a face from the newspapers, a face from much reproduced oil paintings was actually breathing in the tawdry flesh of a fellow creature just across the room. And it was a bit of a shock too, he was older than she had imagined and wore spectacles and blew his nose a great deal being as full of unruly fluids as any of the most averagely healthy of his subjects.

They were all seated very informally around a table in a corner of the great library overshadowed by cliffs of learning. Vangrannicus stood up, fetched another chair and said, 'Please sit down Mrs Simpson.' It seemed there was to be no courtly etiquette, thank god, (Millicent had not even had time to dread the possibility of it anyway) she would have loathed having to make even the most peremptory of curtseys, especially to such an unprepossessing figure as the rather sad Dagobert IV appeared to be as he collected some books into piles very protectively, much more nervous than a head of state should ever appear to be, and darted hesitant looks at the police chief and then herself.

Millicent could not have known that she was seeing Frederick in one of his worst moments, he was more ill at ease than ever he was normally and this was because he had had very little sleep for several days, going over and over his discussion with Johnson, trying to decide what was known and what he believed about the unicorn, trying to decide what he thought of Johnson, agonising over whether he had done the right thing in his instructions to that strange man, dreading the possibility of ridicule if that discussion and those instructions ever became public knowledge. And on top of everything here was Vangrannicus and the Chief of Police with the news that two of his specimen hunters had gone missing. He was intensely vulnerable to the belief that these disappearances were not unconnected with Johnson's performance at the recent zoo audience in the rotunda, and yet he did not want to mention the possibility to such pragmatic men as these since it would involve introducing a mythical beast into a police investigation. As he listened to the police chief he was trying to remember what reaction the missing men had had to Johnson's performance at the rotunda. (He could not recall them saying or doing anything). And, above and beyond everything, he was wrestling with his burgeoning inclinations to believe that a mythical beast was not mythical, but might have been seen trotting about the forgotten quarters of his kingdom. The fact that he had persuaded himself that this was a clear possibility made him begin, now that he was sitting at a table with Vangrannicus and Inspector Horrocks, to question his own sanity and wonder whether he had worked himself up into some sort of mental exhaustion. These were not the sort of men that ever strayed far from the most solid, sternly toe-stubbing facts. If their children had ever been read fairy stories it would have been their mothers that had done it. He shaded his eyes with his hand, managed a peremptory nod to Millicent when she was introduced to him and bade the inspector carry on.

Horrocks outlined, in the best and most prosaic traditions of a police notebook, the circumstances, first of the Right Hon. Willoughby's disappearance – his being by far the most important case – and then those of Trevor Simpson's. As he began, Millicent was doing two things at once, something she was rather good at. She was listening to Horrocks but also taking this rare opportunity of studying at very close quarters the illustrious and venerable and much loved (if you believed the popular press) head of state, His Royal Majesty King Dagobert IV. Every pub had a picture of him, mostly in full royal regalia, ermine collar and ungainly crown – big as a gas oven and plastered with supposedly priceless baubles. There was one version which you would have thought the powers that be would not have allowed to get out, but which somehow had slipped through the censors and was indeed very common on public walls – it showed, if you looked closely, the great headgear very slightly lop-sided and bringing pressure to bear on the tip of the royal ear which was discernibly somewhat squashed, the whole effect being endearing but more in the style of one of the seven dwarfs than the implacable head of the armed forces.

Millicent was reminded of it now as she sat opposite his naked and somewhat thinning bonce, looking at a man on the verge of old age, going grey, bloodshot eyes and no discernible autocratic feature about him. It was said that he was not that keen on being King himself anymore, but there were still plenty of people who did believe that the institution of the monarchy was divinely ordained and that this distinctly unimpressive, though perfectly amiable, character naturally represented in himself the will of the Invisible. She marvelled at the whole ridiculous idea, and she marvelled at the certainty that she would find it irresistible to tell people that she had been sitting with the King in his private library at a table just inches away from him even though that meant nothing more than that she had been sitting in a room with a particular man who was, as a man, no different from thousands of other men. Yet there remained many, especially amongst older people, who regarded Frederick as a human being so special, so apart from the rest of mankind by dint of his ancestry and of his history and the history of the kingdom, that he was sanctified, a living relic, for all practical purposes a species apart, a mythic being. People were capable of believing some very unlikely things, she thought.

Horrocks had explained that the Hon. Willoughby had seemed pre-occupied on the morning of the fourteenth and had gone out wearing some old clothes borrowed from the servants. The gatekeeper at the zoo, one Joseph Wainwright, had seen him leave the zoo at approximately 4.30 on the same day in the company of one Grimes, Culvert, another menagerie employee. They had been asking where a man called Johnson lived (no one knows his forename – even in the Human Resources Office) – also an employee but largely on an extra-mural basis it seems – and the two walked off it is believed towards a lonely cottage on the other side of the great meadow which Wainwright thought to be a place often visited by Johnson.

Vangrannicus was unhappy about such an impromptu meeting, the King should not really have been subjected to the unscheduled presence of an unvetted commoner, but he had had no choice. As the wife of one of the disappeared he had had to keep her close so that she could give evidence immediately to himself and the police, and he had had to get down here lickety split in order to ensure nothing had happened to Dagobert. (In fact if he told the truth to himself he had to recognise that he had come close to panic, had he not?) But he now wished he had been able to manage things differently, this was not right, for the monarch to have such a casual *ad hoc* meeting with a commoner. He preferred to pre-arrange any casual *ad hoc* meetings with commoners himself. Any attempts to impose some sort of formality on this little very private audience however could never come to anything. The soft yellow light, low over the book table, beyond the reach of which the rest of the library appeared to be almost in darkness gave a cosy atmosphere to this corner of the room and it was natural that conversation was always going to veer more toward the intimate than the officially minutable.

He sat back in his chair and eventually relaxed a little, allowing himself a measure of relief at the non-abduction of the King and lit another cigar as Horrocks moved on to the case of Simpson, Trevor, and even responded to Millicent's pleading eyebrows (Millicent's eyebrows pleaded very effectively) to offer her one from his case.

There was only one flimsy sheet of typing paper for Simpson, T, and that was only sparsely typed upon. Horrocks dutifully read out the name, age, birthplace, education, job history and religious affiliation of the missing man and a statement Millicent had made in her local police station three days ago. There were also other witnesses quoted, including Jemima Cake, the croquet umpire, and a familiar name: Wainwright, who once again seemed to be the last person to have seen the missing man. Millicent looked from one to the other of these supremely powerful men, Chief of Police, Lord Chamberlain, Reigning Monarch, and expected discussion, strategy decisions and a string of orders to be issued directing the immediate allocation of men and resources to the necessary manhunt. But what there was, to start with at least, was a moment of silence. Then the King spoke, nervously, she thought.

'A good man, Simpson, his men are bringing the maleo you know, should be here soon. In fact had anyone checked that he's not simply gone down to the docks to prepare for its arrival?'

'Yes, Sire, we've checked, some of his zoo staff are there but there's been no sign of him down there and they say they haven't seen him, though they expected to,' said Horrocks in a businesslike tone, pleased to appear thorough.

Vangrannicus smoked on, not looking as involved as he ought to be as far as Millicent was concerned.

Then the King asked in the hesitant tones of someone trying to appear to be less interested in the answer than he was, 'Did Wainwright say Simpson asked about, er, what was his name? The man they were going after in the other case, Johnson, was he too going to look for this, er, colleague of theirs, Johnson, perhaps?'

Vangrannicus looked at the end of his cigar.

Horrocks said, 'Yes, I believe Wainwright did say he told Simpson that Willoughby and Grimes had gone to find Johnson, Sire.'

Whereupon the King put his head in his hands and let out a sort of groan.

The Chamberlain looked up at the sound and putting his head on one side allowed himself a bit of a quizzical look at his sovereign.

It did not quite yet occur to him that the source of the King's disquiet was the likelihood that various of his zoo-men had begun to wander off in search of a mythical possibility, and the concomitant likelihood that this mythical possibility might therefore no longer be a secret, whereas the King was desperate that it must not be made known, for fear he himself would have to cease to believe in it. A bead of sweat appeared on the royal forehead, which his late wife would have read as a sign that agitation was beginning to cloud his mental processes.

Millicent was going to ask who Johnson was but then she remembered, Trevor had told her about the strange man who always wore an old bowler hat, who seemed to have an unusual way with animals but was not much interested in people. She had never met him, but as far as she could remember what she had been told about him he was not the sort of person people would go out of their way to meet.

Vangrannnicus reluctantly remembered Johnson too – he was that scruffy disrespectful old codger, the one who was either never there or if he did turn up no one could make out half of what he said which was usually very little. He was one of those that had been around too long to sack – that is, hopelessly inefficient (or at least Vangrannicus assumed him to be inefficient) and offensive in his general slovenliness to the dignity of a royal office, but one who had been in the job so long, and his father before him, that sacking him would represent an irritating contradiction of the tradition of continuity which Vangrannicus so much respected and upon which indeed he regarded the legitimacy of the state ultimately to rest.

And then suddenly, a jolt! An electric spark suddenly reconnected two parts of his brain – oh dear, the brass-buttoned boy was getting old, how could he have forgotten? – he suddenly felt very annoyed with himself when it came back to him that only a few days ago, after the last rotunda audience of the specimen hunters, the King had asked for this same Johnson to be brought to him, brought to him here in this very library. And yet the King said nothing now about it. There was something strange here. He had asked Vangrannicus to keep the meeting dark, had he not? He looked again at his royal master who was so obviously tired and ill at ease. What on Earth was all this about? He had thought that the King was simply concerned about the mad old duffer and might have been going to retire him, but no, perhaps there was something else. Johnson had thought he'd seen a unicorn. My god it couldn't be something to do with that could it? He looked again at the King who was smiling wanly at Millicent.

Horrocks, who was a very large man, outlined the pattern of police enquiries. Except for the lack of wool or tusks it was just as if a woolly mammoth had been introduced to the library, Horrocks had a massive head that jutted its lantern jaw over his white starched collar, he loomed from the darkness, his shiny bald pate reflecting the candle light, and spoke in flat deliberate vowels which supported thick, truncheon-like consonants and the effect was as the building of a wall – each word a brick laid firmly down to block the possibility of any contradiction. The police enquiries apparently largely consisted of 'investigating the Johnson man' and keeping an eye out for the missing persons. His ponderous and deliberate assertion that there was no reason to suspect foul play might have made you laugh if one of the persons in question wasn't your husband. There was some rather inconsequential questioning of Millicent about what sort of man Trevor was and what sort of things might he get up to which she didn't know about – which also almost made her laugh – questions about did he have any money worries? Were the children well and accounted for? And then to her utter astonishment, the sudden matter of fact reeling off (reading directly from the typescript) of all the innocently subversive organisations the young Mrs Simpson had subscribed to in her distant revolutionary past. Some of it was partly true. Millicent was astonished, as much by his gall in reading it out in her presence as by the half-baked idiocy of the analysis, and gave the officer a pitying look before accentuating her deep sigh with a slump of the shoulders and an exhalation of blue smoke. Everyone present, probably even Horrocks himself, knew it was utterly irrelevant, but the Chief of Police could not help hinting at how efficient the Royal Constabulary was and how much more they knew about you than you might suppose.

'Very well,' said the King, which meant they were all dismissed.

He started to pile up his books and the blank look in his eyes made Millicent feel suddenly sorry for him and wish she could tuck him up in bed. The Chamberlain and Horrocks marched away into the unlit gloom towards the door, Millicent was slower, picking up her handbag and pushing her chair back under the table a little awkwardly with her free hand, which still had the cigar between its fingers. The King had half risen to his feet and was flipping the pages of a book to find the place he wanted to mark and as he dropped in his leather bookmark she caught sight of a plate representing a medieval white unicorn in a rose garden.

She couldn't help saying, 'I saw one of those on my way here!'

Horrocks was already marching down the corridor.

'Mrs Simpson,' called Vangrannicus from the doorway.

'That will be all!' called the King in his direction, but to Millicent he said quietly, 'Wait a moment, what was that you were saying?' and put a hand on her arm.

Vangrannicus was confused and annoyed but had no choice but to withdraw and close the door though he did not stray far from the keyhole for a long time.

'You saw one of these?'

'Yes, just like that.' He was frowning and she was smiling but they were both puzzled, he still had hold of her arm and moved out from behind the table to look earnestly into her dark eyes.

'What, on your way here, you say? Just now? When exactly? Where exactly? Is it far? You must take me there. Have you told anyone else? What was it like exactly?'

Was he a bit mad? Was he having some sort of an attack? She was quite taken aback. This was the King, and he seemed to be going nutty about a unicorn. The protectiveness she had been beginning to feel was for a second or two almost undermined as she wondered whether there were aspects of his private personality which might be unimagined by suburban commoners. But then he seemed to realise he was frightening her and calmed down.

'I'm sorry, I get a bit excited sometimes, even at my age' he said, looking again into her dark eyes.

He still had hold of her arm, though his grip was now warm rather than tight, and she had a frisson of a new feeling which was unexpected and might be thought laughable but was strangely enlivening as she looked back into his eyes and said, 'It's not far, come along I'll take you.'

'No, no,' he whispered. 'This is the quickest way out,' trying to guide her by the elbow.

'But we're not going out,' she laughed, 'it's just down here and round the corner.'

Frederick stopped and looked puzzled and disappointed but then followed her saying, 'I don't understand.'

She smiled, 'Honestly, its down here, the unicorn. Don't be disappointed, its very small.'

He seemed to relax a little and half smiled, and in fact felt something like relief when, having encountered no one on the way, they entered the anteroom and Millicent said, stubbing out her cigar in the marble ashtray, 'Its in here, see if you can find it.'

Already it seemed all vestiges of royal mystique had evaporated for Millicent.

Frederick looked quickly round the room then went straight to the painting and peered at it from close up for a minute or two before exclaiming theatrically (he was noticeably cheering up) 'Aha, eureka!' pointing to the tiny white unicorn lurking in the forest in the background of the picture, and she was laughing and said, 'Did you think I meant a real one? Did you think I was saying I'd actually seen a real unicorn?'

Instead of answering – and she herself did not know whether it was a serious question – he said, 'it's a Girardi Boldoni, one of my grandfather's acquisitions, rather a nice picture isn't it, romantic and sort of intricately vague, with that misty light hinting at a moon that isn't there. Good isn't it' The King's propensity to surrender to enthusiasm – in almost any direction – which could be exasperating for some people, but was endearing to others, now showed itself in all its runaway vigour as he waxed lyrical about Boldoni being unappreciated and not enough notice being taken of his exploration of the hinterland of impressionism long before it was ever thought of. Then, however, he suddenly changed direction.

'But, you know, as I look at it now... you know it was always assumed to be an Italian pastoral scene, but, swop me bob, if you...' (Millicent came closer and stood next to him) 'do you know I don't think I've ever really looked at this painting properly before... look, if you imagine it without the trees up there and remove the hunting lodge from the top of that hill it could be... do you know I think I may have been there.'

Millicent peered hard and eventually whispered, 'Yes yes, I feel as if I know that place too. How strange. Imagine that! We must have the same dreams.'

Impulsively but carefully, Frederick lifted the painting from its hook (it was not a large work and in spite of its ornate frame not too heavy). 'Come, Mrs Simpson, we shall have some brandy.'

She could not refuse, he was the King. She did not want to refuse. It might be getting late but the kids would be having a fine time sleeping at their granny's house and poor old Trevor was, well he was wherever he was, and hell, brandy with the King, who'd have thought it. In his private apartments.

CHAPTER ELEVEN

The brandy was delicious and very old, the King was lovely and not as old, when you saw him at ease at home, as he looked when everyone was looking at him and he was forced to parade about somewhat and assume a modicum of pomp which she saw was entirely alien to him. Or indeed when he was tired and worried, alone in the dark of his library.

For his part he soon decided that Millicent was extremely intelligent, very witty and perspicacious, and, dammit, a very, very fine looking woman. He was close to becoming 'Frederick' to her rather than 'Majesty' or 'Sire.' Indeed a seed of mutual liking had germinated in double quick time and would soon rise to the surface – breaking through the crust of forms of address – where its bloom would shine for each of them.

After the third VSOP he decided to tell her everything. All about Johnson and the unicorn. She did not say anything at first, staring at the painting for a minute or two then looking back up to Frederick, and then glancing through some of the books (mythological and zoological) which he had brought with him from the library.

'It's not impossible you know. Do you know about the coelocanth?' he asked.

Yes, she had heard of the coelocanth, the prehistoric fish found happily swimming about the Indian Ocean one day very much un-extinct. 'But,' she said tentatively, 'there is no fossil record of the unicorn, is there?'

'Well, not as such. That may just be because no one has yet found it. Or identified it properly. It is not a reason not to believe.' He said perhaps rather too earnestly, almost giving *believe* a religious overtone.

'Your Majesty' and indeed 'Mrs Simpson' were heard no more and it was 'Frederick' and 'Millicent' all the way now. She found herself mischievously wondering, as she felt sufficiently relaxed and warm inside whether it would ever be Freddie and Milly. He was a lot older than her, well, no, not a lot. He was older than her but not, as kings went, so much older than her than his father had been when she was a little girl. The mature and enriching spirit once more glided over her welcoming tongue, and the warm grey eyes she looked into wondered what put the twinkle in her own. Logs crackled in the hearth and when Millicent shocked herself by boldly asking if there might be such a thing as a small cigar, he pulled a cord and someone appeared and in a minute or two brought a box of the things.

She looked across at her coat with the astrakhan collar which lay draped over a chair. It had, with that collar, something of the look of those huge coats that adorned the ample matronly figures of dowager duchesses and queen mothers in sepia photographs. It was not something she habitually wore, indeed ever wore normally herself, it languished in the wardrobe waiting for funerals, receptions and the other rare formalities that punctuated life, but it made her now think of Frederick's female line for it reminded her specifically of his mother, Queen Gertrude, who had been a familiar figure in the rotogravure of her childhood. Now deceased of course, she remembered the funeral on the radio. The wireless, the wooden story box, and here she was amongst the dreams which had come out from behind the fretted walnut cabinet which she'd listened to with her head on a pinafored lap, here she was amongst the people on the other side.

And then she wondered – and all this took only seconds, it was whilst her host was opening the cigar box and looking for a cigarette lighter – what had become of his wife? He had been married of course, there was the famous Princess Daphne, heir to the kingdom (god help it, was the popular opinion) but his wife must have died, there was no Queen now, and yet Millicent could remember nothing at all about her funeral. As an adult she had never been much of a royal watcher, but to miss an entire state funeral... it would have been impossible. There must not have been one. Very confusing.

Turning back to take a cigar from the proffered box she was faced again with the painting resting on a chair and her mind returned to the matter in hand. Boldoni she had come to appreciate only very late in life. As an art student she had condemned what she had perceived as his reticence and his traditionalism, but in maturity she had come to understand the poetry of the ethereal, the numinous, that pervaded his subtly slanting vistas. She would be ashamed now for anyone to know the venom she had heaped upon his work in her youth, when she was preparing herself to plough up what had gone before and eclipse the whole canon with new and blinding wonders. She could not help making a few appreciative comments about the artist's technique, his colours and brushstrokes, which intrigued Freddie but before he could inquire whether she was herself an artist, she dived in and asked with raised eyebrows, 'Are you wondering whether the unicorn might not be a fanciful addition to the landscape at all, but actually painted from life?'

'Well... yes, do you know, I suppose I am.' He turned again to the painting and stared into it. 'You might say that could not possibly be the case because if they were so much a fact of life in the area then their presence must have been reflected in the written record of the time and there is no mention of them of which we are aware. But, what if the situation was just the same as it is now? Unicorns not thought to exist in reality. Someone sees one, knows no one will believe them, mischievously sticks one in his painting. His painting of the area where he saw it.'

'You mean if anyone saw one nowadays they wouldn't say anything because no one would believe them?'

'Yes. Except for Johnson of course.'

'Who is a bit mad, and would not give a hoot if anyone thought him mad?'

'Yes.'

'But. Surely if there were sufficient of them to breed and continue over all these years they must be seen from time to time, even if rare, they must be seen sufficiently often that people would have to talk about them. They would have to become real again and accepted as fact. Surely.'

'I admit,' said Frederick, 'that it's all very strange. I just do not think Johnson made it up. I do not think he would tell a story to his King. He's odd but there's nothing devious about him; he might have secrets and secret ways, but there's nothing of the sly schemer, the trickster, the joker about him, nothing at all. Those are people traits, and he barely exists amongst people.'

Millicent suddenly remembered that the Queen had died young, abroad, was it? Or of something that wasn't talked about. Any way it had all been very low key, no state funeral or anything, maybe she had been buried abroad, was that likely?

'You know,' said the King after another sip of brandy and running his tongue all round the inside of his mouth and an exaggerated pouting of the lips which was both reflective and savouring, 'I think I should, that is, I don't think I'm ever going to put... to put this thing to rest, until I've gone... until I've gone to look for it.'

Millicent smiled broadly and turned away from the little photograph in a silver frame she had spied on a distant little table almost hidden by a vase of flowers. 'Could you do that? Surely they wouldn't let you? You're the King!'

'Exactly, I'm the sodding King and I can do anything I like,' and they both spluttered into spontaneous laughter.

Oh what friends they had so soon become. By the end of that night Millicent felt as if she'd known old Freddie all her life. He was lovely and a marvel. And his castle was a marvel too, it was fantastic, fabulous, in here with all the stones and oak and spiral staircases and pictures and mullioned lights and lackeys and free cigars at the snapping of the fingers and Indian rugs; anything was believable, there were probably magic wands in that chest in the corner, without a doubt a great many more bizarre things seemed possible here than they did in 38 Dumbleton Close. Find a unicorn? Of course, why not? She would not have thought twice about it in her art school days, just lit another reefer and taken off after the spectral beast, leaping straight over the trammels of conventional science as if they weren't there. There were things 'They' did not want you wondering about, there were things 'They' did not want you to know about, and a unicorn may well have been one of them. And then in the middle of it all she had a feeling of suddenly remembering herself, a sense that all these years she'd rather betrayed herself, that her true nature had been prematurely buried, buried in family life. This is what she had been meant to do, look for unicorns with a drunken King. And she was heaved up into elation at rediscovering herself and plunged into disappointment at the thought of all the lost years, and all the time there was a little demon who she knew was sitting there waiting to remind her that she had not thought of Trevor since they had left the library.

Then she re-focused and suddenly realised that her cigar ash was very long and Freddie was picking up another book and reading a description of the temperament of the Chinese unicorn.

'"Always gentle, beneficent, delicate in diet, regular and stately in pace," and with a call "which in the middle part thereof is like a monastery bell." Marvellous, eh?'

As well as unicorns, however, they talked during that night – largely at Millicent's instigation – about what is was like to be King. Freddie hinted that he did not like it, in spite of not really knowing what the alternative was, never during his entire life having been a private citizen, he intimated that the whole rigmarole was a bore and a pain. He was in a very mellow mood and he had not met anyone he liked as much as Millicent in a very long time, but he remained a little circumspect about actually coming out and saying that if it wasn't for the zoo he would abdicate. Thinking about it reminded him of the other reason he had not yet done it – in case they tried to make Daphne Queen, which they would, those bastards, and that would kill her if she did not manage to run away. No, if he gave it up the whole damn shooting match would have to change and that was a big operation, that was revolution. And it had so far proved beyond him seriously to contemplate its fermentation. All he seemed capable of was little erosions of the frippery and flummery, nibbling at the decorative edges of the formality of the institution.

Millicent marvelled at the strictures there were upon his life, it must truly be like living in a straitjacket. She shuddered, how could he stand it, but then she reflected, and simultaneously the King said, 'Well everyone's life is restricted, isn't it though? You can't do just exactly what you want to do can you?' and she was amazed at the congruence of their minds; of course Dumbleton Close had its rules of behaviour, its timetables, its mores, its tight little conditions everyone had to acknowledge.

'But at least here the freedoms you do have are enormous freedoms aren't they?' she said. 'You can indulge yourself to your heart's content with paintings and zoos as long as you appear when and where you are supposed to appear in the right clothes and wave the sceptre and make the right little speeches, can't you?' She looked around the magical apartment again and stood up, which operation was not as easy as it normally was for some reason, and asked if they could go out onto the battlemented parapet and look at the view. Which they did. Taking the bottle with them.

Freddie had a voice which, without being over-loud, had a resonance far beyond that which his relatively slim frame would lead you to expect. There did not seem to be enough space inside him to reverberate the warm baritone sound which emerged. It was a lovely friendly voice, a voice clearly enunciating but in a very slightly lazy way which, without ever descending into a drawl lent a measure of friendly informality and even avuncularity to his utterances which Millicent for one could happily close her eyes and listen to for a long time, whatever he was saying. And some of the things he said were very quaint and unusual and made her laugh. His talk was littered with turns of phrase, little bits of archaic slang and curious metaphors which had fallen out of use even before her grandfather was born, and which, outside of the King's conversational speech, were only now to be found in old dictionaries of unconventional English. He said things like 'Swop me bob' (which she assumed had once been 'So help me god') and described some unfortunate woman as 'fustilugs'.

On their way up the stairs to the battlements Millicent found herself in a fit of giggles prompted by, 'I suppose I'll always have to give my head for the washing.'

He smiled at her and when she'd recovered she asked him how he came to use all these weird old expressions.

'Oh I know, I'm sorry, I just don't seem to be able to help it, I'm very old fashioned, I know. One had nurses, you know, some of whom were of a certain vintage and may have been recruited from rural districts where language progressed only at the speed of the slowest ox; and they weren't always quite top drawer, don't y'know?'

And Millicent could see that he made fun of himself but also that he was at odds with himself and his position.

'Some old sycophant once said to me that it must be because of my position at the apex of history, at the top of the pyramid of culture that our noble nation has slowly erected, like a great muck heap of thought and art and ideas, that because I was born out of it and into it, there must be all these little bits of cultural shrapnel, fragments of ideas and arcane and quirky speech that have been lodged within me and cannot be expunged,' he laughed. 'Not that I've tried. It is strange, I'm sure, but in the ordinary course of things, nobody pulls me up about it you see, because I'm the King and whatever I say goes, even if its "humgumptious". Maybe on the contrary, its incumbent upon me to keep these little things alive. "Ob and sol", as they say, or have I made that one up? Please don't ask me what it means.' He sighed. 'Lots of things are incumbent upon me, you know.'

She smiled and involuntarily touched his arm as they reached the top of the stairs and emerged into the starlit night.

The view from this vertiginous turret was probably always magnificent but tonight it was also something else, it was strange. It encompassed more than one vista, for the west and the east displayed oddly separate moods tonight. The occident was sable carpet of incalculable silver stars, dark and bright and mysterious hanging over the even blacker lumps of solid forest which bunched in clots over the land which stretched into the Lanes once it had disappeared over the horizon, but here, where you could still see it, it was not quite the Lanes, here it was still mapped and intermittently inhabited by people like you and me. In the Orient, and over the moody river stretching away to the north and the sea, was fog. And the fog made this land, this very familiar land – for within was shrouded Dumbleton Close – look very very strange. It was impossible to imagine Dumbleton Close just quietly hiding in there and still being Dumbleton Close with its garden gates and washing lines and rabbit hutches – tonight it was impossible to know what was in there at all, but whatever it was, it was something that had not been there before. The suburb was now transformed into something unknown. The visible tip of the steeple of St Michael's must now belong to some exotic temple hidden below the cloud, altogether different from the building Millicent had left behind that afternoon.

As she looked and tried to see into the mist and enjoyed its opacity and the hints it gave of things which it would not reveal, and looked at its drifting thick veil she felt it was like a huge animal or spirit rolling in its sleep, one great dream blotting out lesser imaginations and reaching back and forth across millennia to offer grim but exhilarating revelations to those who could abandon reason and their ideas of themselves.

They were quiet for a while, the King looking about him with his hands in his pockets, with a slightly sad expression which was at the same time ready to brighten with hope at any moment. Millicent found herself thinking, as her gaze swung slowly back and forth between fog and stars, that if there was such a thing, whatever the unicorn was like, it would not forget its children, and she admonished, in her imagination, a milky foal for not polishing its little stubby horn. She must go. She must be back before morning. But her stockinged feet (where were her shoes?) felt pleasantly cool on the old dressed granite and Freddie tipped 'one for the frog and dichter' into each of their glasses perched on the uneven top of the wall.

'Your husband, ma'am,' toasted Freddie, and they sipped Trevor's health. 'He's a very nice man and very knowledgable, very conscientious, I can't wait to see this maleo bird. Wherever he's got to I'm sure it must be in the line of duty. He'll turn up any day now and surprise us with something, I'm sure.'

It had suddenly occurred to the King that he ought to be reassuring Millicent, he ought to be more gallant, he'd allowed himself to be put off balance rather by her attractiveness, she was a lovely woman. He got a grip on himself and attempted to retrace his steps back onto the firm dull ground of the dutiful sounds he was supposed to make. 'Yes, I've enjoyed his reports on the flightless birds and he's an eminent specimen hunter – very experienced, the others look up to him, you know.' He was not entirely sure that this was true, but at the time it was easy to persuade himself that he believed it, so he said it anyway. And he could never entirely dissemble, generally he found himself exaggerating but rarely actually outright lying.

Millicent had no real wish to discuss her husband with the King. She had come to the castle (yesterday as it now was) to demand to know what had become of him and what steps were being taken to find him, but not to discuss him in any intimate way. She loved Trevor, she reflected, nursing her glass and looking away from Frederick. Even if he was changing into someone a bit different from the man she had first taken from the box, unwrapped and played with exhaustively, the man she had married, he would still be Trevor. Indeed it was a love which was all the warmer for being now an old and familiar and habitual love, and as such well able to encompass the gradual appearance of a new profile, lit in some new and unseen way by a light that had never caught him that way before. Of course she was worried about what was happening to him, both out there, wherever he was, and in his head. Something was going on in his head, she knew that. Some sort of mid-life thing probably. She was helped to know it now by the thing which was going on in her own head. The thing which she realised for the first time tonight.

There had always been a strange counterpoint, a balance of opposing forces about their relationship which had choreographed a delicate dancing course up hill and down dale and taken them to places each would never have been alone. When they'd met it had been an attraction of opposites. An artist and a scientist, a man of punctilious observation and detail (he'd been an entomologist then) a woman of fiery emotion and dramatic, brash, passionate gestures strewing huge canvasses with panic and tragedy. The meticulousness of the interlocking parts of the dung beetle and the shocking form of the naked human psyche plastered in blinding heaps of colour. But they had fascinated one another, they had seen the miracle of the unexpected in one another, they had been each a revelation to the other. Over the years of course, after the euphoria of the discovery of these fabulous unknown animals which were each other, they had recoiled somewhat one from the other, still fascinated, but sometimes more content to look from a distance, and lately, but only very lately, they had been surprised by a measure of mild repulsion. Whence it came they could not say. And now, well now they each seemed in some measure to be recoiling from themselves. Perhaps it was natural in homo sapiens. Trevor could tell you what was natural amongst the coleoptera and the hymenoptera, the trichoptera and the diplopoda, and by now he knew chapter and verse on everything the ratites, struthioniformes the palaeognathae and lithornithiformes were likely to do, but he found it increasingly difficult to predict his own behaviour.

For her part Millicent was remembering the demons which had once so troubled and excited her but upon which she had closed the cupboard door as if putting away her childish things – love and death and the agonies of the human predicament – swapping them for childish things which were rather lass abstract but just as dramatic – chicken pox, bullying, tantrums, missing bits of Lego and costumes for the school play. Now she did not paint at all, but tied shoelaces, did up buttons, wiped noses and attended PTA meetings. He had moved away from insects, up the food chain as far as cassowaries and the like, but though there were more and more things on which he was an expert, there seemed to be one thing that he knew less and less about and that was himself. And there was one thing, one danger, she was more and more frightened of, and that was the danger of forgetting something altogether. She felt she was forgetting who she used to be.

She came out of her reverie to hear Freddie speaking quietly now of the Horn of Ulph and the unicorn as a symbol of the moon. It was as if he were addressing the stars.

She had the royal limousine (piloted by a very drowsy chauffeur, rousted from his bed) stop about a mile from Dumbleton Close – she did not want to excite the neighbours' imaginations by being seen emerging from a great black motor with a royal crest – and as she walked through the wispy fog, which was beginning to disperse now as the promise of the dawn brought light winds from the south, her mind was full of entirely unexpected things. She had thought her home-coming would have been in time to retrieve the children from Granny and put them to bed, and that she would have been relaying to her mother-in-law reassurances from the police about lines of enquiry and suchlike, whereas... She had been out all night drinking with the King. Who was, it turned out, a republican. And rather nice. She had been looking at a hitherto unseen Boldoni, a mysterious dreamscape with its beams from an invisible moon and its hint at flesh and blood mythology. And she had seen, had she, had she really seen what she thought she had seen in that small photograph in the silver frame?

The lamppost she approached was visibly shedding the foggy possibilities it had been wrapped in all night to become once again, in the light of the day, just what was expected of it, just a lamppost. The mask was lifted from Dumbleton Close to return it to its allocated character as a place of enduring ordinariness.

Which was the way most of those who lived there preferred it. Indeed they had no idea it was ever anything else, since they rarely peered into the veil of night prepared to notice the twisting of perspective that their imaginations might have fed upon, given free rein. However, Millicent was proof that there was one at least who found herself resident there (by chance and circumstance) who could still dream. Who could dream of other places and of lampposts with bears' heads, of lampposts erupting with roses and mottled with pulsating phosphorescence. But who now must walk the quiet streets, marvelling at the stultifying banality of it all as dawn's routine reclaimed it.

An early riser waiting for the kettle to boil looked out over the inert bricks and tarmac, the lurking moggies and the dank shrubbery of the cul-de-sac – ah, there was Mrs Simpson, coming home, it seemed. Very early. And wearing a very oddly posh coat. It was only a familiar woman in a coat going through her own front door. But that coat, at this time? Where has she been? The kettle whined and knocked and spat and stirred itself to the drone which came before the whistle which would penetrate the locality.

Millicent hung up her coat and looked at the clock. She had an hour before she should collect the children, and lay down to nap. After a minute or two of drowsy semi-consciousness she found she suddenly understood what was going on. Trevor had gone after the unicorn. Bloody hell, of course of course that's what had happened, it wasn't another woman, it wasn't his mid-life thing, it was a mythical beast. Freddie suspected him of it but was not sure, and hence had not quite said it outright; he was not likely to admit to people like the Chief of Police and the Chamberlain that he believed in a storybook animal, even if he was the King, but in his evening with Millicent he'd let drop a lot of clues. He was quite candid, in discussing the Boldoni painting, that he was open to the possibility that the unicorn might very well exist. And he had not been joking when he'd said he wanted to go and look for it. He was serious. All these zoo people going missing, they must have been taken with the possibility too. These animal collectors. Collectors. It was obvious. Though it was unlikely they had seen the Boldoni – it was this weird Johnson bloke who had started it all for them. Yes that must be it. She felt enlightened now, but as if she must have seemed a bit stupid last night. But then, the unicorn had been introduced as an entirely different topic hadn't it? It had been introduced, as far as she remembered, with the brandy, so perhaps she might have been excused for not making the connection immediately. How was she to know what was going on. The police obviously didn't, they had made no mention at all of mythical beasts.

Before she could get off to sleep properly she heard the rattle of a latch key and calls of, 'Milly! Yoo hoo!' 'Mummy!' 'Where are you!'

CHAPTER TWELVE

The man in the breakfast room said hello but barely looked up as he did so and seemed not to want to catch her eye. He was wearing a heavy corduroy jacket with leather elbow patches and trousers of a rather familiar green colour which attracted Daphne's attention. It was just like the bottle green livery which marked out so many of the royal household. Oh god, not already surely? But no, they would not send anyone in uniform, they would be plainclothes.

Partly out of perversity – he obviously did not want to be engaged in conversation – and partly to make sure he was not to be worried about, she decided to talk to him. And having decided to talk to him it was a short step to persuading herself that there was something interesting about him – he had nice thick brown hair and manly stubble. And although he could not be said to be ill at ease, he had the look of a man with something on his mind.

There were 'hello's and 'Did you enjoy your breakfast?' and 'Yes thank you very nice,' and then a long silence, in spite of her fetching little smiles (which at one time she used to spend ages working on in the mirror) and the man started to push his chair back.

'I'm here on a field trip,' blurted Daphne. 'Entomology you know.'

'Oh really?' Trevor sat back down and gave the girl a searching look.

CHAPTER THIRTEEN

Nobody now knew where Johnson was. Some thought they knew which direction he had gone off in, but for anyone who knew him that would not necessarily be an accurate clue as to where he had got to, his course was ever zigging and zagging and subject to mysterious exigencies such that it could never be susceptible to objective projection. But, anyway, there wasn't really anyone who knew him. People could tell you what he looked like – his bowler hat was a familiar mobile relic making its stubborn glide through narrow streets toward the zoo – some few ancients could tell you who his father had been, but nobody could tell you what he liked to eat or whether he was married or religious, whether he had his own teeth, drank, or what, if any, school he had gone to. Consequently there was no one who could either nod sagely or express disbelief if told that he was now in a meadow beside a river.

Nor could they tell you it was the same meadow his great great grandfather haunted once, coming along and dumping to the ground a huge burden he had carried here on his back through heath and forest and weald and fen. Having marched many miles to get this heavy lumpen thing and many miles to bring it here, to wherever he now was, beneath tall lime trees and squabbling rooks where the sun hid amongst odd shaped little clouds which came and went as if they might be the same ones circling in some satanic ritual.

What was it in that sack? A sacrificial victim? He might be capable of believing strange and ancient things... Or a messy mass of umbles cut from unfortunate ungulates, ready to be spread and read for the prophesying according to the lore of the sybils; would the sack steam when he cut it open with the stench of the insides of lives still subsiding and not yet cold? He threw his burden down and its shape wobbled visibly as it met the hard earth beneath the grass before resting inert and softly bulky.

But it was not to be opened yet. Or not here perhaps. There were other things to do. Or rather there was one very strange thing to be done. A paramount thing. It was the dance. There was the dance to be danced. The dance that must be danced. The dance that must be danced when orbits coalesce and when the apex of the arc of the season makes its invisible shadow over the eccentric point of an historic eclipse, and when the moon runs like a scythe through the constellation of Monoceros. Congruences not divinable in any printed almanac but only triggered in the instinct of those of the Johnson's ilk who stalk the planet by lights the feeble multitude are blind to. (We say 'of Johnson's ilk', but were there many others of his clan extant? His race may have been numerous in some golden age, but it was certainly of a nobility sufficiently primitive to have dwindled by now to poignant survivors, striding onward toward extinction, ever at odds with populist religions, kitchen gadgets, pasteurisation, electricity and tabloid newspapers.)

The dark square solidity of the ancestral Mr Johnson adjusted its bowler hat and was then motionless where it stood in the grass for a time, the sun coming and going in the mysterious way peculiar to that particular place. And then the strong arms in the black woollen coat were slowly raised to stretch out to either side, north and south. He was for a while like a black signpost against the rich green, spotted yellow and white and red, of the meadow. And then... and then the dance began. A sight never seen by another mortal man, as rare as the rising of the phoenix, as obscure and incredible as the elephants' graveyard, as mind numbing as the cascade of a million lemmings: the field dance of an animal-man; the vigour and the mystery of all earthly life, the immense and intricate and incalculable simplicity of the essence of existence took hold of Mr Johnson that it might now be manifest in a ritual which was itself a concinnity of grace. Things no scholar could ever truly grasp with the dumb gloves of reason were gradually exposed in a slow – at times imperceptible – pre-historic choreography that would have chilled the blood of anyone at all had they stumbled upon the sight. The serene steps, striding high, of the oblong boots, the precision of the placement of the hob-nailed heel, gently compressing the dandelion it caressed with the great but compassionate weight balanced above it, alone in the meadow the thick figure dances, such poise in the expressive gestures of the squat fingered hands as largo the torso twists like a crane, then the planetary head with its ring of black brim remains steady and still before jerking to the quarters in a rhythm so controlled that its force is channelled in a flood to the hands as they rise and wave and turn and wing to the music – which makes no noise but which is heard by everything growing in the field – and the whole of Johnson pirouettes on a steel toe-cap and the cigar smoke whirls in a spiral about the grim face and the stern white eye.

In the very centre of the dance – which went on steadily spinning and weaving until the sun went down and the moon came up – amongst much that mesmerised, amongst the baffling signs and gestures and inflexions and nostril flaring, a great secret was depicted. It was a secret most never know, some few, some very few, briefly experience, but no one could ever speak of. And if they tried they would probably stutter words like 'magic' before surrendering to the impossibility of the task. For it was something which could not be said. It could only be danced or possibly swum, or occasionally dreamt, or perhaps glimpsed in a line of inspired poetry.

He grew darker as the heavens grew lighter – it was now neither day nor night, each was put aside by a new time thrust down to intersect the familiar sequence – and all the tiniest details of things became all clearly visible in a precise luminosity so that each of the myriad long grass stalks, meadow foxtail, reed grass, Yorkshire fog, tufted hair grass, meadowsweet and all the tufted perennials, each of the myriad wild flowers, yellow and purple saxifrages, agrimony, great burnet, lady's mantle, dog rose, bramble and hundreds more were all individuated where they stood and weaved together in an intricacy colonised by beetles, earwigs, spiders, snails and worms and field mice and moths and creeping things of all descriptions and everything, everything, and every part of everything, was in clear focus and all visible at once, blaring forth in a great bright harmony of wonder and beauty that it would have hurt to look upon, making the eyes ache with the unveiled miracle of the meadow, its surface bejewelled with diamond daisies and thousands of buttercups and poppies and butterflies.

Then, quite suddenly it was over. The last arcing prance and then the boots were slid together, the arms lowered to his sides and the true dawn was allowed to resume its course over the horizon. He was still, for the briefest of moments, and then turned and took up his burden again before striding off out of the meadow and into the trees.

The hare, whose odylic eye had all the time been staring through bluebells, leapt very high, turning in the air, and ran off to some secret place.

CHAPTER FOURTEEN

Johnson's great great grandfather was only four ancestors away from Johnson. Four human spans holding hands to stretch across the years and keep things connected. Remarkable though it sounds, it is but necessary to follow the chain of people along a little further, a mere dozen or so will take us almost back to the medieval age, when there was no doubt that unicorns, though rare, definitely existed.

CHAPTER FIFTEEN

He drained his coffee cup and was getting up to go when she suddenly felt she did not want to be alone and fell victim to one of the impulses which so often pricked her into unconsidered actions.

'Have a nice day! What will you be doing today? Are you here on business or is it a walking tour? We're near the Lanes, aren't we? I think they call them, are you going in that direction?'

He had closed his haversack and made it half way to the door but his natural and instinctive politeness would not allow him to escape without a little conversation. 'Er, yes, its just a little sort of holiday, a walking holiday, yes.' He lifted the pack onto his shoulder.

'I'm sort of the same thing except I'm an entomolgist, bug-hunter you know, sort of a little field trip, thought I'd see what I could find.'

Why did she say this? There was no need to mention this camouflage, which should have been kept for emergencies or to answer suspicious questioning authority, she could have said anything, would it rain, what a nice rucksack.

Trevor at once turned fully round and looked at her. He could not have told you why, not in that instant anyway, but there was something about her which made it difficult for him to believe that she was an entomologist – even the rankest amateur. Did entomologists always have a particular look, or a uniform? No of course not, they came in all shapes, sizes, genders, ages, but, even so...

'Oh really? How interesting. Are you looking for anything in particular, do you specialise, er, is it butterflies, or more beetles and creepy crawlies and things?' He hated the term 'creepy crawlies' and only said it as a way of luring her into the belief that her subterfuge was safe – that he knew nothing about the subject. Then a fly buzzed across the room. Unseen and unconsidered whilst it stood wherever it had been standing cleaning its forelegs but once it took off the familiar noise, which made cooks and kitchen staff reach for a swatter and look to the meat-safe door, had Daphne and Trevor searching the air for the switchback doodling course of the intrusive creature. Daphne was on her guard immediately.

Trevor knew it at once for *fannia canicularis*, the Lesser House Fly, rather than *musca domestica*. If it were to come across a lampshade it would happily fly round it all day. Daphne would have blithely called it a bluebottle, which it was not. Trevor suddenly found his precise, superior knowledge rather burdensome and was not moved to call Daphne's bluff by cross questioning her on the nature of this specimen. He simply said, 'Well no difficulty in finding *him* anyway.'

Daphne smiled and wondered briefly whether it was a 'him' before searching for something to say which would change the subject.

The fly itself looked round and down and sideways and this way and that and over and across and saw a world unknown to mammals. His compound eyes saw more kinds of light than people saw, and some things, for example a descending rolled up newspaper, appeared to him to approach in slow motion, like a log felled in the forest, so many images did his complex eyes transmit per second. But he did not see particularly clearly; though he was very acute when it came to sensing motion, his focus was not good. And he could not, of course register the little signals which indicated subtle shifts in human emotions. He did not even know a face was a face rather than an arse or an elbow. He was aware of large and lumpy beings which were alive though never quick, smelt strongly of all sorts of things but not at the moment of food, and which were intermittently making what to him sounded like booming and scratching noises to no obvious purpose. The mass of them was so incomprehensible in form – their limbs so huge and few, there were no recognisable palps, thoracic hairs, wings or ovipositor. He swerved and spiralled up to a dusty curtain rail, not realising that he flirted with danger – there were cobwebs and arachnids lurking behind the pelmet – but after only the briefest of settles (upside down) he spied the holy grail, a milky glass bowl hanging from the ceiling by black chains, a fitting abandoned and left high up here by the tide of some half-hearted redecoration many years ago which had never reached the ceiling – nobody noticed it now, people do not look up often (what's 'up'? the fly would have asked from his inverted perch gripping the smooth underside of the glass) – inside which were the desiccated corpses of several of his species, but there was no bulb in there now and he began a blissful gliding flight about the ritual object, mesmeric in the way its smoothness was strangely uninterrupted by the extremely abrupt turns which should have been impossible to accomplish at this velocity without skidding arcs, but instead they were no more than a change of direction. His movement was like the easy and precise tracing made by the point of a baton in some cosmic hand for whom speed and direction were at once the same and different things. He made an age old traditional pattern which he and his forebears had been weaving since millennia before the invention of light fittings, when dangling fruit or lianas or ape droppings had stood in for glass bowls. If you'd asked him why he did this he would have said he had no idea, he just always did it. And it was very calming.

If you'd asked Daphne why she had blurted out the thing about being an entomologist she could not have told you either – though it was nothing to do with habit or instinctive ritual. Perhaps she just wanted him to wonder about her as she wondered about him? Perhaps she just wanted someone, anyone, to wonder about her, wonder what sort of person she herself was. That would somehow make it easier to be herself, it was hard having to invent yourself all on your own without any feedback. And without any sycophancy. Perhaps also she wanted someone to help her in her adventure, perhaps she needed a bit of advice, she was already beginning to lose sight of exactly what she hoped to achieve out here, she had probably lost the bowler-hatted man's trail. She was beginning to feel a bit lost herself and she did not like this inn.

Left, along, back, right right along along left, left, along along, over across and back and up a bit and left and right again and up a bit and right again and down and... all to the mellow little buzz that his wings always made, how glad, how utterly fulfilled felt the little fly as he buzzed in his own pattern beneath the circular glass bowl and all his troubles evaporated in the age old dance.

Trevor looked up at him and remembered trying to catch flies alive when he'd been a little boy, with sugar lumps and lassos of the finest cotton. Funnily enough what he could not remember clearly was whether it had ever been successful. Had he ever roped and thrown a bluebottle? Probably not. He rather hoped not, for any such attempt would almost certainly have damaged or killed its object and he prided himself on never having been the sort of kid who had pulled the wings off things.

'At least the weather's not too bad, not that I mind a bit of rain, you've got to take the rough with the smooth, and I love a good storm don't you?'

Trevor was thinking about ways of catching things – he knew all about nets and traps of course, he was a pro – but he was thinking about more naive methods which had been used or at least written about. For instance that story about catching elephants by creeping up to the tree they leant against whilst they slept and sawing it down (it was a medieval misconception that elephants had no knees and must therefore sleep standing up). Pits for heffalumps, lures and baits and decoys and mist netting. He was suddenly overcome by a feeling of revulsion about the sneakiness, the dishonesty of his trade.

'Which direction will you be going do you think? Or have you not made up your mind yet?'

'Oh, sorry, no not sure really, probably toward the Lanes, I expect.' Of course in reality, like Daphne, he did not know where to go next. Reports and hunches had lead him to this village which seemed by its situation to indicate the Lanes as a likely direction for the elusive Johnson, but you could never be sure with him, he was quite likely to have doubled back or just to be sitting quite comfortably high in the branches of a lime tree until you had gone.

A woman came in for Trevor's plate and returned a minute or two later with a very old fashioned red and white tin fly spray. With her mouth turned down in a frumpy grimace she pumped it vigorously and viciously up toward the ceiling and the little fly was suddenly engulfed by an asteroid belt of fast moving droplets of DDT. He had no chance of avoiding all of them and was soon dead and plummeting like a small black thing which no longer buzzed, no longer flew instinctive patterns and might have been any sort of dust or detritus. He hit the lino not far from Daphne's foot and she saw it and could not stop herself giving a little sigh and saying, 'Oh dear.' She wanted to talk to this man but found herself distracted and staring at the body. Its noise had fled, it was just a bit of dirt. It had not been a pleasant thing you might say, when alive: annoying, a health hazard, obsessed with faeces and lampshades, but now that it lay like a small black cinder suddenly quiet and quite dead – deserted by its juiciness it looked as if it could no longer be squashed, it could only be crunched – she could not help but be brought up sharp by the instantaneous passage from one state to another. And this began to open the door in herself she knew she ought always to try to keep firmly closed. But never could.

Trevor looked down too and said, 'They only live for about a month you know.'

'All the more reason not to kill them, don't you think?' said Daphne, who wondered how he knew.

'They should never be allowed near food,' said Trevor, who knew quite a lot of other, very unpleasant things about them, but had no particular wish to speak ill of the dead.

He looked at her whilst her attention was taken and concluded that she wasn't bad looking, nothing like Ms Cake of course, nobody could... oh god, get a grip, but she also looked somewhat familiar. He was sure he had seen her somewhere before, but he could not think for the life of him where. She was dressed a bit oddly, was obviously a bit nervous, probably not unintelligent, but... what was she really doing out here on her own – she definitely was on her own, he had no sense of a partner just gone to the loo or something, she had been sitting at the little table by the window, the table for commercial travellers or lonely aunts in transit.

The dead fly had been cut down in its prime. But then just as Trevor was asking her something she heard a new buzzing and looked up and there was again a fly performing a jerky orbit of the lampshade. It was just like the other one. Exactly like it. It appeared to fly in exactly the same pattern. With the same glee. If it landed on some horse manure its behaviour would exactly replicate that so often exhibited by the dead one. Neither fly had or had had any concept of individuality or identity, they both responded to exactly the same stimuli with exactly the same instinct. So you could say

that this buzzing fly was just the same as the one that had lately
ceased to buzz. She could not tell the difference and neither could
the flies. The sensations of life felt by the one that now flew were
precisely the same as those that the one lying still on the lino had
felt. It was reincarnation. Sort of. It was duplication. It was life
going on. Not ceasing. It was just jumping from there to here. It
was succession.

He followed her gaze and saw and heard the new specimen. 'Oh,
there's another one. I wonder if the woman with the Flit will let it
live.'

The thing she did not allow herself to think about was rising up
and she felt herself beginning to think about it. Her left hand shook
slightly.

'I was just saying, will you be going into the marshes at all? I
shouldn't wonder that there are lots of insect specimens over there,
dragonflies and mosquitos and water boatmen and the like.' He
was being a bit mischievous. But then a worried frown descended
on her features and she suddenly looked very vulnerable and a
little frightened and all his paternal instincts came to the fore.

She looked up into his face with large round eyes and said,
'Yes, yes, I shall be going into the marshes and fens, where are
they exactly, would you know?' but it was obvious she was still
preoccupied by some great unease that had settled over her like a
black cloud. He wished he could dispel it.

'To the south, I think, although people say the marshes move.
Areas dry up and others flood so the borders are always shifting.
I've never been there myself, they say it's a ghostly place, but of
course that's the reputation of the whole region is it not, that's what
keeps most people away. I shouldn't wonder that there might not
be undiscovered species lurking in those wetlands – you might
become famous, you could discover something and name it after
yourself, *sympetrum alisonii*, if your name happened to be Alison,
just a guess, don't suppose it is.' If he could make jokes he would
have done, just to try to set her more at ease, she was chewing
a fingernail and looking from him to the fly up above and back
again. She did not appear to notice that he knew the Latin names
of insect types.

A previously unseen servant of the inn entered, just as dismal looking as her colleagues and also sharing with them an indefinable air of being just sufficiently polite but not quite friendly. She proceeded to sweep the floor vigorously and Trevor and Daphne both rose to leave.

Having collected their coats and bags they descended again to the hallway where they were met by all of the three women, who looked old now though they were not if you looked closely; from a distance at the end of the rather dark corridor as they stood together where they had been discussing the visitors, there was something of the norns about their grim expressions except that they had no particularly profound understanding of anything and knew nothing of what fate had in store. They were inclined to look sideways at people on their own with magnifying glasses. They preferred people called Harry who drove diggers and played darts and were 'a good laugh.' In the absence of such at this time of day they each displayed resolute frowns which may have been assumed with the sole intent of assuring visitors that they had much more important things on their minds than insignificant tourists, and even the business of taking the money seemed irksome to the one that undertook it. This inn, in a little village on a narrow unfrequented country road set in woodland interspersed with sheep meadows ought to have been rustic, poetic, knowingly slumbering in layers of history and folklore, but it was less than it promised. It was not yet a precursor of the ghostly Lanes, even though it looked as if it should be, for the cultural tentacles of the city extended even as far as this and invisibly surrounded it, and the disappointment, mundanity and sourness that tainted much of urban life was evident in the bar-rooms of the Black Widow which should have been peopled by characters sucking pipes and dreaming quietly of oxen, but instead was patronised by men smoking cigarettes obsessed with the price of petrol and intent on bringing back the birch. The Lanes did not begin here, oh no, not just yet, not so soon, there was a way to go before the Lanes began.

As the pair stepped out into the road they found it newly wet, with a smell of dust – there had been a light shower whilst they had been talking in the breakfast room – and both of them saw a large snail in full sail on top of a brick wall beside the road. Trevor stopped beside it for a moment and thought what a rigid but limited range of things it miraculously did. Slithering, eating, reproducing. The women in the inn were similarly corralled by habit; any of them would recoil like a scorched eye stalk if confronted with experimental poetry or a vicar with an earring.

And yet, any one of the women might equally sometime ask of themselves 'Why do I always put brown sauce on my sausages? Why not ketchup? They might, just for the hell of it, or 'for a change' say 'No, I shall take no sauce today'. Any human being had the capacity, not always activated, but it was there, to do something unusual simply because it was unusual; to amaze their peers and/ or themselves. Any human being potentially had the imaginative impulse to do something that hurts just to experience the pain. And any human being could have an opinion about snails – slimy, strange, edible, beautiful, revolting, pestilential, predictable. Any human being might go mad. Trevor might now himself in the next minute, decide to give it all up and run away with this rather odd girl. Free will, that's what we've got, he thought. But then, almost immediately, he thought, no! these women do not have free will – they would ever be slaves to one sauce. People who regularly examined their will to see if it was free realised that they did not have free will. People who did not so examine, if asked whether they had free will would have replied, 'of course.' People who changed sauce just to demonstrate that they had free will inevitably realised in the end that in so doing they were just as programmed as unthinking single sauce-ers.

He was going quietly mad.

'So which way will you be heading?' asked Daphne, shucking her shoulder bag and dealing with the slight awkwardness of putting on her floppy hat with her left hand. (She was managing the black menace surprisingly well it usually took a lot longer to get the better of it.) But before he could answer she surprised herself by going on to ask him if he'd happened to see a dark man in a black bowler hat anywhere on his travels. Trevor who had been looking at the snail and at her hat and then up at the sky was quite startled and just stared at her for a second or two.

'A dark man in a bowler hat?'

'Yes, have you seen him?'

'I don't know, er, who is he, do you know? Why, are you looking for him? Who is he, do you know?' He was quite put out, to the extent of repeating himself without realising it. 'Have you seen him? Where did you last see him, was it near here? Does he live near here?'

Daphne immediately knew that Trevor knew this man, and judging by his consternation he was either looking for him himself or did not wish to be found by him, she was not quite sure at first which it was.

A rook looked down from the upper reaches of a lime tree, a twig in its beak which it had stolen from a neighbour's nest and would soon insert into its own without a twinge of guilt as soon as its attention ceased to be taken by the people below. Should another rook be discovered in an attempt to take a twig from its own nest however, all hell would break loose. That's the way it was with rooks. Very gregarious but very argumentative thieving and quarrelsome. Perhaps they were gregarious because they were argumentative thieving and quarrelsome. Or was it the other way around?

'Perhaps I should not have mentioned it, don't worry. He's a foreign gentleman. I have some business with him. I thought he came this way. It was a long shot of course.'

'A foreign gentleman? Are you sure?'

'Oh yes, I think he may be Italian'

'In a black bowler hat?'

'Yes.'

The rook turned away hopped up onto its own nest and gave the twig to his wife who grabbed it impatiently and began threading it roughly into the thatch.

The door of the inn was closed with a slam which may have been the draught or it may have been a slam. Daphne was quite a lot calmer than she had been inside; her hand had stopped twitching, she had mastered the rising black tide now and sent it back down to where it dwelt within her. She felt she would be ok unless she was confronted by another dead thing. God! It was only a fly. Flies.

Why was he being so snobbish about the women in the pub? He was not a snob. You could not expect them to smile all the time, they were at work after all. It was the ordinariness of the place, that was it. The unexpected ordinariness. He had been quietly working himself up with thoughts of the otherworldly possibilities of the unicorn. He had allowed his imagination to wax unrestrained as he had progressed further and further from the city and in the dark, as he had approached the black gables and chimneys of this tall old building last night it had become a storybook place for him – some gave them white bread and some gave them brown – this little place perhaps was the very town where they had fought all around, the lion and the unicorn. He had hoped to be losing himself, to be sloughing off the weary realities of his forty year old life, and he had awoken to find it was all just the same out here. The same trashy newspapers, the same idiot conversations about nothing. He began to admit the possibility that he'd been a fool even to entertain the idea of even the remotest chance of a unicorn. It was just like believing Ms Cake might fall in love with him, ha! and he was maddened by the stubborn impossibility of the unreal, the unreal which suggested itself continually all around him but stayed out of reach and out of focus all the time.

In the light of the morning's bright and disturbing perspectives, having found himself and his hopes undermined and his confidence collapsing again, it would have been too ridiculous now to pursue the Johnson conversation they'd started to have earlier. And, partly because Trevor had been so agitated on the subject and had now ceased to mention it, Daphne ceased to ask him about the bowler hat, thinking now that it might have been wrong to mention that man in the first place. Trevor seemed like a very nice man, but she knew nothing about him. So the dialogue which they now entered into was a strange one, having as its subject which way to go, but omitting any reference to the object of their journey. (It had somehow become an unspoken accord that they would walk off together.)

They turned west, past the garage with piles of tyres and a shiny black patch outside. It should have been a forge. Smoke and cinders and horse dung would have been so much more pleasant than oil and rubber.

A very morose cat on a dustbin looked at them with deep suspicion as they passed and the little river flowing under the unnecessarily ugly bridge at the bottom of the hill was very muddy.

It was with relief that they each found it was going to be alright not to talk all the time as the silence that accompanied their progress up the hill into the wood on the other side of the little valley proved to be quite a comfortable one and not in the least awkward. Daphne was in fact trying not to think of anything – she thought her brain could do with a rest. It wasn't easy but she was more or less managing just to look at things and let questions and concepts lie fallow for a while. Trevor had suddenly remembered that once again he had forgotten to phone Millicent.

Yet they did speak from time to time, at first in little flurries of discussion on the subject of something seen or glimpsed in the trees or the hedgerow, but later, as they descended a rolling road which dipped between thick colonnades of trees whose branches met above their heads to cloister them in a dark shade, they began to loosen the stays of their reserve and allow more personal topics into what gradually became a real conversation, the secret semi-darkness of the enfolding boughs encouraging them to speak in whispers.

There was no mention of course of Daphne's black horror, and nor of the grenadier in Trevor's pocket which he gripped and stroked increasingly, but a sensitive and independent girl in the grip of something, probably some family difficulty, began to emerge for Trevor; and Daphne saw dimensions added to what was becoming a picture of an intelligent and fatherly (though he was not old enough to be her father) bloke, educated and trustworthy. She liked him. He was almost certainly married and not supposed to be going wherever he was going.

There was something about the way her mouth or teeth were configured which made a little whistle when she pronounced the 'sh' sound – it made him smile, he couldn't help it. (It was not like the back of Jemima Cake's knees – that sight did not make him smile at all but brought down a grim portcullis of desire over his usually amiable features). For Daphne's part she liked the rugged solidity of his canvas knapsack with the worn leather straps, which, like him, had been about a bit and knew a thing or two but had nothing at all pretentious about it. She liked his grey linen shirt which was clean but creased. She liked the lightly tanned skin of his face which was clean but beginning to be creased with light creases which in time would perhaps become deep gorges but would never be ugly, they would always speak of life and outdoors and warmth and sunlight.

It was very quiet under the dark trees on this black road (or was it a lane?) and any rustle in the ferny verges would have startled them. But a rustle, some quarter of a mile further on (probably a blackbird) was all the more startling because it was accompanied or caused by human voices. Not coming from the road but up above, over the back of the earthy bank which was knotted and ribbed with the huge gnarled roots of the lowering trees, were the words of a bad tempered exchange being conducted in the German language. Trevor and Daphne stopped and looked at one another. Trevor had next to no German, Daphne had a smattering of Wagner thanks to an adolescent infatuation with the character of Brunhilde, but could not generally understand normal conversation.

Then amongst the distant gutteral argument suddenly a raised voice had Trevor wide-eyed with a mixture of fear and wonder when it enunciated clearly enough, even for the most benighted monoglot, the word, 'Einhorn.'

Had he had the presence of mind or the ability (it was very steep) Trevor would have scrambled up the grotesquely racinated side of the road to get a view of the irritable Teutons who seemed to be mentioning the unmentionable. His mind raced – did the foreigners know all about the unicorn? Was it not at all for them a myth and a mystery? Did they, of course, know exactly where it/they were to be found and what they ate? Would they surrender themselves to full bellied roaring hilarity when the extent of the childish bewilderment in which the Englischer wandered was admitted to them? More than that. Much more and much worse mortification would have been his if he had grasped the earthy tendrils and risen up to peep at the figures on the other side. This was because neither party to the conversation he had heard originated from anywhere remotely near the Rhine, in spite of the language they had spoken.

In fact, one was Willoughby and the other was Culvert Grimes.

CHAPTER SIXTEEN

What had happened was that Willoughby had hit upon speaking German as a means of confusing his persistent and incorrigible companion. He had to do something. It was like being chained to a madman, the sort of terrible fate visited upon some class of sinner in a special circle of hell which had escaped Dante's attention. It had been obvious for a very long time that Grimes knew perfectly well who Willoughby was and Willoughby was increasingly convinced that he knew why he was looking for Johnson, though so far each had forborne from mentioning the unicorn. Willoughby was clinging to the fragments of possibility that Grimes could not be a hundred per cent certain about it being the purpose of this escapade; whilst Grimes looked as if he understood and relished this very uncertainty of Willoughby's and prolonged it simply to maximise the discomfort of the aristocrat and possibly as a means of recompense for the disdain with which he had been treated over the years by such as he.

Many times Willoughby had been tempted just to throw the whole thing up, run away home, throw off his ridiculous and superfluous disguise and simply ask of his fellow zoo people whether by now, having had time for reflection, they gave any credence to Johnson's rantings. Even approach Frederick himself. But so far he had remained a prisoner of his own indecision, too protective of his own dignity to do anything other than to continue to roam around with Grimes's huge eyes staring into his face, his gargoyle grin and his questioning conversation which constantly threw at Willoughby the very things Grimes knew Willoughby was desperate to discover, and he asked his mischievous queries in a way which hinted that he might himself know something of the answers to these questions but found it amusing not to reveal anything. 'Did Johnson come over this way do you think, sir then? Could the way be over that hill? Is this, might you say, a Johnsonian path at all?' Willoughby could have throttled him, and on a couple of occasions had come near to it.

And so it was that as a spontaneous, but arguably pointless reaction to having this demon shackled to him, Willoughby had just started speaking in German. The damned fellow seemed to know or sense so much, he seemed to be able to bore into you and wriggle amongst things in your head that he had no business being privy to, and he found everything so bloody amusing. Guessing that a foreign language would be something he would not know, and for no other purpose than hopping onto an island where Grimes would not be able to follow him, Willoughby began speaking, or, at first declaiming, German, right into the fellow's face; see how he liked his own medicine. And it worked. To start with it bemused him. He was confused, the smile did not disappear, but it faded and he was silent and his stare was suddenly much more passive, rather than aggressive. He was wrong footed and he did not like it, and when Willoughby saw it his heart was glad and he was able magically to recall great chunks of Goethe.

After a while – and perhaps Willoughby might have foreseen this if his language shift had not been so desperate and impromptu – Grimes, after an hour or so of giving silent attention to Willoughby's every utterance, began mimicking him.

It was obvious he did not understand what the words meant but he was able to copy their sound with remarkable accuracy and a reasonably acceptable accent. Willoughby tried speaking faster and then just saying the longest most complicated words he could remember or even make up but the damned fellow just gave it back to him. It might have been amusing to a disinterested observer, but Willoughby did not find it funny. Still he did not give it up. He continued to feel the German built something of a wall about him. He even thought it made his thoughts more secure than just thinking them. Speaking them in German kept the interloper out and he felt safer. Trouble was – and the realisation of this was devastating to Willoughby – after only about three days it began to be apparent that Grimes was in fact beginning to understand. He was in many ways, as we have seen, a freak of nature and it was now revealed just how annoyingly efficient his peculiar brain was, and what remarkable feats of processing and memory it was capable of. He began to respond to Willoughby not with just the infuriating parroting, but, and his smile grew into a threatening leer as he did it for the first time, with a conversational response.

Resigned to his fate and just because it made the whole thing feel a little as if it weren't happening to him but to somebody else, Willoughby carried on speaking in German and as the days passed and the idiot became more and more fluent and had the effrontery to enquire about vocabulary there inevitably came a point where their whole experience became, if it were possible, even less real. Certainly Willoughby began to feel as if he were a character in a play. It mattered less and less what he said or what Grimes said, being as they were, far from home (somewhat lost if the truth were acknowledged) and therefore unrecognisable, and *sprachen Deutsche*, which further camouflaged them even from themselves. It was also inevitable, given these developments, that the 'secret' came to be openly acknowledged. Willoughby, without making any pronouncement or statement simply began making remarks about Johnson's belief in a unicorn and it was implicit thereafter in his utterances that this was the reason he was looking for him.

Curiously, once this elision was made it was with no sort of glee that Grimes received it – in fact he did so with no overt acknowledgement of any change in the realities of their search.

'Es gibt einige moglichen Quellen fur die Einhornlegende: das Nashorn, der Oryx, das getrennte horn der Exzentriker der Natur, horn-drehen, ein missdentete kunstagung, der dreibeinige Arsch, und lunarer Mythos,' muttered Willoughby as they went along.

'Kommandieren Sie ja, phantasticher Chef,' was the enthusiastic and respectful response.

Mostly of course they continued to say 'Johnson' much more than they ever said 'unicorn' but they did occasionally say 'unicorn', that is to say, 'Einhorn'...

CHAPTER SEVENTEEN

... And so it was that Trevor heard the fateful word in German floating over the bank and through the leaves and boughs and trunks that topped the declivity wherein he and Daphne crouched. He had put his finger urgently to his lips and grasped Daphne's wrist with his other hand. If he only could have seen them, once he had got over the shock of recognition, he would probably have guessed they were on the same conjectural mission as himself and he would probably have made his presence known and they would have had an awkward conversation and... well, who knows what they would have done, what conclusions they would have come to having pooled their non-existent knowledge of the habits and whereabouts of the Johnson man? But as it was, Trevor naturally assumed he was hearing Germans speak German, he could not have been expected to recognised the voices of his colleagues, not in a foreign tongue, not at this distance. And thinking therefore that unknown persons were in this very vicinity on the track of the unicorn, and that these unknown persons were of the very thorough and no-nonsense Teutonic type, Trevor made the leap to instant belief in the reality of the unicorn. Johnson might be mad, but Germans weren't; very many scientists were German, they would not have come all this way if they did not know something. It may be that it was their expedition that Johnson had got wind of and that was how this whole thing had started. Yes, that was in fact very likely.

Daphne heard the guttural clanking consonants of invisible speakers and stared through the dark ferns at the knotted, twisted bark that jutted elbows and eyes through the dim red earth, emerging and diving down again in a maze of roots knitted through all the long grim years of this ancient lonely roadside and heard trolls, black and arguing for certain about whose sack the girl was to go in. She began to try to pull Trevor away up the road, 'Come on, let's go, let's go, they're after us, I'm sure,' and was getting agitated as the fairytale fear gripped her. Trevor was desperate to get up the steep wild bank and see through the trees to espy the Germans, but he could see he would not be able to climb it and he could also now see that, largely hidden by the undergrowth, there was barbed wire. Maybe it was easier further up. He surrendered to Daphne's tugs and they ran together up the hill. They were going in the same direction but one thought he was running towards something and the other thought she was running away from it. The voices had quickly become two very different things in their minds. Trevor was going towards the respected language which conveyed the possibility of a breakthrough in palaeo-zoological research, and simultaneously Daphne was going away from the grim terror of huge fanged shaggy trolls with warts and claws and axes eager to drag people off and eat them in a cave. That same terror which, it has to be said, in one manifestation or another was always waiting for her.

'Come on!' said Trevor.

'Come on!' said Daphne, and they flailed arms trying to grasp the wrist of the other and finished up hand in hand.

By the time they got – breathing heavily – to the top of the hill and the levelling of the terrain the trees thinned out to reveal a meadow to the right which dipped and rolled away but there was no sign of people in it. Or trolls. In fact Willoughby and Grimes had done a bit of a dog-leg and gone over a stile and into a different little wood which was not visible from the road. Trevor looked about him with frustration but it was not to be. There was no physical trace of scientists. The fleeting distant snatches of German conversation, the second hand syllables, had flown away into the breeze, faded into the air which was too thin to hold them, their only echo the one Trevor's intense effort to seal the sound in his memory created.

Einhorn, they had definitely said *einhorn*. Hadn't they? Yes, he remembered it clearly, it was einhorn, like that. And that was unicorn. 'My god,' thought Trevor. They gazed across the countryside, he looking steadily in the direction he had thought the conversation had come from, Daphne at his side looking nervously around in all directions, suspicious even of the sun as it now emerged from behind a cloud.

Then there was a cyclist coming along the road mumbling, coincidentally, the Ode to Joy from Beethoven's Ninth and Daphne leapt up as he came into view, grasped a fence post which happened to be lying there and scrambled to the road just as the figure slowed on the incline and reached the corner at the top of the hill. She jumped down the bank and smashed the post two-handed with the practised accuracy and might of a medieval knight onto the head of the man whose song was cut off by the dull crack of his skull as he crashed to the tarmacadam, felled amidst the percussion of spokes and mudguards and the brief pathetic jangle of the bell. He was quite dead and did not twitch.

'Holy Christ! Jesus!' What the hell, what the hell had she done?

Then Daphne said, 'Come on, this way, through the copse!' and lead the way across the road and began to climb a gate, and when Trevor, who was quivering with shock, followed after and looked back in the act of swinging his leg over the top bar of the gate he saw that there was no corpse, there was no cyclist, there was no bell, there was only the empty space of the lane.

A sudden frenzied figment had jumped into his mind. And yet what could have prompted the imagining of it? He had not known Daphne long but it was inconceivable that she would brain a passing stranger out of the blue for no reason. Is this perhaps what it is like when you start to go out of your mind? Mechanically he followed her, even though this was not the way he wanted to go; he felt dazed by the thunderclap vision which had come and gone in a flash. There was the weathered wood of the gate and here were clumps of nettles and a sprung sapling which she failed to hold back for him, but all he saw was the merciless psychopathic blow, utterly abrupt and subitaneous, unheralded by any shout or warcry. Which had not happened, dammit. He had looked back into the lane and there had been nothing there. It had been a strange sort of daydream which had gone off in his head like a firework.

But they had said 'unicorn,' they had definitely said unicorn. Whatever else had not happened there could be no doubting that 'einhorn' had. He had total faith in it.

But... perhaps it had been a premonition. He watched the back of the figure in front of him bending and swerving under branches and around tree trunks, and the blackness of the floppy hat began to insinuate dark possibilities, the awkward long limbs began in his eyes to assert themselves in a malevolent insectile way and hint at the unlikely power they might conceal. Perhaps what he had seen was a warning vouchsafed to him by some protective angel; on some unknown future date on some unknown road he would be cycling up a hill or coming round a corner and she, this shy and vulnerable slight figure of a girl, would leap out from above and batter his brains out with a paling stake.

What he did not realise until later was that by this time they may have already crossed the invisible border. It may have been that they were actually in the Lanes when he saw what he saw. And this was perhaps just the sort of irreconcilable thing, in this case a vision of phantom brutality, which contributed to the reputation of the region. A reputation which was unspecific but always darkly numinous.

He stopped for a moment, shivered and shook himself and reached in his pocket for the grenadier which he clutched tightly. Into the very next telephone he came across he would speak urgent, profound heartfelt apologies to Millicent and the children. Only half a mile further on, however, fantasies about Jemima Cake were allowed to drift about him and were welcomed since they obscured the insane vision of brutal murder, and he tried deliberately to divert himself with the memory of parts of the croquet Queen until the scratchy trees and undergrowth and losing sight of Daphne forced him to stop.

This was not like him. What had become of the steady, controlled Simpson of Large and Rare Birds, the respected much travelled zoologist, deeply knowledgeable, adept at planning research programmes, quietly and firmly organising people and resources, dealing with budgets, dignitaries, and crises minor and major, the modest but self assured family man with the beautiful wife and two adorable little ones? Well that façade had already been shaken by the shocking realisation that he had arrived at middle age, by a perspective of disillusionment, by creeping boredom, by a ridiculous infatuation with a girl half his age. And then this unicorn business had erupted. It was as if, softened up and made vulnerable by the mid-life crisis, the strange utterances and then the disappearance of Johnson, and then the disappearances of Grimes and Willoughby had conspired to push him over some sort of precipice; he had been blinded by a childish competitive urgency and he had begun to lose his aplomb, his *savoir faire*. Even his reason. He should not be here at all, he was going about things all the wrong way and he knew it. This impromptu dashing off toward the Lanes was a compulsive and ill considered idiocy. He must regain control. Of himself. Of this girl. Of this expedition. Of his head. It was no use careering wildly through woods in panic flight. The first thing to be done was they must find those Germans, make contact with them, identify them – and whichever direction they had gone in it was not this one.

'I say! Daphne! Hallo! Can you come back here, please! We are going the wrong way! Hallowooo!'

She did not come back, but she did slow down and he came up with her just as they emerged at the other side of the trees where they thinned out and gave way to a rising heath.

'You mustn't be frightened, there's no one chasing us, the voices, those Germans, well I think they must be an expedition looking for the same thing I am.' He was a bit out of breath.

She just stared at him for a moment and then said, 'The man in the bowler hat, you're looking for the man in the bowler hat. So am I. The Italian.'

'He's not Italian –'

'Of course he is, or he's in the pay of the Italians, don't worry I know what his game is. Who exactly are you and why are you looking for him? Exactly what sort of a person are you? You haven't told me anything about yourself, you know. You could be anyone, for all I know you might be an escaped convict or something.'

This was in contrast to the nervous but friendly and trusting girl Trevor had met at the inn. The innocence which had been attractive was beginning to be tainted as Daphne started to exhibit worldly considerations like suspicion and by implication an interest in herself which had not seemed to be there before when she was pretending to be an entomologist and eager for acceptance and not looking him in the eye.

Unnoticed for the moment a huge wild boar sow and her striped piglets trotted through the trees about a quarter of a mile away, the mother sniffing the air and snorting.

'Yes, you're quite right, I am Trevor Simpson, I am a zoologist and –'

'Oh god, oh no! You're a bloody zoologist! That's all I need, for Christ's sake, a sodding zoologist.' She took off her hat and flopped to the ground. A look of weary disdain took over her features and immediately made her appear about ten years older. She sighed and shook out her hair making it clear she could no longer be interested in anything he might have to say.

Trevor was quite taken aback. As we know he was generally feeling rather undermined, and this reaction – quite unexpected and unusual, most people were impressed – rather nonplussed him.

'Yes, a zoologist, what's wrong with that might I ask?'

'I should have known!' She had taken one shoe off and was massaging a foot. 'You know all about flies, don't you? You don't work for my –' Christ she nearly did it, nearly forgot herself catastrophically, but recovered quickly – 'I mean the university, or whatever it is, of wherever it is, do you?'

The sow now had their scent wafting thickly down to her and she did not like it. It was people-smell and all people were nasty. They butchered piglets and ate them. This was not going to happen to her family. Not if she could help it. If there were half a dozen of them with guns she would sell herself dear, but if there were only one or two, unarmed, she would just rush over there and kill them as thoroughly and as mercilessly as her huge teeth and the crashing force of the whole half ton of her could accomplish. The forest was for pigs. Everyone knew that. The sapiens lot had no business here.

A change had definitely come over Daphne, the foot massage was vigorous and expressed the sudden irritation that she now felt.

'Don't you like animals? Most people are quite interested in them?'

'Well I'm not.' She looked directly up at him in what could only be interpreted as an unfriendly way as she put her sock back on. 'Not at all.'

Trevor was confused. He had been about to take command of the situation, had been preparing to resurrect the Simpson who managed and organised, the Simpson who knew more than his underlings and would now explain what they were going to do next, but the rug had been pulled from under him by this sudden recalcitrance and he was at sea again wondering whether this dissension might reflect a hidden capacity for violence which...

She got to her feet brushing off her trousers and said, 'Look, do you or don't you know where I can find this dark man who wears a bowler hat? I can't be shilly-shallying about here with zoologists I –' She stopped at the moment she became aware of a noise, not loud, but rhythmic, hard and propelling something. It was a drumming of hooves but in the quarter second it took for the urgency of the situation to flush her with adrenalin all she could comprehend was a muscular whirlwind of tusk and gristle tearing through turf, snapping aside the underbrush and showering divots as something which required her death moved irresistibly up the slope straight towards her. She ran as fast as ever she could, clutching her hat in her hand. The experience was exactly heart-poundingly parallel to that of an infant gazelle chased by a lioness.

Trevor saw it too. And saw it for what it was, a wild boar with a litter, very angry and supremely dangerous. And yet... could he trust this image? Was it going to be real, or a false *coup de foudre*, a lunatic imagining in some way generated by this place and the uncertain state of his mind? He found himself wondering whether it was necessary to stare at events to ensure that their aftermath did not evaporate and have the laugh on you. Was this animal going to be terrifying but un-sustained and without consequence? Stunned into an idiotic brinkmanship he stood there as the great beast thundered toward him, only at the last minute did his brain lurch back into self-preservation reflex and allow him to flee something which might not be there. But it really was there. It kept coming, after him now, not Daphne, which was a misjudgement on the pig's part because Daphne had run straight up the heath and could have been caught quite easily, whereas Trevor ran back into the trees and dodging trunks he could use them like a matador's cape.

CHAPTER EIGHTEEN

Daphne looked up at the clouds which loomed and rolled like black and steel-grey gods across the immensity of the heavens. She hunched herself inside her coat against the sudden chill of evening and spots of rain and dropped to her haunches beside a lime tree wondering what had become of Trevor. Had the pig perhaps even killed him? It was possible that, even moderately ripped, he would have bled to death – they had been a long way from any human help. Animals kill you. A lot of them, that's what they do. You can catch them and feed them and breed them, but some of them will remind you, given half a chance, that they inhabit a different realm, and live by truths too deep for science to plumb. People might have evolved themselves onto some sort of intellectual island where they were marooned and in the grip of their quandary, their minds whizzing in ever accelerating circles, which had driven them mad without them realising it, but beasts were always beasts and all the sounder for it. They might be nasty but, if you left them alone, they were honest.

She wished he were still with her though. In hindsight she saw him again as she'd first seen him, a pleasant, personable, intelligent chap, avuncular and chummy. She'd gone into a mood when he'd said he was a zooman. Well she couldn't help that. Regretted it a bit but she could not help it. And there must have been a time when he was not a zooman, a time before, when he was just a young man. Did it matter that there had been a time when he was not a zooman? Fifteen years ago, say, what would he have been then, a student of some sort? You might as well ask did it matter that there had been a time when her mother yet lived?

The rain had thickened from spotting to pittering and pattering audibly on leaves. In a little while her hat would be weighed down with moisture. But she just squatted there in the long wet grass without moving, staring back in the direction she had come and thinking of her sadness. Until she thought again of breeding programmes: both animals in the zoo, and the other type – political alliances between states, cemented by marriage and requiring princesses to be virgins in the traditional way – could you believe it? In this day and age? She was little more than an animal in a zoo – and she thought of the evil, dark bastard in the bowler hat and she fed on the energy the anger aroused in her and she rose up and looked up at huge elemental cumulonimbus and it was as if they acknowledged her. And now she knew the way to go. Here, down this path, which was suddenly revealed to her amongst the trees.

And men, she thought, men were very like dogs. Often they were very nice and perfectly friendly and good with children, but you could never tell which of them would suddenly turn, just right out of the blue, and rip your throat out. You could never tell.

CHAPTER NINETEEN

For those men like Simpson, who were afflicted by the indefinable quality which tipped her attractiveness over into irresistibility, Jemima Cake's stylish spectacles had the curious effect of enhancing her attractiveness by the very daring of their juxtaposing to the classical cheek bones and immaculate skin the hint of a flaw in the divine creature, the suggestion of her being subject to one at least of the imperfections most human bodies were heir to. These reading glasses said, 'Yes, she's a goddess, but she is in human form, she has a physicality like yours' which was calculated further to inflame the ardour she inspired in her devotees by making them conscious of the actual possibility that the laws of science would not be infringed by the concept of such a body being brought into proximity with ones own. Alas, or perhaps just as well, Simpson was not here to see Ms Cake in her study reading by the soft glow of the lamp on her desk, her clear brown eyes speedily scanning the text before her, and her fist now brought up to support her slightly dimpled cheek as she peered more intently at a particular paragraph.

On the other side of the door, her acolytes, Pippa and Willis, were measuring the wing of a bat – an awkward manoeuvre involving holding all the ungainly and tiny parts of the animal still and manipulating a tape measure which required the co-ordination of all twenty fingers and both brains – but they were eager to have the job done, the animal back in its cage and their minds freed to consider the matter of the moment. Which they believed was the question of mermaids. This must be what Jemima was researching so intently behind the door, protected by the 'Do Not Disturb' instructions which had been so forcefully given that morning.

'What do you think it is, Pippa? Anything? I mean something new, or just a seal or a walrus or something?'

'I don't know, a dugong, maybe aren't they usually dugongs or manatees, these supposed mermaids?'

They had finished the measurements which Pippa noted down

carefully in the bat ledger while Willis gingerly restored the tiny
beast to its box, saying thoughtfully, 'Yes probably, but you never
know, we shouldn't rule things out, it might indeed be some sort of
Melusine or Atargatis,' as she hooked the catch on the box, darting
a mischievous smile at her friend.

'What?' laughed her colleague. 'What are they when they're at
home?'

'Creatures of legend, half women, or goddesses anyway, and
half fish, I've been reading up a bit.'

'Have you indeed? And so do you believe there can be finny
people, or finny apes, mammal-fish?'

'Er, no.'

'But you never know, eh?'

'There are more things in heaven and Earth, Horatio...'

'And wouldn't it be something to set before a King!'

They both fell to giggling and Pippa threw a rubber bung at
Willis who let out an involuntary shriek and they remembered the
stern requests for quiet their leader just behind the wooden door
had made and they put their hands over their mouths and were
beginning to creep away when the door opened and Jemima was
suddenly there and looking rather serious.

Jemima's style of leadership was always friendly but always
firm; there were jokes and banter but it only took a reversion in
the particular cast of the boss's eyebrows to let the assistants know
in an instant that everyone was to be serious now, and no more
nonsense would be brooked. It was a style which reflected Jemima's
personality, she was always several jumps ahead of everyone else
and fully in command of all the psychology that hummed about
any particular situation; and it was a style which was more than
effective in that it seemed to inspire dogged dutiful self sacrifice
and volunteering for overtime, and – certainly in Pippa and Willis
– a devotion that tipped over into heroine worship and beyond.
So any admonition that was to be given would be received with
passionate *mea culpas*.

But Jemima looked preoccupied rather than irritated and surprised
her assistants with a very strange question. 'Willis, Pippa, please
tell me what you know of Mr Johnson, I want to know about Mr
Johnson.'

They were somewhat taken aback. 'Mr Johnson? You mean scruffy old Johnson who wears a bowler hat and disappears for ages and nobody likes much?' Willis laughed nervously thinking she might have overstepped the mark – he was after all, technically the same grade of zoo-keeper as Jemima.

'I don't think anyone knows that much about him, Miss. He's… well I think we all have to admit he's rather strange,' said Pippa. 'To be honest he frightened the life out of me when I first joined. I thought he was one of the casual muckers-out until he came up behind me once and grabbed a pangolin I was carrying, told me I was holding it all wrong. I remember he called me an idiot schoolgirl. Under his breath, but I heard him. I can't say I warm to him.'

'Yes, yes,' said Jemima, but do we know anything of his background, where is he from, where does he live, what, if anything, was his education?'

'Oh no, Miss, nothing like that. Neither of us has had anything like that sort of conversation with him. I get the impression he doesn't hardly talk to anybody – well not to people at any rate. One of Mr Simpson's men told me once he'd heard him murmuring with a coati mundi,' (stifled giggle) 'and I've seen him when he was looking as if he were talking to a badger, not actually saying anything but…something about the way the badger looked at him, it was as if it were listening to him.'

'So beyond the fact that he's a queer cove we know nothing about him or where he might be found?' A little impatience was creeping into Jemima's tone and it did not go unnoticed.

'Er, no, Miss, sorry, no we don't. Perhaps we could ask in the office.'

The sudden re-orientation of the priorities of Jemima Cake's platoon, from the investigation of reports of unlikely marine mythological survivals with finny fundaments to a preoccupation with Johnson's particulars and whereabouts had come about, unbeknownst to Pippa and Willis, the day before, when Jemima had had a chance encounter in a corner of the castle gardens…

… She had first been accosted by music, the sound of a cello, mellifluous but mournful, wistful and wafting over the apple blossom. So affecting was it that she had sought out the source of the sound and re-directed her steps down the red brick path into the maze of pergolas, bowers and parterres. She failed actually to find the musician himself, or herself – such a maze it was down here – but sat on a stone bench to listen to the rest of the piece (Elgar, she afterwards thought it was).

With the very slightest inclination of his head the cellist acknowledged her presence even though she was behind several hedges and therefore physically invisible, and then closed his eyes as he continued playing.

When the music stopped she made to depart, intending to re-orient herself to the exigencies of the day, but as she stood up she saw a pair of boots sticking out from behind the statue of a faun. This was a strange little corner of the garden. The music had lured her into a place she'd never been before; she had never even noticed this path and the secluded corner with its neat little box trees and then a small orchard with espaliers against a wall and a sun dial and it all delighted her – with its hiddenness as much as its intrinsic charm. Ms Cake was as susceptible as most people to music, and she was sensitive as well as intelligent but it was probably true to say she was not quite as at home in the world of whimsy as many of her peers; she had read poetry but kept little or none of it in her head and her acumen was exhibited for the most part in the practical realms of science. And the management of staff. Oh, and she was quite good at the finance side too. It was therefore a little unusual for her to be so taken aback by the charms of this garden and the lilting vibrato of a violoncello. It would not be appropriate to describe her as wrong footed by the experience but she had nonetheless been gently detached from the purposefulness which usually characterised her activities. Whilst she would never ever have thought in terms of having been brought here by some mysterious fate or force, it remained true that she did not know quite what she was doing here, and found she could suddenly no longer remember where she had in fact been going before her diversion down the red brick path toward the music.

The boots behind the faun were large and brown and highly polished.

'Beautiful music, Miss, beautiful music, isn't it? Don't they play well?' It was Ruscum, half rising from his bench clutching a cheese and tomato sandwich in some grease-proof paper to his lap and affecting an awkward sort of half nod half bow from behind the faun's hooves. 'I often have my lunch here if I have the time, in the hope that they will be playing. Please, sit down a moment. They will probably play another.'

He could not believe it. It was the new animal collector, Ms Cake, and up close she was even prettier than they said. In spite of his having left the moon-struck-calf years a long way behind, he could not help being knocked somewhat sideways by the presence of this woman; he was, it seemed, in the camp for whom belief in her mortality was severely challenged by the perfection of her flawless form. He was an immediate convert, even though he knew full well he was joining a club whose subscription consisted in abandoning one's dignity and self possession. His efforts at restraining any obvious look of sustained astonishment must have been effective, however, because she did not snub him when he lurched into a conversational gambit.

(In fact Jemima had, of course, got quite used to her effect on certain men, and from time to time she was not above knowingly using it to her advantage. Though not without a sense of regret, merit ought always to suffice, and dealing with those who got a bit carried away could be very annoying. And she could never understand why it was just some men. It was many men, but why not all? Or none? That was a question which intrigued her scientific sensibilities.)

'Lovely and peaceful here, isn't it? What a beautiful garden, a real escape from the cares and woe,' said Ruscum with a smile.

There was an honesty in his eyes which would always give him away if he ever attempted any subterfuge or misrepresentation, and his humble origins, reliability and straightforwardness immediately reminded Jemima of her father – a plodder, true, but one with a clear conscience and qualities of dutiful industriousness that would always be envied in the end by quicker wits who thought they had a shortcut to the easy life.

'Yes it is nice here, isn't it? There are so many corners to discover, I never seem to have the time.'

'Yes, you're new at the zoo, aren't you? I think I saw your appointment papers.'

'Oh really –'

'Yes, I'm with the Chamberlain you know, his factotum, sort of thing. Secet'ry some call me. Oh aye we've got a finger in every pie, not much gets by us.' He smiled tapping his nose with a forefinger.

Jemima immediately thought to herself how useful this chap might be, but buried the thought under her genuine liking for him, and proceeded to chat about the castle and the difficulties of getting to know a new place etc.

Ruscum wanted to be the wise old man who had seen a thing or two, the insider with knowledge of state secrets the ordinary citizen could never imagine, but found himself also lapsing involuntarily into Cupid staring at Psyche.

Jemima, hardly aware that she was doing it, shone at him with bright admiring smiles and a little flick of her fringe which she knew was juvenile and reprehensible, but she couldn't help it, and pretty soon in the privacy of this little nook, Ruscum was relaying things about the court which were far from common knowledge. A lot of it was of no interest to Jemima however, celebrity trivia which Jemima was disappointed to learn Ruscum deemed worthy of relating. She was disappointed indeed that someone of Ruscum's own stamp, a man of character with his own qualities, in whom she had seen parallels with her own esteemed blue collar father, should think the daily doings of accidentally privileged folk should in any sense be more important than his own. But her attention revived when she learned that Mrs Simpson had been to the castle. And had had a very long meeting with the King. Some said she'd been there all night alone with him (wink). Jemima was not interested in the wink (which Ruscum, as soon as he'd made it, wished he hadn't) – it further disappointed her – but she was set to wondering about the wife of a senior zooman having an urgent meeting with the King at a time when Pippa and Willis were gossiping that her husband had not been seen for some days. Then Ruscum said his boss and the chief of police had been involved.

The distant sound of the snapping of the catches on an instrument case indicated that the cello was on its way out of the garden and there would be no more music. The sun was now indeed past its zenith but Ruscum was for once reluctant to get back to his desk.

By now he had dipped deep into his store of forbidden knowledge and was in full flow with a rumour about the death of the late Queen which was so explosive that it had to be expressed almost entirely in hints, innuendo, and conspiratorial facial expressions involving much nose-tapping and exaggerated winks. Jemima whose prized currency of communication was bald facts, gleaned little from it. Though she stored up the information that amongst the body language there was here some sort of a skeleton in a particularly posh cupboard. She was more interested in what Ruscum said just as he was leaving, when the clock on the tower chimed the half hour and put him into a flurry of consternation, stuffing things into his pockets and stamping the foot that had gone to sleep and quite put out that he would not be able to take his leave with the dignity that his regard for Ms Cake demanded.

What he said was – and she was never sure whether he only mentioned this just as he was leaving because he had not really meant to mention it at all, or whether it was because he assumed it was something she would know more about than him and therefore was a topic to be avoided – what he said was, 'And there's something going on about that Johnson bloke as well isn't there. Have the police been to see you yet?'

'The police? What about? Why on Earth should the police be coming to see me?'

'Ah, well. Perhaps they won't,' he said enigmatically, not quite knowing himself what he meant by it. His coat was now buttoned and he was soon into his hurried but exaggerated farewells and, 'Do hope to meet you here again perhaps, it's been so nice talking to you, Miss, anything I can help you with!' and all that, as he backed out of the arbour.

'What do you mean? What is it about Johnson?' and suddenly thinking she ought to excuse her ignorance added, 'I've been rather busy lately.'

'Er, what was it, er, well I think, and I should not really mention this...' He wished now he had not uttered the name, he had only the vaguest inkling that Johnson may have been secretly called to the royal presence, and less understanding of why, and if he was going to mention it at all he would have been much happier doing it in circumstances where he could milk it with wry nods and shakings of the head and raising of eyebrows and meaningful silences. Blurting it out now when he must scurry back to his office put him entirely off balance. 'Ah dear, sorry must dash, blimey, look at the time...' and he was gone.

Jemima was alone until a robin riffled through the air and was suddenly on the branch of a cherry tree beside her. She stood holding her chin in finger and thumb, the other hand supporting her elbow in a classic pose of deep reflection. Ruscum had revealed himself as a man who rejoiced in secrets and in the privilege of his position in the Chamberlain's inner office. Johnson would seem to be the subject of something secret, but perhaps a secret not all of which Ruscum was privy to, or perhaps he really just did not have the time to tell it. She had only seen Johnson once – at the monthly audience not long after she had taken up her post – and he had had that story about a unicorn at which everyone had sniggered. Hmm. So it seemed that – and it may have been on the very night of that audience – witnesses saw Johnson admitted to the Royal Library and it was thought he met the King himself there, and was there for above an hour, in the middle of the night.

Though Jemima did not know it, the zoo and all its doings were in themselves matters of no moment beyond their importance as the King's hobby as far as the Chamberlain was concerned, and this prejudice had naturally been passed on to those of his entourage. It was therefore only the unusual and apparently clandestine nature of this midnight meeting with the smelly old man that had made the event worthy of remark by Ruscum, who had sought rather lamely to hint that there might be more to Johnson than met the eye and that his position as an animal man might be a cover for other activities involving lengthy periods of disappearance and un-minuted reporting direct to the monarch.

Jemima did not think Johnson was a spy. He did not exactly blend in, did he? And spies had to do that. She needed to know more about him: whether he was an idiot, whether 'unicorn' might be his way of referring to something real but rare.

She sat down again and watched the robin flitting between branches. A remarkable and beautiful creature, small and seemingly delicate, but in fact robust, vigorous and fierce toward its own kind. And she thought what a strange garden this was, with its lumpy red-brick paths and little stone cobras on the gate posts, and indeed what a strange little kingdom this was, what strange people – that is, though they seemed perfectly ordinary, almost all of them had something surprising about them to spring upon you as you got to know them; almost no one was completely predictable. Even Pippa and Willis, who, on the face of it could not be more conventional – eager young assistants of 'good family,' clean, well presented, polite, well spoken – but... Willis for instance kept a voodoo altar locked in a shed in the garden of her cottage and Pippa, unbeknownst to many, as a child had very ingeniously and effectively (in the most mitigating of circumstances) poisoned her stepfather.

But no, everywhere was strange, everyone was strange, the robin was strange – red, precise, fierce, delicate, intricately and mellifluously strange; all birds, all creatures were wonderfully strange. To see anything as one first saw it was to render it strange, however familiar it usually was, and to see anything as new and strange was to delight in it.

Jemima's mind ticked on busily, moving along to review the things she had to do, and the things she had to contemplate, the matters of the moment, which now included this Johnson business, as the robin was joined by a blackbird on the ground under the hedge, and a pair of collared doves flew into the arbour, one of which momentarily alighted on the crumbling head of a cobra. She suddenly felt a little tired and as if the air in this garden, sweet though it was, was somehow slowing down her thoughts and even giving them a tinge, a roseate hue they were never normally clad in. She looked around to make sure there was nothing going on she was not aware of, someone spraying something for instance, which might explain this unaccustomed ambush by the forces of relaxation in the middle of the day, but all was perfectly still and she was perfectly alone. The deep green of the boxwood hedges together with the soft red brick wall and its elongated pear-bearing branches bounded this hidden little corner of the castle gardens and kept the quiet in. And it seemed to be a quiet which for the moment blunted the edge of Jemima's all-conquering logic and sought to seep dreams into a consciousness that was made drowsy somehow by the sun and the stillness.

She dozed... She was leading a long, single file expedition into a mangrove swamp pervaded by a none too distant, dark, sustained growl... But that soon faded and she was half awake again in the peaceful garden. So peaceful now, almost like a graveyard, her eyes closed again as a bee hummed and zummed its ranging looping way behind her head and she imagined herself beside a grave which may have been that of her late father. He was wearing Ruscum's polished boots, lying there just below, never to speak but solid in his still and dependable presence. A presence enhanced by the mystery of his death, and that understanding of what it was all about which he would now be privy to. His identity persisted but not his face. He was a steady but invisible force, to be referred to, to be mused upon, to remember. And this force was a reminder of the rope of ancestry stretching and coiling deep into the ground and measuring out past ages. Far far away where time had different names and then no name at all. And everyone was a different shape to their present shape and the sky a different colour. Her father, now a part of that great dark 'before', was suddenly at her ear and giving her advice... and her dream rolled then to the days when he yet lived and quietly embodied the benign moral certainties... and to classrooms and Bunsen burners... and she passed the examination and all was well, except there was one thing she had never understood and she had never admitted she didn't understand this one thing and she hoped no one would ever find out that there was this thing, this one thing...

To be dreaming in a garden about schooldays and the dead was not something that had figured on her schedule at the beginning of the day – and generally never would. But she was beset by airy forces and could not bestir herself to the business of the moment because she felt something important tugging at her from nether and invisible realms where the writ of science did not run in the ordinary way but was refracted by processes only truly comprehended in other states of being. She was becoming unsettled, anxious and intrigued by the hint of something strange. She was on the point of having something revealed to her, but it was a revelation lucid only at the moment in dream, one which she was not allowed to transport back with her; something which the waking brain was not quite allowed to grasp. All this was unfamiliar ground. With an effort she broke the spell and urgently checked her wristwatch.

Jemima discovered for herself, in conversation with a llama keeper later that day, that as well as Simpson, one of his bird men had also not been seen for days and that it was rumoured that Sir Willoughby too had gone off somewhere. The penny dropped.

Following up the llama keeper's tip-off she took out her bicycle and boldly presented herself at Willoughby Hall where a worried butler was most helpful and eager that such a smart young lady should concern herself with his master's disappearance. He had no compunction in the circumstances about showing such a personable colleague the actual books Sir Jolyon had most recently been referring to.

Jemima very quickly cottoned on to what was likely going on. There was a race afoot. People had obviously come to believe that there might be something behind Johnson's wild assertion and were careering off looking for him. Well, they'd certainly changed their tune. Most of them had done nothing but poke fun at him following the rotunda audience. This was not what she was used to. This was not her style. If they really were going to elbow one another aside to be the one to grab whatever it was Johnson had found and push it out before the King with a, 'Look at me, aren't I clever, am I not the best specimen collector?' she was tempted to let them get on with it. If Johnson had found it he should get the credit. Even if it *was* a unicorn, she smiled to herself. She thought how unusual people could be, but also how disappointing human beings commonly were. She was still only just beginning to realise how much personal kudos attached to any animal discovery here, which made true co-operation a rare thing.

CHAPTER TWENTY

The Gardening King had laid out these terraces. Legend had it that he had gone out one day with his spade and laboured until he disappeared in an orderly jungle of potatoes and lettuces and fruit trees and pergolas and rhubarbs and serried lines of gooseberry bushes. And all was Elysian, the home of the blessed. It had been augmented and altered by generations of his successors and trees had grown sturdy and venerable and hedges thick and square and sometimes sculpted, and when Jemima had wandered through it delighting, but also wondering, following Ruscum's hinted revelations, about the things that were come to light and those that remained hidden and those that would remain hidden, probably for ever, she had not known that there was a particular horrific secret very close to where she had walked in the green and architectured beds and steps and statues. And it could not be further away in form – for it was ugliness and despair and menace and decay, and it lay just half a little mile along a path beyond the garden wall, over there through that door and then down by the castle wall, and down some stairs and under those bushes and back on the lower level round the buttress.

In a dark and weedy corner, below the huge bridge pier, below the castle ramparts, below the riverbank, lapped by the tide when it was high, amongst black-brown mud and old half bricks, the remnants of a coat slushed in each little wave and tried to leave, tried to float away, but could not. The chance that it might free itself and be washed gradually beyond this place and off down river to foreign seas and fresher climes was a real chance, in theory the poor black rag might just as well go as stay. But, caught up here in the back eddy with sodden and slimy forgotten things and the sad dirty vegetation and blobs of worms that fought blindly to survive in their allotted slippery crevices, truth was, it was never going to move. It would be frayed and steeped and tugged and slopped at here until its warp and weft were thinned to final dissolution without ever feeling anything of the salty tongue of wider waters.

It was a fitting ragged standard for the invisible misery that inhabited a hole very nearby. Unknown to any of the hundreds that crossed the bridge each day, in the deep shadows beneath, behind a rusty heavy iron grille set deep into the massive stonework, there dwelt something with a story so sad and remarkable that few would have dreamt it could be true. It lived down here in its own special darkness, a darkness imposed by tragedy as well as stone, hemmed in where only the most meagre wisps of grey light could sometimes penetrate to play a teasing little watery dance upon the dripping ceiling. In this dank black hollow the poor prisoner lived.

He had no name now. The name he'd once been given was never uttered. It would have enraged him, perhaps, to hear it, and of those very few that knew it, most thought him long dead and others, with a shudder of horror and sharp pangs of guilt, could not help sometimes wishing him so.

Looking through the tiny window in the thick oak door, it was difficult to make out anything more than a shape, a shape with a smaller shape which might be a head. It was still and stirred not at the presence beholding it whilst water dripped into the foetid, matted straw. He whose duty it was to feed this beast – almost as forlorn and forgotten as his charge – pushed a tin dish through the feeding hole and waited a few minutes to discern any sign of life. Or death – that was all now that could occur down here that would have any meaning, the only thing that could be reported, the passing of the shape. There was a very low and steady hum of breath that the guard could barely separate from the rumble of distant traffic on the bridge high above them and the steady sluicing of the river water racing round the bridge pier. His arm was beginning to ache with the effort of holding up the lantern and he tapped his keys on the window grille. 'Ho, ho there, you alive old fellow?'

Very slowly the head shape began to rotate and two eyes, red like coals glowing in the blackness, surely the eyes of a demon, rested for a moment on the tiny aperture and then turned slowly back to the wall.

'There's your grub old boy, eat it up,' and relieved to be able to get going, the man lowered his dim yellow light and trudged off into the gloom toward the long spiral climb to the rest of the bright world.

Were there any thoughts left in that black shape, that black head in that grim oubliette? Had the mind been hollowed out, the darkness seeping in to erode all memory, or was there an identity yet clinging somehow to the forlorn shadow? But perhaps by now it was just breath. No more than a finite number of inhalations and exhalations until the wheezing of the last one and a stifling victory for the great stone blocks of the dungeons that destroyed life by always outlasting it?

The grizzly old fossil who fed him was actually a brass buttoned boy – you couldn't tell it to look at him, his blue coat was very old, patched and filthy and only one very tarnished button remained on it as it now hung about him a little as time had begun to shrink his aging frame. His beard was grey and carried crumbs and grease and spittle. He had been allocated this grim responsibility years ago, and he who had appointed him was now dead. No one ever sought him out or had orders for him or inspected him. It was a strange job for the old gaoler who was all but forgotten himself. Even Vangrannicus, the great controlling Vangrannicus himself, was unaware of the existence of this prisoner and even of the location of the hole into which he had been cast. It would not take much, it would only need a whisper from this old gaoler – who lived alone and rarely spoke to anyone – on his deathbed perhaps, to create a myth. A hint of a strange man-beast lurking amongst the foundations of the ancient citadel, deep by the river moat, might easily be passed from mouth to mouth and become a storybook monster. A tale to be embroidered and built upon and contorted as generations replaced one another, and frightened one another and mystified one another with half told truths and imaginative interpretations of insinuated things. A process which strained out the sadness and distilled the horror to full strength.

It was certain that if the old man were to die without telling where his charge lay, he would never be found; would starve away to his cold death and his skeleton would slump into the rat riddled straw. Never perhaps to be identified. The name and his true history evaporating into nothing, like the old coat rotted away in the river.

Jemima was oblivious to the poor prisoner but, for a long time after that afternoon in the garden, she felt a little strange, beset by things which would not conform. It was as if, in that place on that particular afternoon, she had become aware of gaps in the veil, opportunities to see through chinks in the habits and rituals and conventions of life, and to appreciate that usually dormant possibilities stirred amongst the fruit trees and flower beds and ornamental marbles. She was quietly thrilled by feeling ever so slightly out of her depth.

'There are more things in heaven and Earth, Jemima Cake...'

She could imagine her father saying this, assuming a playful gravity as he tapped out his pipe on the fender, and there were of course more things in heaven and Earth than she knew – even she did not know everything – but not things that could be said to be undreamt of in her philosophy because her philosophy was reason and science, and she was therefore a believer in something which was infinitely adaptable and which contained, if only you knew where to look for them, and to formulate them, the theories that would rein in all and any manner of peculiarities.

So she was safe and would not be startled into any wide-eyed abandonment of principle and law, but she could not deny the feeling of having been invaded by some extra sensitivity, of having an inkling of some invisible and rare dimension hitherto absent from her life. And it was this feeling which had influenced her as she had mused on her way through the rose beds laid out along the garden wall (the other side of which lay the path leading in the opposite direction to buttressed obscurity and the dark stone cell) and out of the castle grounds.

And it was this same feeling which influenced her as she walked quickly back to the zoo from her interview with Willoughby's butler – deliberately taking a detour through the castle garden again – and thought about how one thing leads to another and one thing makes another and eons of the slightest differences become accumulated into whole new creatures. And some of them die out and are forgotten. But some are only half forgotten. And maybe some of them were unicorns. And maybe there remains one which is still a unicorn. She thought of that funny old poacher – that's what he looked like to her, a poacher with a bowler hat – Johnson, and smiled and shook her head as she clinked the latch and closed the green garden door in the wall thinking that he himself was a little like something that ought to be extinct but wasn't, and she picked up her pace and marched down the straight path to the zoo.

The nearer she got, the more the residual scent of roses was routed from her nostrils by a vigorous air pumped full of the pungency of camel and tapir and binturong and she thought of the man who had first seen signs in the muddy rocks and astounded everybody by saying here was an animal that lived long ago but is no more. A creature we will never encounter in the flesh, which has bequeathed to us the shadow of its bones so that we shall know that it walked once upon a time here on the Earth.

CHAPTER TWENTY ONE

Johnson's bowler hat was again abroad, moving steadily along a lonely and forgotten lane which meandered for no obvious reason across a flat landscape misty at the edges, a lane which, simply because it continued and extended itself looked as if it ought to lead somewhere, but seemed to the expectant traveller more and more to refuse to do so; increasingly it was hinting that viewed from on high it probably assumed the configuration of a fistful of string which had been cast down by some disgruntled god rather than something intended to connect places to one another. There were crossroads which teased with the possibility that they had been previously encountered from another direction. Johnson could never look puzzled or confused or frustrated however – the set of his face was geological and changes in it and to what passed for his expression were wrought only by time and erosion rather than emotion, so whether he was close to being lost was unknowable. It was difficult to be sure whether he had an image of his destination in his mind. Like a badger snuffling purposefully along its path he continued on without a pause. There may have been an element of religious faith amongst the instinct in his system of navigation, faith which itself brought about the certitude that a white house with pointed windows would eventually allow itself to be found once more. He believed things about the house he sought and about its principal inhabitant – things which remained un-revealed to other people.

Nettles caressed his moleskin trousers as he stepped up on to the deeply wrinkled old timber of a stile which led from a wood to a meadow. Who knows but that it might be a meadow not unknown to his great great grandfather. The arguments of rooks echoed above his head and as cattle slowly turned their necks to follow his progress across their domain, they looked strangely as if they might know him and could guess his purpose, but through the slow cud-chewing they appeared dubious about the whole affair. The surmise any human observer might make as to his thoughts, however, would almost certainly be wrong. Any such conjecture would be repulsed by a force which Johnson – especially out here, in the wild and peculiar places – collected about him, an aura which translated the oddness he projected when in the town and amongst organised and hierarchical humanity into something altogether different, an intimidating and mysterious sort of priestly authority which would give his rare utterances the daunting impact of holy writ rather than the pathetic and inconsequential character of misguided nonsense emanating from an unfortunate mind.

His utterances were very rare out here though, there were very few people to address and even fewer that would care to engage the bullet-headed stern-eyed figure as he tramped steadily onward, onward with a restrained urgency, that would not brook interruption. Was Johnson perhaps not entirely human? Or rather was there something in his makeup which was suprahuman? Was he hybrid spawn – the unique offspring of an unimaginable liaison entered into by some Olympian with a secret inclination? Was the element in his constitution which was interpreted by men as obtuseness perhaps the manifestation of incorporated supernatural forces? Supernatural forces from which all reason would inevitably recoil, would bounce off, blunted, to resound only to the echo of comic disdain, which was all that was within the range of the inferior, purely human, intellect?

As yet not many people had really taken the trouble to contemplate him at length or with any seriousness, but when the time came more than one would discern something of the centaur about him, something which gave him a grim passion and a stony and alien morality, something which gave him an active link with the forces of creation and even of immortality.

Before he came to the white house with the pointed windows, Johnson stopped as he crossed a heath and cocked his ear to the wind. He could hear voices flying faintly by and he took off his bowler hat and cupped it to his ear so that he might magnify the whispers which had travelled a long way, mixed up with the weather, and had been thinned until they were on the point of disappearing.

'Wir müssen sich beeilen. Wir sind verloren. Wenden wir uns wieder. Niemand kann uns dabei helfen.'

He firmly replaced the hat on his head and turned his hard eyes in the direction of the very faint voices for a moment or two before continuing on his way.

Did he understand German? From the look of him, you wouldn't have thought so, but it was probably dangerous to assume that there was anything he couldn't do. He was about to conjure food from his thick coat – it emerged in the form of a ragged boulder of black bread which he hacked with his pocket knife and munched furtively behind birch trees, arresting the circular grinding motion of his great jaw from time to time to listen again in the direction of the whispering wind.

CHAPTER TWENTY TWO

Johnson's somewhat stone-age persona was belied by the deftness with which he negotiated the little garden gate, carefully latching it behind him. The path's mossy stones, one by one, introduced him to the sage green front door which, like the house with its little pointed windows and white walls and unusual chimneys, was neither urban nor agricultural in character, but looked as if it had arrived here by chance, from somewhere with a slightly different architectural accent.

He rapped the brass knocker and the large lady opened it immediately and stood still for a moment, resignation in her grey eyes, before shuffling away, and almost at once the beautiful maiden was there and her bright clear eyes looked upon Johnson and he said, 'Will you come?' and she said, 'Is it for the unicorn?' and he said, 'Yes,' and she said, 'Yes,' and then she followed him, stepping down the path between the bright flowers in the sunshine in her elegant little boots.

CHAPTER TWENTY THREE

King Dagobert IV felt a coolness infiltrating his loins as he walked along and glanced down to see that the flies of his corduroy trousers did indeed gape to afford the royal underwear a rare exposure to the outside elements. He stopped in between lampposts to make the adjustment, looking round to make sure his embarrassment was not noticed. He was trying to look ordinary and had found some clothes his valet deemed no longer wearable (which did not mean that they were worn out, not by most people's standards). By no means as used to dressing down as his daughter was (Freddie would never have attempted any sort of complete theatrical disguise) he had stumbled and fumbled into them hurriedly and without any help and he wondered now whether his look was truly that of a 'man in the street' or 'on a bus' as he put his hands in his pockets – not a thing it often occurred to him to do. One of the fly buttons pinged off. 'Botheration!'

But he must remember that he was in a hurry – he had something extremely important to say. Two of Horrocks' men followed him at a discreet distance but did not seem overly apprehensive of any immediate danger to his highness since one gnawed on a chicken leg and the other angrily tapped with a forefinger the folded newspaper he carried (some sporting outrage). Frederick knew trying to give them the slip would only bring more of them swarming after him, probably with sirens and searchlights and things, so he did his best to pretend they weren't there. He found the street with its neat enamel sign mounted on two concrete posts, Dumbleton Close. It was a cul-de-sac with a neglected shrubbery at one end; the houses had been neat once, just a few years ago in fact when it was all new, but now some of the paintwork was becoming a little neglected, not all of the hedges were as closely clipped as they might be and there had been unfortunate accretions here and there: plastic fencing had been defiantly stuck around number 14 and elements of mass-produced statuary had unaccountably failed to imbue numbers 23 and 17 with instant classical elegance.

As the King approached the dead end of the road looking about him for number 38 he became aware of animals crashing through the bushes and then heard whoops and shrieks and high pitched laughter as two children chased one another out from beneath a mulberry bush and then stopped suddenly before him looking a little astonished. One of them wore a black mask, the other an extemporised cape which was really a towel, they both wielded loaded sticks.

'Hallo there,' said Frederick.

They both continued to stare at him and then the taller one with the cape said, 'Are you Magnus's uncle?'

'No, I'm afraid not, are you expecting him?'

'No.'

'I am here to visit a fr–'

'Your boots are very shiny – are you in the army?'

'He hasn't got a uniform,' piped up the smaller one in the mask, which he now took off, the better to see and quiz this alien to the Close.

'Actually, I sort of am in the army you know, but I am not allowed to wear my uniform all the time.' This was not the sort of remark he ought to make when he was supposed not to be drawing attention to himself, but Frederick was not a natural dissembler, especially with children.

'What sort of gun do you have?'

'It's usually a sword they give me actually.'

'A sword! Are you in the cavalry? Do you have a horse?'

'Great big white one – look here, I'm looking for number 38, do you know which one that is?'

'Yes, we know 38, that's it, over there. Are you the King? He's got a moustache look, I think he's the King.' They did not really believe he was the King, but it was more fun if, for now, he was, and they spontaneously launched into a shrieking rendition of the national anthem, arching their backs and shouldering their sticks. For these children, time and perspective did not exist; there was only today.

As he looked at them, Frederick found himself both searching for his own history and vaguely reflecting on their future.

Memories of infancy may be vivid and lead us to want children to understand as we ourselves did, to be as we once were, long ago, so that we can for a moment live that part again, and so live a little longer; or at least stretch our appreciation of the time allotted to us. But though time may appear to unfold a little more of its length at times like these, may promote the idea of a circularity, of a chain of being, or of batons being passed from gnarled hand to small smooth and white hand, this is all an illusion. Though children and an old man appear to be looking at one another as an old man who used to be a child and as children who would become old men, nonetheless they look not forward to their future or back to his past but across a chasm. There can be no crossing, and all that is to be seen in the distance is a mirage, the fruit of different imaginations.

And, besides, there are things in the minds of old men which are hidden, things which are indeed very deliberately hidden, things which must never be called back into the imagination. Things which the children will never know or guess either, though they stare at the wrinkles and stroke the bald pate until it grows dark and they must jump down and go to bed. So though a person may be sufficiently old to believe he has now some perspective, some view from the top of a hill, of course he can never really see things as they will be in the future, and when he looks back, for the most part he can only see where the sun shone, for he has seen to it that he has forgotten the dark corners in which he once lurked, and blinded himself to events which must never be re-lived.

And yet it always appears, to the old man, to be so magical to be on the first cobbles of that road winding away into a story book distance; surely that, of all places and positions in existence must be the best one, that beginning, never to be surpassed in later years? To be back before the bad things, which second time around may not come to pass after all. He remembered a biscuit tin – green and black with a motto on it – a toy truck and a bear stained with porridge. An old mind cannot resist the struggle to reconstruct its own innocence, or the fiction of its own innocence. Suddenly there came into Frederick's mind the story of William Tell shooting an arrow from the head of his son, and in a bizarre flight of fancy he was assailed by the impossible image of himself taking aim at a precarious Bramley which moved perceptibly up and down with the nervous breaths of the diminutive figure beneath it, which was himself, in short trousers...

'Frederick!' – an urgent high pitched whisper made him jump, the apple fell off, and he turned round to see Millicent beckoning him from her front door and looking anxiously to left and right. He said goodbye to the boys and shuffled as quickly as he could down the path.

There was a pile of ironing on the table and fragments of a model railway on the floor, but it only required the swift gathering up of a cardigan and a newspaper to free the best armchair for the royal nates. He was not expected, but Millicent was not the type to be embarrassed about untidiness or the modesty of her arrangements. In any case, she had no bourgeois perspective, she saw things lying around with an artist's eye and was as likely to rearrange them as put them away, and anyway, by now (they had had three separate trysts since their first meeting in the castle) Frederick's status (as someone too august to suffer imperfection) figured almost not at all in their relationship. And Millicent, we know, was not like that anyway. She liked the luxury he lived in, but she was decidedly not ashamed of the lack of luxury she lived in. There were occasions indeed when she thought perhaps she preferred looking at the luxury he lived in to actually contemplating living in it.

He did take the opportunity – whilst she went to make the tea – to gaze about and marvel at the delicious ordinariness of everything. He marvelled at the space-saving cupboards and the way pretty much everything took place in these two tiny rooms. He was not often privileged to see this sort of thing first hand. It was almost like being in a very far and foreign country.

She came back carrying a tray looking over Frederick's head out of the window to see if there was anybody about. Though she did not care what they thought as such, if her neighbours were aware of the royal presence they would become confused, gossip would germinate and life would quickly become very tedious. She couldn't see anybody – not even the two children from next-door-but-one who had in fact forsaken the shrubbery to infiltrate her garden and stood even now beneath the window sill.

It was not only Horrocks' men who shadowed Frederick up the Lane to Dumbleton Close that night of course – the unicorn was close behind the King, and quite beside him at times. Inevitable, once it had been called from dormancy in the library and the sleeping consciousness of the nation, that its hooves – muffled for the moment – should follow where he led. Freddie had spent the better part of several days amongst his books. His brain, which swam with anatomically unlikely beasts and the stories that were told about them, was a very crowded place which also had to make room for governmental doings and the annoyances of the daily rituals and the wearying preoccupations of the persons that organised them, as well as all the accretions of an unusually active and educated mind. He encouraged the unicorn because it grew by the hour and pushed unnecessary things aside and, he fancied, rather frightened people away. But it also stirred things up with its great white horn. It brought things together and confused them with one another and made the familiar look odd and cast doubt upon the accepted order of things. Without ever telling lies – it was a beast made in such a way that its mind simply could not digest a lie.

Freddie was the sort of person who was often ambushed by ideas. Successive revelations often lay in wait for him as he marched slowly along the corridors and beside the parapets of his castle, squinting thoughtfully at gargoyles and gazing abstractedly at paintings as he passed. Sometimes these radical new understandings stayed for a while and invigorated his conversation with insights which bemused and nonplussed his friends, sometimes they faded away quite quickly. These could be concerning almost anything, philosophy, food, his daughter, politics, the weather, the zoo – all bumping into one another and piling up and then dropping off one by one, sometimes coming round again of course, but not all of them; with the growing of the unicorn however (he was already discernibly taller than a carthorse) everything was becoming much less muddled. It was as if the soup in his head was instantly cleared by the swirling of the animal's holy horn.

The unicorn was indeed beginning to conjure a feeling that it could bring him to the cusp of some sort of paradise, a supreme limpidity, in fact, hitherto unknown, but amidst this exhilaration there were periods when everything wavered and he feared the beast itself might suddenly disappear; at all costs he must not allow that to happen. He was sure the great white animal with his long beard and the slightly Asiatic slant of his eye had coloured his contemplation of life and death as he had wandered down Millicent's garden path, and the idea crept upon him, as he sat and talked in that little suburban room, that it might indeed be the entire architect of his life, and that the building of a sublime and enchanted rainbow bridge to Valhalla was not in the least impossible now, but the chance had to be seized, it would not come again.

She poured the tea and admonished him for turning up unannounced with a motherly wrinkle of the eyebrows. But since what he was about to announce was quite sensational, his purpose could not be impeded by the mores of Dumbarton Close, and this was apparent in the way his grey-blue eyes looked steadily at her over the rim of his tea cup. (Which, he was delighted to note, did not match the saucer.) He launched himself into his subject, that is to say, he un-dammed the lake of folk lore, palaeontology and excited conjecture that had been bubbling within him for days. And it was to be in that very next moment, even whilst he continued in full flow, that he realised...he realised (and it was almost certainly the unicorn which awoke his realisation) as he looked up at her, that the lightly tanned skin of her face, the large dark eyes, the dark hair falling in just such a way, a mole on her neck, a plaster on her thumb, her pullover, her jeans, the dimensions of her ear lobe, the actual mechanics of her idiosyncratic body movements had all now for him assumed the unique and dazzling magnetism of a being who existed quite apart from the rest of humanity. He had liked her from the first meeting and he had been strongly aware of the little feelings of sexual attraction but as he sat here preparing to reveal his strange intentions to her, he was properly aware for the first time that he was in the presence of one of the focal points of his life and that his contemplation of events, of himself, of the future would be anchored now always by reference to this marvellous woman. Was it only he (and the unicorn) that saw it, this particular and special formula, this coalescence of qualities and features and characteristics which together made a being the like of which had never walked before? To be looked upon benignly by that womanly presence was to be enchanted, to be raised up.

Even though he would not allow himself to believe that he was in love with her, and could aspire to no sort of conjugality, he was a slave to her smile, and her slightest grimace consigned him to a disproportionate discomfiture.

Perhaps also contributing to these revelations, there was something curious in the atmosphere, not just in the room, but something which affected the light in an odd way, some sort of daytime northern light phenomenon which shimmered far away and crumpled light waves in distant stratospheres sufficiently to infect the weakish sunlight as it strayed and played between the scudding clouds with tinges of colour rarely depicted in the heavens in these latitudes – watery shades of green and then a deep magenta which penetrated the window of number 38 and glimmered on a fragment of model railway track. He reached the denouement of his speech, 'We must go and look for it,' he said, putting down his cup and clenching his fist triumphantly but rather self consciously in a passionate but uncharacteristic gesture as he sought to inspire her with his determination. 'I want us to go and look for it – the unicorn – I want you and me to go on an expedition to find it!

'The living unicorn, wherever it has its being,' he added, unable to resist darting a look up at the one standing now clearly beside the ironing board as he spoke of its flesh and blood counterpart.

A tiny plastic figure of Superman now looked in on them from the window sill, book-ended by two cherubic heads which looked weirdly infantile and ancient at the same time in the bizarre light which shone from a sky continuing to experience the rarest of meterological concatenations. And there were further contortions in the character of the day – an unidentified sensation – not quite a smell, not quite a sound, not quite a glow – had crept into the Close, into the garden, into number 38; and affected those present in the little room with an enlarging of the heart, a soothing and softening and strengthening of the pulse, a ballooning bliss.

She said, as only she could say it, 'Yes, of course Freddie, of course I shall come.'

The children, who were supposed to be spies and were challenging one another to make out what was being said in the room, were interrupted by the sudden appearance of an earwig moving purposefully toward them along the window sill. Its determined scuttling and its menacing pre-historic pincers excited and terrified them. It was a well known fact that it was a beast ever governed by one paramount desire – to wriggle into the nearest human ear and eat through the brain until it emerged at the opposite orifice grimly satisfied not only by its repast but also by the incidental torture it had inflicted. In a faint and ghostly echo far away the voice of Trevor Simpson exclaimed, 'Ah lovely *dermaptera*!'

Millicent's fondness for the King – for this King who would not be King – was also to undergo a transformation that day; though not quite of the same order as Freddie's *coup de foudre* it was nonetheless significant. It was during this impromptu afternoon tea that Millicent became aware (how could she not?) that her friendship was more important to him than some honest but precarious infatuation and she pondered the shifting balance of their relationship not without a little passing unease. To be toyed with, to be playfully lusted after, to be taken up and dazzled, all could be coped with and she would be pleasured and amused but in the end unaffected; but to be a deep and necessary friend, to be a permanent influence on the wellbeing of this complicated human being was something much more, and she knew she was drawn into a responsibility which went far beyond cigars and whiskey on the battlements, one which would wrench her life and those who already shared it in unconsidered directions. (The thing it was most like, she considered fleetingly, was having another child, so late in her fecundity.)

The social barriers that others might have expected to keep a distance between them had never survived their first meeting, if they had existed at all, but with the level of intimacy offered now by Freddie she did feel a wariness about the inevitable consequences. She saw that she would be dizzyingly promoted in the national pecking order, the man-King-child (who was making no effort to conceal the esteem in which he held her) being himself a demi-god to thousands of his subjects who followed his royal doings as they would a soap opera. She would now be in danger of stepping onto that stage. However she might try to keep out of the limelight, she would be a part of his life and inhabiting a niche in his personal pantheon of friends and relatives. Some pleasantry from him, now smiled at in passing by Millicent, would be treasured and rehearsed a hundred times if it were vouchsafed to many of his ordinary subjects – and this raised her up to the level… the level, she mused, of those in the popular rotogravure, but also of those in silver frames in private apartments. The family icons that adorned his private rooms. The mystique of monarchy – flimsy in the extreme as it always had been for her – would finally evaporate as she seated herself on monogrammed toilets and sought out her own likeness amongst the snaps of dressed-down nobility on the regal tallboy.

Trying to slough off these uncomfortable implications for herself, she returned to contemplate the reality of Freddie as he looked up from the tower of sugar cubes he was building during his enthusiastic talk of mythical animals and uncharted territories both cultural and geographic (which continued on), and she marvelled again that in spite of all the auras others concocted about him he was himself; in spite of everything into which he'd been born and all the constant grinding erosion of a succession of Vangrannicusses, some inner quality in him was so resilient with such a rubbery sense of benevolence and modesty and enthusiasm that he bounced above all the nonsense and invigorated the little living room at Dumbleton Close with an excitement of the possibility of unicorns and a certainty that they would find Trevor and she put down the teapot which she had been absently cradling and sat down and a measure of rapture inhabited her beaming smile. How she admired a man of patient resilience who could quietly sustain himself with a zoo instead of doing what he was desperate to do: which was chuck the crown in the river and declare from the burning battlements that all subjects were now citizens. He was her own little tea time Hamlet. A tragic prince with a sideline in Snarks. How would they travel? Hooded, under the cover of a moonless night? How would they start? Which precise direction? Straight to the scene of the Giradi Boldoni painting or some other way? Were these things discussed? It was surely to be expected, but perhaps they did no more than agree on an auspicious day, knowing that everything else must follow.

The 'spies' could not have told you what transpired because, like a primitive beast from another epoch, unaccountably and unfairly miniaturised in the face of these milky puppies, the earwig was fighting back. Averse to the prospect of being squished to no purpose it scuttled suddenly and fiercely and unpredictably and startled Simon into keeling over backwards into the vegetable plot and banging his head on a watering can. His Batman persona was immediately shed and he started to wail. Lionel went over to him to see if there was any blood, and the earwig disappeared in a flash down the nearest thing resembling an auditory canal that it could find, which was a broken plastic toy trumpet lying beside the dustbin.

But there was another thing that happened there a little later that afternoon, in the stained-glass light which mysticised the ironing. It was the beginning of the unearthing of something hidden, something which would flex itself beneath the surface of that strange day sufficiently to make her aware that fate had cursed Freddie with a secret – just one, but the implication was that it was neither amusing nor heroic. He had stopped building sugar cubes and was sipping his Assam with a faraway look in his eye (there was often a faraway look in his eye – there was almost always a faraway look in his eye) and she, emboldened by the understanding that their friendship had graduated to a new footing, asked him as she appeared to look absently out of the window at next door's kids screaming about something in the garden, 'Freddie, what happened to your wife? You were married weren't you? Everything about you is public isn't it, must be impossible to have any secrets, but I don't seem to be able to remember anything about your wife, I don't mean to be nosey – I'm sure I should know, but I don't. Its just that if we're looking for my husband while we are looking for the unicorn, well, I was wondering about your wife. I should like to know about her.' She turned to look at him, 'Sorry to bring it up if its painful, Freddie.'

The bizarre tints to that strange afternoon light persisted and as he lifted his face to her they gave it a faint purplish tinge and exaggerated the furrows which suddenly appeared in his brow and he answered in a tone she could not remember him ever having used before, half apologetic and half defiant, 'She died. Some years ago. A long time ago.' It seemed that there still lurked, in the unicorn soup, darker things, which could not quite be persuaded to sink out of sight for all the purifying power of the spiral horn. Then he just changed the subject. Flatly ignored the question, and went on about Boldoni, and map making.

His scarcely disguised evasiveness convinced Millicent that there was something wrong here. Something very wrong about the death of, what had been her name? Queen Isolde. No, Iphigenia. She resolved to find out what she could before their expedition left. So weirdly uncharacteristic – how could such an amiable, lovely, avuncular old King have even the suggestion of tragic scandal lurking in his past? It was so unlike him to be anything other than disarmingly open about everything. Was it something which had been intentionally kept dark or was it just because she was not a follower of the monarchical family doings that Millicent knew nothing about it? About what? What could it have been? Drugs? Infidelity? Satanism? Her fancies began to range over the unspeakable excesses of all the evil empresses and iniquitous consorts she had ever read about, but no no, she must rein in her imagination – more likely it was something very unfortunate which would have been awkward for the decorum of the respectable press to report and too challenging to the patriotism of the gutter press – mental illness, or a disfiguring accident. Something just too painful, yes that must be it, simply too painful for Freddie to recall. She must see what her mother, an irritatingly faithful worshipper at the shrine of royalty, remembered.

In due course, Freddie left to snag up the invisible line which connected him to the secret police. In fact the men were caught by his sudden emergence, lounging against a wall, rather morose, and looking quizzically at the ends of their cigarettes as if they hoped the tail end of their conversation had not been overheard.

The earwig, quiet in its trumpet, thought of warm soft brain parts and the taste of people's dreams.

CHAPTER TWENTY FOUR

Millicent knelt on the floor in the hall of the little house after Freddie's departure and watched him through the letter box flap as he turned the corner. She liked sometimes to frame the street in this little oblong trap, as if by letting go and snapping back the darkness she could consign the image to oblivion, but this time she held the tiny horizontal door firmly and closed it quietly in time with the disappearance from sight of the sandy corduroys and the Norfolk jacket with the rip in the pocket. She subsided to the floorboards and spent some minutes gazing at a corner of the huge painting which she refused to put in the garage and which she would not let Trevor hang in the living room. It impeded passage through this hallway, and was itself stifled and frustrated by the space it was crammed into. She could never quite re-attain the mental state from which she'd brought back this huge, dense, criss-crossed image, but she often crouched here staring at it, and losing herself in the mystery of it; the mystery of the painting itself, and the mystery of its creation. And, as she looked, her mind sank into the rough ochre, ridged like plough furrows, and she floated through the cubism on into another painting, deep into pigments, and then she slowly emerged, to be surrounded by, to inhabit, another painting entirely: the Boldoni painting she had seen in the castle, which she could now see magically before her in its entirety and in every detail – that masterly vista of quirky nostalgia that so intrigued and teased. Boldoni was boasting with his perspective of having sat in a special place, at a special point, from whence he had seen what you never have. It was the valley that hung secretly on that wall in the castle, barely appreciated and little understood for a hundred years or more. Señor Boldoni had whispered a little bedtime story; in the corner of his picture, beneath some trees and poised on deep green grass, he had said, and was saying still, 'Once Upon A Time…long before you came, there breathed and snorted here a wondrous beast, white with a long horn and beard, and I say to you: I saw it here, just like this.'

CHAPTER TWENTY FIVE

There were farmers in the Lanes, of course, but they were usually only ever seen from a distance and it was impossible to know what sort of a conversation you might have with them, or indeed whether they would talk to you at all. They rarely showed any sign of having noticed you. They were remote and, the traveller felt, probably unfriendly, having a prosaic relationship with a land which one assumed they ought to be at odds with, it being magical and they being stolid and mechanical. How could they be always there and yet appear to be in themselves alien to the numinosity?

Getting on with whatever it was doing, a tiny grey tractor droned far far away on a little hill, piloted by someone whose mind it was impossible to know, but whose morose dreariness it was easy to assume. Daphne was irritated by it. And by quite a few other things. The bread in her hand was stale and there was a suspicion of mould on it, which disgusted her. Trevor was moaning again, that low but insistent plea for relief accompanied by a prolonged grimace which had the effect on Daphne of freezing up her well of sympathy and wishing she had left him where the pig had left him. The red stain on the shirt wrapped round his leg was getting bigger and she thought, soon he won't be able to walk at all, even with the stick, and she did feel sorry for him but she just could not cope with this, it was not why she had come here, he was very nice and she liked him, but this was all horrible and it was not the problem she was supposed to be dealing with and things were all going haywire and she wished she was somewhere else. Just exactly what is gangrene? What does it look like? Would she have to saw his leg off with the little pair of scissors in her rucksack? Would he die? And (looking round suddenly) where was the pig now, for god's sake? And what if she sawed his leg off and it wasn't gangrene? And she imagined herself watching him smiling, swinging down the street toward her in the sunshine on his crutch like Long John Silver and it was all her fault.

'Don't worry,' said Trevor though still with his eyes narrowed against the pain, 'I don't think its as bad as it looks. I'm lucky really, she could so easily have killed me. You know, I think she deliberately let me off, I really do... Just need to keep it clean before it can be sewn up.' He looked at her and briefly considered asking her to lick the wound; it was well known that the bacteria in the human mouth had a strong antiseptic quality and it was common practice amongst more primitive peoples to lick the injuries of their tribe-mates, and dogs of course always licked themselves. But his glance happened to fall upon the excruciating grimace that disfigured her face as she found thick blue mould on the underside of her remaining crust of bread and he thought better of it. Then he settled back into the powerfully analgesic contemplation of Jemima Cake's soft but firm pink tongue repeatedly stroking her divine healing spittle into the red gash in his own raw flesh.

Daphne cast the vile bread aside where it tumbled amongst nettles to await the attentions of small and nasty things or simply to succumb to the imminent rampancy of the fungus it had already generated. Its character as a piece of crusty wholemeal would soon begin its dissolution. It had avoided being eaten but was fated for a more lingering, less dignified end. It was similar with people, some of us are killed, some go mouldy. She decided she would go for help, yes that would be the best thing, go for help. She did not allow herself to consider that she did not know what help was, or where it might be found, nor did she allow herself to acknowledge the convenience of the possibilities that by the time she got back he would either be dead or recovered and she would be absolved of responsibilities, amputational or otherwise. But a sense of that convenience worked somewhere within her as she got to her feet and said, 'Look here, I think I should go for help, don't you? You just rest there and I'll go for help.' But frowning and gingerly shifting his sitting position he reminded her that the sow was still probably somewhere around and it would be dark in a couple of hours; an early owl twitted from up in an unidentifiable direction and after some irritable rearranging of the contents of her pack she sat down again, gloomily scraped her heel abstractedly in the earth and was silent, as he went on to explain that his wound was not as bad as it looked, had almost stopped bleeding and since he had cleaned it with the small bottle of antiseptic lotion he always carried, everything would be alright and he hoped to be able to walk again by morning. Meanwhile, he went on in fatherly, reassuring and calmly practical tones, it was looking a bit like rain, they should sit out the night here, build a shelter and collect firewood. After a bit of a sulk, Daphne eventually responded to these wise and gently optimistic words and foraged successfully for firewood – hardly any of it green he was surprised and delighted to see – and even had a bash at commandeering saplings and encouraging them with string (from Trevor's pack, she had no string of her own) to assume a protective roof-like shape. She was quite pleased with it and her mood changed, lightening as the sky darkened and a crackle was engendered amongst twigs which she soon nurtured with obvious delight into real warming flames. Trevor was pleasantly surprised to discover that she was good at fires.

They put on their warmest jumpers and settled before the campfire in the time honoured way of travellers, of drovers, explorers, tinkers, highwaymen, runaways and pilgrims, enjoying that special sort of camaraderie ever engendered amongst strangers clustered round the exclusive little sun of flaming sticks. The flames worked their magic on the pair as they stared into them and warmed their hands before them and there was a subtle change in the character of their conversation. The holy flames in the silence of the dark night stoked a confessional spirit within them both and each was moved gradually to set aside the mask they presented to the world and themselves in the daytime bustle of life in zoo and castle and city, and slowly to release little truths, haltingly at first but nervousness was soon dispelled by the reality that only they two existed in the world and all the rest was darkness.

'I'm not really an entomologist, you know. I just tell people I am so they won't bother me. If people think you're a bug hunter they think you're harmless and stop wondering why you're wandering around being a stranger.'

'I knew that. I used to be one.'

'Really?' She smiled. They both smiled; and glanced at one another in the red glow.

'A bug hunter I mean, not a stranger.' He poked the fire with a stick.

'Ha ha, well, we can't really help being strangers,' she said, picking up her own stick and accidentally jousting with his and then recoiling, 'we're all strangers to one another, don't you think?' She loved being in the dark, in this dark, almost alone but not quite. He was a strong but pliable and safe link to the world and she knew she could talk or be silent and it would not matter.

'Well, in a way, I suppose you're right, we never know people completely, do we?' he said, thinking simultaneously about his recent self examinations and confusion and being a stranger to himself, but also that this was not usually his area of conversation and that there was in this circumstance, miles from anywhere alone with this girl, there was a danger that 'therapy' might arise, and this filled him with apprehension, and then he suddenly wondered whether the soldier was still in his trouser pocket but he didn't check, it was the pocket on the bad leg and the necessary squirming was out of the question.

She decided quite naturally to confide in him and surprised herself with how relaxed she was as she told him, camouflaging in easy matter of fact conversational tones the startling nature of her revelations, (which she thought, though it had not been her intention, actually enhanced the shock) that she was really the Princess Daphne, only child of King Dagobert IV, with a string of titles of her own, most of which she had difficulty in remembering, was heir to the throne and a fortune and was on the lam.

'They're trying to marry me off to some Italian prince, or duke, I forget which.'

'Really? An arranged marriage, I see,' he nodded slowly and contorted his face into a look he intended to express sympathetic distaste, but it was not really within his repertoire. He did not believe her. Why was she telling him that she was a princess?

Out here she did not need to be a princess, she had come here to get away from being a princess and she could have made up anything or talked about other things rather than herself, why did she do it? Ironically a quick way of establishing her specialness, that specialness for which she craved recognition, would always be hinting at the royal blood which seemed to cast a spell over ordinary people but which actually threw a thick veil over the real Daphne and was driving her mad. When people seemed slow to recognise Daphne's individual worth in the end she often could not rid herself of the temptation to bring them up short with the revelation that she was the daughter of the King (not quite understanding that it might equally establish her as deluded in the eyes of the wary and suspicious). It was part of her confusion that she found herself having to deny her true self in order to get people to pay her attention and this was a cycle which had the potential to become a dangerous mental vortex jostling with the other maelstroms round which her poor mind rushed. And yet here, with this man whom she had no need or desire to impress, she was not revealing herself for those usual reasons, she was, she found, doing it because in this impromptu confessional that fate had so strangely engineered, she realised that it might be the first step to the acknowledgement of many things, and a new understanding which might involve the final shedding not only of royalness but also of much else which stood in the way of her redemption.

Trevor picked a large timber (part of an old gate-post) from the fire before it had properly caught and banged it vigorously on the ground to encourage the evacuation of all the tiny denizens who were about to be immolated. In the dim light he managed only to see a wood louse (*armidillidium*) and a small unidentifiable spider, before he tossed it back and settled it amongst the sparks.

They were silent for a time and Trevor decided as he stared into the flames that he did, after all, believe she was the Princess. He had no reason not to, and he might as well be sitting by a campfire with a remnant of the old order as anyone else, so he let himself go and allowed himself to believe it. Smoke issued in a thin steady stream from a small hole in the gate-post – possibly the same hole previously home to *armidillidium*. It did not somehow occur to him that she was his employer's daughter, such connections and relations seemed irrelevant out here. Even if elsewhere he might find it more difficult to credit, here in the firelight she could certainly be a princess; the red and the white and the blue flames and smoke and the spit and the crackle brought ghosts and 'phenomena' back into the range of people who in the daylight or the town were usually more prosaically focussed. The gate-post looked as if it might once have been just such a piece of heavy wood as insane people might use to brain passing cyclists did it not? Perhaps that was it, perhaps in the past a cyclist had been murdered, with this blunt instrument, and it was some ghostly re-enactment which had clutched at his passing psyche and assaulted it with the psychopathic possibilities in persons of one's new acquaintance. Or of anybody. A flame he'd been enjoying changed from blue to red as a rustle of breeze lifted Daphne's sapling canopy a little. His leg was certainly getting better.

The discovery of a tin of Spam which had been forgotten in the bottom of Trevor's bag gladdened them immeasurably. Daphne foraged for suitable sticks to spit the rough sculpted slices Trevor's penknife hacked from the lump and soon the smell of processed animal fat rose in the bower, no doubt causing Olympian nostrils to twitch in their long sleep in remembrance of the heady days of sacrificial entitlements. The hot browned and blackened greasy gobbets were juggled and gingerly jawed, smiling eyes sharing the fun and the delectable taste of what in another time they would have turned away from, pitying those into whose lot such provender fell.

Afterwards they were silent for a while and then Trevor, snapping some branches and adding them to the steady smoke and crackle, mentioned the man in the bowler hat.

'The man in the bowler hat...' he began, and Daphne immediately turned from the fire to look sharply at him, 'is called Johnson. Just Johnson, not even Mr Johnson – nobody knows if he has or ever had a first name – and he works for the King's zoo. He's a specimen collector, just as I am. Although I've never had anything to do with him, he's a colleague of mine.'

'What? What man in a bowler hat? You can't mean the one I have been looking for? He's something to do with the Italians, he's an agent, a factotum, a spy, trying to arrange things with my father, hardly an animal man, I think you're confusing people.'

'No, I don't think so. A scruffy man, black coat, large boots, shabby bowler, strides quietly about like some surreptitious primeval fascist, never speaks, I promise you there's only one of them.'

Daphne thrust a stick with which she had been scraping mud from the sides of her boots into the fire and they both watched its progressive metamorphosis as the flames flared about it and fed on it and digested it and its stickiness was lost in swift successive waves of incandescent colours until, in the end, only the fragile ghost of its white shape remained and then even this collapsed and was lost amongst the ashes.

They were silent as they looked, but both Daphne and Trevor thought of transfiguration and the startling speed at which things cease to be themselves, and Daphne thought of a funeral and of sack-cloth and ashes and the fiery demons that suddenly appear and destroy people for no reason at all except that they themselves have no reason. And Trevor wondered whether his mind had begun to flare up recently not because he was about to begin himself again but because he was coming to the end, and what he was sensing was the imminent ignition of the process of his sparkling into nothing. He was even a little dismayed that the thought did not frighten him.

There was a faint rustle of wind, a distant bark of fox, and they looked at one another again, and Daphne wondered what it would be like to kiss him, and she thought what a desperate act it was to kiss someone passionately, people pouring themselves into one another in fierce and frantic hope, sucking reassurance from one your fevered desire would have you believe loved you as you did yourself. People never love you in the end as they say they do. Never. And yet you must believe that love is possible because it is essential to be loved. The alternative, the negative of love is death. And the two together, when they come together, love and death, the love of death, dying in love, dying for love, dying of love… loving death… She imagined a tiny figure leaping from the mountain cliff at the end of a log, through the red flames and into the incandescent ash.

Perhaps he would die soon. Perhaps that's what these strange feelings of discontent intimated – mortality. Imminent mortality. People did die. Some people died suddenly and relatively young. Oh god. Well if he was going to die what did anything matter. Certainly he would die one day so why was his life so constrained? Why did he not seek out Jemima Cake and love her or die in the attempt? Oh no, he did not want to die of embarrassment. He mentally squirmed at the prospect of making a fool of himself. At least as things were she might even attend his funeral, as a colleague, if the rest of them were marshalled to go as they probably would be, for appearances sake. What would Millicent think? About the funeral. Would she want it a particular way? Would she guess what he would have wanted? What would he want? He suddenly saw the smokey plume of a black horse and a whole fiery cortege behind it; he would not want tears, would there be tears? He winced as his hand fumbled in the pocket of the bad trouser leg for the wooden-headed soldier, and such mental consternation and the need not to think of his children dressed in mourning sent him off on a distractive flight of imagination wherein he reflected on the impossibility of harnessing six ostriches to pull a bamboo hearse up the steep stick which was about to collapse in a shower of sparks.

The fox was heard again, more distant now, and then, very faintly, very very faintly – but not so faintly that a strong flat nasal quality could not be made out – the sound of a human voice. Daphne did not hear it, but Trevor did, or Trevor thought he did – just the faintest, briefest sudden faraway snatch of language carried somehow to him, leaving the rest of whatever utterance it was part of behind, muffled by climate and acoustics. *'Wir durfen nicht den kopf verlieren...'* Ghostly, it sent a shiver down Trevor's spine. It was German, but somehow it was not the German of the sought after German men of science – this was a different sound, it was the sound of men who were oblivious to concepts, and who concerned themselves not at all with enlightenment.

Thus the quiet fire in the night of the forest, alternately conjuring and soothing the fevered meanderings of troubled minds, and the universal circumscribing dark which belittled all the measurements and theories of smart astronomers with one slight whispered fairy fragment of an unsettling German phrase – *Wir durfen nicht den kopf verlieren.*

CHAPTER TWENTY SIX

The sun shone bright and big, warming the morning with a holiday excitement, and pumping a sort of quiet mirth into the briskness with which Millicent prepared for the expedition. There should have been more of the character of grim determination accompanying the strapping of her bag since she was journeying in search of her husband who had been missing now for about a fortnight and might be suffering some dire fate – or indeed have suffered some dire fate – but the rare prospect of travelling to strange and quirky territory, travelling with good old Frederick, more than adequately provisioned (would he bring cigars?) and free from all her daily responsibilities together with the prospect, however far fetched, of walking into a fairy tale and coming upon a breathing, panting four legged myth irresistibly imbued her with a girlish gladness she was by no means inclined entirely to suppress.

She sidled past the huge canvas in the hall and with a bang she pulled firmly shut the door (still scarred with the scratch marks of the dog which had died some years ago) and made her way through the quiet street which seemed as ever to be defiantly bunkered and blinkered against the untoward. The norm here was never to look up and never to let anything in. A large tabby cat sitting on a wall eyed her with a look which intimated some understanding of the outlandishness of her escapade, but showed no inclination to join her. She excused it – it was, after all, only a cat, not even a Cheshire cat. And it lived in this rigid cul-de-sac, which gave no sign of ever entertaining any caprice or quirk, and where all contrariness was looked upon as dangerous and the harbinger of ruin. She felt a familiar twisting mixture of sadness and anger tightening inside her as she walked down the road past all the white paint and frosted glass and the half hearted gardening, and gnomes perpetually delighted by crazy paving, which was only slackened when she emerged from the knot of Dumbarton Close into the open and the greater vistas at the top of the hill, where all the valley and the river and the old town and the castle were laid out before her. And she could see right across up into the distant hills, beyond which lay the Lanes where an altogether different air was breathed, which blew clear and chill and was cleansed of cement dust and barbecue smoke.

She continued on, and was swallowed up by the maze of historic streets which became twistier and narrower. The houses were made of brick, just as the houses of Dumbarton Close were made of brick, except these were older, mellow and mossy, not sharp cornered and starkly new. They reconstituted themselves before Millicent's sparkling eyes into a huge brick sphinx which promptly devoured Dumbarton Close in one gulp. Bricks here and bricks there are the same things except to the extent that poetry and ivy cling to them according to their age and the character of the place they are piled up in. In the end, of course, the wind will hack away at their mortar, and walls will fall, for everything comes to an end. Flesh will do so long before clay. Could there really be one thing, thought Millicent as she walked down the steep streets, which had not ceased, and would not cease? Was there a beautiful thing which lived unseen, unknown and undying? The unicorn whinnied and began to toss its head and wave its horn for her as it had for Frederick.

As she continued to descend into the old town, she saw the jumble of roofs and gables, all different colour slates and tiles and the buildings all different sizes and she became aware that some of these streets were just as they would have been in Boldoni's day – except for the air and the patinas and patched repairs, and the light, the light might well have been different (wistful pastels appealed to her across the years) – and Boldoni himself might well have walked this way in stained velveteen on his way to paint the unicorn, and she was filled with wonder and expectation, and she was not at all worried about Trevor because she knew she was on the brink of marvels and revelations and Trevor would emerge to be part of the thaumaturgy which would soon fulminate about them, marshalled by a rejuvenated Frederick wielding Prospero's wand. (The warm heart which cradled such magical optimism moved steadily down the streets and was carried across the mighty stone bridge beneath the great portcullis and through the gate into the citadel. And as it passed this way it remained in stark and ironic ignorance of the sad dungeon and the unobserved iron grille set into the stone in the dark shadows only a few feet below, wherein dwelt the unfortunate prisoner. Bright expectation and abject despair, momentarily so close to one another, each for the moment dumb and blind to the other. It ought to have been impossible for such opposites not to affect one another in some physical, planetary way.)

Half an hour later, Millicent emerged from the ramshackle part of the other side of the town, where 'civilisation' trailed off into smallholdings – agriculture of an unkempt, intermittent, half-hearted style, requiring many ruined sheds and collapsing outbuildings – which then gave way with relief to plain fields and wide open land. At the appointed crossroads beyond the wide meadow (very close to Johnson's cottage though she did not know it) there stood a strange contraption on four large wheels, something of a cross between a *kibitka* and a black maria, a single large and muscly carthorse in the shafts, and a hooded figure standing beside it and looking out for her approach. She quickened her steps and a smile spread across her face as she prepared for the gentle and slightly diffident embrace which had come to be their norm but which disguised within it warm and more intimate undercurrents which they both quietly thrilled to.

But there was no embrace. The hooded figure she realised at the last moment was not quite the right height and was wrongly and annoyingly plump in the middle.

'I'm sorry, Miss, you can't go any further. Who are you and where did you think you were going? Got any ID?'

She told them her name (two more uniformed men had emerged from behind the van) and that it was none of their business where she was going, adding that they had no power to stop her. She was a free citizen, going about her private business, and would they *please* leave her alone.

'Now, now, Miss, you're not a citizen, by the way, even if you think you are, you're a subject. We've 'ad a lot of people going missing, so we need to be sure everyone knows who they are, Miss. Commissioner's orders, Miss, all strangers to be stopped and verified during this emergency.'

'What emergency? I'm not a stranger.'

'Begging your pardon, Miss, but you are to me. As I say, we've 'ad a lot of people going missing and...'

'I know, for god's sake, my husband is one of them and your commissioner knows all about it, I had a meeting with him only the other day, I'm going to look for him.'

'I'm sorry Miss, but its us wot does the looking, oo you might or might not 'ave had meetings with is neither 'ere nor there, we can't have you going missing as well can we? We need to know where everybody is, and not who they say they are, either, nor oo they might claim to 'ob nob with.' (Nasty little grins appeared on the mouths of his minions at this.) 'But they must have their personalities properly documented. Otherwise, my orders is to arrest them.'

Millicent did her best, but could see that this Dogberry was actually the most dangerous sort of idiot, capable of wrestling any logic to a standstill with the sheer strength of his brainless intransigence. How did they come to be waiting in this exact spot, she wondered? Had something happened with Freddie? She looked all around again, but there was nobody else anywhere.

Then, without any warning, the fat man suddenly barked out something and his men grasped her arms and in panic she looked for help from left to right and started to cry out 'Fred...!' But she was addressed in bludgeoning official words, a loud brutal mumble saying something about 'undrarrest...saynthingmebyoozedagenst... and 'bypowers vested in me...' and then her full name was uttered in a formal staccato by somebody else, and the next thing she knew she was inside the dark conveyance between two men with silver buttons on their tunics which shone in the gloom and the thing swayed and they were in turn all jolted sideways and then lurched forward and then thrown forcefully back as the great heavy wheels lummocked over the grass and then found the road and ground on whirling and crunching behind heavy pounding hooves toward the castle to the occasional crack of a whip and calls of, 'Heyah! Hoop hup hup haa!'

CHAPTER TWENTY SEVEN

She was bundled along a corridor and into a small room which, when a candle was lit, was revealed to be a cell. They had put her in a cell! Mrs Millicent Simpson – artist, wife, mother, confidante of His August Majesty and reluctant stalwart of the PTA – in a cell! She called out, she called out, she tried to shriek but could only wail, she banged on the door, she woke people about the place and some in the houses and tenements nearby, but they did not do anything, what could they do? They knew neither who she was nor where she was nor how to get there, nor why she wailed and the remoteness of her wailing subsided into their dreams.

Time was dead, 'suddenly' it was gone; she realised that she had unwittingly experienced the end of that entire dimension. The wall was the wall. It did not continue to be the wall, it simply was the wall. Had there been a fly, perhaps, to crawl over it, things might have been different. But there was no fly.

Millicent stared intently at the point where the remaining three dimensions made a point in the corner, and she was able to conceive of it in the abstract as an imaginary point 'A' and she concentrated her unique and powerful forces of cogitation, polished her many facetted sharp and shining wits which so often caught so many little reflections.

She saw that the marshalling of fat men in uniforms to manipulate the unwilling into tight little airless cubicles was itself dependent upon imagination; there was a mythic idea which gave legitimacy to the bullying and imprisonment of people, for without the ideas about the kingdom and its ordering which Horrocks and his clan had grown up with and believed to be the natural and right way of things, Millicent could not have been snatched and put away. She was here because of imagination – a perverse imagination, stunted and curtailed, often frightened of its own shadow, but one which had at its root a myth, the myth of the monarch. She was not one to be deceived by false dichotomies and knew that fact and fiction were twins which could not exist without one another. Those who had imprisoned her could not know that her imagination was a thing apart from their imagination, was in itself a thing full of wonder, a thing of a capacity that could not be guessed or measured and could never be locked up, neither for ever nor for now. She would experience the history and texture and physicality of the circumstance she found herself in, she would dwell upon some flaked paint and a piece of cotton under the bed to rebuild the passing thoughts of those who had been here and gone, she would use the smell of the blanket to recreate the weather which had rolled about the harvest of oats which had fed the colossal horse that had pulled the wagon that had brought her here; she would enter the grain of the yellow wood on the leg of the bed and see the wrinkles on the skin of the mother of one of the fat blue-buttoned men, she would interrogate the sullen flagstones of the floor and know some of the boots and the bare feet they had felt, that had crunched and slapped here, and she would follow the ghostly spoor of guilty men; she would be ready to receive the knowledge that the innocent were also culpable and that goodness declined as the light failed and that the misery of the dark was a punishment undeserved for a crime that was shocking but misunderstood.

She did not dwell on the immediate cause of her predicament, of her disappointment – she had been thrown round a sharp corner and must deal with what was before her. But had she done so, she would have worked out that she was probably here because the picture she had unwittingly painted for Horrocks and his men and those who manipulated him (the shadowy rich fat men cocooned in the status quo) was of a woman, a common woman, of dubious inclinations who had become intimate with the King – who had usurped in fact the sort of intimacy that they ought to have with the King but had not – and was on the point of spiriting him away on some clandestine mission which would endanger the royal personage, and thereby also the institution of the monarchy and the stability of the state. She was an enemy of the way things should be, she was a force intent on worming her way into the fabric of the structured hierarchy, the armorial pyramid, which they and their clan saw as a sort of tent to keep bad things out.

They, these people and their ilk and minions, had taken Freddie and made a sign of him, a little crown with a lion on it, and put him on everything – he was stamped on the tin bowl and on the bed, he was small and yellow and stitched onto the collars of the fat blue men, he was black and smudged at the head of the notices pasted high on the wall, he was on the doors of the black maria. In this way they sought to make him omnipresent, to make a prayer for his approval of everything that was done – for it was all done in his name. Many of them had hardly ever seen him and some in fact had never seen him in the flesh, but they all believed in him, believed that he was right and good and unquestionable and generated by divine forces because his father had so been and his father before him etc. The whole of authority was sanctioned by a fairy story, a heavily embroidered history wherein the scarce truths were heavily stitched over and no longer visible; which boldly declared in all the school books that Freddie's progenitors had been the foundation and the saving and preserving of the patria and anyone who said otherwise was wrong.

Millicent was now locked in the dark heart of this story and cast as a bad goblin, a threat to the very time upon which the once was and had always been. But it was not the only story and Millicent was about to begin a powerful tale of her own wherein she played a different part; she would twist the fable before your very eyes and reveal villains that had so far evaded all the familiar chapters and when they were brought out into the rigid rays of the great round sun shining over the wooded hills of the last page they would be shamefaced, hangdog and in chains.

She had found a stub of pencil in her pocket and had been drawing on the wall representations of many small items and utensils. She was shading the perforated edge of a tram ticket. It was a ticket for the tram she might have taken across the town on her way to meet Freddie, whereas, instead, she had walked. She had drawn, low down on another wall, the coat she might have worn had the season been otherwise; and high up, beside the door, the telephone in Dumbleton Close, which would ring unanswered in the distant ear of her mother in a fortnight's time if she were not returned. There were other items, of more private and obscure significance. And there was a donkey. She did not understand why she had drawn the donkey.

The process of the evolution of each image etched away at the shadow of Chronos, giving a length and span to what she drew, and making a sort of time, not the sort of time you could properly notice or count, but it was a sequence and the next thing was that she lay down to sleep. Lay down upon the stained and dusty ticking which had been indifferent to so many troubled dreams, and impervious to the anxieties of its many ghostly guests. Tears had seeped upon it, but all were dried and rejected, mere salt among the mildew; the imprisoned mattress was neither innocent nor guilty, and cared nothing for those that were.

Then, in the middle of the night – which persisted outside – the door was opened and time itself re-admitted to the cell. Just the slightest clunking of the bolt and then a quiet creak as it swung only a little way open. No voices, no footsteps, it was as if it had done it by itself. There was, however, a figure in the passageway, standing still and silent some yards off, his outline vague but discernible, sketched in shadow by some feeble illumination that glowed from round the corner beyond him.

When Millicent looked and hesitated round the thick edge of the door he beckoned and moved off. Gripping only her pencil she followed, wide-eyed and in a turmoil of silent gratitude and wonder at the power of her art.

At each corner the figure beckoned her on. They began to descend flights of steps and the air became damper and damper until in what must surely be the lowest passages there were drips everywhere, and the walls smelt of rotting seaweed. There was hardly any light, the floor was uneven with loose flagstones rocking as she stepped upon them and there were some slabs of stone just lying in the way – she stubbed her toe several times and when she cried out her cry had an echo which was lower pitched, oddly distorted, and sounded more like a moan than the yelp of pain which had given rise to it. Which was very strange. The beckoning figure held a lantern and was too lithe and youthful to be truly ghostly. Who could it be?

Then he was no more. She had turned a corner to find only his lantern left on the ground. Ghost or not, he had spirited himself away into the darkness. Cautiously she approached the lantern and took it up. She saw, as she did so, that she was standing beside a door; a door not unlike the one to her own cell but much much older, dirtier, rustier and even more forbidding. Was it to this door that she had been lead? Was that the beckoner's purpose? Had it been he who had let her out? Had he a key? Who had he been? She was lost and at a loss down here. She had been, with Freddie, much aloft in the great castle, she knew the apartments of state and the high and private rooms, she knew the battlements and certain turrets, but she had never been taken down amongst the black roots of the place, never thought about the dripping foundations, tunnelled and creviced with forgotten holes and sad and wicked histories. Where was she? Could she ever find her way back? Most importantly – why had she been brought here?

The unsteady flame of the lantern flickered its yellow light across the silver of the dripping stones and, when she lifted it up, licked the thick rust of the iron grille high in the door.

She stood still and listened. Was there a way out? She ought to be seeking a way out of the castle, she needed to find Frederick, but somehow she found herself motionless beside this grim door listening to the wet walls and the squeak of an invisible rat.

The mysteriously youthful beckoner, meanwhile, made his way along a low tunnel which slanted steeply upwards and ended at a little door, which was not locked. He passed quietly out into the night, making his way along a path which lead circuitously to another door, in a wall, which admitted him to a garden: a garden now not unknown to Jemima Cake, a garden wherein Ruscum was wont to take his lunch.

Behind and beneath a mulberry tree a donkey waited patiently. He may have been asleep, it was difficult to tell, the garden itself, under a stilled effervescence of stars, was dreaming, slowly ranging through its own history, delighting in itself, but unable and unwilling to regret things which happened beyond its bounds.

CHAPTER TWENTY EIGHT

Millicent was not tall enough quite to see through the grille in the door. She bethought herself of the stone block that had hurt her foot on her way here and, taking up the lantern, made her way back to find it. It took all of her strength to lift, stumble and drag it by degrees to the door. She doubled up, hands on hips to catch her breath after the effort, and as she regained her equilibrium she became aware of breathing other than her own. She mounted the block, and before she looked she put her ear to the iron and listened. There was a heavy sort of snoring which rose and fell in tortured lumbering arpeggios punctuated by a wheezing as of a blacksmith's bellows. She turned and put her eye to the lattice of square holes.

At first she could see nothing at all. Then slowly, the thinnest wash of grey was introduced to her straining eye as the distant dawn was reflected and refracted from an invisible sky to the underside of the bridge arch, to the surface of the river and then, like some interloping elf, up again through an ironbound aperture and obliquely onto the ceiling of the cell. Suddenly straw was kicked by the shuffling of heavy limbs, there was another movement, and then, in the limit of Millicent's craning vision there was an eye. Sad and red in a huge dark head.

Even in the difficult circumstances of standing tip-toe on a lump of granite with the side of her face flattened against cold rust and her neck protesting against the unnatural contortion, she could be sure it was not a human head. Very like a human head, expressive like a human head, but not a human head. She was, from the very first moment the dim light had begun to reveal the prisoner, filled with pity, for the head was sad like a human head, sadder indeed than any merely human head could be. There was something more fundamental, more heart rending, more deeply sorrowful about the face than could be seen in any mere human face: there displayed was an innocence which had been betrayed in the cruellest way. It had been offered a salvation it had no need of, and then brutally punished for failing to understand what it could never understand – the predicament it had been lured and goaded into.

Millicent watched for a while. The poor beast was awake but it hardly moved.

He was in an old place. He inhabited an old darkness and had done so for what must surely have been a long time, and that time must of necessity be by now an old time. The sorrow and misery that palpably overlay everything in and around the cell had a thickness and a depth that could only have accrued amongst the layering of seasons without number. He must surely, thought Millicent, be very old – even though the blackness throws a veil over what he actually looks like. Anyone, indeed, peering into this gloom, would have believed they saw a prisoner of time itself who had existed here a lifetime.

She wanted to speak to it but could not begin, it was after all an animal and would not be able to reply. She banged lightly on the grille with her fist – he stirred, she thought – and she said, 'Hello,' in a whisper as the red eyes were slowly turned toward the door, turned with no great expectation or curiosity.

He was an ape: male, very large, despondent. It was obvious to the acute Millicent that his faculties had been eroded away until there remained only the most feeble mental pulse, his mind had all but ceased to function, all he could do was look, look at the wall, look at the door, look at the straw, look at a rat; he could imagine nothing, he could hope for nothing; his history, his mother, the long sequence of life before, was all lost to him; everything had dwindled to sitting here amidst nothing, even the diurnal routine of light and dark had no meaning. Her heart ached for this poor creature and its plight totally eclipsed her own as she wondered what on Earth she could do. Could she get him out? Could she feed him?

The dreadful peace was intruded upon by a noise of distant clanking, the swinging of hinges, the rattle of a lock, ponderous footsteps. Had she been alone, she would have run back into the dark tunnels, but somehow she was not inclined to leave this cell door, it would have been cowardly, as if she were abandoning a child. She had entirely forgotten her status as an escapee and was eager only for information about the creature's plight and to be told who was responsible for the injustice. So she waited as the footsteps got nearer and a light appeared round a corner.

A subterranean constellation came into being when a light swayed and twinkled far off in the tunnel and made a Pollux with the Castor which was the little pool of light from Millicent's lantern. The new star approached steadily and did not seem alarmed by the appearance of an unwonted entity in the darkness. There was a shuffling sound of the dragging of old boots, and, as this and the light got closer, a sound of old and laboured breathing. There was no shout, no challenge, the bent figure of the old warder said nothing until he was within a yard of Millicent when he raised his lantern with difficulty and she could see the bald head, the grey beard, the blotched red skin oscillating slightly in the swinging yellow light and could smell his old clothes and the secret flesh within, which longed for, and may already have begun, the long process of mummification.

'Now then? Now then?'

She was still standing on the granite and was considerably taller than the old man anyway so he might have been excused some trepidation but he evinced none at all; a sort of tired annoyance was the main feature of his tone. Millicent formed the impression that he could not care less who she was, he just wished she was not there, and the sigh which punctuated his utterances was a resignation about something having arisen which would impede the steady grinding out of his routine.

'Now then?'

He could have gone on with, 'Who are you? What are you doing down here?' but for now, he left it at that, having faith in the little phrase to carry implicitly such baggage, and more beside.

She looked on at his decrepit hunched figure, the dirty coat, the huge vein throbbing visibly on the smudged bald head, the tumbleweed beard, matted in parts, frizzy and free in others, branches of it progressing in different directions having grown indifferent to the face that had once so long ago been their seedbed, and she saw the long black nails on the gnarled fingers and looked into the dull eyes and felt as if down here in the slow decay of the black deep dark insides of the ancient citadel the medieval age crept on, clung to itself, refused to implode into the dust of history and continued to be oblivious to the time that might pass elsewhere. This man might have been slugging through these stone corridors since the fourteenth century.

The warder had not encountered another human being at all in the last fortnight, and could not remember ever having seen anyone in this particular tunnel, but his being was by now largely impregnable to surprise, and abandoned by any sense of wonder. He remained susceptible to irritability, however, even if the energy needed to give proper vent to it was largely lacking.

'Now then.'

'Who are you? Are you in charge down here?'

'Nay, oo are you?'

'Is this poor beast in your care? If so you should be sacked. It's an outrage, it's utterly inhumane, you should be ashamed of yourself.'

'Whaaaa? Shut thi gob! Ooojoothink you are? Choodooin ere anyway?'

'Have you brought food for him? Come on, open up, I want to see the poor thing.'

'Never open up!' (A snort which may have been representative of laughter.) 'Never open up, ee'd kill yah!' (Another snort as he put down the can he'd been carrying in his other hand.) He kicked open the sliding hatch at the bottom of the door and pushed the can with its dark sloppy mess through the hole. All the metallic and gritty noises raised the insignificance of the little daily routine to an echo greater than it would have merited in less lonely caverns.

'Who is this animal? Whose is this animal? How does it come to be down here?'

'Eurggh?'

'Who owns it? Who put it down here? Does the Royal Zoo know about him?'

'Eurrggh? Choowant? Taint yorre bizziness missus. Get back upstairs. My job eer, get raff.'

His use of speech had got to be as rusty as the iron on the door, and he was making words up, though he didn't know it.

Millicent Simpson, however, made it known that she was not inclined to 'get raff', and insistently repeated her questions. Herself miraculously a prisoner no more, in the aftermath of the weirdness of her dramatic incarceration and the surprise of her release she found that, unbound, she was suddenly become more powerful, even as if she might be physically enlarged, and this sad dark old fleabag would not prevail against her.

The ape, stimulated by Millicent's bang on the door, stirred now to the noise of the food can, and to the voices. The great head rotated a degree and the heavy lids lifted slightly. There in the unknown, beyond the door, there was someone – not the old man. There was the sound and smell of a female human. He was like a desiccated plant surviving an eternity of drought, which senses moisture in the atmosphere. It was not in itself enough to remind him of hope, not enough to make him believe in anything beyond straw and darkness and the long death, but his ears were instantly revived and listening as acutely as they could, stimulating the stagnant brain to prepare to remember these rare, precious sounds. People yet lived and could come near him.

Millicent was agitated and determined to get to the bottom of this appalling cruelty. The animal must be rescued from this terrible place and rehabilitated in the zoo or somewhere. She must do for it what the mysterious young man with the lantern had done for her, if she did not or could not, then she ought to go back and lock herself up again, for she surely did not deserve to be free.

'How long has he been here? Who brought him down here?'

'Moirrghhh,' shrugged the old man.

'How long have you been here? Was he always here? Were you here when they brought him down? Speak? You must know, come on!'

His feeble attempts to turn and shuffle off, his dismissive grunts, were not to avail him any relief, and after a while, inevitably, he gave way like a sandcastle before an incoming tide. The things he said, however, were not what Millicent expected to hear. At first the responses she managed to cajole out of him were just mutterings without even any spaces between the words so she had to keep repeating her questions and she only just stopped herself from grabbing hold of his shoulders and shaking him like a naughty child. But then, in a mixture of surrender and a defiant desire to be let alone to go back to whatever private hole he lived in, he raised his head and said, 'King!'

'What? What do you mean?'

'King. This 'ere is the King's animile. Ee brought it 'ere. All the animiles is iz. Yort t'know, that anybody knows that.'

'Well, yes, of course the zoo and all its animals belong to the King, but I'm asking about this ape here, who brought this animal *here*?'

'King!' he said with a hint of exasperation, and seeing his effect, adding with a little resurgence of his recalcitrance, 'Ooo are yooo anyway, yavn't told me that yet av yer?'

'Do you mean the King himself *personally* brought this animal here?'

'Aye, I doo, I sawrim.'

We're all crazy left to ourselves; we cannot be crazy together, because when we are together, all behaving in the same way, whatever we're doing, however senseless, is normal and therefore sane. But the sanity which rises to the surface of a lone man's mind cannot be so called because it does not conform. This lonely sanity is a unique and maverick animal wandering its own path, deeper into the woods farther and farther away from the farm, charting the recondite bends in its own uniquely logical path.

Through the years and the isolation, the old chatelain had grown within his head an image, a fabulous amalgam of the character of the castle and the persona of the King and the kingdom which was somewhat his own. Though it had begun the same as everyone else's. The personage of the King had become for him by now utterly conflated with the motif of the crown and also and most particularly with the lion couchant which surmounted it. He could not now separate the physical breathing entity which was Dagobert IV from the heraldically stylised figure of the red lion. In his mind when he recalled, as Millicent asked him to do, the night the ape was brought, tightly roped about the arms, down to this dungeon, he saw before his mind's eye a lion rouge with fierce eyes and a long wavy tongue manhandling the packaged beast with only the help of a couple of footmen.

'Arrr aye aye, I sorrrim aawrright, all a-roaring and a-shoutin' and im, im,' (he waved the back of his hand at the door) 'screaming and screeching and baring iz fangs. They weren't noice y'know, neither of erm, black and red beasts.'

Millicent held the lantern up close to his face and frowned intently.

'Took three on 'em, lion and two gert footment with truncheons.'

'Why? Why did they bring this animal here? Why did they lock him up here? Why was he not taken to the zoo? Where did he come from, where did they get him?' asked Millicent insistently. She was greatly puzzled and intrigued and not a little disturbed. Could she believe Freddie had personally manhandled a great ape into a dungeon? Nothing could be more uncharacteristic. And... he had never ever mentioned an ape, never spoken of having an ape, of there being an ape of any sort in his collection. He was a man who needed no encouragement to regale you with epic and minute descriptions of anything from a lovebird to a binturong, a man proud and obsessed with his menagerie almost to the exclusion of everything else it seemed at times – and he'd never ever mentioned a huge chimpanzee. This was peculiar. But her witness, though his age, decrepitude, and remnants of uniform gave him an incontrovertible authenticity as having belonged to these black tunnels for years and years, was not an easy subject to extract information from. Millicent wanted facts and dates, but she could see that he only had memories, memories into which his mind may well have twisted and weaved dreams and gossip and half-truths until the story as he told it was likely to be more myth then record. But she persevered and the warder forgot that he did not know who she was, and losing sight of considerations like what right she might have to be here, he gave himself up to the conversation.

In the end – he said it so often and believed it so plainly – she accepted it: that the King had indeed himself brought the unfortunate ape down here. And its name was Nicodemus.

When she began to ask where the animal had been brought from, this elicited some grins and some hectic short nods but at first no words. She gave way now to her previous inclination and grabbed his elbow and shook it gently, and his connections flared back into life and he said – and he sounded a little surprised – 'Oodeneden Abbey.' He said it again, as if he had just remembered it, 'Oodeneden Abbey' and the grin came back.

Everyone had heard of Oodeneden Abbey. It was the royal retreat, the country estate to which generations of monarchs and their extended families had taken themselves for extended summer holidays and extended Christmas breaks, each invariably affording an 'informal' photographic opportunity for the press. There was usually a dog and a tartan rug somewhere visible, to emphasise how casual the royal relaxation could be and the classlessness of picnic accoutrements. There had never been, as far as Millicent was aware, an ape in the picture.

Millicent looked again into the cell. The prisoner had moved closer to the door and looked straight back through the grille. Millicent was deeply moved once more by his plight and clenched her fists.

'This is monstrous! Why on Earth is he locked down here? What about all the other animals in the lap of luxury up in the zoo? Why did the King bring this one down here and treat him so badly? Do you know? You must tell me?'

The old man's Oodeneden grin had gone and he turned his beard on one side as he looked up at her with his tired eyes and said in a soft hoarse whisper, intimating in the one word that he had seen more death and unpleasantness in his long life than she could imagine, 'Dangerous.'

Millicent stared back at him with a questioning frown.

'Killed'un, didden 'e? S'what'ey say. Killed'un.'

She was shocked.

And he felt a tremor of satisfaction at her discomfiture and then – an unfamiliar feeling, one which in him had come close to atrophy – a sympathy for her. And with the trickle of sympathy there then began to rush upon him, miraculously, a sudden quickening of sorrow. The routine, the dusty cruel and imperious heraldry, the long wait for the inspection that never came, imagined trumpets, the clean white clock he so often dreamt of, all the drab cornerstones of his life were suddenly shifted and belittled. Some spirit touched him and he suddenly regretted all his long years down here like a pit pony in the moral darkness. It was a revelation. The darkness was not a blanket of legitimacy, but a smothering of sin and cowardice. He was stabbed by a pang of loathing for the red lion with his long tongue and his ancestral mastery. Holding up his lantern, he looked at her again, into her dark and sparkling eyes and he wondered if she were an angel, and he was aware that with her coming there would be an upheaval, there would be cataclysm and the quiet, dripping, black, interminable numb certainties would be prized open and the light would shine in and he would be examined, and chaste and holy knights would put him to the sword for he was too old for true repentance, and his bowels churned and sweat trickled in his dirty grey whiskers and how could it be that what was right was wrong and how could the red lion betray into error his loyal men?

'Killed who? Who did he kill? Are you sure? When was all this?'

Millicent had to wait for her answers which could arise only slowly out of a mind which was in the throes of squelching from the sludge it had been sunk into for a quarter of a century.

''E killed 'er. Killed the Queen. I think she was the Queen. Yes, the Queen – it was. We wasn't supposed to say anything about it. Ever to say anything about it. Only us knew. Yes it were the Queen. Oim sure it was 'er, as 'e killed. Only ever the four on us... own'ee the four on us as knoo.' Thus did a secret kept sleeping for a generation blunder back into life. 'Well five if you count 'im, but oim not sure you can count 'im.'

Perhaps its secretness had been less in the end than his failure to remember it, and the absence of anyone who wanted to know. Though he said it somewhat uncertainly, as if he were in the act of recalling a dream, there was no doubt about what he said. It was Millicent's black eyes that had done it, shining brighter than the lantern, they had by the power of their stark honest beauty opened the old man like a tin-opener slicing into the feeble metallic stronghold of dead fish. After so many years the pungent aroma, the challenging tang of a shameful skeleton, had been released once more into the world. But in this case the skeleton had flesh on its bones and shuffled on its knuckles toward the door.

The ape listened. He listened to the people, there... just outside. There were two; there had never been two, always only one, the same one, the old one. The other one was a woman. He was at the door.

His breath was heavy now and full, and Millicent could hear

it, wafting straw fragments across the iron grille. It was suddenly now the most important thing for Millicent to secure the release of this animal. She did not understand the situation or its origins but she was sure that, beyond common humanitarian considerations, there was a great importance attached to freeing the ape.

CHAPTER TWENTY NINE

There was another fire in the old town. Men ran with ladders and a bucket chain was formed, people cried, 'Where is the engine? Call the engine!'

There was altogether a great deal of noise in the night down there, shouting and then singing and chanting were heard, and there were people wearing masks cavorting about and upsetting people and there was excitement and crowds and running this way and that and people looking anxiously out of windows and people throwing things out of windows and people throwing things into windows and at windows and breaking glass and stealing things and dogs barking and horses kicking down their stalls and the ringing of bells and the sound of a hurdy gurdy on a roof top.

Perhaps the burning down of the bakery, some time before, which the powers-that-be had almost forgotten, had been indeed a sign, a portent, an omen. For amidst the drunkenness, amidst the scuffles the cuffing and buffeting and kicking and the settling of scores, the random and playful vandalism that had erupted alongside this new fire (in a wool warehouse) there was sufficient desperation and enough natural captains down there to marshal it, that there could well develop from it something with a very long historical shadow.

The fire had actually been an accident but there were those that watched for just such a moment, just such a time, and *Carpe Diem* was the word amongst the clubs and gangs, saints and demagogues, who burnt their candles in the attics and derelict outhouses of the old town and who had long wanted to lend a shoulder to the up-ending of the world.

It was not just the cranked and the cranked up, not just the revolutionists. It was not just the hard up and the disadvantaged – though there were plenty of them. There was no shortage of the put upon, many were poor and a lot were at the end of their tether and desperate to throw a brick at something or somebody – but there was something else, something which might easily ally itself with political discontent but which was indefinable and whose origin could not be traced. It was something natural and cosmic. Like an eclipse in that it disturbed the diurnal certainties of life on the planet, except that it was invisible. There was something whose time had come round, had revolved and evolved and nothing could stop it, no amount of orders in council or new tax laws or tinkering with import duties or fines or punitive sentences or royal beneficence could avert the rumbling of the sinkhole that was preparing to open up below all the age old certainties of the kingdom. It was the time for cataclysm.

No matter what little thing began it, or appeared to begin it, it was the time for the times to change – and for some they would go suddenly and alarmingly backwards and for yet others it would seem as if they were being catapulted into the end of days. The upheaval was inevitable, ubiquitous and shocking, like lemmings or flying ants.

There had long been a mood in the old town, a special mood unprecedented in its weight and pervasiveness, a sort of mass despondency, a smouldering communal unrequitedness, which had inched now to the brink of terminality, and no amount of bread, circuses or exemplary punishments would alleviate it. But no one either involved in it or watching from a safe distance could say what actually brought it about, what made it inevitable; no one had been quietly able to observe the long term concatenation of events and say this will tomorrow explode like a firework or unfolding rose petals, there were no intimations, no precursive events, no repeating historic pattern, no symptoms, no particular outrage, no perceptible tipping of the scale, no pattern of history repeating itself giving rise to wry nodding smiles; so the sudden beating of hundreds of terrifying drums brought at first neither tears nor laughter, but a sort of startled jubilation which promised a new madness for all to enjoy – though they could not be certain they would survive it.

CHAPTER THIRTY

Freddie poured himself another whiskey and sat down and immediately got up again, to look out of the window, but turned back before he got there and sat heavily down again, raising the glass almost to his lips but then putting it down, and putting the second finger of his right hand across his lips as if he would chew it and resting his forefinger vertically on his cheek. This pose too was short lived. He thought he heard someone in the corridor and jumped up. Expecting a knock at the door, he backed toward the window and looked intently at the brass doorknob. There was no knock, and now he did turn, picked up the glass again and looked out of the window.

He sipped the ripe and round old whiskey and tasted the rich golden distillation, the patient potency of something which had lain hidden through the drifting years until at last it had, in the dark, accumulated to itself the natural histories of water and peat and wood and barley to generate an elemental life. A life of sleep, recollection and dark realisations which imbued the drinker with a silent understanding of the earthy land as it stretched out before its King, here beneath the sun and there beneath the skimming rain. There, far below, lay the expanse of open country, painted with coloured moorland, stippled with forests and etched with waterways, into which he should have been trekking – in search of that which was believed not to exist, the truth blanketed in myth, which he knew now would bring atonement and absolution, purifying his existence with a touch of its magic horn.

According to history as it was written, this country belonged to him, it was by his leave that anyone lived in it or did anything on it, so walking out one morning to meet his friend and wandering where he would, ought not to have been subject to any sanction. He was himself the fount of all sanction. Yet, of course, he could not do as he would wish to do, not openly, not with anyone watching. He would have to sneak out, having made himself unrecognisable, at a time when he was least likely to be seen, (like some respectable burgher in a mackintosh on his way to meet a lady of the night, he thought resentfully) and to this end he had planned his assignation with Millicent quite carefully... only to have the way barred by Vangrannicus's intervention in the form of a reminder of a tedious and insignificant event: an informal reception for veteran embroiderers who had spent lifetimes stitching the great tapestry in the Castle and were coming to take coffee with him beside it in the long gallery.

This annoyance could easily assume the right shape to fit into the jigsaw of paranoia which increasingly he could not help toying with. Did 'they' know what he was planning? 'They' as he thought of them, were the rich and undeservedly decorated, the ugly, hydra-headed lump of malignant courtiers which found the monarchy a useful crutch for the onward march of their aggrandisement, but had no respect for the King, made fun of him behind his back, mocked the rites and rituals and were a thorn in Vangrannicus's side. There were undoubtedly amongst his personal entourage those in their pay, who watched and reported, he was sure of it, though he could not point the finger with any certainty at any particular culprit. Lately he found himself watching for the watchers, and had begun sometimes to peer at those with downcast eyes, to catch them out in a darting glance, or a sidelong look at papers on a desk. He had not used to do this, but felt lately driven to it by those who mumbled amongst themselves and then laughed loudly, in the King's presence, and were surely seeking to undermine him. The great white beast himself had begun subtly to reveal to him how, though everything might look in order, the once holy atmosphere of the court was now come to be curdled by base and venial men.

It ought to be inevitable that Vangrannicus must be at odds with these men, yet he seemed to choose not to see them, and never talked about them. Freddie had never been able to surmount the barrier of correctness with which the Chamberlain surrounded himself, and so could not confide in him over this. Exasperatingly, even though the brass buttoned old man wrapped himself in *comme il faut*, he seemed to be stubbornly blinkered both to the demeanour and the burgeoning menace of this plutocratic faction. That was the way of it with him, nothing else, either less or more, could be expected. As Freddie saw it, Vangrannicus had blinded himself to what was going on, he obviously believed that if he just kept up all the rituals any change would be kept at bay – even the plutocrats' encroachment on power. Another version would be that it was only Freddie who had the vision necessary to pick up all the little clues (some of them very little) and understand the lie of the land.

Vangrannicus was for the King and for Tradition. He believed in the personal ascendancy of the ruler, and that the person transcended the office, and that eccentricity in a King was an expected characteristic of authenticity – any King worth his salt should build a zoo or fiddle with clocks or invent superior windmills, but nonetheless the prospect of King Dagobert IV out in the countryside in mufti without minders would have him quickly in a state of irritated consternation. Freddie's passing thought that Vangrannicus had concocted this embroideresses' reception to stymie his departure was swiftly rejected however – he could not possibly know anything of Freddie's intended escapade. But the fat hangers-on, the tubs of slime with their medals and ribbons, 'they,' might well have wind of it. He could not say how, but he felt all the time now that 'they' knew or suspected what he was thinking or planning, and he had an irresistible feeling that they would put every obstacle in his path that they could.

They must not prevail, these vile goblins, these sly and smiling gangs who laughed at zoology and libraries and believed only in their cushions and their caviar, ostentatiously mouthing their prayers and bowing low, the hypocrites; he knew each of them was in fact their own god, and that they made fun of all the offices of state, and slyly schemed their selfish greedy schemes.

He took another drink of whisky. It was, of course, to a great extent all his own fault. His ambivalence towards his role and its ridiculous responsibilities had led to a perpetual mental flirtation with abdication but not so far to any decisive strategy for constitutional change, only to his spending more time on his zoo and in his library. He had been an ostrich. He played his part, wore the costume, but then sloped off at every opportunity to manage his menagerie and delve obscure tracts. The tragedy was that while he was being an ostrich he had known he was being an ostrich. When he brought his head up from the sand, things had not gone away. It was his own fault. Instead of calling for revolution and jumping ship in a blaze of glory and defiance, instead of taking the reins – and then throwing them away – instead of gathering about him men of talent and ambition who shared his liberal views, he had done nothing, and like a poisonous infection these vile caterpillars had coalesced into a huge fat pustule contaminating all the vital organs of state. Their manoeuvring had been subtle and designed not to break the surface but it was obvious to those involved, and he knew all about it, oh yes, of course he did, you couldn't fool the King. And it was all his own fault.

He was like a dog tethered in the yard, seeing dark things sliding over the walls but cursed with an inability to bark. That door behind him was not locked. There was nothing to stop him wandering down into the street if he wanted to; nothing but decorum, and five hundred years of the way things must be seen to be done. He was manipulated in the shadow of the great awkwardness threatened by any out and out confrontation he might attempt to initiate.

He took another gulp of whiskey and stared out over the land, imagining that his eye might magically light upon the small and determined figure of Millicent striding toward the rendezvous, a tiny detail in that wide vista, an ant of supreme importance, and if he did see her he would know all would be well. But he was far too high up, it was all a long way away.

The door clicked and a nervous footman started to utter the apology which must precede what he had been sent up to say, but before he could finish the King, swallowing the last of the whiskey as he went, held out the empty tumbler, dropped it into the man's startled grasp, and strode out and along the corridor, disappearing down the servants' stairs. Two floors down he skipped into a little corridor and through a tiny secret door and emerged five minutes later between geography and topography in the gloomy but sanctuarial library. There would be disappointment and perturbation amongst the embroideresses, but today he could not help that.

The dark and the smell of the books acted immediately like a cold compress on his panic and he decided he would hide here for a little while and decide what to do. It was good to be invisible. Whilst Freddie was invisible, the King both exists and does not exist, he decided. Without him, these evil forces would be much more exposed; they needed him in their clutches, to be paraded about, to acquiesce, to be seen as collaborating. As long as he continued to exist but could not be found, then things could not be changed so easily. (The fact that this was the ostrich mentality in another guise was lost on him for the moment.) And if they did not know where he was, they could not say he was dead, and he could not be definitively usurped. If that's what they were plotting to do – and increasingly he was convincing himself, in his wilder, whiskey-fuelled moments, that some of them at least would even go so far.

He was on his haunches in the gloom beside the Rivers of South America, tapping his temples with his fists, gurning and grimacing – a dark period was beginning, he knew it. A blanket of nightmare was going to be thrown over everything and old certainties would be invisible and then uprooted and removed from the reach of desperate fingers. But he would not give in, he must prove as solid as the statues of his ancestors, defiant against any tide, be it sweeping in or out, forward or backward. He would not allow the glorious golden dream of the unicorn expedition to be snatched away from him by these vile exigencies, by tawdry turpitudes, by guilds of needling women, and the little worldly ambitions of little worldly people, by the cowardly baying of a pack of slavering oftcomers and parvenus – the most detestable moral cripples, all of them.

Gaining strength from his little whispered tirades, and the whiskey, whose flame continued to glow within him, he hauled up his great pocket watch – it was eleven minutes to eleven – and made a plan. Find some old clothes and make his way through as many unconsidered little alleys, vestibules, aisles, secret doors and corridors as would be persuaded by his memory to make themselves available to him, and so to the little gate that led into the garden and thence out through the door in the wall that opened onto the river bank, but not under the bridge, no not that way, don't think about the bridge, turn left and then he could skirt the town and be out over the meadow by mid-day and Millicent would still be there. Perhaps, perhaps Millicent would still be there. Of course Millicent would still be there.

Freddie pictured her in the appointed place, standing there on the appointed ground, looking anxiously about her. And then her person dissolved into empty ground; he saw the earth and the sky, and the breeze wafting freely through the reeds which grew around the space where there was no Millicent. (What he did not envisage, was the sight of Millicent, standing there in the proper place, serious but with a strange half suppressed smile of expectancy and surprise, holding hands with something.)

It was barely noon but the sky above the garden wall was dark and looked thick with bulging black cushions of smoke. There was a strange noise too, like a continuous groan, and then came an intermittent cracking noise, like whips or something. He hurried along and found the door in the wall. As he went along the little path and passed quickly near (but not beneath) the bridge he looked up and saw straggling groups of people running over it, then a few hesitated and turned back and others appeared, running from the other side, some carrying children. He heard someone scream and then a large stone struck the parapet a glancing blow before making a heavy thumping plunge into the water pushing up a high lazy fountain which hung in the air before falling slowly back, releasing drops which blew onto the ground just behind him with a raking patter. It was unusual, it was strange, but he was not curious, he could not concern himself with a little riot just now, he had far too much to think about; he passed quickly on his way, pulling up the collar of his coat and searching for the little alley which would take him on to the little lane that skirted the town and would deliver him to the open country.

When he found it the little alley had 'Anarky' (sic) chalked on the wall and there was an old settee up-ended and leaning on a barrel. A large black rat scuttled through the weeds along the foot of the wall and then calmly turned to stare, one paw in the air, as he passed by. There was the sound of people shouting, but it was some way off and he could not make out what it might be about, and then smoke suddenly filled the alley and made his eyes water before a gust of wind dispelled it. He was startled by another rat and stepped in a deep puddle, wetting his thick woollen socks and causing him to curse ('Scrounch it all!'). As he progressed down the lane, which did not quite wind, but persistently kinked (in not always alternate directions) and retained its high old wobbly brick walls on either side, he was further assailed by many hidden things: a burst of loud ugly invisible laughter from somewhere very close at hand; drumming and marching feet from somewhere more distant; a loose horse which looked up from the scruffy patch of grass it had found and looked at him half warily and half expectantly, as if it had had enough freedom and would really like now to be caught and taken home but was not sure that Freddie was the one to do it; and then, at the end, just before the walls stopped and the way opened out with what ought to have been relief on to a common, several small children were sailing a model yacht in a tin bath and looked up to stare in unison. They seemed totally oblivious to the drumming and whooping and clattering.

Their King was now oblivious to it as well and passed by hurrying into the open country.

Thereafter commenced a Royal Progress through some of the more obscure parts of his little kingdom, unheralded, unaccoutred, unmarshalled, unacclaimed, which saw the determined old man, King incognito in old clothes, carrying a little knapsack and wielding a stout stick, tramping with expectation and foreboding in equal and alternating measure, occasionally nodding to the wise words emanating from an invisible presence at his side. But the journey was not supposed to be a solitary one and the place it actually began from was one of immense disappointment – the clearing at the crossroads just by the little white bridge over the tiny river Front, by the chestnut tree, just two miles or so beyond the castle walls where Millicent should have been waiting, but was not. Here he had looked all around, far and near, in every direction, had thrown down his pack and sat on the ground and took out his monster watch, and put it back and took it out again and then he'd sighed deeply and stood up and folded his arms and disconsolately peered around at the ground to see if perhaps she had left a note or a clue or anything.

Despondency welled up around him and within him. Mr Simpson had been found, or come home. She had no further interest in or need of unicorns. He kicked a dry branch. She had simply changed her mind – she had children to look after, she had no servants at all. He had been mad to credit her with the same enthusiasm he had, she had had to go along with him of course, it was the damnable

King thing again! No, no, he would not believe any of that, this was Millicent, Millicent – the most marvellous, dark eyed woman in the world! Artist, goddess, counsellor…red lips, smoking one of his cigars…a meaningfully arched dark eyebrow… the elegant sensitive fingers… Then he had taken out his hip flask, swigged, and proceeded to shuffle carefully and infinitely slowly over the whole ground, peering intently. It was only then, when no trace of the richly desired Millicent, she who was to have been his inspiration, helpmeet, encouragement and support, had been found, that he trudged out of the clearing, which was now the very pit of vacuity. It was to be a good many miles before he was finally persuaded by the unicorn – who before he did so had at times faded almost to nothing – to carry on rather than retreat and forget about the whole escapade.

But carry on he did – after first hurrying back to the clearing and writing a note, which ran to three pages torn from his notebook – with several crossings out and two insertions which had to be forced into tiny spidery occupation of the margin – which he carefully lodged in the fork or a tree. Standing back to make sure it was visible to anyone casually inspecting the area, his tongue still extended in concentration, he might have noticed a plume of smoke rising from the distant town and a glinting from an upper turret window in the castle which was reflecting flames down below. He might have noticed them and been concerned, but he did not and was not. All he saw was his message in the tree ('Scrounch it all!' he murmured as the breeze dislodged it and he hurried forward to set it right.)

He might not have noticed it, but others did. Jemima Cake looked up as she crossed the yard outside her office in the zoo; Newsome, butler to the missing Willoughby looked up from his pantry doze; Prince Antonio frowned as he looked up from reading his correspondence on the terrace of his suite; Ruscum looked up from his cheese and pickle sandwich and ran, still chewing, back through the garden, staring at the sky and stumbling through the door in the wall; old Joe at the zoo gate looked up from staring at a puddle in the ground, smoking his pipe.

And Millicent looked up at it as she heaved open the heavy red door of the phone box in a sedately residential street. A very large black ape gripped her hand tightly and would not be separated from her so that they were squashed together inside and the door could not close on them. She had to fumble one-handed and crook the receiver awkwardly in her wrong ear as she dialled, heavy primate breaths filled the quiet kiosk, and then the clank, clash and whirr of Button A momentarily startled the beast, who delivered a single retributive thump to the black box and then clasped Millicent with renewed strength and would have climbed into her arms if he could.

'Hello, Mum? Yes, yes, I'm fine... Not sure, soon I hope... And the children?... Oh, she'll be fine she's always doing it, don't worry... Look, Mum, can I ask you something? I know you know all the history and everything and I thought you would know this, well probably everyone does except me...yes, ha ha...but you know the King is a widower right?... The King, yes the King... What actually happened to his wife? I can't seem to remember a funeral or anything, I know I was probably quite small but I just thought, you would know of course, what did she die of?... Oh, oh, I see... very strange... and they never... no, well, I don't suppose they could, really... oh really? Goodness me!... and there was never any... no oh, I see...but you say people didn't believe it?... some of them... so what were they saying?... You're kidding, I've never heard that before...oh right. Look, thanks Mum, thanks very much for that... I'll tell you later, and thanks for that and thanks very much for everything... I'm sorry I've really got to go now... I'll call you later and be back as soon as I can... What? Oh a few days probably, love you, bye.'

The door swung slowly back with a low grinding squeak and a dull thump as they stood in the deserted avenue, Millicent looked again up at the lowering sky and then down at the red eyes, still moist with tears, which looked back in grim and desperate adoration; yet as she felt the strength of the grip of the hairy hand she sensed – and it may have been implicit in the grip itself, or it may have been her own intuition – a quiet warning against inconstancy.

CHAPTER THIRTY ONE

Millicent's arms on the ape's body would have looked puny and pathetic, like some malformation, the tragic outcome of some terrible syndrome. The ape's arms would have looked ridiculous on Millicent, a waxworks' or taxidermist's joke. Nicodemus was covered in black hair, matted in places; Millicent was covered in a kahki parka. Even so they stood together on the pavement and there was a warmth and a common animality between them; their posture was mother and son. A bus passed down the road and the two or three people riding on it, clutching wicker shopping baskets, stared as blatantly at the unusual couple as only those within the safe confines of a double-decker can stare. What they saw was a lady with an ape, and they must have admired the sight if they had known what they were seeing which was a lady with an ape cautiously waiting to cross the road before continuing their perilous and uncertain journey into the strange hinterland of civilization. In the no-man's-land that they would shortly lose themselves in, reunions, like all else, were unpredictable and it was not beyond the realms of possibility that history would double back on itself and repudiate lifelong and fundamental assumptions – for the territory they were travelling into certainly bordered on impossible realms. And harboured an increasing number of unusual people, which it was busy making more unusual.

Millicent lead the ape round a corner and they descended a steep crescent of tall villas built for the comfortably wealthy of yesteryear, which had aged to a pleasing softness. Their haughtiness had been largely worn away and its residue now seemed to be overlain by a sort of wisdom, accumulated through the passage of time, so that they were somewhat more friendly now than they had been designed to be. Yet they remained imposing, even if no longer expecting tradesmen to know their entrance. The street stood as a sign of the way things used to be, and of the way thoughts about old times could persist in architecture, and of how difficult it was to eradicate the character of a place. They had three (and sometimes four) storeys, high chimney stacks, elaborate porches and were made of dark red bricks which harmonised with the mood of the mature gardens with their lawns, black trees, evergreens and stone birdbaths. Ivy climbed the high walls, and aspidistras in brass planters obscured the secret drawing rooms from all inspections but that of the imagination. The avenue continued winding down the hill, which became very steep, and moss colonised the cobbled roadway as it did the stone gate-posts and the edges of the steps leading up to the heavily knockered front doors. However inevitable it might be that these residences would at last slide into the sump of dereliction or suffer the cruel disfiguring of modernisation, on this day they yet retained something of their grandeur, and clung to their sedateness, forming a high canyon of gables and turrets and dormer windows and pediments and stone balustrades which towered above and overshadowed the tiny figures of Millicent and Nicodemus. A stern and morose bank of cloud was punctured by sunlight, making the stones, and slabs and dark green leaves, wet from a previous shower, glint and glisten. And yet, though physically dwarfed by the setting, the pair were by no means belittled in dignity as they walked slowly but resolutely down toward the sudden end of the town. This neighbourhood – once so often festooned in patriotic bunting for any little royal occasion – if it knew where Millicent was going, would have taken a modicum of reassurance that the old values it had once hypocritically adorned itself with were not yet entirely dislodged. Indeed, a breath of mild redemption gently stirred the gunnera and quieted the consciences of dead denizens as she passed. The ape did not impinge on the place because he was too short to show up over the walls – had the place been aware of him he would have raised more disquiet.

All the passing impressions, the mute ghosts amongst the wilting palms in the gazebos – some of whom might still be alive – the sad eyed Pekinese confined in upper windows, the history and the declining times, which Millicent was thoroughly aware of but on this occasion could not allow to distract her – indeed she appeared hardly to notice anything as she walked thoughtfully down the street along the residential nave of this fusty bourgeois cathedral – all these impressions, the fascination of the sad facades, could not have had a meaningful impact on the ape, could it? For him, the shapes and styles and textures and colours of the houses and gardens could have no redolence beyond their physicality, could they? And yet... For there was, here and there, a passing resemblance to portions of Oodeneden Abbey, was there not? Where he was said to have spent his formative years. Who indeed is to say just what he saw? What connections he was capable of, as his mind slowly stirred from the petrifaction of imprisonment? There was in fact, garden carpentry on view in exactly the same style that adorned a certain lavish summer house in Oodeneden.

There was a distinct possibility that this large black ape had played a little known, but dreadful, part in forming the character of the Royal Family so respected by the loyal inhabitants of this avenue, and Millicent herself, thinking hard about what her mother had told her, was coming to suspect there was more to the ape's history than the cruelty inflicted upon him. The ape's passing by would have terrified the district if they knew all about him, or indeed anything about him. For these very villas, in their august and self satisfied prime had been the very spine and fabric of the respectability on which the old traditional monarchy seated itself. It could not have occurred to those who built and first lived in these houses that there could ever be, would ever be, anything other than that which had always been. And the King was that-which-had-always-been incarnate. (And 'god', they supposed, as something of an afterthought – religion was really just a sauce to the main course: loyalty, flag, crown, royalty, anthem.) Down this faded thoroughfare of old and solid simple sampler morality – blinkered to the plight of the slave and the foreigner – walked a revolutionary artist, a commoner, (currently in the throes of seducing his royal highness?) and an ape who had... but she was not yet sure that he had... or quite what he had... Notwithstanding, they were forces of disruption and disrespect, and they slid boldly down the avenue, the avenue whose old ethos applauded any brave expedition to find the unicorn, for it accorded with the dusty, colourful storybooks in all of its nurseries, full of pirates and goblins and pixies and dragons and rainbows which were now only stared at by moth-eaten teddy bears and airedales on wheels. (It was from these nurseries of course that rich children, having been taught to believe in impossible things, subsequently graduating to staunch faith in monarchy and primogeniture.) What was by now little understood was that the reality of the unicorn might be more than any nanny had ever bargained for. And the invisible ape, scuttling beneath the coping, the animal ape, neither was he for show or amusement.

The crescent became a lane, which dwindled to a smaller lane and soon they were across a little bridge over one of the great river's little backwaters and out upon the great wild prairie meadow and in sight of Johnson's cottage though they knew it not. The ape asked for nothing by sign or gesture though she knew he must be very hungry. Even without food, however, the novelty of the open country was reviving, and he began to look about him. It was always windy across the great meadow and the breeze lifted the black hair on his arms and propelled the smells of the country into his broad nostrils and a dry leaf into his midriff – little overtures from nature, which was eager to reclaim him.

Behind them, in and about the great citadel, all the people of the town were doing what all the people of the town generally did: some were doing the ironing, some were running riot in the streets and throwing stones at the police, some were not doing anything in particular, some were indulging in a bit of playful vandalism, some were cutting their toenails in the bath, some were plotting the overthrow of the government (which many of those doing the ironing were thinking would be no bad thing), some were ineptly trying to set fire to things which would not light. It must be escaped from, repeated Millicent to herself. The town and all its doings must be pushed back, with a strong arm, for they must get away, she and the ape, away to the blue lanes, they must reach the King, they must find the unicorn, rescue it from extinction.

The cloud of smoke rising above the town did indeed seem, gratifyingly, to decrease in significance the further they got away from it. And at the same time somehow the nature of the expedition itself was changing. She had been intrigued and excited by the prospect of finding an animal which was supposed only to exist in fairy tales, she had been eager for a jolly illicit jaunt with Freddie, but now, suddenly, this quest seemed to be much more than fun and fossil hunting, and casting about for the errant spouse, it now carried with it a huge responsibility of great importance for the future. There was suddenly no question of the unicorn's existence, shc believed in it utterly. Millicent saw a huge canvas stretched before her, beyond the trees, towering into the sky, with great pots of purple absolution waiting to be daubed upon it. If the hope of the unicorn was to be gained at last, they must hurry through the long grass and get where they were going; get to the place which would bring them to itself as long as they gave themselves up to it. Millicent quickened her pace and the ape eagerly lurched and rolled along beside her as they passed Johnson's cottage and found out the track to the little river Frant. They no longer looked back; neither the artist nor the ape. The temporally unstable and guilty serenity of the majestic crescent of villas, the tight, tasteless confined cul-de-sac of Dumbarton Close, the motley old city, alternately raging and sleeping it off, they all were sinking back into the mist which rose from the river and began to roll now across the meadow.

Jemima would travel by bicycle. She had a robust machine, and she had thigh muscles which, as well as being objects of desire for certain men in the hot abstraction of their lust, were also anatomical engines of some considerable and surprising power. They were very capable of propelling a fully loaded bicycle at impressive speeds up dauntingly steep inclines. She had loaded the capacious pannier bags with a thoroughly practical inventory of the necessary and the conceivably useful, having carefully considered all possible eventualities and weighed everything's usefulness against its heaviness and its foldability. The machine was checked all over and oiled. Oiled almost as liberally as the certain men in the abstraction of their lust would desire to oil her thighs.

Pippa and Willis would want to come. Would they be useful? Would they be company? Would they get in the way? She snapped a strap tight on the luggage rack and tried to imagine them pedalling and giggling along behind her through the mysterious lanes. They were certainly capable of pluckiness, and they were good scientists – they could be relied upon to analyse pellets and droppings with accuracy, they were practised and capable in tracking and had been well drilled as sample and note-takers, but... but, there was something which told Jemima they might be *de trop* when it came to this particular expedition. They might not be able to keep up, in more senses than one. So the next morning, just before dawn she checked her watch, settled her foot into the toe clip and pushed off from the kerb alone, and full of a feeling not just of the usual scientific anticipation, but augmented this time with a special sense of adventure, tinged with trepidation, which could not easily be shared.

A long and comprehensive note had been left for her two assistants, emphasising the fact that they were now *de facto* in charge at the menagerie, with so many people mysteriously absent, and listing all the duties they must not neglect whilst she was away. They should be glad of the chance to prove themselves with this temporary promotion – she would have been.

She rolled along beside a high brick wall at the extremity of the old town, on the opposite side of the castle from the disturbances, where it was quiet and not a soul was to be seen in the narrow lane. Turning sharply right, she went under an arch between two round towers and across a short stone bridge spanning the little river which fed into the great river as soon as it rounded the bend past the menagerie. Everything here was quaint and pleasant, swans glided between the bridge piers, rooks squabbled in tall elm trees and the low early sunlight was just beginning to warm everything as the sudden judder of the cattle grid was left behind and the quiet hum of her tyres found the comfortable harmony of a steady ten miles an hour. The open country beckoned.

Twenty minutes later, Jemima had somehow found out a very secret little road which, with a surprising turn, deep dip and sudden rise, took her behind Johnson's cottage, giving her a glimpse of the rear elevation of that modest dwelling not seen by travellers crossing the wide meadow at the front. Rarely seen in fact by anyone. She did not know it was Johnson's cottage or she would have stopped and knocked and made enquiries, but she was sufficiently intrigued by the homely, overgrown and dishevelled dwelling to pull up as she reached the top of the rise and peer through the boughs of elder and oak. A tiny woman in some sort of cowled cover-all was hanging washing on a line. There was no sort of horticulture carried on in the garden, which was wild with grasses, nettles, brambles and ancient neglected apple trees. Though her sharp eyes spied a grass snake emerging from the thick ivy which all but consumed the rotting water butt, her keen powers of observation, honed to a rare acuteness by their lifelong scientific application, must have been in some way befuddled or befogged, for only then did she realise that there was a gigantic rabbit standing on the kitchen step. A rabbit displaying none of the timidity of the species and, looking for all the world as if it had a larger range of preoccupations than the average *lagomorph*. A gigantic rabbit surveying the scene, indeed, with a proprietarial air, one who seemed to approve of the washing, yet without deigning to notice it.

Jemima stood astride her bicycle rooted to the spot, watching the quiet scene for some minutes. The little woman, with a mouthful of pegs, progressed steadily along the line securing grey combinations and thick socks until her basket was empty and then she took up from the long grass the long pole with a notched end which was to prop the soggy laundry rope up into the breeze. Jemima, with all the excitement that usually accompanied the crucial stage of some laboratory experiment, waited to see whether the rabbit, as by far the taller of the two, would lend his assistance. In the event he turned his head slowly in the opposite direction, sniffing the air as if he had detected something which might just be worthy of his refined consideration. Having accomplished alone, with a bit of a struggle, the manipulation of the very long pole, the little woman picked up her basket and went indoors. The rabbit looked up at the sky and then, incorporating a surprising little balletic skip into his about turn on the step, himself went inside. Jemima remained for a few moments looking at the washing. None of it would fit either of them, she thought.

As she moved on along the road Jemima began to look about her with a new circumspection; she realised that in this place her powers of observation must be enhanced with a greater receptiveness to things that were odd. Not things that were impossible, necessarily – anything ostensibly impossible her normal powers of scientific appraisal were capable of dealing with – but things that were more than unusual, or rather, things that were unusual in unusual ways; the dilapidated cottage had been enough to awaken her to a category which she had previously had little or no experience of – the subtly bizarre incorporating the downright incongruous, and she correctly surmised that the character of the territory she was now entering had many such components. It was not just things like suddenly noticing surprisingly large and unobliging rabbits, it was also auditory – the unusually flat pitch of a blackbird's song, for instance, or the blood curdling bleat of a lamb – and it played havoc with one's sixth sense, inculcating unaccountable periods of nervousness and then returning things to normal. She pedalled on, humming the air which she remembered hearing in the castle garden, and hoping that she had what it takes to be uplifted, rather than permanently unsettled by it all. It was, after all, enticing, fascinating, intriguing. Why had she not been here before? Then she found herself feeling – quite powerfully – that she had.

She swept along round three more corners, wobbled with alarm as a scarecrow cropped up in her peripheral vision, then through the sound of her own deep breathing – occasioned by a sudden incline – detected human voices: the sound of conversation of some sort. At the top of the hill she stopped and dismounted. Listening hard she looked all about her. The talking was intermittent: rising a little in volume and then fading away, and then coming back again. She could see no one, even though her practised powers of observation were focused systematically on each segment of the surrounding country, which was an odd mixture of irregularly shaped fields and paddocks (parallelograms, rhombuses, pentograms, etc nothing so commonplace as a rectangle) abundant copses, and out and out woodland. She kicked out the stand on the bicycle relinquishing it to close her eyes and listen intently. Some faint words wafted up from below the hill; faint but distinct, distinct but unrecognisable – they were, she was sure, in the German language.

'*Es war einmal…*'

She could hear only snatches, and the phrase that stuck in her mind was the first one she heard: '*Es war einmal.*' The memory of the sound of these voices swirled around her on top of the hill for a long while after she ceased to be able to hear them. And the scene itself, the patchwork fields, a distant windmill, forests and winding roads, looked especially colourful as she turned a full circle on her vantage point and really began to feel the obscure and puzzling character of this country. Deep in thought, she re-mounted and rolled down the road as it wound its way lazily onward. She found herself imagining her father, looking down on her. He had no experience of expeditions into the unknown and potentially fabulous, and would have been impressed and proud. But also just a little bit jealous, and therefore inclined to let something just a little bit patronising creep into his hesitant smile as he observed the venture – as if the hardships and demands might in the end be less than those he had had himself to endure in far less glamorous endeavours. She did not resent his condescension, it contributed to the myth that he was still greater than she, which is what kept her striving for perfection; Jemima was indeed glad to have him with her for a while, and kept up a sharp lookout hoping for a sight that would impress him.

The ghostly parent was, however, to be denied anything spectacular or conventionally disturbing at the moment – the Lanes waylaid Jemima with quirky sensations but they were quietly wrought by a subtle dappled light on tree trunks for instance, or the moody shadow beneath a lumpy mulberry bush shaped rather like an armchair, and suchlike oddities which were difficult to point out. Nothing as striking or immediate as a very large rabbit – which she was beginning to think now she might have imagined... no, no she had not imagined it, it had been there, no doubt of it. Whatever else befell her here in these blue lanes she would not betray herself to the extent of starting to make things up. She was first a scientist, and might conjecture on the basis of evidence, but she did not make things up. She resolved that on the way back she would investigate the nature and causes of that rabbit.

Meantime she must remember why she had come. Somewhere about here were various people earnestly hoping to see a unicorn. But she doubted their searches would be as methodical as hers. She had made a plan. She had assembled the sparse information available, seasoned it with reasoned assumptions and made conclusions about the best places to look for a mythical quadruped. It was most likely to be equine or ungulate. Almost certainly graminivorous. Since it was so rare as to have been thought extinct for many hundreds of years and yet if all the time it had been breeding sufficiently to continue to exist, it must be extremely shy and secretive – possibly nocturnal. It may indeed be migratory – giving rise to occasional sightings at long intervals which would have eroded credence in its reality. This farmland, sparsely populated as it was, would not hide unicorns of any normal horse-like proportions, even if no one ever saw them the damage and depredations of large hoofed beasts with normal appetites would be obvious. Perhaps, just maybe, it was in fact much much smaller than the traditional image of itself; perhaps it was no bigger than a roe deer for instance. Or perhaps it did not live here at all but much further off and merely strayed here in ones and twos from time to time.

She made a plan. She would spend some time hereabouts watching in likely places for a diminutive unicorn, before moving up country and ranging more widely for a larger species. Her first objective would be locating the sort of woodland which an animal of the projected proportions would find conducive as cover and a foraging base. She covered several leagues that first day on her trusty bicycle but dusk found her dismounting in a very satisfactory location and making her bivouac amongst young oak trees in just the sort of place an informed observer might expect to see, if they were lucky and very very patient, a shy and secretive four footer who had successfully hidden itself from humanity for the past six or seven hundred years.

Having put up her tent and eaten a cold supper, nightfall found her sitting half inside her canvas shelter thoughtfully sipping milk from an enamel mug and staring into the black night which shrouded the trees, listening to the anonymous nocturnal sounds – mysterious and even unsettling to those that did not recognise them, but all instantly familiar to one of Jemima's experience. She had a camera beside her and checked its settings with her torch. To see anything on the first night would be just too weird... but you never know, if there was anything here she was as likely to see it tonight as the next night, statistically, she thought, pulling on a thicker sweater as the temperature began to fall.

How long should she watch? This first night. The first of very many probably. Her legs, now warmly trousered, ached a little from the cycling and the cross-legged watching posture did not help. But she concentrated and overcame the discomfort. Her father would not allow such wimpishness. An owl. Long eared, probably. The sudden shock of a nightjar's churring, which however often you'd heard it was always peculiar and unsettling. Some distant pattering and thrashing of the undergrowth – badgers. The just detectable snorting of cattle as they stood statuesque and invisible in a corner of their field beyond the trees. She began to make a mental map of the dark neighbourhood, and to list things she might have expected to hear but so far had not. All quite routine.

Expect for those voices she'd heard this afternoon. Were she to hear that sound again in the still of the night she was not sure how she would react. There had been something more strange about it than its being simply in a foreign language. The way it had seemed to float, as if the speakers were revolving in the air or something, the way it had come and gone, faint and near and faint again. Now that she had the time to reflect on it she found she was a little frightened and would not wish to hear it again, certainly not in the dark. *'Es war einmal...'* she had made out, what would that be?

The moon was waxing, but weak and thin and veiled, so the darkness held sway between the trees and only the whites of Jemima's eyes were visible when the cloud shifted enough to light them. She was become a thing which might have frightened her had she been outside herself. Two white eyes staring from the gloom of her little tent. She was very still, always listening, but also wondering what sort of German speaking spirits were abroad and why, when there was a sudden heavy rustling and then the cracking of branches and the slight but extensive pattering of many feet moving through the leaf litter of the forest floor. Jemima stiffened and strained her ears to get the precise direction of the noises. Then, very careful to make no sound, she slowly rose from the tent, picked up the bicycle and backed towards the substantial trunk of the biggest tree, which she leant against holding the steel framed machine in front of her. Although nothing could be seen she knew very well what it was – pigs! Wild and always dangerous.

Science could tell you what was likely to be out there in the dark, it could tell you that a mad axe man lurking in the trees with the express desire to dismember you was statistically so unlikely as to be beneath consideration. But what science also told you, in the dark, was that with no possibility of definitive evidence for the absence of a mad axeman lurking under the trees, said axeman remained a possibility. This was the way the dark worked on human sensibilities. Deprived of eyesight and with almost no sense of smell, homo sapiens was often the victim of an uneducated aural ability and an intellectual imagination hugely inflated in such circumstances by the fear of death and the association of black night with that negative state of being.

Jemima was probably less susceptible to such terrors than the average person. She had an ear attuned to the natural world, and, in daylight at least she would have told you she was reasonably confident of her ability to calm and disarm any averagely deranged character she might meet. But even so, and notwithstanding she knew all about pigs and the chance was they would pass peacefully by, and she could climb the tree if necessary, there was something about this particular night in this particular wood which was rather beginning to play upon her equilibrium, something seeking to undermine her. Something itself unseen of course. Was it a little black imp crawling down the bark of the tree to hop onto her shoulder?

She did not believe in such nonsense of course. Silly superstition had no place in her philosophy. There were no such things as black imps. No such things as spirits. (Except, what about her father? Who was currently having a doze in the little tent. Well that was entirely different.) She wished now the pigs would come, fending off wild boar with a touring bike was more straightforward. But they did not come; they had rustled and grunted off in a different direction and Jemima was left with the silences, the owls, the distant cattle, and the persistent disquiet of the possible revenance of spectral Teutonic voices.

When she had made her assessment of this expedition and decided against bringing her assistants, Jemima had lost sight of the fact that, vastly experienced as she was, she had never actually been in the field totally alone overnight, never; at least not since she was a child running about the common with a net and a jam jar, but that was not overnight, it was just because she had lost track of the time and not noticed it getting dark. She had been subject to the loneliness of command of course, she was used to that, but there had always been other physical presences whom she could condescend to chat to, it had never before been quite like this, alone with herself and whatever was out there. And whatever was inside her, and mentally keeping her company.

She made an effort to concentrate, but kept finding she was drifting from observation into a kind of meditation. There was no wind now and the stillness began to leech strange thoughts from the cracks in the back of Jemima's brain. The Italian prince sidled into her croquet embrace, as it was when she had demonstrated to him stance and grip that day. She smelt again his eau de cologne and felt again the warm dark skin of his meticulously manicured hands. She wondered what had become of him, where was he now? Was his visit still going on or was he back in Venice? She realised that he sidled into her thoughts with increasing frequency lately.

An owl screeched. She wondered what time it was, but five minutes later she had still not checked her luminous watch. What would her father think of the Prince? It was difficult to know, and contemplation of the question brought out some of the contradictions in the paternal character. He would have been a little dazzled by the style and exoticism, but would have refused to give in to them, dismissing the expensive clothes and European manners as superficialities; he would have been embarrassingly polite if introduced, and totally fazed by any likelihood of foreign languages being uttered. On the whole he would have attempted to divine the inner qualities of any prince and have resolutely assessed their worth on the basis of character rather than wealth or birth. He would not have considered it beneath him to hobnob with an aristocrat but if due respect were not afforded to him in return the veil of decorum would be slashed by some brutal sarcasm. He was generally intelligent enough to recognise his own prejudices and keep them in check, but it would always be the case that royalty and the use of eau de cologne were not things which recommended themselves to him in the normal course of events.

(The badgers again, on a different track this time.) Would he have happily stood in a freshly pressed suit, carnation forced into his button-hole, to give his only begotten daughter, the apple of his eye, his beautiful scientist with letters after her name, to 'give her way' before the altar at St Luke's in Rowleybottom, to this unknown doge, this suspiciously well groomed Adriatic adventurer? She longed for the owl to screech again, and was rewarded by the high pitched, saw-toothed bark of a fox. Normally she never thought of marriage and such things. Not that they were beneath her, it was just that she was too busy. And candidates were thin on the ground – they would have to be as intelligent as she – and preferably qualified in the same field. She smiled to herself at the bizarre meanderings of her mind, the Italian prince would never come into the frame. But he had very nice skin. And lovely eyes. Oh what ridiculous thoughts rose unbidden to her mind that lonely night. What unexpected questions tugged irrelevantly at her mind and set a blank screen of mental pre-occupation between her watching eyes and the dark trees.

Her father could have told her that the mind locks up the senses and turns the gaze inward when the body is tired and all alone. He could have told her how it can be perfectly pleasant sitting out alone, watching the birds, but then you are always, as homo sapiens, eventually assailed by your own thoughts – and they were likely, for no physical reason at all, to undermine the serenity of the day with black reminders of one's shortcomings, flawed reputation, and fast approaching demise. (Could have told her, but he never had.) Jemima, now alone and called upon to be in command of no one but herself found her authority wavering and though her eyes were wide open she was not seeing into the night before her but into an unfamiliar night within her. It was inevitable that, in spite of the reluctance of her consciousness to let itself plummet any further into this unknown territory, she would lose her grip, and so find herself falling miles into a far from dreamless sleep, wherein was panic and exultation, terror and ecstasy, all pulling and lurching her this way and that.

She woke to find herself still sitting cross legged, her body slumped over her water bottle, her hand gripping the barrel of the torch. Her legs were so stiff it was difficult to get up and she ached all over. She was glad no one could see her. She felt disappointed and ashamed. How she would have admonished Pippa or Willis if they had gone to sleep on the job. And the sleep she had had was not the restorative sleeping bag time she had planned and would not sustain her long into the next day. Oh damn and blow it.

But much worse was to come. As she stretched up and stamped out the pins and needles she noticed that the tiny tent was sagging rather in the middle. Then she noticed there were marks in the ground right beside her bivouac. She bent down intrigued and excited. Hoof marks! Hoof marks! Oh my god, what was this? What could it be? Get the measuring tape. Camera. She fumbled in the bag. Quick. Not a horse. A foal? Were there wild ponies here? She had not seen any so far. And then she saw something else. There was a small hole in the canvas of the tent. A small hole just beside the hoof marks. A small hole just such as might be made by an exploratory poke with a sharp straight horn. She sat down and began to cry.

This was what happened when you dream of men. The shame, the indescribable disappointment! The measure of dereliction was such that, had it been Pippa or Willis that had committed it, she would probably have had to be restrained from physical assault. She herself, Doctor Cake, had snored here under the influence of sexual fantasies while something – just possibly the rarest animal in the world – had approached, come right up – its breath would have been audible, its breath would have disturbed the air about her, it would have been felt on her neck even whilst an Italian prince breathed upon it. The quested beast its very self had poked and prodded about her camp. Its ears twitching, its head nodding and shaking, its foot softly stamping the soft turf. This turf. Its white straight horn swirling secrets and mysteries into the acquiescing night.

It had stood so very close. It had not been the least bit wary of her. Had it not seen her? She was sufficiently upset almost to blame the animal itself for having failed to cause her to wake. As far as it was concerned she might just as well have not been there at all. There was no doubt, however, of its deliberate attentions to the tent – it had paid her no heed but it had clearly sought to skewer the somnolent spirit of her late father.

She sat down with her head in her hands, looking through the tears and the cracks in her fingers at the hoof marks in the ground.

CHAPTER THIRTY TWO

Prince Antonio was hunched over his guitar plucking delicate, trilling little airs out of the stillness of the morning as he sat on the window seat of a chamber in the highest tower in the castle. Occasionally he looked up from the strings and glanced out across the town far below. The music, the view and his thoughts vied with each other as some sort of harmony between the three struggled to come into being and resolve the vague unease which had peremptorily arisen to toy with the balance of the most serene, relaxed and self satisfied of souls. His plaintive arpeggios conjured images of his Italian home and built sunlit palaces between the sooty chimneys; an arresting chord had the image of Jemima Cake resonating before him; a questioning grace note softly twanged the memory of dining with the enigmatic but innocently appealing Princess Daphne. He shook his head and suddenly interposed some fortissimo flamenco rhythms. This was a strange and ill mannered little kingdom. Where was His Majesty? No one seemed to be able to tell him where his host was. No one in his entourage, none of his diplomats knew what was going on, or whether his state visit was at an end or not; all communication was in such circumspect and non-committal and evasive florid language, that utter confusion ruled. Of course no one knew where the Princess Daphne was either. At first he thought they had been told not to say where she was, but it was by now apparent that nobody knew. She had run away. She often did, he learned. Now strumming lackadaisically, he decided he would quite like to run away too. Anything to alleviate this boredom and idle uncertainty. But it was not something he would actually do. He knew himself very well. His self indulgence tended to run on comfortable, relaxed and mostly indoor lines. Whilst he could be taken over by an emotional piece of music or an inspiring work of fiction or, indeed – and very often – a beautiful woman, so far at least his raptures had not had him running barefoot across moors or climbing mountains; he was an armchair – and boudoir – romantic.

He put down the guitar and stood up and stretched, the habitual and involuntary flirtation with the maid who came in for his tray being stifled by a yawn. What would happen today? Where would he go, what would he do? Who would he meet, what would they say, what would he say? God help us if it was like yesterday, when the answers were: nothing, nowhere, nothing, nobody of any consequence or interest, nothing of any consequence or interest, and nothing.

He tightened the cord of his dressing gown and strode out onto the terrace, snatching up a dazzling fedora which he assumed at a provocative slant, and calling over his shoulder for his people in the insistent, somewhat petulant, but always musical tones of his native tongue.

When he paced lazily back into the room, ennui was apparent in every shuffling step: elegant deportment could not be sustained when the body was subject to such purposelessness.

Eventually his secretary appeared around the door. He was not yet wearing a tie; it was early but even so, this degree of laxity exemplified the extent to which the local slovenliness into which this benighted little northern kingdom was crumbling had infected the standards of Antonio's entourage. This particular amanuensis was in general a stickler for proprieties, and even as he came in put his hand to his throat and looked embarrassed. What strange creatures human beings were, how peculiar and pointless were the intricacies of their hierarchies and the punctiliousness of their rules and habits and mores. And yet... without them what would there be to distinguish him, Prince Antonio from all the non-princes? He sighed a would-be self-satisfied sigh which came out as just a sigh and poured himself another coffee.

The man promptly excused himself and came back a moment later immaculately cravatted.

The two smiled silently at one another, for different reasons.

The prince had no instructions, he resumed his seat by the window and invited the secretary to sit down with him. They remained together contemplating the view, without speaking, without even smoking, for several minutes.

'Shall we go and watch the rioting?' suggested the secretary.

'Is it worse? Many dead?'

'I'm not sure any one has actually been killed yet. Come to think of it though, I don't think they generally get going until the afternoons.'

'Oh well... I don't think I'm in the mood really anyway.'

They continued to stare out over the slates and tree tops and into the cloudy distant hills, each silent in a different way, Antonio seeking some quiet, satisfyingly reflective mental nook into which he could rest his mind and guard it from the annoying dissatisfactions which lately had shuffled up to lay siege to it; the secretary, as he often did at times like these, assuming a mien of reserved alertness while thinking his way meticulously through a chess problem.

More of the Italian entourage came in ones and twos onto the terrace, like rooks coming down to perch in the same tree, until the whole gang was assembled and an air of expectancy was generated: would they rise up together and take flight to pillage a crop somewhere, or would they hop about here from branch to branch, squabbling and bantering and pointing their bald beaks at one another? Of course they waited for Antonio to pronounce the fate of the day. They were all bored with this castle, and they were all increasingly annoyed at being ignored – there was no mollifying diplomatic euphemism for it – they were being ignored. The Vangrannicus character and his minions were very polite but seemed extremely busy and any schedule of events which might once have existed for this visit was obviously in shreds. Something had happened to the King. Most of those on the terrace thought he had been quietly assassinated.

Antonio plucked the cigarillo from his lips briefly and decisively to say, 'Let's go for a ride.'

The suggestion was greeted with noisy approval.

It was a good idea but it could not come to pass. The only limousine Ruscum could find was stagnant and moribund in a tomb-like vault of a garage and one look at its tyres confirmed that its sleep was not to be disturbed. He offered a carriage but the Venetians were nervous of horses and then the Prince's next suggestion brought about a tumult of applause and laughter – they would take a boat trip! They could indulge their homesickness with a return to the water.

By early afternoon, two large skiffs, each with two sets of oars, were seen progressing down the little tributary beneath the castle walls heading for the great river, a Venetian flag in the stern of the leading vessel and fine Italian tenor voices plaintively jubilant in barcaroles resounding across the water. As they passed the zoo they were watched: a cud-chewing camel reserved its admiration but paid them close attention as the little fleet passed by; bandicoots twitched and a musk ox glared. Pippa was close to the river mucking out the warthog, mopping her brow with a muddy forearm and not looking her best. Willis boldly waved from the terrace outside the office, but then shyly sidled behind a tree. An enthusiastic man had been despatched, prior to their setting off, to invite Jemima Cake to join the outing, with any of her girlfriends who might want to come along, but had returned to report that Cake was not to be had, and her underlings, though they had dithered perceptibly, had declared that they could not abandon their posts.

The boats ploughed on, down toward the little river's confluence with its big brother. The broad sweep of the great river came into view as they came out from beside the citadel, and after listless days filled only with enervated badinage the release of a good work out with oars and lungs as they rowed and sang, sweetly and lustily invigorated not only themselves but any who saw and heard them. The large flag flew and flapped and fluttered and made the little fleet reminiscent of royal progresses in days of yore. The wind was freshening, however, and ruffling the surface of the water as well as putting a chill into the air – especially for those not rowing.

As they rounded the great bend – the downstream current pushing them at a steady pace which they would never be able to replicate when they turned for home – a middling sized cloud suddenly slid over the sun, blotting out warmth and cheeriness and emphasising the wetness of the drops of water which splashed upon them. The singing faded until there remained only the lonely effort of one brave soul at the helm of the second boat, soldiering on as if he would combat the wind with his lungs just as he fought the river with his rudder. Willis, who had emerged from behind her tree to watch the boats row away, could still faintly hear him a minute or two after they were all lost to view round the bend, and she was almost overcome by an immense sadness.

CHAPTER THIRTY THREE

King Freddie stepped doggedly on, his deer-stalker (flaps down) giving him something of the air of a bloodhound. He wore thick woollen trousers tucked into high boots and a padded Norfolk jacket which was complicated with straps and belts and collar buttons and the like, designed to allow its transformation into at least three different characters depending on the clemency of the weather and how well versed the wearer was in its manipulation. There was at least one button in the wrong hole, and he had contrived to half secure one lapel into storm position whilst its fellow flapped, expecting nothing more than a fresh spring day. He was unwittingly exhibiting his inner turmoil in the way his jacket was thus wrenched uncomfortably about his person. He shambled in confusion away from his household, his citadel, and the history that had moulded him, groping his way, he hoped, toward what he had lost and the strange promise the world now held out in this, its forgotten corner.

He shook his head, flapping his dog-like hat ears, and once again stopped and looked back to see if, after all, there was any sign of the longed for Mrs Simpson, but she was nowhere to be seen. He went on a few paces, and stopped to watch a very large, and very dark, toad lumber across the path. It looked up at him with a meaningful expression which was a mixture of a vague disgust and pity. *Bufo bufo*. Freddie was pleased he could remember the Latin name, and then he thought he would go on to see if he could remember his own names. Not a simple task, there were an awful lot of them, so many that a few frequently got missed off official state documents – the only place you could expect to find them all together. He knew Dagobert, Alphonse, Maximillian, Frederick, (one of his nannies had used to refer to him as 'little Damfy', until she was reproved for it by an ancestor of Vangrannicus) but struggled with the rest of them. He was pretty sure he was also Simeon, and very probably Louis; he also had a vague memory of Clement Lancelot, but that may have been a cousin and not him at all. The toad went on its way and disappeared in the grass just as Freddie remembered Gofton. He was the only person he'd ever heard of who had ever been called Gofton.

The weather was short-tempered without being in an absolute rage. It did not rain but maintained a tight-lipped greyness occasionally lightened – though not brightened – with an off-whiteness which failed to raise spirits because rather than presaging sunshine it felt uncomfortably like an admonishment, as if the dark monotony of celestial disregard for all lonely sojourners was broken by a sharp reminder that though it could be otherwise, this was the weather the world deserved.

The young deer that he then encountered stepping through some bracken tinkered with his train of thought to introduce Daphne into it – by representing youth, femininity and vulnerability – and thence commenced an inevitable short sequence of associations which presented him with another name: Nicodemus. Not one of his names; ah, but it was the name of someone very dear to him once upon a time. A name which conjured such colourful nostalgia. They were both gone, it seemed, Daphne and Nicodemus, no more to be found. Daphne wandered off, and poor Nicodemus... who could not be suffered to remain. It was an episode never more to be stirred into life; it must remain buried with those who were buried with it. How so be it, he saw now in his mind's eye the noble chimpanzee himself quite clearly...but all about him was a thick fog. Oh dear, what a web he had woven about himself, Dagobert, Alphonse Maximilian Frederick Louis Simeon Horatio Clement Michael John Gofton Walpaert. But it had been for the best, hadn't it? He'd only been trying a little experiment... with existence, to find out what it was; surely there could be nothing wrong with that. To find out what it was to be – to be an ape, to be a man – slowly to discover how the difference between things could be evaporated and everything could be made to understand everything else. Anybody would have done it given half a chance. It had all gone wrong but no one had been to blame really had they? Oh what had become of his smart and handsome *pan troglodytes*? He no longer knew, simply could not remember.

Before this moment he had not thought of Nicodemus for a very long time. It was almost as if he had not been allowed to remember?

But he had been wrong to think him dead – that could not be. No, no he was not dead.

Where, oh where, was the divine Millicent? Surely she too had not abandoned him? He searched desperately for his unicorn, which was visible (a ghostly form at the moment, the outline clear but the body translucent) drinking from a pond a little way ahead. No doubt the same pond on which *bufo bufo* had been intent. They go, he thought, but they none of them come back. Iffy had been the first to go. And afterward Nicodemus, Daphne, Millicent – all gone. Yes, Millicent too, it seemed. Freddie then began to twirl around and around holding his arms outstretched like a child trying to make itself dizzy and started to laugh uncontrollably. Stopping quite suddenly, as he fell to the soft earth, wide eyed, he knew before he hit the ground with a joyous thump, that the unicorn, when they found it, would surely bring Nicodemus with it. And he lay there with his eyes closed, a smile on his face now, fully expecting the sun to come out from behind a cloud and bathe him in warmth and light – which it did. He would bring the unicorn back, and surely the others would all follow.

Something blocked out the sun and made a shadow pass over Freddie's closed eyes. Millicent! He sat up and looked all round, hoping he was loomed over by the wonderful darkness of the artist. But there was no Millicent. He was suddenly in the umbrage of a small but oddly shaped cloud which threatened to grow.

CHAPTER THIRTY FOUR

There was certainly something which overcame strangers here. Something which quietly but effectively bewildered them and often induced instability. Whence precisely it emanated no one knew – but it was something which infiltrated the minds of most of those distracted souls who crossed the border, and in so doing it revealed something to them. It could not really be described but the attempts people made tended to use words and phrases like 'startling,' 'twisting', 'refractive,' 'subtle but insistent' and most said, surprisingly perhaps, that though there was a sense of shock and surprise that went with it, it was a sort of beauty.

A beauty less stridently romantic than Wordsworthian landscapes, a beauty which was unlooked for and unimagined but which seeped up from the blank topography and wrapped the visitor in the remnants of tragedy, which made them question history ever more ardently even as they understood it less and less. A beauty which transcended any previous definition of the word, but was no other more apt to apply to its poignancy. Quietly effulgent emotions were conjured through senses inexplicably enhanced by mundane stimuli and there arose hints and clues to fulfilments unlooked for, wherein old fears might become embraceable. Anguish itself was distilled to a piquancy which exhilarated the traveller as he found within his longing that which lay deeper than his desires and undermined them with revelations. Some were tempted by a vision of restful ecstasy. It was assuredly a country that fuelled meditation and conjecture, for here the bounds of credibility were in ruins or indiscernible and certainly those with a particular cast of mind, or those on the cusp of a psychological rite of passage had ever been attracted to it. Some avoided the place precisely because it was believed that what was elsewhere repressed, dismissed and denied, was here likely to creep forth, and might run amok. However it was wrought, it was uneven in its pace, this magic of the Lanes. It took a while to affect some travellers and some, it must be said, were not affected at all.

Millicent, for her part, rather took to the place. (There could be little doubt that she had been here before.) She soon recognised things, and one of the things she recognised was the incongruity of looking for a particular person in a land which she strongly felt attached little importance to where people were, or who they were for that matter, and her search for Freddie, though it never lost its earnestness, became altogether less flurried. The ape was much calmer now (whether that was because he was here, or because he was farther away from where he had been, was not clear) and whilst he always kept close to his rescuer, he had relinquished his anxious grip of her, and was beginning to look happy, she thought. Happy to look about him, seeming to delight in birdsong and grasping handfuls of foliage from the hedgerows which he licked, tasted and occasionally relished.

They needed provisions, however, browsing would not sustain them, and Millicent had resolved that she would ask to buy some food at the next farm they came to, but before they got there, just down a sudden dip in the road, tucked beneath some oak trees with a little apron of grass before it, was a little shop. An old advertisement for something in a tin, very faded and peeling, had been pasted on the end of the building, probably before Millicent was born. There was a cat asleep in the window and a bee buzzed and then crept silently along the dusty pane. She signed the ape to sit on the bench which ran round the middle of the tree that was in the middle of the green and went herself and opened the door. There was a jangling and she stepped onto the bare floorboards of the dark and dusty interior. An old woman in a pinafore and with a black eye-patch sat squinting at the newspaper amongst a jumble of things which Millicent was pleased to see included loaves of bread and bottles of milk, as well as tins of spam and soup and suchlike, but there were also gardening implements, coils of rope, buckets, rabbit hutches, bicycle parts, rubber hoses, and rolls of chicken wire. Next to the counter was a tall pile of yellowing magazines.

Millicent bought milk and bread and a tin-opener and some tins and some apples and oranges, but was disappointed by there being no bananas. She glanced through the dirty window and saw that the ape was lazily swinging from a low branch by one long arm. Assembling the coins and the woman's counting the change took a minute or two and Millicent happened then to look down at the pile of magazines. They were very old and the top one was a 'Special Edition' and had on the cover a large black and white photograph of Freddie's wedding – he and his bride were stiffly waving from an ornate coach whilst a small crowd of flag-wavers indicated their loyal joy. The line of policemen, Millicent noted, however, nearly outnumbered them, and one of the flunkies clinging to the back of the equipage was clearly stifling a yawn.

'Oh bless you, you can 'ave it dear, I've been meaning to get rid of them for ages, take as many as you like,' said the woman with a smile, when Millicent tried to buy it.

She grabbed half a dozen and thrust them into the carrier bag she'd been given, saying, 'Goodbye, thank you very much,' as the bell continued to jangle and she stepped across the unkempt sward from dusty commerce to the primitive and bizarre responsibilities which she suddenly realised were to be her lot for the foreseeable future. What had she taken upon herself?

He casually cast himself off from the end of his bough and plummeted down to knock her heavily to the ground and scatter some of the purchases. Here was a very boisterous sense of fun, she thought, pleased that it could be resurrected so soon after his incarceration, but trepidatious about the implications for her bruiseable body and its breakable bones. The semi comatose, almost dead, forlorn figure slumped beyond hope in the black dungeon had given way to an animal that seemed suddenly to be years younger. Freedom and sunshine had transformed him, it was quite remarkable, a miracle. And not a little daunting.

The apples brought forth such appreciative noises from the ape, such excited 'oo-oo-ing' that the pinafored woman could be seen through the window for a moment directing her good eye across the green. But she was not moved to emerge from behind her counter and was soon absorbed in her crossword again. Millicent took up the commemorative issue of the illustrated paper, settling down against the oak tree to chew at the wholemeal loaf and immerse herself in the account of the nuptials of His Majesty King Dagobert IV and Princess Iphigenia of Heligoland, all those years ago. Intuition and what she remembered of the garbled rantings of the ape's warder told her to keep the pictures away from the animal's inquisitive gaze and she tossed him another Granny Smith which he caught with a long lazy arm prior to swinging happily up amongst the higher branches.

It was all predictable guff about how beautiful she was and how accomplished and noble he was, and how marvellous he looked in his uniform, and her lovely dress, and little descriptive pieces about the romantic chocolate box kingdom she had been brought up in, and true love and such like: tosh beloved of all hacks on such occasions. It was unlikely of course that Millicent would come across here any clues as to the fate that befell the lovely Iphigenia many years later but she idly persevered, looking carefully into all the feast of photographic plates the *Illustrated News* was pleased to present for what it assumed would be the nation's drooling and worshipful delight.

She was rewarded on page nine, where a small picture of the carriage returning from the church, probably taken from the roof of a neighbouring building, surrendered to Millicent's very sharp and determined eye a small dark figure looking out of a small very high window. Almost certainly the photographer himself and very probably the editorial and printing staff had never noticed it, they would have been intent on the principals. Although it wore a suit and tie it was clear to Millicent – even though it was not quite in focus – that it was not a human child, it was a chimpanzee, and must surely be a baby.

'Aha!' said Millicent partly to herself but not minding if anyone heard.

What was he doing dressed like that? And in an upper room in a house in the centre of the town, quite close to the castle? She looked up to where he sat on a branch, sucking the juicy apple. Suddenly he returned her gaze and the menace momentarily eclipsed the pathos. She was not afraid of him, but she went over in her mind what the old gaoler had said, and she could not be sure what she believed. He had been like a child when she had brought him up from that foul underworld, as gentle as a lamb and desperate to be embraced and to feel, as they went along, the constant security of her hand. Now he appeared as a strange mixture of sadness and strength, of anger and loneliness. And whilst he had seemed to be very young again, gambolling on the green sward and bounding amongst the branches, as she looked at him now and the way the thick bough on which he sat swayed dangerously under his weight, he looked huge, far bigger surely than chimpanzees usually were.

She turned back to the illustrated paper. But... Was he ever actually in the menagerie? She would have liked to have asked Trevor, he would know. But Trevor of course was missing. The King was missing.

Digressively, she put down the paper and her eyes clouded over as she momentarily thrilled to the idea of the sudden isolation of every individual. She wondered whether there were as many different types of isolation as there were isolated people or whether all isolations were essentially the same. That was the point really – if we're each isolated we cannot know whether we are all thinking the same thing or not. And that seems to bother us, or many of us; as if there is something which we are all supposed to be thinking. Like ants. And cut off from that something we have no purpose. (On the whole in this instance she herself did not believe there would be any synchrony of thought. The King would be thinking about her, Trevor would be thinking about himself or some species of egret, she was thinking about this.) A light gust of wind shushed through the leaves, played with her hair and riffled the pages of the magazine. The bough above was vigorously wafted up and down as the ape shifted his position and then swung himself up to another branch. The sepia-toned images of elaborately dressed people conducting strange rituals seemed utterly unconnected with the reality she sat in, the green of the grass, the slight noises of wind and tree, the stoic presence over there of the one-eyed shop-keeper.

Her mother had said Queen Iphigenia had died of food poisoning, or possibly typhus, whilst on a visit abroad somewhere and because of diplomatic niceties and the danger of arousing any sort of xenophobic mania amongst the masses the obsequies had been carried out back in the country of her birth and the whole affair had been deliberately played down at the behest of his Majesty.

The old duffer in the dungeon of course had had a different version. He had stated as plainly as he was capable of stating anything that she had been done in by the animal whose foot now dangled immediately above her and whose toes were playing with her hair. She looked up at him and he grinned down at her, the lips pulled back to display all the teeth in a facial gesture (incorporating something of the grimace of a Chinese dragon with the amiable naivety of a George Formby) which was certainly more abstruse, she thought, than it appeared – she did not understand these things but fancied that facial gestures amongst great apes invariably involved affirmation or otherwise of the individual's position in the hierarchy of the group. She trusted that she remained top in this little group of two. But would he eventually forget about being rescued? All those years down there in that black hole must have had their effect, nothing could come out of that horror unscathed. He swung down and snatched another apple giving her a playful – but very hard – slap on the shoulder. And he had been put there for a reason. Which could surely only be – in such an animal-loving regime as this one – something as serious as homicide. And yet, as she watched his sad eyes looking at her over the green orb of the fruit, she mused on whether what the old warder had said could really be taken at face value. He was old and seemed confused about so many things did he not? Perhaps he'd fantasised the whole thing. She peered again, even more closely, at the tiny figure in the corner of the little photograph. With his suit and shirt and collar and tie. He did not look to her like a killer.

She mused on the innocence of animals. They relied on instinct rather than moral choice. They were still in the garden of Eden, no one had given them an apple. Except that she had, innocently, just done that hadn't she. And other people, it seemed had given him things – a suit of clothes, a room at the top of that tall building perhaps. Had the poor animal, plucked from its natural habitat as a baby, had human accoutrements thrust upon it, had he been dressed like a doll and encouraged to mimic the idiosyncracies of the upright hairless tribe? Was that how all this had come about? Had he been worked on, had he been intensively reared with repeated lessons and examples, exclusively amongst those not of his own species, to see what would become of him? To see perhaps, if he were bottle-fed with interminable repetitions and treats, he would renounce his chimpanzeeness and mature into some freakish semi-human thing that could watch television, eat with a fork, and ultimately perhaps speak?

Dreaming it all out there on the seat beneath the oak tree Millicent had such faith in her intuition that she felt sure she was on the right track. Freddie – it must have been Freddie himself – had been trying to bridge the divide between humans and animals. Not content with collecting the rarest of the rare he had hoped to actually create a being, a being which was capable of both experiences, beast and man, someone, something, that understood the whole true gamut of evolution from forest to library. The whole project would in the end culminate in the great revelation – some great leap forward in understanding from whence the acquisition of intellect and morality arose. Freddie would stretch consciousness between the worms and the stars. The ape would be the first child with one foot in the wilderness and one on the ladder of learning and reason, and King Dagobert the Fourth would be his father.

Was that how it had been? Was Freddie capable of such grandiose and hubristic thinking? Hmm. But then this was quite a while ago, he would have been a young man and young men think big and are ambitious. And often regret things in later life when they are content with less, and more ambiguous.

The ape no longer wore a suit. He had forgotten his table manners. Landing heavily on the grass beside her and grunting loudly he snatched the entire bag and emptied it onto the ground, throwing what was not immediately edible over his shoulder with some force. Millicent wondered whether she should admonish him, like a dog or a small child, but found herself just watching him and marvelling at the strength and the delicacy – one tin of spam had flown a good hundred yards, the choicest segment of an orange was precisely and cleanly released from the skin before being savoured. Was he a brute, wanting in reason, or an intelligent animal only a chromosome or two from herself and sharing very many attributes with people? Except language of course.

She looked deeply into his eyes as he appeared deep in thought, eating another orange and she thought to herself, 'Yes, I bet Freddie tried to teach you to speak, didn't he? Or communicate in some way.' All previous ideas about brute beasts and the god-like homo sapiens would have to be abolished if it were ever established that an animal could have communicable thoughts, could grasp or form concepts and frame them in some sort of syntax. The more she thought about it the more convinced she was that this had been what Freddie had been about down there in Oodeneden. He had been trying to bridge the gap, looking for the secret that dwelt in that gap, which once revealed would change the way the world and all life was understood.

It had gone wrong though. In some horrible way it had gone wrong. It was useless to conjecture. She must seek out Freddie and ask him. She did not know definitely whether the ape had killed Queen Iphigenia, nor, if he had, in what circumstances and whether he had been driven to it – subject to stresses and torments his benevolent experimenters were unaware of perhaps, in their eagerness for things to be proved in accordance with their prejudices and preconceived theories, with their unshakeable belief that he would be happier as a man.

Food for thought, as they say. She picked up another magazine and lazily marvelled at the sorts of washing machines they had then.

CHAPTER THIRTY FIVE

Jemima's efforts to apply science to her predicament, to inspect and assess the evidence and to formulate a proper theory of the possibilities were at first half hearted. Her usual control and objectivity, her capacity to rise above the petty demands of the selfish psyche, had been ambushed by an ugly creature at least as frightening as any that might dwell in the wild. She was cornered by the sudden emergence of a something within herself which she had known about but which she had thought insignificant and completely tame. It had now grown up and would be ignored no more. It was very inconvenient. No, it was more than inconvenient, it was a monster. She knew she would never get it back in its cage, and struggled with the need to concoct an emergency regime wherein it might at least be quietened and its interference rendered less than constant. She was faced with recognising both her desire for Antonio and the catastrophic effect of that desire, which had been to deny her possibly the most important zoological discovery of all time. It was difficult to assimilate this new urge inside her and recognise it as inevitable and natural since its first eruption had had this tragic effect. It was a genetically driven urge of course, which was generated from within her and yet it was nonetheless alien to her nature. No doubt there had been myriad papers written on female development but she doubted that any exactly documented her circumstance. This biological interiority arose like a parasite with its own self preservation programme which might be designed for the propagation of the species but was entirely at odds with Jemima's purpose; she had not been created to recreate but to understand and interpret, to research and to demonstrate. Nature's overarching plan sought to impose a tyranny of hormones on her which was totally at odds with her personal well-being and fulfilment, she was sure of that. Things had always previously been within the power of her intricate and calculating mind. But now that mind was faced with something which obstinately would not respond to logic and it seemed wanted to upset everything, to kick over the careful and intense work of her determined and dedicated life so far. It had upped in a moment and looked like it had deprived her of that which would have been the culmination of a brilliant career. She understood that she ought not to kick against it, that this thing, this desire, this passion, was a common phenomenon which totally preoccupied many people, and it now seemed that it was one which she was not, after all, going to be able to side-step. Her exemption had finally lapsed. It was a dilemma. Equally as strong as the passion she felt for Antonio was a negative passion generated by the concomitant crippling of what she lived for: science and her achievement of perfection. Antonio she knew had little to do with perfection, except, perhaps, in his physical form.

There was one solution perhaps – would everything get back to normal if she were able to put an end to him in some discreet way? ('To do him in', to express it in parental plain speaking.) It was an idea she did not entirely discount. Would it be so wrong? Sometimes unpleasant things had to be done for the greater good, did they not? She had humanely despatched lots of animals in her time. Antonio was, as we all are, just another type of specimen.

Assisted by severe and belittling admonishments from the disappointed spirit of her dead father she had after an hour or so managed to calm down and to start properly to immerse herself in the job in hand. All was not lost. Whatever sort of beast it was, the chances were it would not have gone that far, it would still be here somewhere to be tracked down. And by god, she would do it. Laying out measuring tape and taking hundreds of meticulous photographs, writing copiously in her two notebooks, scouring the terrain for tracks leading to and from the camp, minute inspections of hoof prints and calculations as to the weight of the animal occupied her all the morning and by the time she finally took a break for something to eat and drink she was fairly exhausted. As we know, she had had little proper sleep. Taking up her mess tin and spoon she ambled away a little distance and sat on a fallen tree trunk. The progress of each porridge laden spoon from tin to mouth (those same exquisite rosebud lips which excited Trevor and so many others) became slower and slower as she stared into infinity and wondered what it was like to be hanged; was there still the death penalty or had they abolished it? She could not remember.

CHAPTER THIRTY SIX

That same day, when the sun was at its zenith and Jemima's mapping of the area which contained her camp had encompassed a circumference of some hundred yards in all directions, she was to be rocked by a startling discovery. It was so startling that she repeated her whole inspection of the ground, paying especially close attention to the examination of the whole periphery. She re-checked her map, on which she had meticulously plotted all the hoof prints and, separately, all the hoof-print-like marks which might or might not be hoof-prints, and went slowly over the ground verifying their positions and that she really had not missed any. Then, at long last, with wide eyes and a puzzled brow, she sat down again on her log. She was toying with a conclusion which her zoological expertise would not countenance. There were no hoof-prints beyond fifty yards of the camp. None. Anywhere. There was no track signifying arrival and no track signifying departure. Either whatever had made the prints was capable of such a prodigious leap that seemed entirely impossible given the anatomical projections she had been able roughly to make on the basis of the size of the prints – which were relatively diminutive for a quadruped – or... or... She began to laugh to herself. And then – and this was a sign of the state she was in – it might have appeared as if she had gone a little mad because she got up and ran, ran as fast as she could all through the trees and round the tent and over the log, and as she ran she flapped her arms vigorously. And she laughed and she whinnied at the prospect of a winged unicorn.

But later, when the laughing had stopped and she was again upon the log, her chin in her hands, she was as much inclined to believe in its spontaneous eruption into being as that it could fly. The only four legged things with wings were definitely imaginary. Though the process itself was unpredictable evolution did not generally go so... so sideways. If you'd evolved wings and feathers you would have no reason to morph an extra pair of legs – which anyway would make you too heavy to fly – and if you had four legs on the ground there would not be any free limbs to change into wings.

Could it climb trees? Or (and this was not yet something which Jemima thought – it would be a very difficult thing for her to think, and there would be different schools of thought as to whether she would be enhanced or diminished by thinking it) had science actually come up against a manifestation which was not amenable to all its laws? Was the unicorn a thing that was sometimes there and sometimes not there?

It looked like she was going to stay here another night at least. She set about re-adjusting the little tent, tightening the guy ropes and making sure the poles were straight. Her bicycle was leaning against a tree, and the sight of it brought forth more idiotic ideas shamelessly to expose themselves before her open mind. It was a mind which was more than open, it was gaping and stretching to solve this problem, a mind in serious danger of dislocating itself. Only people and possibly some apes could ride bicycles – no mythological animal ever had. But perhaps one could have been carried, or ridden on the shoulders of a cyclist? Assailed by such thoughts and the introduction of the colossally disappointing possibility of human agency and deliberate trickery she crept slowly into the tent, where she lay down and had to force herself to think seriously about the animal being brought here. Of course she had to concede that, even if it was unlikely to have been by bicycle, it could certainly have been carried here by persons unknown: dragged here, drugged in a sack perhaps. Then they would have waited for it to come to (or possibly they gave it an antidote) encouraged it to cavort about the camp, and carried it off again. That was possible wasn't it? She was afraid it was. And yet, as she lay on her back and looked out of the little tent at the upside down trees, she felt for the first time in her life as if the more physically plausible of the explanations was the least credible.

CHAPTER THIRTY SEVEN

A winged lion with its right fore paw resting on an open book lay on a cold and rocky shore, oscillated by the little rippling rhythm of the water in the pool where it found itself. Still attached to the broken post which had adorned the transom of a large rowing skiff, it was a forlorn fragment evoking tragedy and the sad fate that ever threatens to overtake those who go down to the sea in ships.

This Venetian flag would have been a grim sight for any admirer of Antonio had they been walking on this lonely Northern shore. People, however, were the rarest form of life here. No one ambled to and fro for relaxation in these chilly climes. It was a shore which lay beyond even the sketchy cartography of the supposed unicorn territory. People had ideas and theories but no one was quite definitely sure that the same sea into which the great river ran stretched up and round and over in this direction, and it had hardly occurred to anyone that you might be able to get to it by starting out at Johnson's cottage; but if you were prepared to trek and to climb and to scramble and to endure for many long days, actually you could. If you were prepared to do those things and to keep doing them you could actually get practically anywhere, of course, assuming you were not eaten, or frozen or starved on the way.

Those who had sung their rollocking way down the river under a flag such as now languished here amongst the cold ragged seaweed had had no intentions to explore new lands or find new routes, they had simply set out for pure pleasure. This would deny their disaster the nobility ascribed to the fate of intrepid adventurers, and yet the lackadaisical, impromptu character of the Venetians' voyage, embarked on solely for the enjoyment of the water and the moment and the air and the sun, made what seemed to have befallen them so unfair that the tears that would be shed for them would be more poignant than those for more conventional heroes.

Feelings of natural justice allowed that hubris might attract a measure of cruelty in recompense, jollity never should. But as yet there was no mourning, no one knew. This place was so remote and beyond almost everyone's ken. It must have been a storm of a particular and most sustained ferocity which could have driven them so far. So far away from the city, and many leagues from the idiosyncratic country to the north of it where kings and artists and apes and animal hunters roamed and searched and began to lose themselves, knowing nothing of the sea and its icebergs and its seals and its bears and a forlorn and broken flagstaff clunking sadly against a rock.

CHAPTER THIRTY EIGHT

Trevor's leg looked terrible but he was staunch in his pronouncements that it was getting better and they had found a conveniently shaped branch which, suitably trimmed with the clasp knife, could function as a crutch, so that the next morning they set off again on their search for the bowler-hatted man. The bowler-hatted man whose image was become the motif of their wandering. Daphne had combined their belongings in one pack (save for some small secret things she privately nestled inside her clothing) which she insisted on carrying – indeed Trevor's protests had been rather lame, he might be able to walk but he knew he wasn't up to bearing any sort of load. There was no discussion as to what direction to take, they certainly had no wish to re-visit the place where they had met the pig, so they naturally continued on the path that lead gently uphill through the thin woodland. This path eventually became quite sandy and the wood ever thinner and rockier. Very large old stones protruded through the bracken and gave rise in lively imaginations such as Daphne's to thoughts of giants' buttons or dinosaur eggs, or the last mossy remnants of some ancient temple to a forgotten but once colossal god. After a little while a particularly flat one suggested itself to Trevor as a seat and he gratefully flopped onto it holding his bad leg in both hands and stretching it out before him. She asked if he was alright, was answered with a nod and a cross between a grimace and a smile, and then put down the pack and wandered ahead to the top of the rise before them to see what was on the other side.

After a night by no means free of doubt and sorrow it was rallying to find that one's history looked back at one somewhat more reassuringly in the morning light, which obligingly sought out the optimistic facets, the signs of hope which could be made to twinkle, in the long train of events which had delivered her up to this day. She was reassured that she was doing the right thing, even though she was in a peculiar place with no real idea of what she wanted to happen. She stared out over a wide plain dotted with small trees. There were no habitations and she could not make out any roads. It seemed less outrageous today, amongst the lichen covered boulders and the bracken and the suspicion that there might be adders and the stridency of the grasshoppers and crickets, to suggest that the bowler-hatted man might not be Italian, or even to do with the Italians. She mentally confided to a passing jackdaw that she had quite liked the Italian prince. She was in a mood amenable to the gentle introduction of new possibilities. Yet nothing would entirely oust the bowler hat from her fixated mind; it might very well be that it had lost its original significance but it was still the thing she was following.

Looking down over this inviting bit of landscape where agriculture for some reason was in abeyance, and the faint sound of a cuckoo was heard, everything was relaxed and prepared to take its chance, and the mystery of life exhibited a more enticing aspect than it had in the grim and secretive solemnity of the firelit night. For the nonce at least it appeared she was granted remission from her turmoil; troubling things were uncannily eclipsed by nature, which reclaimed her as an independent animal. An animal ever prey to anxiety it was true, and one which was, given a sniff of its own quarry, ever prone to over-excitement.

Trevor took up his crutch and hopped along to join her on the brow of the hill and they both looked inquisitively down into the multitude of discretely foregathered clumps of trees and amongst the far distant blue hills of the horizon for clues and encouragement. In the far, far distance, two very tiny figures walked along a winding path, but it was not by any means certain that they would catch the eye. Had there been a glint of something – a piece of jewellery, a silver topped cane – their motion might then have become more apparent but there was none and it was entirely due to chance and the random ranging of Trevor's keen eyesight honed over years of expeditions that brought the momentary movement of the pair as they appeared and then as suddenly disappeared behind different little copses, to his attention.

'Look! Down there,' he said, grabbing Daphne's arm.

She could see nothing.

He waited, expecting the figures to reappear along the line of the path where he was guessing that it ran. But they did not.

She stared in frustration and eventually declared there was nothing to be seen, he had imagined it, the trick of a shadow.

He said nothing, then rummaged in the bag for his binoculars, which once levelled remained glued to his face for many minutes, the crutch under his armpit steadying his stance. 'Oh no, they were there, definitely, two of them,' he whispered.

'What were they like? Who was it? Did one of them have a bowler hat? Is it the dirty old man? Can you see anything? May I have a look?'

CHAPTER THIRTY NINE

Trevor was trying to keep up but found that a flurry of short crutch-hopping steps always needed to be punctuated by a momentary rest, especially if they were going uphill, and it was as he slumped to catch his breath behind Daphne on a little ascent that he spied something on the ground. Something which he went to great lengths to pick up.

Whatever it was, it had bounced away from the path and come to rest beneath a bush. The manoeuvre involved dropping the crutch, lowering himself gingerly to support himself on hands and one knee and then with grunting, groaning, a stretch of the arm, flexing of the fingers and finally grasping the object, he struggled upright, hopping to lean against one of the huge boulders and examine his hard won prize. It was a leather bound notebook with many interleaved pieces of paper all held together by a thick elastic band. When he removed the band some of the loose papers cascaded to the ground and he brought forth an oath. He would get them in a minute. Turning to the flat surface of the great stone he laid out his find and began to examine it.

The pages were covered in manuscript, some in pencil, some in ink, sometimes both together on the same page. It may have been the same writer throughout but there was a change in the style of the handwriting as the thing progressed, and its size and legibility varied hugely. Sometimes it was excited and urgent and dug right into the paper, in other places it was small and exceptionally neat. It was essentially, he discovered, a diary. One which recorded the doings and reflections of someone over many years, beginning in childhood. Little whimsical drawings were sometimes interspersed amongst the text. There was no name but it must be Daphne's. It must have fallen from her bag or a pocket as she climbed the hill.

Should he read it? No, it was a private and personal document. Did he want to read it? Not particularly, it would be for the most part, dull, and then intermittently embarrassing and rather pathetic in places. People's ideas of themselves were always disappointing.

Then he saw royal arms embossed in the faded and battered cover. So it was true – she must really be the Princess. He felt that this put a different complexion on the matter; it contorted the ethics of the situation and removed the book from the realm of the personal and pushed it slyly into the category 'historical document.' It would still be boring but he had a duty to read it. Posterity peered over his shoulder and demanded it. It had this effect even though Trevor was by nature averse to the idea of the institution of the monarchy – he worked for it but he didn't like it. It was a wrongheaded idea, a model which could never work properly. The actual figureheads would always be at odds with themselves because their selves must be inseparable from the myth they represented, otherwise they lost all credibility. And yet they could never be inseparable. It was one of the many fundamental flaws in the institution, he thought; people were not remotely god-like (even the most saintly) and should never be persuaded so to exhibit themselves. Having been so persuaded they could not complain if people read their diaries. And people would always read their diaries because it was like looking into the gap, into the crack between nature and religion, which was always going to be shocking and full of relentless schadenfreude.

He could not read it now, unfortunately, because she was calling to him from the top of the hill. With difficulty he collected the fallen pages and folded them back inside, then he stuffed it into his trousers and resumed his hopping walk. One thing from his skim though the diary, however, stuck in his mind: a meticulous little drawing – which demonstrated no small artistic talent – of a child holding hands with an ape or monkey which was dressed as a little school boy with a jacket and tie, in a garden with a fountain.

Trousers are not the best place to keep anything literary however and it was inevitable due to the wrenching motion of his locomotion, that the little book (it was quite small) would eventually fall unseen – and unread – with a soft bounce onto the grass. There it lay awaiting a fate all too common: slow decay, preceded by a peculiar existence as a material entity intended to convey the immaterial but utterly incapable of having any meaning for the ants and woodlice and things which encountered it. The complicated sequences of letters just lay there, keeping unimaginable secrets from the field mice and voles that passed it by, indifferent, living as they are assumed to do, entirely beyond the reach of ideas.

Trevor had indeed spied distant figures, even though Daphne had not been able to make them out. They might be invisible again now but they did exist and did continue to pick out their path amongst trees and hedges and little streams where, for the moment, they evaded all magnification. Trevor's attempts to guess their likely course and focus his optical ambush on the right spot for their reappearance were not so far proving successful and Daphne was frustrated.

'Can you see them now? Can you make them out?'

'Erm, hang on... no, not yet...'

'Were there two of them? Did you say there were two?'

'Yes, definitely two... hold on, I wonder if they went behind that clump...'

'Any bowler hats? Come on let me have a look now.'

Frustration was enhanced by what the searchers would never have imagined, which was that the path of the pair of figures was extremely erratic. For some reason they did not take a straight line. They often retraced their steps and went in circles of varying sizes, as if they were deep in discussion of some great and very abstract philosophy and could not concentrate both on that and where they were supposed to be going. There was nothing urgent or agitated about their progress, however, they maintained a steady andante. It would all have been perfectly normal if they were strolling to and fro in the beautiful garden of a country house, but somehow it was odd out here, so very far from any habitation or refreshment.

After several minutes Trevor allowed the glasses to be wrenched from his grasp. Daphne's ranging and focussing was fevered and encompassed territory a long way from the locus of the first sighting. But it bore fruit.

'I can see them!' she whispered excitedly after a few minutes. However it was only one figure that she saw and it promptly went behind an outcrop of rock and was lost to view. She lowered the binoculars, 'No bowler hat – a woman! In a sun hat. A woman.'

'Well there must be someone with her, I definitely saw two people,' said Trevor.

The elusive and very tiny people remained out of sight. Would they appear again? Perhaps they were resting in one of the little woods or behind one of the tumulus-like hillocks which Trevor and Daphne's careful observations had by now made familiar.

Trevor smiled to himself as he wondered whether God had ever looked down on the Garden of Eden and not been able to locate the Man and the Woman.

'Come on let's go – we know roughly where they are, let's just head down there we're bound to come across them,' said Daphne.

'Are we sure we want to come across them? We have no idea who they are.'

'Precisely – we need to find out who they are. And if it isn't the man you call Johnson we must ask them what they know and whom they might have seen.'

'Interrogate them, you mean?'

'Why not?' She was the Princess again in this little exchange, whereas Trevor's commanding adult, scientist persona was severely undermined; he was in danger once more from the uncertainties which assailed him. He was no longer sure he wanted to find Johnson. Could they not simply rest for a bit. He wondered what was the best way to capture a unicorn, and whether it should be undertaken at all. Whether it was possible indeed, as well as whether or not it might be a dreadful sin, to bring down curses upon one's head. If it were possible surely someone would have done it by now? If it was Johnson down there what exactly would he say to him?

'Oh come on!' said Daphne through gritted teeth.

They toiled on and descended the slope, Trevor's leg dictating the pace much to Daphne's frustration. She frequently climbed up onto one of the huge rocks which persistently dotted the landscape (it was now a very unusual landscape) and scanned the horizon and the land in between with the thoroughness of a seaman looking for icebergs, or whales, or survivors. She was now and then rewarded with a glimpse of straw hat, or what she took to be straw hat, and less frequently with a sighting of the black-coated figure escort. It was sufficient to keep her excitement at a high level and she kept up a torrent of commentary as to what she could see and what she could not, and when they went on there was no let up in her exhortations to Trevor to keep up.

After several hours, however, by which time the menagerie man was dangerously exhausted, dishevelled, sweating and with blood again trickling from his bandaged wound, a look of incomprehension coupled with despair suddenly came over Daphne's face as she slithered off one of the boulders and said, 'They're not getting any nearer. They're just not getting any bigger. They're still the same size as when we first saw them.'

Trevor, who was slumped against the rock, managed to say 'Well, obviously we must not be gaining on them. Perhaps they're just too quick for us, I honestly cannot go any faster, and all these brambles...'

'No, no, not only are they moving very slowly, they're still going round in circles, and sometimes they seem to be coming backwards, we should have caught up with them by now. There's something strange about this. Why are they so tiny still? They seem to be permanently consigned to the distance, magically unapproachable.'

She was staring him in the face, frowning, very agitated, her look appealing to him, in the name of justice and the laws of physics, to do something about it.

Trevor stared back with resignation and thought that what was being contravened was less likely to be the laws of physics than the laws which state princesses shall have what they want, and have it immediately. He took the glasses from her and began to swarm as best he could up the outcrop.

'Over to the left, toward that tallest tree, there's a pond I think, or something shiny, over there can you see?'

He could. He could make out a little ornamental pond with a fountain. Here in the middle of nowhere. As the phrase was. Who would have built that fountain? It did not seem to be, or have been, part of anything. There were no discernible ruins nearby. After about the third, 'Can you see them?' from Daphne he was able to answer yes. They seemed to have stopped by the fountain. It was the most sustained view of them he'd had. It was Johnson, yes, even at this distance, it was definitely Johnson. He was dipping something into the pond, aha, his bowler hat! And offering his companion to drink. She declined. She was, even at this distance, quite beautiful, and he was aware of a serenity about her which was not diminished by the intervening mile, half mile, whatever it was. What on Earth was Johnson of all people doing with such a companion? Emotions of surprise, perplexity and jealousy erupted in him and tangled themselves up as he stared with ever greater concentration trying to understand what he was seeing.

'What are they doing now? Can you still see them? They're miles away, aren't they?'

Trevor could see them quite clearly, they were not 'miles away' (she was a strange girl) but he did feel a certain inapproachability which may or may not have been magical. It was more likely to be just shyness on his part, and a general reluctance to tackle the mysterious Mr Johnson. And or it may have derived from the rather daunting self containment and perfection of Johnson's companion. But his observations were suddenly perverted and overridden by a strange and compelling idea. The scene, the setting for these little characters, was one he had seen before. Not so long ago either. He was overcome by the feeling that the little ornamental pond and the soft grey stone of the fountain were the same as he had seen depicted in Daphne's diary. He had had only a glimpse, but surely it was just like it, it was the same place she had portrayed in her drawing. The distance and indistinctness of the real prospect were even represented by the sketchiness of the style of the drawing. Neither was a perfect rendition of itself but there was no doubt that each was the other.

Still looking through the binoculars, he turned to peer down at Daphne who appeared as a fuzz of different colours. She was neurotic, maybe a little insane. He could definitely feel himself slipping in that direction too, well probably more insanity than neurosis. An outright manly lunacy. Down there, Johnson was very likely mad. It felt rather as if all sanity had been left far behind, or faded away to be replaced by a new rationality which did not overly concern itself with what two and two made, but had altogether different priorities. Then he put down the binoculars and searched for the little diary in his waistband. It was not there. He rolled over and stuck his hands down his trousers and then searched about on the surface of the rock and looked down at the grass but it was gone. He looked up, grabbed the glasses and roved left and right until he found the pond again. The people had gone. But there was the little fountain, beyond the brambles and willows, in a halo of light green grasses with an apple tree or two behind it. The pencilled fountain, on the other hand, to his great chagrin, was lost. Never to be seen again. He was, however, even without it, taken aback by the abiding notion that he seemed to have experienced someone else's déjà vu. Daphne herself seemed not to have recognised the scene – at least she made no mention of it, she must have forgotten it. Had the diary drawing been done not from life at all? Was it just something she had imagined? And never ever been here? How can a place make its way over great distances and lodge an image of itself in your brain?

He did not want to be blamed for losing the diary, which was quite likely to happen. He could not go back and look for it, his injury and her mood would not allow it – he could see she would brook no excuses about going back when they were actually within sight of their quarry. He decided to say nothing about it for the moment. He suggested they stop for lunch.

She pointed out that they had no food left, and she would not stop unless Johnson did.

He said they had better find some food otherwise they would not be able to keep going.

She said, 'Look, just wait here, will you, I'll be back!' – she was uncharacteristically decisive today he'd noticed – and marched peremptorily on down the path where she was soon lost to view in the tall bracken.

As she walked she thought to herself, Johnson was now in sight, it was only Trevor's injury which was keeping her from catching and confronting him. Therefore does she need, any longer, to keep company with Trevor? His wound did not appear to her to be getting any better, despite what he says, it is still bleeding, he might still die. Whoever Johnson was, he was now located, and if she looked sharp he could not give her the slip – she might be wise to dispense with the companionship of Mr Simpson. She hurried on along the thin path which was more and more encroached by small trees and brambles and bracken, and as she turned a corner she suddenly thought: If Johnson is indeed nothing to do with the Venetians, not a man in their pay negotiating with her father and stipulating virginity, if, on the contrary he is something to do with her father's zoo, why was she following him? If he represented no designs on her as an international marital chattel and she therefore had no reason to belabour him, why was she still following him? The only reason there could be must be that she was following him for the same reason that Trevor was following him. And she did not know what that was. He had not said. Had she asked him? No, she could not remember having asked him, and if she had she could not remember the answer. So her anger with the bowler hat, her fixation with the need to track him down, had outrun logic and persisted only as a matter of momentum.

She had actually slowed down considerably now. 'If he dies, I'll have no idea why I'm following Johnson.'

Trevor rolled onto his back, on top of the great slab of stone, rather like a sacrificial victim he thought, and allowed the sunlight to play over his closed eyelids as he enjoyed the stridulations of the crickets and grasshoppers (*orthoptera*).

'What the hell,' he thought. Then he drifted off into daydreams of Millicent and the children which took place in a peculiarly twisted cardboard version of their house in Dumbleton Close, except that it was not in Dumbleton Close, it was on the edge, right on the edge, of a an immense white cliff with blue sea and crashing waves far below. It was a bit like being inside one of Millicent's paintings. But suddenly he was not in the house he was outside it, walking up a sandy path toward the house and he was not alone, the beautiful girl, Johnson's beautiful, otherworldly companion was with him. She was telling him, explaining very simply as if she were talking to someone not very intelligent but trying to be polite, that Johnson is her uncle, that she follows him, she does as he requests, for he is very wise and knows what must be done. She is reluctant to look at Trevor, who feels very insignificant in her presence. He realises that since he is dreaming this is an instance of a place from afar transporting itself into his mind and he is infected with an urgent desire to sketch the house, it is wrong to experience places without having first seen a drawing of them, he must draw number 33 Dumbleton Close quickly, before it falls into the sea. He wanted Princess Daphne to see this drawing, and to recognise the place.

CHAPTER FORTY

Vangrannicus looked up at the goat-sucking cherub in the large painting on his office wall and once again thought it knew something he did not. He paced up and down for a while and then sat down at his desk, hunched over, steepling his fingers, pursing his lips, deep in thought. Ruscum spied on him through the crack in the door, waiting for a flurry of 'urgent' orders, and 'immediate' orders and 'top priorities,' but the sitting and the thinking seemed just to go on and on. There was still no news about the King, no sign or sighting of him, no one had any idea where he might be, even Vangrannicus's spies had drawn a blank. Nor, come to that, was there any news of his daughter, the heir. So there arose the real prospect of the extinction of the line, the end of the House of Walpaert, after all these generations. A sudden, totally unexpected and utterly unaccountable snuffing of the noble candle after almost five hundred years. It was unthinkable.

Vangrannicus assumed that the nation shared his perturbation, but as a whole it did not. Some had not even noticed that the King was not there. Some had, but did not care. There were some few genuinely worried about what had become of him, but then there was a not insignificant number – growing, in the wake of the recent discontent – who privately relished the chance of a clean sweep and a republican coup.

The rioting, which had seemed at its beginning to be the earthquake which would churn up the entire anthill and leave nothing unchanged, had – to almost everyone's surprise – subsided, and this new and unexpected contortion of the course of events had been wrought by concatenations of happenstance and the peculiarly gusting forces of invisible winds which stretched some things and slackened others and pushed things back and sideways. It was as if the road of history had suddenly turned a corner and revealed a track less rough and less steep, less injurious to travellers for the most part, but one which soon showed itself to be uncertain as to direction and unsettling as to the threats it might conceal. No one, at the time, knew how it had come about. Certainly apathy, the old ally of the status quo, had crept slowly out and spread like sludge into the cracks and fissures through which the idealists with their sledgehammers had hoped to entice progress. But there had also been specific odd chance events which crucially undermined the impetus of the insurrection. One of the most dedicated and ruthless of the anarchist faction, moving carefully along the street, gingerly carrying in a delicate parcel a round black bomb, was so charmed by the music coming from an upstairs window one day that he could not help stopping to listen. Entranced by the song, his death-dealing errand was so delayed that the dignitaries whom he was to have despatched had long since passed down the avenue and round the corner by the time he came to himself. The gramophone on the windowsill, playing a scratched but poignant melody, had perhaps begun the end of the revolution.

On the other side, Commander Horrocks, Chief of Police, had discovered that his daughter was secretly engaged to one of the ring leaders: a boy he had found sufficiently intelligent, brave and accomplished that the revelation about his politics failed to scotch entirely his status as a prospective son-in-law. Once the forces of repression and insurrection were espoused in this way it signalled not the end of family rows particularly, but the dilapidation of street barricades and the dissipation of armed outrages.

Things would not be the same though. In spite of the sympathetic and repentant noises the government made, issuing messages about 'new departures', 'once and for all', and 'at long last', into the 'realms of justice and equality', and in spite of the fact that those responsible for these monumental and historic sounding pronouncements did indeed believe their own utterances (Vangrannicus, the chief fount of them, certainly did) nothing of that ilk was in fact likely to occur. Nobody really knew how to do it. Instead, the changes that did come about were spontaneous, and not ordained by any establishment, instead rising up from ground level and growing as vigorously and as obstinately as weeds – weeds which had had their menacing beauty revealed to them and relished the quietly disruptive role, which they were suddenly able to understand and glory in. The troubles had not resulted in a *coup d'etat* but seemed to have had the effect of calling into being a sort of recalcitrant poetic sensibility which began to pervade the generality of the people. The under-class now made a proud and disdainful cloak of its poverty and wrapped itself in it defiantly. A principled and superior reluctance to conform to the mores of society began to take hold, people refused to do as they were told, and a cultivated fecklessness was everywhere apparent. Bohemian attitudes interrupted and belittled the normal course of economic activity and it all came to be rather more alarming for the bourgeoisie than the rioting had been. All in all, having discovered that the forces of reaction were spiritually vacuous, just too stupid to be taken seriously, the populace, having taken a false step toward conventional revolution, now retreated from it, conserved its energy, cultivated renitence and was thus ripe for something more significant, for something unknown and unprecedented and bizarre. All the nation seemed to be waiting, waiting with an eager trepidation, a barely contained excitement, which might easily rise in its nervousness to lap dangerously close to hysteria. It was a time when people were susceptible to rumour, and even though they were mostly reluctant to do more than hint at what they believed exactly, many of them started to say, 'Something is coming.'

Vangrannicus liked to control all the buzz and the whisper and the evulgation, and in happier times it had been his office which had been the source of most of the stories that went around. His men, even now (especially now, in fact) were still busy sowing rumour (and provoking confusion by simultaneously sowing counter-rumour) in the taverns and pie shops and laundries and at bus stops and butchers shops – wherever there was a queue there would be a brass-buttoned boy in mufti reciting the carefully rehearsed sentiments that had been dinned into him. But they had an uphill struggle. People would stare into the distance and then turn to look the fresh-faced agent in the eye and say, 'It may be, it may be as you say, but I myself have heard different things.' Or they would simply gaze at a pile of horse dung steaming in the street and shake their head and smile. Others would guffaw and say, 'Get away with yer, pull the other one, it's got bells on!'

Those others in Vangrannicus's pay whose job it was to spy, to slink about eavesdropping and slyly interrogating the mood of the people often heard strange things, and Ruscum, assigned this role one dark night, crept into one of the lowest and dingiest ale houses in a corner of the oldest part of the town, eager to unearth some sentiments that might startle his superior. However, as far as the mood of the nation and the air of alarm and the prophecies of the imminence of either doom or spiritual resurgence which buzzed up and down like alternating swarms of manic bees were concerned, this place appeared at first to be a backwater largely untouched.

Ruscum looked around with a sigh of disappointment. In a corner sat a lumpy, bearded man, very old and unkempt, taking regular pulls at a glass of strong beer and occasionally spitting into the fire with a muffled oath. Had the light been better, Ruscum might just have recognised (as he did in the end) an ancient version of the uniform he himself wore when not undercover. But it was dark; in this corner there was no reading done, there were no pictures on the walls, and the customers had no wish either to stare at one another (people took exception to this) nor to be recognised. And those ladies who sometimes here hawked their brevity of bliss also preferred their charms to be spared too close an examination.

The denizens – their number belied by both the dark and the grim silence which mostly prevailed in the room – were stirred not at all by Ruscum's clinking of the latch, and continued contemplating their drinks, or the floor, or their own sad histories which rolled around once more before them, and once more demanded another glass before they would accept the explanations being offered (offered mostly in frowning silence but some mumbled and muttered to themselves, occasionally breaking out into an audible oath). It appeared Ruscum would be able to report little from here, there was no conversation at all, just coughing and grunting and then the intermittent low crooning of some old song, the few words remembered being repeated *ad infinitum*.

The barman gazed in a sphinx-like stare, the fierce eyes of his diminutive wife darted to and fro as she filled the beaker. The smoke and fumes and fluids of the desperate relaxations of many generations were absorbed into the black beams and creaking boards of the place; stepping carefully round the form of a sleeping bulldog he took a seat by the fire and began to experience an edgy fascination for this slough of despond as he looked furtively across at the creature on the other side of the fire place.

Barkstein, whose chin had almost slipped down onto his chest in a not unfamiliar attitude of submission to liquor and the accumulated exhaustion of his years, suddenly lifted himself up a little as he caught Ruscum's eye and made a noise which the latter interpreted as some sort of greeting.

'Evening,' said Ruscum.

Barkstein made another noise then hoisted himself up and spat again in the fire, settling back with a grin as if he might have made a joke. Ruscum smiled a small and rather tentative smile.

Silence then prevailed once more for a good few minutes, even the wistful dirge – half sung, half moaned – had finally collapsed back into the sad void from which it had arisen.

'Bit chilly out,' said Ruscum who could think of nothing better for his opening remark. Barkstein neither moved nor spoke, except that the heavy beer glass cradled in his two hands rose and fell on his belly with the breathing which wheezed in and out from him with a sound like some rusty and derelict piece of farm machinery pushed to and fro by some idle hand which might at any moment tire of such a pointless occupation.

'Nice fire here though,' Ruscum persisted.

This most innocent of gambits, like a fly cast hopefully onto still waters, somewhat surprisingly caught the eye of the deep lying, ostensibly somnolent old fish, and Ruscum watched and waited for Barkstein to rise.

Eventually he broke the surface, 'Aye, aye guffire,' and then made a noise which might have contained an element of chortle but was mostly bronchial readjustments – it concluded with another copious spit into the hissing logs. His mouth was crooked into a smile but the eyes which he turned on Ruscum as he sat back again remained serious, rather threatening in fact, as he said, 'Berrathan dahn theer, berrathan dahn theer, in t'damp.'

'Down there?' asked Ruscum, tentatively, full of interest, his head on one side in an inviting gesture.

'Aye, dahn theer. Ah wo underground fer years, years and years since… tha wudda bin nobbut more'n a bairn when I fost went dahn.' And his tone was somewhat accusatory, as if the cowardly Ruscum, by his failure to suffer the same fate had somehow contributed to it.

'Ah, I see, you were a miner!'

'Miner? Nah, pshaw! Miner? Norrabluddyminer. Never a bluddy miner! I guarded t'beast, guarded t'beast!' And he suddenly remembered it was a secret and put a gnarled and twisted forefinger up to his mouth and looked sideways into the gloom of the inn in a surprisingly theatrical gesture.

Ruscum leaned forward in his seat and for the first time made out the one remaining tarnished brass button on Barkstein's coat; even in this light Ruscum was sharp enough to recognise the crown it bore.

'Oh aye, you guarded the beast,' he said quietly, and respectfully, hoping to set a conspiratorial tone and to tempt the other into revelations.

But it was not going to be as straightforward as that. Barkstein might be gently poked into a talkative mood, but understanding what he said was by no means a simple matter. He jumbled words and syllables, invented his own haphazard syntax, interposed obscure and incomprehensible oaths and his diction itself had slumped into a slur of sound whose original components remained largely recognisable only to the speaker – this was no doubt derived from years of talking only to himself, 'dahn theer'. He also had an annoying habit, similarly derived, of assuming his interlocutor already knew what he was talking about.

Of course, Ruscum ingratiated himself in the time honoured manner – attending to the man's wants each time the glass was drained. The strong beer loosened Barkstein's tongue but made its formation of distinct words even more lazy and anarchic. Eventually, by dint of hard listening, as if he was struggling to interpret an entirely foreign language, Ruscum came to understand that Barkstein had been a castle warder and that for many years he had been more or less abandoned in the deepest part of the old dungeons entirely in charge of something. But quite what it was he could not fathom. Sometimes he thought it was actually a man, at other times he thought no, he does mean an animal, a large and potentially dangerous animal, but one with mysterious and unlikely qualities.

For years and years, Barkstein had remained silent, rarely in truth having the opportunity to speak to other people, but dutifully guarding his secret when he did, it having been so impressed upon him at the time of 'the event' that he must keep his mouth shut on pain of death... But now he was old, so very old, the beast was gone, he himself was up again, up amongst the living, and it was almost as if he had passed into another existence, where old truths might now be set free with a whisper across the hearth. And as he spoke he often forgot that what he spoke were secrets rather than dreams.

There was a recurring element in the tale, however, which further hampered Ruscum's understanding. This was the 'loyon', presumably an actual lion, that was involved in certain crucial events. It seemed it was the 'loyon' that had originally captured the enigmatic beast and brought it down to be incarcerated deep into the castle. What this lion was, remained a mystery to Ruscum, as well as how it managed to give orders or whether it was itself wild or domesticated. It seemed to be an animal with a whole array of special powers. It did occur to Ruscum that it might not be real, might only be an invention in Barkstein's head, and that it was he himself, possibly with underlings, who had entrapped and imprisoned the other thing. Since the nature and character of the other thing, the thing that Barkstein guarded, remained so ill-defined, there may be some excuse for that mystery overlapping to obscure the true nature of its adversary.

As Ruscum himself sipped his third glass of the strong beer he was becoming rapt in visions of a huge god-like lion, possibly with the power of speech, overpowering, with the help of minions, a strong and malevolent animal, not native to these climes, immensely strange and possibly representing an alien morality. By the time he sipped his fifth glass (all in the line of duty) Barkstein himself was becoming transmogrified, his human attributes appeared mere vestigial tokens, the hair and hide and broken teeth, the smell and the dark red eyes were those of something which could never have been to school or played cricket or queued to buy a newspaper or applied for a job; it was obvious now, he was himself some sort of throwback, a chance survival of some hybrid race, interbred with something historic and indefinable.

'An angel cum dahn, an angel cum dahn, and took it up,' whispered Barkstein wistfully, waving his beer pot at the fire.

Without understanding, Ruscum lapsed into a slurring repetition of this mantra, 'Nayngel cum dahn, nayngel cum dahn,' before losing consciousness.

CHAPTER FORTY ONE

Pippa and Willis were staring gloomily at the teapot in their little room at the zoo, bereft, and unable to think what to do.

'How long has she been gone? It seems like ages.'

'You know *exactly* how long she's been gone, and so do I.'

'Did you water the aspidistra?'

'Yes. In any case, you can't kill an aspidistra, they'll live through anything.'

'So many people disappeared. Is Jemima with them, do you think? Have they all gone off together?'

'I don't think they all went together, but I wouldn't be surprised if they were all on the same scent. I think they're probably all looking for the same thing.'

They were silent for a while, Pippa resumed her copying of figures from scraps of paper, which she was neatly entering into an accounts ledger. This was always done for some reason with an old fashioned steel nibbed pen which required to be dipped frequently into an ink bottle, and made the scratching noises which underscored the ticking of the clock to emphasise the persistence of time. Was it comforting that time ticked on, ticked on, ticking off in tiny measurements the journey across the monstrous hole which was Jemima's absence? Or did it feel more like the lonely ticking and the scratching would just go on for ever, and never be relieved by that longed for voice, or footstep, or rattle of the brass door knob?

Willis was fiddling with a loose strand of purple wool on the tea cosy. 'Is it the unicorn? Are they all gone in search of the unicorn, do we think?'

'Yes,' said Pippa without looking up. 'That's what we think.'

'But there isn't a unicorn.'

'We can't say that can we; we can say that there is very little evidence for the existence of the unicorn, but we can't actually say, definitively, that it does not exist.'

'And mad, smelly Johnson is evidence, is he? I rather think not.'

'Well, whatever you, or we, think, I'm pretty sure that's where they've all gone. There may be something that's happened we don't know about.'

'Well you're probably right there.'

There was a knock at the door. They looked at one another in puzzlement and with beating hearts for a second before Willis relinquished the wool and got up to answer it.

'Yes, hello can I help you?' Pippa heard Willis say, and the nib moved again, carefully shaping the tail of a nine.

'Sorry to bother you, but my name's Newsome, I work for Jolyon Willoughby, they said at the gate that you might be the people to help me, this is Ms Cake's office, isn't it? You see, he seems to have gone off somewhere, and I'm not sure where, and to be honest I'm getting rather worried about him, I wonder if you might know where he is? Is Ms Cake in? You see, I believe it was to do with his work here, with the animal collecting and everything.'

The tall figure in a camel hair overcoat, paisley scarf and brown trilby hat was a huge surprise to Willis and she was a little nonplussed, both by the overall effect of the unusual personage and by what he had to say, but she managed a rather hesitant smile and invited him in. He was ushered to a stool beside the incubator and offered a cup of tea, but Pippa, pressing blotting paper to her page, said it would be cold and they should make some fresh.

Mr Newsome, it was a little diffidently made plain, preferred to remain 'Mister' Newsome. (His forename had been almost redundant from the first – he was, by custom, by preference and by propriety, a 'mister' or more usually indeed, just 'Newsome'.) For all his distaste for the presuming use of familiar names, he proved to be a very nice man and they soon discovered that their situations were almost identical – a much loved employer, in each case the cornerstone of their daily lives, had suddenly vanished they knew not where. In Newsome's case of course it was a cornerstone of very long standing, for Pippa and Willis it had been relatively newly erected but nonetheless its absence was equally calamitous. Newsome was a methodical man and was able to recount in detail the circumstances surrounding Willoughby's departure – the proletarian disguise, the agitation, the sudden and unaccustomed anxiety and, most crucially he could list the books which had lain scattered about and piled up on the breakfast table that morning – could name them and, following his subsequent wary perusal of them, say something of what they were about: fossils, and animals with a horn. (It was a measure of his concern that he was prepared to reveal private things about his employer – something he would normally regard as an unforgivable breach of trust.) But, crucially, he was also able to reveal that Ms Cake herself had been to see him after his master had disappeared. She had asked about Willoughby, and had been most interested in the books he had been able to show her. That clinched it for the girls and they told Newsome of their suspicions and of Mr Johnson and his performance at the rotunda before the King.

'So that is definitely it, that's what's happened, they've gone off, either separately or together to find the unicorn,' said Pippa, closing the ledger and getting up from her seat to look out of the window, her expression a troubled frown.

'Goodness,' said Newsome, taking in this weighty information wide-eyed and staring sternly at his teacup; this news in fact, confirmed his own suspicions. This was not the same as an organised zoo expedition in search of a specimen; this was bizarre, there was madness, he felt, in this escapade, which seemed to have been launched peremptorily, without any of the usual planning and delegation, it was as if Jolyon had been bitten by some sort of horse-fly which had him leaping into servants' clothes and tearing off with an insane look in his eye which was both hungry and terrified. The serene, self-satisfied composure, and awareness of his station, which usually characterised his master had evaporated in a trice and Newsome was very troubled by the whole thing.

They none of them knew what to do. Their circumstances were of course subtly different – for whilst the girls were worried and rudderless, they had had no orders as to following after, or sending out search parties, or, 'If you don't hear from me by...' they were simply expected to carry on – whereas Newsome, fearful both for the physical well-being and the state of mind of Sir Jolyon felt he probably ought to embark on some sort of rescue mission, but had not the first idea how to go about it.

They sat together for the greater part of the afternoon, reassuring one another, or trying to, and a bonus for the ladies were insights into the home life of the remote and snooty Willoughby (Willis in particular found this fascinating) which Newsome could not help revealing in his extremis. Also in the course of their talk, they inevitably said the word 'unicorn' rather often. They were not aware that, the window being open, what they said could be heard on the path outside – the path which connected the most distant cages with the tool sheds and food stores and along which a labourer from time to time that afternoon had occasion to ply his wheel-barrow.

Twice this personage heard the word 'unicorn', once on the way out, and once on the way back, and he was greatly puzzled. But when he crept quietly back later, without his barrow, to hear more, the window was still open but it appeared that they had all gone. And somehow the open window and vacant room seemed now to give a strange echo to that mysterious word, to make him wonder whether he had really heard it, but then the uncertainty made it somehow even more magical and he kept thinking about it.

He could not resist repeating the word that he'd heard, firstly to himself, then he repeated it to his family and to the public bar of the Black Swan and the word threaded its way into this conversation and that and was recognised by persons who had heard it at the rotunda some while ago and began repeating it themselves.

Meanwhile, Ruscum did not understand that, for Barkstein, 'lion' (or 'loyon') was merely heraldic shorthand for King Dagobert himself – if he had realised this he would have been knocked sideways of course and events would have taken a different turn. As it was, he naively carried the strange story from the Pipemakers' Arms into the castle gardens on his habitual visits there and began cryptically hinting to persons he came across about a lion in an underground struggle with a mysterious beast. It did not take long for the two stories to come together. Which they did like tinder and flint, and the bushfire was soon well and truly ignited.

The whole community had had an ear cocked for a portent, for a sign of the coming of something, ever since the rebellion had fizzled out, and the imminence of an apocalyptic pair of giant beasts, mighty in horn and tooth and claw and hoof, coming to wrench apart a dying civilisation was just what they had been waiting for. It was what they all deserved and they were ready and eager to welcome it.

One old woman sitting alone by her high window, having heard the talk, relinquished her knitting for a moment to recite to herself with a sort of delighted sing-song foreboding, 'Some gave them white bread and some gave them brown,' seeing in her mind's eye the colossal godzillas striding out of the nursery to do battle.

CHAPTER FORTY TWO

Freddie stumbled on, singing softly to himself and hardly looking where he was going. Having lain for an hour in a hollow listening to the wind and wishing for oblivion, a sort of sleep had eventually overcome him, but, now risen and on his way again, though he appeared less frantic he was not refreshed and it was not calmness he had achieved, more a sort of stupefaction. In this state it seemed some half remembered canzonet, waveringly intoned, assisted in keeping his perturbations at bay by contributing a sustaining rhythm to his footsteps: 'The rain may na wet me, The sun may na dry me, Hey there, pretty girl won't you come a riding?'

He was very much alone, but he was not unobserved. Brisk, a runaway sheepdog, stared at him through the camouflage of long grass beside the track. This was an animal who had had enough of farmers and of farmer's boys and of whistles and of gates and of continual bleatings. This was an animal intent on un-domesticating himself and in no mood to make contact with people again. He would never more lick their milky hairless paws or look them in the eye in a vain attempt to divine their bizarre needs, he was finished with that species and would be much happier as a dog alone – or a dog amongst dogs if he met the right sort – but never a kennel dweller more. Having set himself free he was re-discovering the natural role of *canis lupus* (they could keep their *familiaris*). This was the true life; he'd found he could get along very well hunting and scavenging, so it was with a rather self satisfied curiosity that he watched this old man, obviously mad, plunging and tottering along the track, looking at the ground, then stopping to stare up into the clouds, and making a quiet purring-growling noise as he went along. He won't last long, thought Brisk. Unless someone finds him and feeds him he'll fall by the wayside; and then I shall have to face the dilemma: am I sufficiently rid of any regard for the bipeds that I could do the sensible, practical thing, and eat one? This reminded him of food and his attention turned back to the morsel of leather he had been chewing. He had been at it for a while, it was something he had found a few miles away lying under the bracken. It had been all square and with neat leaves of paper sandwiched in it to start with, but he had chewed them out and savaged them and spat them out and they now trailed about the area, and blew here and there like fat damp confetti, of no interest to a dog. The leather cover was something to be going on with, however, and he continued quietly gnawing and slavering over it whilst King Dagobert the Fourth became lost to view in the birch trees and his little song faded away.

The next day Brisk was long gone but, it having been a dry night, the many fragments and lumps of paper remained in the grass and across the path along which two figures now made their way.

Very often these men spoke in German, but today, the one in the shapeless hat, said in English, 'Let us not argue any more.'

'No, let us not agree any more,' rejoined his companion. 'Whether or not we argue we ought not to agree, do you not see?'

'What? What do you mean?'

'Well, if we agree all the time there's no point in there being two of us, is there?'

'I don't...'

'Well, if there's no point in there being two of us, there might as well just be me.'

The other stopped and gave him a stare before turning away and saying, 'And how would that happen?'

'Oh, I don't know, bundle you up in a sack and have you carried off by a gigantic bird, throw you down a well, call up a two-headed giant – any number of options really...'

Then he saw the pieces of paper and stopped to pick one up. 'Look at this, what's this, do you think? There's writing on it.'

Willoughby couldn't help but join in and started, desultorily at first, picking up the morsels of paper, which were shredded to various degrees but many of which still preserved readable fragments of words and phrases.

Grimes started reading the pieces out loud and his eyes dilated and his voice got even louder as he delighted in the way these manuscript shards occasionally made a mad syntax together. 'We can rebuild it! We can rebuild it! Collect them all, we must collect them all.' He grabbed Willoughby's elbow and started shaking it.

'Come on, come on! This must be it, this must be the story we've been looking for, ha ha, it must be the story of the unicorn. It will tell us where it is, ha ha!'

Willoughby, who was by now no longer in the least the assured and commanding figure Newsome would recognise, mechanically picked up more and more pieces of paper and handed them to his excited companion who knelt down, smoothed them out and lay them on the grass as he slowly read out each one and looked for something which might follow it, or precede it. When he found three letters together which had been the end of a 'tunic' still attached to the 'orn' which had been part of 'ornamented' (the original phrase from an early part of Daphne's diary had been about them 'making me wear a stupid tunic ornamented with flowers') he whooped, waved it in the air and leapt up to do a little dance around his friend.

Willoughby was, these days, ever bemused and wrong footed by a constant series of such antics, and the strange look that often came over him signified that he was again entertaining the possibility that his companion might after all be merely some sort of *vorstellung*, an invention of his stretched and exhausted mind. But he went on complying with it, and playing the man's games, wondering the while about how it had all come about. He now found himself believing fervently in the unicorn, and prayed to it in the dead of night that it might come and rescue him. In fact, the parts of Daphne's chronicle of her life proved to be eminently amenable to being re-arranged into a fairy story; quite probably anyone's history, with a judicious shuffling of chapters and juggling of sentences and swapping of phrases, could be revealed as the magical tale which explains nothing but lays the mystery of experience before the reader in an enticing and wholly captivating way. And it seemed the unlikely pair had the knack. They went on to divine and reconstruct many stories from the fragments they came across, which would come over time to have a wide circulation. Certain of them would even be set to music. The wild and moon-mad head of Grimes combined well with the detached and crumbling but still erudite and conjectural brain of Willoughby.

Willoughby had begun to take consolation from an understanding that, though all things were possible and most of them bad, there was a wry amusement to be found in the shocks that fate manipulated and dealt out lavishly at every turn. They were not above interpolating and interpreting, and Grimes in particular was often heard to say, 'What was obviously meant here but for some missing pages was...' and Willoughby to say, 'this can't have happened quite like that, surely,' and, 'There's a section missing here, it must have been the bit where...' But in spite of their enhancements and manipulations, Grimes from the outset, and Willoughby eventually, believed what they had written to be a version of the truth. All brought about because The Black Dog Who Had Had Enough of Sheep devoured a book he could not read.

CHAPTER FORTY THREE

Meanwhile the King shambled on, his personal attendant unicorn rather overshadowed at times by the looming memory of Nicodemus now, but still present and buoying him up. There was no rationality as to the directions he took – and he took many, all of them in fact, at different times – he meandered and veered and circumnavigated things and sometimes he was ambushed by the sun or the moon when they and he came upon one another unexpectedly – time, and the notion of a right or wrong direction had abandoned him.

Yet the hope that any moment he might come up with Millicent never diminished and he noticed that, no matter what the direction, the further he went the better he felt, and this had the effect of making him reluctant to stop and so he was quite exhausted and barely wheezing his song – 'Hey pretty girl... won't you... come a-ridin'... Hey pretty girl... won't you come a-ridin'' – when he found himself amongst large granite boulders and tall bracken and wending along a track which lead him to an ornamental fountain in a pond, the sight of which was so soothing, so rare, so odd, so alluring, so enigmatic, so consoling, as to ridicule all convention and expectations, and he flopped down in a swoon praying that it was not a mirage.

It was difficult to imagine the fountain and pond being conceived in the abstract and then constructed with stone and chisel, shovel and mortar, for it had the quiet semblance of something eternal. It was such a pleasingly proportioned thing, beautiful yet unassuming; there was no individual part of it which was odd or unusual particularly but the whole, with its vaguely baroque style (albeit with the effulgence of that idiom gratifyingly subdued) with its dragonflies, bull rushes, water boatmen and the patinas of moss and lichen together with the duckweed in the corners, the gentle mesmeric splashing, the long grasses that surrounded it and the willow trees which befriended it, all became something which embodied peace and reflection and solace.

Amongst the long meadow grasses he slept and his unicorn drank of the clear water, and was refreshed and made considerably more substantial. Freddie himself remained invisible, since the grass was very tall and the circumference of the pond sufficient that it was possible to approach it from many directions without glimpsing dormant royalty.

Johnson and the mysterious girl approached it and retreated from it as they strolled too and fro on the other side, but it was not at all obvious what Johnson and his companion noticed or did not notice for they had a certain air about them which suggested, not that they consciously knew everything, it was more as if everything important to be known already lay naturally deep within them and they were anyway not inclined to feel or express surprise in the conventional way, their cognizance of both past events and what may come to pass deriving from an arcane, and somewhat metaphysical standpoint.

Other persons continued to watch the pond from their distant boulder, though not sufficiently intently to have seen the arrival of the King however, who had made his entrance whilst their attention had been distracted.

If Daphne had seen her father at this point... who can say what would have befallen? But she had not seen him. Neither she nor Trevor.

And then there was a sudden crashing in the undergrowth behind them. The alarming noise of something large lumbering with no regard for stealth through the brush and the saplings, crashing through whatever was in its way.

Trevor slipped smartly off his boulder and, grabbing his crutch, displayed a turn of speed he would not have been thought capable of a minute ago.

Daphne grabbed her own bag and overtook him in the scramble into the tall green sea. They did not care about paths, they wanted to be as far away from the noise as possible and as much hidden from the noise as possible, and all as quickly as possible. Instinctively they ran, not toward the fountain and Johnson and the girl but sideways, away, they hoped, from everything. As long as there was a possibility that it was a pig they would keep going. Not even thinking that they might actually be fleeing from a unicorn.

CHAPTER FORTY FOUR

The little wind tried vainly to stir a stiff line of poplar trees which stood immensely tall in a forbidding rank. Reluctant to shelter anything, they were unruffled by squirrels and harboured no owls. Aspiring with the grandeur of their proportions to hint at the ineffability of a superior genus, in fact there was something disappointing and even vaguely disreputable beneath their bristling reserve, and Millicent was immediately alive to it; these cathedral-high besoms, scratching invisible things from the blank air, gave rise to feelings not of awe but only of narrowness, which gave rise to a twiggy despondency.

Craning their necks from time to time to look up at them, Millicent and Nicodemus made their way through the moribund farmland that lay at their feet, where the fields were half ploughed and full of couch grass, the hedges overgrown and the stiles rotten and covered by brambles; the Lanes themselves here were potholed and penetrated by thrusting weeds, for this was where, like a great fishing net left out in the mud, the rotting edge of the mesh of lanes had frayed away to nothing. The roadways having led nowhere in particular for so many miles, they now gave up the pretence, ceased holding hands with one another and actually deposited the traveller nowhere in particular before fading away.

Millicent was however fascinated by finding herself, as it seemed, at the beginning of archaeology – they were walking along roads which very soon would be roads no more, the incursions and smothering of vegetation and encroaching earth were already advanced in hiding this obscure little byway. She was gripped by an acute awareness of the slipping away of something unique to this place, for the sadness itself would be sunk out of sight before long, and for ever outside the range of anyone's imagination. She would probably be the last person to be in this place as it used to be and feel the keen and penetrating anguish of its oblivion. She spied the remains of a rusty old kettle lying under a bush and it was immediately imbued with all the pathos of a lost generation. It was possible that Boldoni himself might have passed this way, his easel on a donkey on a sunnier day, his equanimity undisturbed by the tall trees, (which might not have been tall then) smoking a pipe and looking into the distance.

Millicent was marvellous, and always marvelling, and on this day, though it was a grey place with a black ape, malevolent spiky plants, damp and sadness oozing from the cracked and punctured and fading road, overshadowed by unfriendly poplars, all beneath a dark sky, still she was able to look at it, to be with and amongst all these things even the desperate decayed and irritating sight of the rusty kettle, to enjoy the flattened emotions of this place and to imagine a past which she re-created with the same longing she put into her drawings. She took what was about her and relished it, she peered deeply into the remnants of the history of the place around her and could so strongly feel its character and its mixed fortunes. This forgotten lane in a forgotten field, these grim and moody monster weeds need only to be looked upon with an open heart to be imbued with a cathartic, subtle and incisive sense of revelation. Through her art she was capable of exalting this nadir of neglect and making it shine in the soul.

It was inconceivable that Nicodemus might be affected by such rarefied feelings of indeterminate loss as she felt, but he held Millicent's hand quite tightly, eyed tall nettles suspiciously, and looked up glumly as the sun was again suddenly buried by grey cloud. She stopped, overcome by her inspiration. Taking out her sketch pad and pencil she sat down and worked quickly for a while, bewitched by a great thistle, haughty, spiked and unassailable, which grew up from the crumbling rubble of the roadway.

Nicodemus soon knuckled over to join her, still carefully carrying the can of pineapple chunks he'd been given a mile back in his other hand. He looked at what she was doing and was fascinated by the marks on the paper and by the pencil moving up and down and from side to side, the long and short shading, vigorous cross hatching, and the long and bold lines joining other lines and changing shapes before his eyes.

Did he see a thistle? Did he see a sense of loss, the slow and inevitable rampage of stark and thorny forces – which is what motivated her? Or did he see merely the graphite marks? She did not know, but she looked into his eyes from time to time as they in turn watched her moving pencil and the mystery of Nicodemus again encroached upon her.

After a little while she folded back her thistle and turned with a bright clean page to Nicodemus, who was sitting now only inches away from her. The unpredictable ape remained still and continued looking into her eyes as they darted between him and the paper. In a very few minutes the portrait was finished and she leaned back and squinted and reviewed her work. Then she moved to kneel beside Nicodemus and showed him what she had done. She did not know whether apes, or any animals could recognise two dimensional representations of things; she could not remember whether those who researched these things held that this was a trick only the human brain was capable of and not available to lesser beings. But she put an arm round him – as far as it would go – and they looked at the drawing together and then Nicodemus looked away from the drawing and stared at Millicent and then she withdrew her arm and started to point at his nose in the picture and then – tentatively, they had not before attained this level of intimacy – touch his nose in reality.

He gave no sign of understanding at first, but he was interested, and or bemused by what she was doing and she moved boldly on to indicate his right ear, and his forehead and his chin. He began to touch her nose and her chin. Millicent quickly rendered each of her own features – as far as she remembered them – on the paper and they looked together. Nicodemus grabbed the pencil in his fist and zigged and zagged in strokes just like those of a human baby except they were so powerful they threatened to rip through the paper. Millicent pulled up a dandelion leaf and drew it and they both watched the ghost of the leaf appear magically on the sheet. This he seemed to understand. He looked at the leaf, he picked it up and examined it; he picked up the sketchbook and examined the drawing of the leaf. He looked at Millicent. She touched her nose, she pointed to the drawing of her nose. She turned the sheets back to reveal his portrait, touched the nose of the portrait… touched his nose.

As a baby ape in the experimental household in which he'd been brought up, these things had been done before. Freddie had sat before a large mirror holding his hand on hundreds of occasions whilst Queen Iphigenia had made detailed notes of every action and reaction of Nicodemus. Eventually he had seemed to recognise himself, pointing to the image and then pointing to himself, and Freddie had been ecstatic – it proved he had a sense of his own identity, that he could think of himself as a discrete entity, that he had a concept of himself in the abstract. Iphigenia had been less convinced and had seen him on subsequent occasions, when left to himself, looking into mirrors and then creeping behind them to find the Nicodemus that dwelt there. But Freddie would have none of it. His own princely chimpanzee had taken a giant step onto the first rung of the ladder which would lead up toward language and philosophy.

Yet Nicodemus now sat in obscurity on a decaying road to nowhere. Instead of being the most celebrated animal in the world he was one over whose existence a dark veil had been drawn, and elaborate efforts had been made to erase him from history. Millicent took advantage of the physical closeness the two now found themselves sharing to look again into his eyes, this time in search of a clue – had he killed the Queen? It was perfectly possible to look into the eyes of a human being and not have any idea as to whether they had killed someone, the inscrutability of an ape would probably exceed that, so her hopes were not high, but she looked anyway and wondered what had happened and who exactly had done what to whom and what were they feeling at the time and why. It was a woman he was said to have killed. A woman such as herself. She was sitting at the ends of the Earth with a powerful animal who could beat her to death quite easily if he were so motivated. She looked and she saw his deep brown soft African eyes with their black pupils, the dark leathery wrinkles beneath those eyes, the characteristic low forehead and pronounced orbits of the skull, the very wide very straight mouth, the huge ears, the grey beard about the chin and the black hair – it was hair wasn't it, not fur? she made bold to stroke it gently on his arm – the nostrils erupting from the face independent of any nasal superstructure. 'Did he know who he was?' was one question. 'Did he know what he'd done?' was another. Could he answer, 'Yes,' to the latter without answering, 'Yes,' to the former? Could he remember, could he remember his own history, or was each morning a new day? And if he could remember what he had done and if he knew that it was his own self that had chosen to do it, did he ever wish he had not done it? Could he understand a word like 'sorry' other than as a sound made when a cup got knocked over or someone was bumped into? And – while she was asking hypothetical questions – what was his idea of her, Millicent? Where did he think she had come from? Millicent felt frustrated by her own ignorance – she could not even begin to answer any of these questions, which must have been addressed by specialists of one sort or another over the years but it had all remained outside her ambit. And then, for all she knew, perhaps the whole concept of identity could never have any relevance whatever to an animal's being; an animal might have ideas which govern its sense of the world which we have no words for and no power to imagine. The imposition of the philosophy of one species (the one that thought it was the only one that could think) onto other species was possibly an arrogant and pointless exercise. She remembered the story of the flamingo and the abacus and let out a little laugh.

What she could do was what she had done, which was release him, and she had no qualms about that having been the right thing to do. They would go on together and find Freddie and all would be well – Nicodemus would be blessed by the unicorn and released into the wild somewhere.

He drained the juice from the tin and she dared again to stroke him and he took her hand and they went on their way. And she felt instinctively that she *was* going the right way, toward the little hill and the trees which were the scene in the painting with the dancing maidens which hung in the castle and also had clearly depicted within it, if you looked hard enough, a small, white horse-like creature with a long spiral horn. She was sure she knew just where to find it.

As they went along, she continued to think and daydream and suggest things to herself until she found she could quite clearly imagine how it had all come about – she could actually see it all before her like a brightly coloured picture book. There was the baby Nicodemus on a rug before a Christmas tree, the doting King unwrapping presents, Iphigenia peeling bananas and the servants of the royal household making faces to one another behind the royal backs. She could see the no-expense-spared nursery, the piles of books on animal psychology, and she could see the little princess trying to like her hairy little brother but in the end resenting him and then hating him. She could see the dutiful consort trying but ultimately failing to keep up her wifely enthusiasm for the project in the face of domestic chaos and continual animal tantrums as he got bigger and more boisterous and never looked like being enlightened by the mantle of humanity continually thrust upon him. Most of all, she could see the King and the ape getting closer and closer until they were inseparable buddies. And then she could see the inevitable brewing of the poison, as the confused animal became more and more jealous of any display of affection on the part of the King not directed toward himself. And then the tragic denoument. Had there been witnesses? Or did some gardener turn a corner and find her Royal Highness flat on her back, wide eyed and oozing red blood into the lawn? Or was she dashed from a tower perhaps, (did they have towers at Oudeneden?) Nicodemus having erupted in a shrieking raging charge and battered her over the parapet, her summer dress suddenly flapping for an unimaginable second in the empty silent air before the dull thump into the parterre? He was all amiability beside her now, chuntering his little chimpanzee talk and pointing at a distant crow, but the hand she held had done the deed, the old man had said.

On that magic hill, however, when they reached it, it was certain that nothing of the squalid and regrettable would remain. They would walk serenely into Boldoni's warm light, a light which comforted with the bizarre tones of a dusk mingled with noontide, harbouring a suggestion of a glow even in the thickest shadows, and the sight of the marvellous white quadruped moving through a distant thicket would gladden and uplift the heart of every wretched pilgrim.

CHAPTER FORTY FIVE

The calendar rolled round at the unremitting and perpetual behest of planetary forces, taking no account of the indispositions of humanity and its arrangements – the royal animal collectors were once again due to give an account of themselves to their sovereign in the rotunda at the end of the causeway. However, since the King was gone mad, AWOL, dead, abdicated or fled abroad according to which rumour was given credence, uncertainty arose as to what could actually take place. This uncertainty was enhanced by the concomitant absence of several of the most senior questing zoologists. But it had not been cancelled, and indeed the event seemed to have accrued heightened importance as a focus for the crises both constitutional and zoological and consequently a larger than average crowd of courtiers and press and hangers-on as well as The General Public (which, though not officially excluded was not normally encouraged at this event) started to stream along the causeway and flood about the rotunda. No one knew who, if anybody, would stand in for the King. Wild stories had whipped up expectations and some actually hurried along expecting to see a real unicorn right there in a halter; there were children who scurried and skipped ahead in expectation of a boxing ring with a lion in one corner and a unicorn in another. Some came with not the slightest interest in animals, real or imagined, but hoping that the gathering might form the locus of an impromptu flexing of the anarchic tendency – possibly a small riot might be hoped for, the de-bagging of a policeman, or the letting loose of something from the zoo, dromedaries or water buffalo perhaps, to stampede amongst the complacent multitude.

A larger than usual crowd of different elements, many of them in unfamiliar surroundings, made life difficult for the officials as the hubbub increased and the clock ticked to the appointed hour. Pippa and Willis were there, very nervous with a bat in a cage; Murgatroyd and his assistant, Proctor, who generally paid no attention to the news or to other people and had not heard anything about the absence of the King or the unicorn hoohah, entered the arena and were at once as bemused by the atmosphere and the mass of people – as was the bandicoot they had on a lead. Mr Kelp looked nervously over his pince nez as he wheeled in a small aquarium on a stand which contained a snail or a sea urchin or something, whose preoccupations (like those of Mr Kelp) could not be further removed from those of the crowd if it or they had been on the moon. There were only a couple more, Wilson and Turner, and then some very junior zoo people assembled; they were thin on the ground without Johnson, Simpson, Willoughby and Cake.

There was a delay, the crowd waited, and the crowd stared, firstly with minimal interest at the bandicoot and the bat, and then at one another, and quickly the muttering rose in volume until it buzzed like a swarm of lumpen flightless things, too high pitched and bleating to be a restful noise, and too human to betoken a preoccupation with anything as pleasant or as pure as honey.

Vangrannicus arrived, looking tired, worn, worried and exasperated. Ruscum and two other officials followed closely behind and they all looked nervously around, taken aback by the numbers of people. They had not brought chairs, hoping to get through the ritual as fast as possible.

Some children and one or two drunks started shouting 'U-ni-corn! U-ni-corn! U-ni-corn!'

Ruscum blew a whistle and Vangrannicus glanced at some notes he held in his left hand as he held his right arm up for attention.

There was a crooked little alleyway which linked the river end of the zoo to the rotunda, but neither place was really visible from the other unless you were a giraffe and tall enough to glimpse a portion of today's proceedings over the top of the things in between, or a large brown bear. The large brown bear had his own artificial mountain and was this morning standing on top of it on his hind legs, rolling his great head this way and that and wondering what all the noise was about.

'Regrettably,' shouted Vangrannicus, before the crowd had quite stilled itself, which it now did seeing something was happening. 'Regrettably,' he shouted each word, and paused between each word – he was not used himself to speaking to such a large and mixed crowd with dubious elements in it and adopted a stentorian, no nonsense, tannoy style. He intended to be as brief as humanly possible. 'Regrettably His Majesty... is... indisposed,' (muttering, some laughter) 'and... cannot... be here... today. Specimen collectors...are henceforth...required to give written... reports... written reports only... until... further notice.'

Murmurings, a little booing, some more chanting of 'U-ni-corn! U-ni-corn,' but it was rather half hearted.

The zoologists looked at one another, shrugged their shoulders, folded their arms, smiled resignedly and some shook their heads.

Vangrannicus referred to his notes and began to say something else – 'Today's proceedings will...' – but the little boy called Simon who had come along with his father and looked out at the proceedings from a forest of legs was not listening. He had caught sight of the distant bear and was fascinated by its size and by the differences between it and the teddy called Bear who languished at home on the little bed they shared. And yet both were bears; and would surely recognise one another.

Looking steadily at the great brown animal who persisted on his hind legs and throwing his head from side to side, Simon, who was a very intelligent child, then looked about him at the people who had been calling enthusiastically for the unicorn and he suddenly thought what fools they were. They knew nothing of the unicorn. They didn't know how big it was, what it liked to eat, where it went in the winter, what language it spoke. How annoyed it might be by crowds of people, and shouting. If it should suddenly thunder into this little arena and start impaling people or bursting them like balloons they'd be sorry. He would not himself be frightened, however, for the beast would know he was different, it would recognise a fellow creature who meant well and was free from sin.

He began to tug at the trousers of his father, he wanted to go home. Thick clouds rolled up from the north to blot out the sun and a cold wind blew in from the river and squirmed through the columns of the rotunda to lift a few collars and have hands darting protectively up to hats. Vangrannicus's cloak whipped and billowed in the squall, rain began to patter, people turned about and began to walk briskly away beneath unfurling umbrellas along the famous causeway, ignoring the statues and cursing the vindictiveness of the elements.

CHAPTER FORTY SIX

Though her nostrils ached for a few threadbare molecules of essence of Antonio, it was only a tide of distant cow dung which crept up to the edge of the woodland and mingled with the nettles and leaf litter and lay like a pungent blanket over the field before her. There was no path here and Jemima pushed and hefted her heavily laden bicycle through the undergrowth and long grass seeking a way out across the black and stagnant ditch. At no time, however, did she cease to look for tracks and prints and signs of the passing of her quarry. Her vigilance was strong and persistent.

Also ever-vigilant was the dog Brisk, who watched her from the edge of a copse on the other side of the field. He was having difficulty with ridding himself of people. It seemed that whenever he saw one he still could not resist watching to see what they were doing. It wasn't that he hankered to be once more by their side with a lolling tongue and expectant uplifted eyes, it was just that their peculiar activities continued to fascinate him – even more so than before perhaps, when they were continually shouting and exhorting and whistling at him. It was as if they believed their strange routines and rituals were the necessary scaffolding for a way of life more exalted than that of everything else, the cows and the sheep and the foxes and the rabbits and the birds – as if their little machines and the boxes they lived in represented a closeness to god which he would never experience. He did not believe it himself, and he suspected that for all their cleverness they believed a lot of impossible things. But he found he could not ignore any of them when they crossed his path, he had to look, because they were ever likely to do something which was utterly unfathomable.

Having crossed into the field and negotiated the worst of the boggy ground, Jemima heaved her machine up a slight incline and onto firmer terrain where the grass was shorter and she might, if she chose, mount up and pedal on towards the gate at the other side. She was about to do this when she was stopped short by something she saw on the ground, which she bent down to examine. A footprint.

There were in fact several footprints, shod feet, the solid deep tread marks of the soles of sensible footwear, right and left, but amongst them were also prints of naked feet, and these were a different shape from the ordinary human ones which it must be assumed were cocooned in the accompanying boots. They had a distinctly thumb-like big toe. There was a large gap between this toe and the other four. It was, she discerned immediately, not a human being who had lost their shoes, but an ape. She pushed her bicycle to the gate and leant it up, returning for a closer examination. What on Earth was an ape doing in this neck of the woods? And escorted by, let's see, yes, definitely a woman. She was perplexed. Could it be something escaped from the zoo? But there weren't any apes. (This had puzzled her when she had first taken up her appointment – it was an obvious gap in the collection, but no one had been able to tell her why the King just did not seem interested in apes.) So whence this animal? And who was with it? It was a conundrum. And they were quite fresh, these marks, it was quite possible the feet that made them were not terribly far away.

Brisk knew what had taken her attention, he had himself caught the unfamiliar scent when he'd arrived here. He did not know what it was, but he did not like it. It was a trail he would follow only with some trepidation.

Could it have been a woman and an ape who had been responsible for the shenanigans at her camp last night? Even more bizarre. In the absence of any hoof prints should she follow these? Her dead father suddenly rose up and began grimly to tell her all about Edgar Alan Poe and the Murders in the Rue Morgue, but she silenced him with a wave of her hand. After a little while, during which she very carefully inspected the surrounding area and minutely examined all the most clearly defined prints, she straightened her back and walked resolutely over to her bicycle. No. It was very peculiar, but it was a red herring. She was not looking for people, she was not looking for an ape. There was no evidence to connect apes to unicorns. Apes, she was sure, did not even dream of unicorns. She would continue with her plan. She looked all about her for the tallest tree, advanced upon it, leant the bicycle against it, took out rope and crampons, packed a small haversack with binoculars and a notebook and pencil and commenced to climb the imposing

Scots Pine which towered above the neighbourhood and had done so since before she had been born.

It took a good half hour for her to reach the topmost branches, and she found she had company when she got there. There was a large ramshackle nest with a huge eagle sitting in it. It did not like being disturbed, and looked sternly at Ms Cake, maintaining a menacing silence but forbearing for the moment from bringing beak and talons to bear. Her reconnoitre was therefore to be a rather nervous one, as she sat on a convenient branch, took out her binoculars and intently surveyed the landscape, watched over herself by that eye, very fierce and very beady.

She peered slowly around the points of the compass, mentally noting characteristics of the terrain, and possible impediments to progress. She stopped after a minute or two and sketched a rough map showing the two little rivers she could see and the position of a distant church tower which would be a useful landmark. She also allowed herself to reflect for a moment on how beautiful it all was. The colours and the clouds and the little hills all came together in a such a pleasing way... but her position was too precarious for her to give in to the mystic mood which had overcome her in the castle garden – although she almost did. She resumed the binoculars and almost at once she saw what she had rather hoped not to see but which did not surprise her. It was the expected irrelevance, and it immediately gave her a sinking feeling: the admittedly mysterious, but dangerously distracting sight of a woman with a large backpack holding hands with a very large chimpanzee and skipping across a little ditch, about three miles away to the east.

Jemima abseiled expertly down the towering tree trunk, packed away her gear, gave her hair a quick brush, and mounted her bicycle with very mixed feelings. There were other directions of course, but she felt drawn to the one taken by the woman and the ape, and not altogether for scientific reasons. She had a sort of feeling which she could not quite assess – though some of it was certainly foreboding – and knew not whence it arose.

She came across no more hoof prints – other than cattle – for the next few miles and was beginning to think about changing direction, when she saw them again, the woman and the chimpanzee, advancing steadily into what looked like pleasantly soft countryside. They were much closer now, and, finally giving way to the strange nagging attraction which had grown into the feeling that their meeting was inevitable, Jemima turned very deliberately onto the rutted cart track that would lead her towards them.

Not wishing to startle them, especially the chimpanzee, by coming upon them suddenly, (Jemima knew very well that calmness and no sudden surprises were the cardinal principles in dealing with animals) she rang her bell when she was within fifty yards of them. It was a surprisingly sharp and grating tinkle, which sounded very out of place in the hush that prevailed here on the overgrown path, and although intended gently to forewarn of her approach it actually startled both the objects of the ring and the ringer herself. Millicent and Nicodemus stopped immediately and looked round, hands tightly clasped.

As Millicent watched the approach of Jemima's loaded bicycle along the narrow path, she immediately appreciated the strength and balance of the girl, and saw at once that beyond the power and elegance was a great spirit, and a disciplined mind. Nicodemus was fascinated; it may well have been his first glimpse of bicycle.

The two women greeted one another, and their greetings were cordial but understandably wary. Both had a secret to guard: the secret of the unicorn, which in each case was a very different secret. The unicorn Millicent sought was nothing like the unicorn Jemima sought. Their visions, understanding, and expectations of it, their conjecture as to its nature and significance, could not have been more opposed.

Jemima had been wary of Millicent and Nicodemus when first she'd seen them from the scots pine. And yet, she'd been drawn to them. Perhaps it had been a compulsion to find out about the chimpanzee. Perhaps – but she would have had difficulty admitting this to herself – she needed company, to be distracted from her dangerous preoccupation with Prince Antonio.

Two different minds, two different types of knowledge and understanding were to be introduced to one another. It was to be hoped that the encounter would not be complicated by trivial and unnecessary misunderstandings – these were strong women, and not easily dislodged or inclined to give way. There was a minute or two when it felt as if they might be content with one another's mute presence only, but then they did begin to talk and they found they liked one another well enough. At first they spoke of the character of the immediate terrain and what might lie ahead. Then, they discussed provisions, fuel and firelighters, drinking water, first aid, cutlery and kettles and all the things Jemima was equipped with and Millicent not.

Ever since the scots pine, Jemima had been a little unsettled by the possibility that the ape might have turned out to be something akin to the very large rabbit, that is, undeniably present, but manifesting a style of existence rather more unusually taken for fictional, and not readily amenable to validation – or rather, invalidation. She was glad, and professionally delighted, to discern that he was what she would have no hesitation in calling 'real'. He exhibited a certain superiority, but only that which derived from his innocence as an animal, and not, thank goodness, that enigmatic air of detachment associated with the affectation of human mannerisms, and deportment, flaunted to unnerving and exasperating effect by the aloof and unhelpful *lagomorph* encountered in the cottage garden.

They went on to whisper about Nicodemus and his tractability – Jemima knew, it seemed, a thing or two about chimpanzees.

The vaguely menacing indifference of the gigantic poplar trees was left behind now, as were any vestiges of metalled roads and any pretence that serious farming was still carried on. Field gave way to scrub and the path they followed was becoming very narrow and frequently disappeared in long grass behind birch trees, only to reappear unexpectedly, often occupied by complacent rabbits who were reluctant to relinquish it. Jemima said with a laugh that she thought she'd seen a very large rabbit standing on its hind legs in a cottage garden at the beginning of her expedition; it had seemed very real, but it must have been some sort of an hallucination. Millicent asked why it had to have been an hallucination, there were some very large rabbits, and it was surely unlikely that it would never occur to the odd one to try to stand on their hind legs.

'But it seemed so very like a person, such human mannerisms,' said Jemima, who sounded to herself as she said it not like herself at all. She glanced at Millicent who looked straight ahead and strode firmly on, and they were silent for a while.

Nicodemus walked between the two women, looking up alternately at each, and occasionally at the bicycle and seemed to be pondering something, or trying to recall something, or someone whose name escaped him.

Jemima was disappointed that the country was becoming such that animal tracks would be very difficult to spot, the grass and bushes and small trees would not reveal hoof prints and could quite easily conceal the actual quadruped if it was small enough and quiet enough, hence she frowned intermittently as she looked to either side of the path, yet she stuck to her task and her science and continued to relish all the possibilities she relentlessly assessed.

Millicent felt more and more that these birch trees would soon give way to rising ground, oaks and lime and beech and eventually to Boldoni's low hill and the magic wood with the chitoned maidens and her faith was reflected in the resolute confidence of the firm steps she took. She wondered whether Freddie too would have been drawn this way, and stifled the dread of his having fallen by the wayside.

Tucked up in bed at night when dreams are dreamt and that tangle of wonder and trepidation and bemusement invades the tired and unresisting mind, personages slide into view, are sometimes identifiable, but if actually spoken to at all are very rarely cross questioned as to their identity or significance. They are usually simply strange and familiar, benevolent and dreadful and continually transfiguring and de-transfiguring. So too here in the unknown real wilderness, at least to the extent that it would have been ridiculous to interrogate one's travelling companion as to their employment, forebears, purpose or beliefs. There was a certainty that the most important things need not be questioned – even if they were as yet incompletely understood – and this certainty grew with the distance they travelled. Indeed Jemima soon found that she was in a state of having discerned, she could not say how, and Millicent found that she was in a state of having divined, she could not say how, the nature of their travelling companion's mission. Neither was yet inclined to mention the name of the mythical beast, however, and not just because it was unnecessary so to do.

They were not to be at odds it seemed, for they were mutually complementary – the one being happily susceptible to unsettling atmospheres and shifting psychic perspectives and the other quite capable of taking matters in hand, whatever the circumstances (as long as Italian princes could be kept at arms length) and together they progressed steadily through the countryside ever inspecting the ground and horizon for signs and movements and looking for the remembered profile of painted hills in the blue-grey distance. Each noticed different things, and each inspected things differently; one analysed and drew conclusions, the other instinctively perceived ghostly histories and metaphysical realities. Nicodemus looked from one to the other as if he wondered for the first time where they might be taking him.

CHAPTER FORTY SEVEN

Freddie's stamina was being severely tested by the dreams and possibilities successively tangled around him. The promise of the unicorn was interrupted at times now with the temptation to believe that his experiments had been vindicated, that the great Nicodemus had only gone away to extend his burgeoning humanity in some rite of passage and the two lordly beasts would stride out of the woods together to astonish the world. But the strain of maintaining such euphoric expectations was very great and in the end he could not sustain it, falling back into a long and troubled sleep.

Freddie awoke and rose up out of the long grass like a zombie, not quite alive and full of misgivings. No one saw the emergence of the tousled hair and the staring eyes however, for the fountain had been abandoned, temporarily at least, by those who had lately visited it. With difficulty he stood up and rubbed his knee. The sparkling solace of the magic fountain filled this place with peace, but it could not, it seemed, extinguish all the smouldering baggage that Freddie carried with him from elsewhere and which had managed to re-kindle itself whilst he slept. The mournful expression that occupied the far-from-regal countenance represented all the sorrows that now had gathered to beset him, plus one additional feeling which was at least as pressing as all the others – hunger. He stared hopelessly about him wishing for Millicent and a pork pie, but expecting nothing. He looked into the water and was at such an extremity that, semi-conscious as he was, he wondered: if he chanced to see a fish should he summon his failing energies and make a dive for it? As he slumped onto the grey wall which surrounded the quiet welcome of the pond he was beginning to think that at long last perhaps the expectation of tomorrows – which is life itself – was very near dwindled out. The ephemeral things he saw amongst the pondweed, darting and gyrating, were too small either to be caught or to make a mouthful.

'Animalcules,' he said to himself, remembering an all encompassing rural term, 'animalcules' and there was an uncharacteristic hint of dismissiveness in his tone. He did not seem able to evoke his great white friend, who had almost faded away and would need to be recalled with stronger cries than Freddie now felt capable of.

Meanwhile, not very far away as the crow flies, his daughter and his keeper of large and unusual birds were sitting together on the ground in an anxious silence, having collapsed into the safety of this little hidden glen panting with terror a few moments ago. A false alarm as it turned out, but they weren't to know that. The fear of the pig at last began to subside and Daphne was able to catch her breath and to speak again. 'We'll have lost them now, we'll never find them again. Even if we find a way back to the fountain they will have moved off by now, we'll have to start all over again!' And she managed to make this sound as if it were Trevor's fault and not the phantom pig's, in spite of the imprecations she ended with, 'Bloody pig! Bloody animals!'

Meanwhile, a middle-aged man, exquisitely turned out in gentleman's outdoor accoutrements of waxed jacket and flat cap, walked rather stiffly, but earnestly, through farmland looking anxiously about him.

Also meanwhile, and again not terribly far away from either of the three scenes just described, two women and an ape zig-zagged assuredly and irrepressibly, so that some god-like observer with an aerial view of everything would have been intrigued and excited by the seeming inevitability of the crashing together of these expeditions, in the un-mapped and un-mappable land, which had the dotted lines of their progressions cornering, accelerating, circling, stuttering until their not coming together in the next hour was inconceivable, and yet still it did not happen.

There was another 'meanwhile', and yet it was not as the other meanwhiles, for it was in quite a different and very far-flung place. It was coming, however, it was journeying steadily towards the others. Not a frenetic and ill-informed wandering this, but a steady, determined, fateful straight line which advanced upon the others with the solid strides of destiny.

CHAPTER FORTY EIGHT

It was difficult to get near Johnson and the beautiful maiden. They were always moving quietly and steadily, or even sometimes merely strolling, but they could never be caught up with or encountered close-to. The unlikeliness of the pair was captivating – black coated Johnson with his firm-set bowler and stern medieval air, and the almost ethereal qualities of his companion whose beauty modestly transcended the archetype. And then the subtle necessity of their disparity gradually came to be realised by the observer. The nameless demoiselle presented a figure whose magical allure also encompassed a strong suggestion that she might, if she chose, manipulate the material world in bizarre ways, though her purity would probably restrict her from feeling the need to do so.

Earthy Johnson, intent on the calling forth of the rarest elements, the deepest burrowers, the oldest rooted things, the lives that were themselves the very perimeter of creation, walked beside her; she was his lodestone, his talisman, his key to the unlocking of a fundamental mystery. He walked with his hands clasped behind his back, the empty cigar holder crunched to a skewed angle in the corner of his grizzly mouth, looking steadily forward and about him, nodding slowly from time to time as if in agreement with the un-stated wisdom of his serene companion whose deceptively languid strides blessed the grasses and the flowers as she placed her miraculous ankle amongst them.

It was only such as Johnson who would know that it was only such as she who could summon the horned beast from the invisible mythic realm where he lay sequestered. Sequestered but enduring and ready to uplift and entrance those he showed himself to, once in a millennium, like a star moving on its own errant course through the otherwise predictable heavens to startle the firmament and stir up stagnant earthly life.

Such were the people in the wilderness striving for the unicorn, in various degrees of wisdom and ignorance. Amongst all the people back in the town and the citadel however there was no striving toward the lost animal, there was simply a surrender to the expectation that it would come, as they had been told it would come, or as they had told themselves it would come, and people waited for it in glee and terror and hope and dread, and some suddenly became religious and some made jokes about it, and everyone spoke of little else. Especially at the zoo everyone spoke now of little else. Troughs were filled and buckets emptied, dung shovelled up and straw laid down as it had been day in day out for many a year, but what filled the minds of the zoo people as they went about these tasks was: where will they put it? Will it go in with the okapis or will it need a paddock to itself? Would it be fierce or tame? What about the rhinoceros? And, most importantly, who would actually bring back this mighty prize and present it to the King? And where was the King anyway? Oh didn't you know? He's out there himself, looking for it, he's actually gone himself.

The belief that, far from hunting the unicorn, the King was in fact dead, was by now, however, the majority opinion beyond the zoo. No one had seen him for ever such a long time. A bizarre story began to circulate amongst some of the more unfortunate and gullible that the unicorn itself would actually be made head of state, because no one had seen the Princess Daphne for ages either. Or, come to that, the Italian prince who they said was supposed to marry her.

Pippa and Willis were sitting on a bench on a lawn just below the castle walls. It was a position with a commanding view, first of the roofs and chimneys and church spires of the old town and then the zoo in the distance, and then the widening river stretching away beyond that under a pink sky, fading to grey where it sheltered unknown lands to the north. A handsome young man and his girlfriend came walking by, gave them 'good day', and sat themselves down on an adjacent bench where they too looked into the distant rosy welkin.

Willis sighed and simultaneously stretched out her legs, clasping her hands together behind her head and saying, 'Look how terribly far it all is, look, just look at the distance... how much distance there is... compared to the little dimensions we footle about in, you know, day to day. Could those be sheep I wonder? By Jove, yes they are, look at those sheep. You know, there could be, how do we know there isn't, someone way way over there, someone just at this minute, somewhere beyond the sheep, just while I'm saying this, who has a powerful telescope trained on the castle and has happened to pick us out here sitting on this bench. Which to them is miles and miles away. I wonder if they're wondering who we are... and what we're doing.'

'Why don't you go and get our telescope, you could have a look back at them,' said her companion who had taken a letter from her pocket and was reading it.

'I say, who's it from?' asked Willis.

'Newsome.'

'Oh really, is it? I think you mean Mr Newsome, where's he got to? What's he say?'

'I'm not sure exactly where he is because neither is he – beyond the sheep, I would guess. Shall I read you what he says?'

'Oh yes, please. Imagine, Mr Newsome, the intrepid butler, who'd have thought it?'

'"Dear Miss Pippa," he begins, "Have made my way, as you suggested, into the territory you believed Ms Cake went off to explore, and though progress has been quite swift, it has not been without mishap."' Not having noticed that she was not a joint addressee, as might perhaps have been expected, Willis instead looked nervously round at the couple on the other bench and signed with her eyes to Pippa that they were overheard, and anything of a confidential nature would be better left on the page.

At the same time, the handsome young man turned to them and smiled and whilst he smiled his girlfriend, who had been looking demurely into her lap where her hands were clasped together, raised her head, and looked over at the girls with a stare which they thought seemed not altogether friendly. The eyes were an unusual dark green and rather mesmerised Willis. The force went out of the young man's smile, though he held the expression, before coughing apologetically and saying to the zoologists. 'Excuse me, I think you should be aware that my girlfriend is the daughter of the chief of police and would feel duty bound to report anything you might say of an incriminating or suspicious nature.'

Willis and Pippa looked at one another, unsure whether to laugh but between them managed to blurt out a couple of confused 'thank you's and then there passed a few full seconds of silence, during which Pippa searched rather nervously for her place in the manuscript.

But before she could begin again, the girl knelt up on the banquette, took hold of her boyfriend's head and, turning his face toward them, said, 'And this young man is a philosopher, rabble-rouser and anarchist, capable of many crimes and accused of quite a few.'

She was very beautiful, with fine cheek bones, perfect skin and long blonde hair cascading in curls over her shoulders. However, of the two Pippa and Willis thought she was decidedly the most unnerving.

Pippa looked at the boy. He did not look like a bomb thrower, on the contrary, his neat haircut, regular features and light blue eyes made him look honest and good. It was of course possible to look honest and good and still throw bombs, thought Pippa. However he certainly looked capable of accomplishing unexpected and astonishing feats, feats which it would probably not occur to anyone else to tackle, some of which feats might well be criminal – the depth of outrage he was capable of feeling would not be restrained by a simple statute. His enigmatic girlfriend's peculiar and, you might think, inappropriate outspokenness, her green eyes and stunning physical presence, were sufficient to nonplus anyone coming upon her for the first time. She was mentally strong, thought Pippa, might well harbour huge reserves of loyalty and be capable of enduring great hardship in the cause of whatever simple truth she might espouse. She was certainly of independent mind, having fallen in love with her father's arch enemy.

Then the girl in question suddenly got to her feet stared boldly at Pippa and Willis and said in a clear quiet voice, 'I could amaze you with a list of his activities.' She grasped the young man's head in her two hands again and this time kissed it repeatedly. 'In the old days, they would all have been capital offences, but my pa says he won't prosecute him, not now that he's my intended, he's not above arresting him and giving him a good talking to, but he won't actually charge him with anything, not now that he's my intended.'

Pippa gave a slow, shocked and rather mystified nod.

Willis stared.

'Now now, steady on,' muttered the boy, whose name they would later learn was Wilfred. Another silence ensued, the girl relinquished Wilfred's head, put her hands in her pockets and stared at the distant vista.

Pippa turned away and, not feeling that she had any alternative, continued reading, though she did not at first have all of Willis's attention which, with her gaze, kept wandering back to the bizarre couple.

Pippa was trying to sound unruffled and noted with relief out of the corner of her eye the girl's resumption of her seat. '"I can only describe this land as unusually ordinary, which sounds like a contradiction in terms, but its hard to describe in any other way – it's nothing out of the ordinary except that it all looks as if it's the first time you've seen it: a field, or a cow or a tree, say, or a very large rabbit all look rather otherworldly. And I have to say it has made me begin to wonder about Willoughby Hall and the life I now feel I may have left behind for good. I do find it all rather difficult to put into words. I know I should not digress about the vague and the indescribable, but its very difficult not to, even though I know what you're interested in of course is the trail of the missing persons. Well I'm sorry to have to tell you there is no trail, not that I can discern or uncover. I've tried asking people, but they just look blankly back at you. They'll sell you a pint of beer or a banana and sometimes say hello, but they wont actually talk to you or answer questions. Almost as if they aren't allowed to."'

Pippa and Willis were aware that the lovers, now relaxed and holding hands on their bench, were unashamedly turned toward them and listening to every word, smiling broadly (they really were both very good looking).

Then Wilfred leaned towards them and whispered, 'Nothing we hear will go any further. Your friend's letter is very interesting.'

Pippa shrugged, even though she wasn't sure she believed him, and having found her place resumed reading.

'"The days can seem very long here – although my watch goes round at the same speed as far as I can tell – and there are other odd feelings besetting you if you are susceptible. The Lanes themselves for instance rarely run in the direction you would like; they appear to be intent on frustrating you and swerving you away from your object. It takes a while to realise that they are just lanes and not the tool of some malevolent sprite – but one's mind is assailed by this and sundry other unsettling feelings very often when you first come here. Where these feelings come from I don't know. Perhaps this is just what it is always like abroad, I am not a widely travelled man alas and must try hard to adapt myself to circumstances.

"I stopped to slake my thirst at a lonely inn. There were no other customers at all. My boots echoed on the bare boards as I approached the counter and the barman looked as if he were waiting for me. Not expecting much of an answer I asked him, as he poured my drink, whether he had seen the honourable Sir Jolyon Willoughby who was on an expedition and thought to be somewhere in the district.

"'Tall, very depressed? Travelling with an idiot who aspires to be some sort of holy fool?' I was astounded to get any response at all, therefore such a lengthy and interested one with descriptive features quite bowled me over, but of course I had to say no to all particulars except for the tall. Whereupon he disappeared into the cellar and any hopes for a more discursive conversation were dashed.

"There are a lot of places here where the atmosphere exudes a sense of its being suddenly empty of something, with a very slight eddy to the air as if something or someone had just that moment departed. I am all the time convinced that I have just missed Jolyon, but equally I am becoming now so accustomed to his elusiveness that my faith in his being found is itself increasingly insubstantial and I fear the very real possibility of its sudden extinction. Nonetheless it persists and I go on. It is impossible to be methodical here, one cannot impose quadrants on the map and slowly eliminate sections one by one. One is instead urged this way and that by sudden compelling instinct or intuition, following an invisible star, wide eyed and expectant, across yet another turnip field toward the certain promise of a clue lying behind that oak tree, behind that hedge. Ever curious, ever expectant but always at the same time knowing there will be nothing there.

"You will find it difficult to believe or understand but I have to explain to you the strangest thing of all – which is that this eternal tenterhooks, this state of belief and non-belief, the continual and senseless allure of the next empty paddock, ruined brick byre full of nettles, taciturn farmer or *no vacancies* sign, all this purposeful purposelessness, well, I actually *enjoy* it! Immensely. I'm not sure I would use the word *happy* – it's a much less conventional feeling than that – but this continual sense of unfulfilled promise and cynical optimism imbue me a with a sort of joy I've never felt before. With little hope of your understanding quite what I mean I feel compelled to attempt to express this to you, not least because your knowing that something bizarre is happening to me might enhance your interpretation of my letters. I am resolved to keep on with my correspondence to you by the way – even though I am by no means certain that anyone ever empties these lonely pillar boxes, or what colour uniform they might wear."'

There was a sound which may have been a kiss or a slap but Pippa was not to be interrupted. She was sure that notwithstanding the odd physical digression the lovers were still as intent as Willis now was on Newsome's account.

"'With great ingenuity I crossed a small river and carried on toward the setting sun…'" (Pausing momentarily to glance down the page and flip it over to confirm her disappointment that the ingenuity was not going to be detailed, Pippa continued) "'… and making my bivouac on top of a small hill beneath an enormous scots pine I took out my telescope…'" ('Aha!' cried Willis with a smirk of triumph.) "'and scanned the horizon and the road ahead. Imagine my surprise when I saw a gorilla lurching along the ridge.'"

At this, Wilfred suddenly tensed and his fiancee neither kissed nor slapped but held on to an ear, it seemed for dear life.

She wrenched his head round and frowned meaningfully into his eyes.

"'I only saw it for a moment before it dropped down the other side of the hill, but it was quite unmistakeable. So it seems there are some exotics injected into this unusually ordinary landscape. I wondered whether there might be other unexpected fauna lurking about amongst the primroses – poisonous snakes for instance – but was confident that my stout boots and the sheer weight of my trouser material would rebut any lunging fang. Then I reflected that it was an out of the ordinary beast that had brought my master here in the first place, and perhaps I should not be so surprised. An ape is not of course as unusual as a unicorn but nonetheless the sight of it refined my appreciation of Sir Jolyon's mission. And served to remind me that it was as well to be on one's guard."'

There was a little flurry of urgent whispering between Wilfred and his inamorata. Whatever it was about it was sufficiently serious to put a stop to all tactile by-play.

Pippa and Willis were intrigued. Willis writhed about on the bench kicking her legs, with her hands beneath her thighs, trying simultaneously to concentrate on both Newsome's letter and the ill-matched, unpredictable and beautiful couple, whilst Pippa too tried, a little more discreetly, to perform the feat of both reading aloud and listening hard. They could not make anything out, but inevitably Pippa's reading slowed down and the whisperers realised they were the cause and there came the moment when everyone stopped what they were doing and looked at one another.

In the silence Pippa peremptorily introduced herself and her colleague, 'Pippa and Willis. I'm Pippa, this is Willis, we work at the zoo, the King's zoo, so you see we're not subversives. Our boss has gone on an expedition similar to the one recounted in this letter.'

'Oh I see,' said the girl.

'You seemed a little put out by the story of the gorilla...' said Willis, not one to beat about the bush, and ever ready to flush out something sensational.

'Yes' said the girl and, 'Not at all' said Wilfred, at the same time. They looked at one another, and then, having been given Wilfred's tacit agreement the girl began to tell them about it. It seemed perfectly natural, here beneath the ramparts of the royal castle for the daughter of the chief of police to recount such secrets to chance-encountered strangers. It was an indication of the effect Wilfred had on people but also a measure of the times, and very probably the influence of the looming shadow of the unicorn.

'It was Wilfred that let it out. You see there was a gorilla, kept in a pit down underneath the castle, and Wilfred let it out.'

'Let what out?' asked Willis excitedly, 'What are you talking about?'

'Yes, what are you talking about?' asked Pippa very calmly, folding the sheets of Newsome's letter and putting them in her lap.

'He let out the animal, the gorilla, it was him, let it out of the dungeon.'

'It was an accident, I suppose,' said Wilfred, 'but not one I necessarily regret. I freely admit to you that I have liberated a few wrongly imprisoned persons in my time, in doing that I was simply an instrument of justice, correcting some of the more outrageous acts of this blundering regime, but I didn't even know there were any animals down there and I certainly didn't intend to let any out. As I say, I'm not saying I wouldn't if I had, but I didn't and I didn't. What must have actually happened is that a lady who they'd arrested one night, for nothing at all, got chucked in the chokey. I got to hear about it, and really had no alternative – the woman was totally innocent. I purloined her father's keys, went along there in the middle of the night, and opened her cell door. Then I left. If there was anyone or anything else down there that got out that night I know nothing about it.'

'It was the woman, it must have been the woman you let out, it was her that let out the gorilla!'

'What gorilla?' asked Pippa. 'Where was this gorilla?'

'Yes,' said Willis, who was standing up, frowning in confusion and flapping her arms by her side, 'what gorilla? The gorilla in Mr Newsome's letter? How did it get to be in a dungeon?'

The girl then matter-of-factly went on to further demonstrate how free she was with secret information. 'No one knew about it, except the King himself and the man who was chief of police before my dad. Apparently there was some sort of monster kept in a cell and it must never be let out – neither it nor the secret of its whereabouts. He, my dad I mean, got to know somehow that the beast was gone, only a week or two ago. He's quite upset about it. Thinks they'll have his head off.'

Do they still actually do that? thought Pippa and Willis in unison – though neither one said anything – and the outlandish thought that they still might, even further enhanced their appreciation of the boldness of this handsome Wilfred. He was a man who dared to right wrongs, and had boldly wooed and won the daughter of his arch enemy. He was very brave and she was very beautiful but to say that neither of them in the least conformed to any sort of stereotype was understating the case. He had every appearance of being totally honest and open, and yet for all the blond hair, the smile, the regular features there was a feeling that there was something going on inside his mind which he would never tell you. And you could not be sure whether it was something simply odd and mildly surprising, or whether it was something deeply disturbing. In her case, she was the policeman's daughter who seemed to think nothing of publicly betraying the scandal of her father's negligence and her fiance's culpability in it and letting out state secrets for all to hear – and in between it all, childlike, she toyed and stroked and caressed with a far away look in her eye and more than a suggestion that the pinnacle of her devotion would be to follow his tumbril to the scaffold.

Either Pippa or Willis would be a better partner, they each silently thought, for Wilfred; they would not undermine his nobility in public so much. But it was a fleeting thought and one they knew better than to linger on. And they could not help comparing this girl to Jemima Cake, who rivalled her for physical perfection but towered above her in decorum and whose sex appeal was polished and enlarged by her intellect, her modesty and her authority – attributes Wilfred would appear to have ignored in his search for Miss Right.

The story of the gorilla remained a ruined story, a dismembered story, incomplete, with fragments sticking up here in portions of Newsome's letter, and there in the anxieties of the ill-assorted family of the chief of police, and it should have set Jemima's girls thinking.

But it seemed not to. Instead the just visible ribbon of fading white light in the very far far north which was the disappearing river on its way to the great sea, sparked a vague but intense regret in their hearts and conjured the reprise of an Italian song and the gentle rhythm of dipping oars. The light was now become sub-crepuscular, the pin-prick sheep dimmed and disappeared and the cold distant north lands were soon hardly visible at all. There was a chill in the air and this combined with the gloom that descended on the horizon to render resting on these benches a suddenly unattractive alternative to home and hearth. Yet they stayed sitting there, all of them, for quite some while.

Pippa no longer read from her letter which was folded up and put away; the unlikely betrothed couple looked into one another's eyes and then with resignation searchingly into the darkness, and all were silent and cold, as a bell tolled from one of the highest of the many towers, to disturb ravens who had been roosting amongst the old and shaggy ivy and now took slow and circling flight uttering intermittent deep throaty calls above the suddenly uncertain quartet.

CHAPTER FORTY NINE

Not very far away, behind some thick stone walls, up a couple of staircases and along a long panelled corridor smelling of polish, Vangrannicus sat wrapped in his cloak beneath the goat picture in a state of anxiety, holding a cigar he'd forgotten to light and sweating slightly. He seemed to be continually afflicted with anxiety these days, by a feeling that things weren't quite right, that everything was sliding in the wrong direction. A sense of doom was beginning to invade him, even though there wasn't any rioting any more, the bakery was working again, the sun came up and went down in the expected places at the expected hours, and he himself largely conducted the day to day running of the country (so it was difficult to find fault with that). So what was it, this gloom that had crept inside him and would not go away? The tragedy of the disappearance of the Venetians had been very upsetting of course. But there was nothing to be done. Though she had been missing for a long time now Princess Daphne's escapades were not unusual – she might well still turn up. The missing zoo men could be replaced quite easily, he was sure of that. He had no time for silly stories about unicorns, which apparently were the craze of the moment. So what was it that was upsetting his equilibrium? For a dyed-in-the-wool brass-buttoned boy it could only be one thing – the spirit-sapping on-going mystery of the King. Where on Earth was he? How could things go on with no King? Vangrannicus could not settle, could not be content, could not stop thinking that everything would fall apart, that chaos was about to ensue unless the King was found very soon and brought back from wherever he had got to. He was the keystone in the arch of history, he was the thing that held the town the castle the city the country the laws, the people all together, he was on the money, and stared from the stamps, it was his seal which was on all the great big important documents (destined to be historical documents, remember) it was he that held everything in its place and kept the whole thing working as it had always worked and must always go on working.

Vangrannicus was beginning to chew his nails, for there was a little worm, a worm that had got into his head but which on no account was to be listened to, and it was this little worm which was really the source of the Chamberlain's discontent, for this little worm kept wanting to whisper that everything is as it was, that nothing is wrong, that people live and die just as they did in the old days when the King was here, hiding in his library, and this thought, if allowed to wriggle right inside his head would drive Vangrannicus insane, he knew it would. For it would implant the germ of the unspeakable idea that the King did not matter. Whether he was here or evaporated to Timbuktu it did not matter. Vangrannicus had always known that he did not really do anything, of course, apart from parade about, smile and wave, but Vangrannicus had long since been convinced, as a matter of faith, that it was not in doing things that the King's crucial importance lay – it was in being the King, and everyone believing in the King and the King sitting at the centre of things for everything to revolve around. There was a sort of abstract clockwork which secretly made everybody and everything continue doing what they were supposed to do and it emanated from the King, from his crown, from his throne, from his ermine robe, from his orb and his sceptre. Without him it ought to be inevitable that it should all go wrong, all the sins of humanity should bubble up and destroy the quiet order of the world. But nothing had happened. Nobody seemed to mind that he wasn't there doing nothing in particular. It was beginning to look as if his presence had always been superfluous. This was the equivalent to Vangrannicus of the denial of gravity, it was as if he was discovering that things just stayed where they were for no mysterious and fundamental reason at all – they just stayed where they were because that's where they were. He roused himself and called Ruscum in.

'The King must be found, call out the guard,' he said.

But it was not going to be as simple as that. Ruscum stood rooted to the spot.

Vangrannicus looked him up and down and said it again, 'Call out the guard, they must go and search for the King.'

Ruscum's stiff stance was deflated as his body sagged and the truth was allowed to escape from him at last with a shrug: 'I don't know how to, sir.' Vangrannicus looked steadily and quizzically at him as Ruscum continued, 'I'm sorry, sir, excuse me, sir, but in all the years I've worked here, sir, I've never had anything to do with the guards, I've never called them out, I don't know where they go to when they're not here, I don't know anything about them. I don't know how to call them out sir, and I'm not at all sure that they'd come if I did.'

Vangrannicus reflected. In fact, everything that Ruscum had said was true for him too. In all his long years of service he'd never had any dealings with the red-coated figures who stood here and there, in corridors, outside doors, in the corners of quadrangles, beneath the portcullis. They were just always there, he'd never looked closely enough to tell one from another and he'd certainly never spoken to one. All of a sudden, the business of calling them out seemed rather daunting. Who was their boss, general, captain, whatever you called it? What best to do? He glanced up at the goat, paced up and down with his hands behind his back for a minute or two and then lit his cigar and said, 'Perhaps you could bring some tea.'

A little while later, Ruscum was back with a tea tray but also with that look on his face which he was never conscious of wearing but which Vangrannicus recognised at a glance and knew that it signified he was up to something and was rather proud of himself. Equally Ruscum could read his boss like a well thumbed almanac and had sized up the situation. 'Er, Corporal Trenchworthy is without sir.'

'What? A soldier? I thought you didn't know any of their names?'

'So I thought, sir, but it transpired when I went to get the tea, Corporal Trenchworthy was in the corridor guarding the urn, sir, and happened to take his mitre off sir for to wipe his brow and I recognised my old pal Nat, him who I play cribbage with in the Apple Tree. Fancy him being a castle guard and me knowing nothing about it.' It was obvious that Ruscum had suspected all along that the Chamberlain shared his complete unfamiliarity with the military.

After a preliminary sip of his Darjeeling, Vangrannicus said, 'Send him in.'

'Now then soldier,' began the Chamberlain, after putting down his tea, wrapping himself in his cloak and glancing involuntarily up at the goat and the cherub. 'Who is your Commander in Chief?' He tried to adopt a tone which suggested that he himself of course knew the answer and that he was asking the question for mysterious reasons of his own.

Trenchworthy, who was not quite sure whether he was supposed to be at attention or not – the Chamberlain being a civilian – opted for a sort of attentive slouch, somewhat supported by the huge old flintlock he was obliged to lug about, and with his old fashioned mitre a few degrees askew snapped, 'The King, sir!' with a momentary but half hearted twitch toward the vertical.

'Well, yes of course, but I actually meant who…'

'The Sergeant, sir, and if you want to know who commands him, sir, it's the Captain, sir, and above him it's the Colonel and then the General, and he takes his orders directly from His Majesty, sir.' There was just a hint of world weary satire in Trenchworthy's tone though not quite enough for him to be reasonably accused of insolence.

'Well, you see Corporal, Corporal, is it? Yes, the thing is, Corporal, that by an oversight, His Majesty has temporarily forgotten to keep us quite informed of his precise current location and we er, need to… we need to make contact with him. Could you ask your Colonel, or General perhaps to…'

'No, sir, with respect, sir, the only person of a higher rank I am allowed (with permission) to address would be my Sergeant, sir. And might I say, sir, there won't none of 'em be interested in looking for the King if that's your drift sir, with respect, sir.'

'What?' Vangrannicus was looking sternly at the Corporal. 'And why not, pray?'

'Well, sir, 'e's the King, sir, and wherever 'e decides to be is the right place for 'im to be. It's not for the likes of us to go looking for 'im; the act of looking for 'im, do you see, sir, would suggest that we thought 'e was in the wrong place, sir. And we would never 'ave such thoughts, 'e moves in iz mysterious ways, an' all that, its not for us to wonder where 'e might be or 'ave an opinion about where 'e ought to be.'

'Yes, but don't you see? We need to know where he is.'

'Do we sir? Why sir?'

'Well… affairs of state and all that.'

'With respect, sir, we're all taught that 'e iz the State, sir. And above the law, sir. With respect, sir, if he aint told you where 'e was going 'e may have had iz reasons, sir.'

'Oh, get out,' said Vangrannicus.

Corporal Trenchworthy lumbered obediently toward the door, leaving in his wake a strong memento of his presence in the form of the stale tobacco fumes and heavy scent of schnapps which habitually hung about him. Disconcolate, Vangrannicus wandered to the window seat and sat looking glumly into the courtyard below. Ruscum sidled over and said quietly, 'It's the unicorn, sir, isn't it? That's what everyone is saying: the King has gone to look for the unicorn.'

Vangrannicus smiled half heartedly but did not look round. Ruscum persevered. 'If that's what everyone believes, in the absence of any other suggestion or any evidence to the contrary what's wrong with us believing it too? We might as well, at least it would give us something to imagine about what he's likely up to, even if we don't know his map reference.'

There were roses in the courtyard and it was a measure of Vangrannicus's state of mind that he allowed them to remind him of embroidery and medieval pictures and knights and damsels and dragons. He was by no means a fanciful man and he had no idea why his thoughts should turn in such a direction, but he was suddenly taken with an intense wish to see a delicate ivory-skinned courtly maiden in a pointed cap, long gown and plaited hair moving serenely amongst the flowers softly humming to herself whilst musing on love poetry, or perhaps a theorem of geometry.

His dream slowly vanished as the magic of the courtyard was snuffed by the encroaching dusk and he turned back into the room to see Ruscum busying himself with lighting the lamps. 'Tell me then, Ruscum,' he said, with a weariness which sounded just a little affected, 'what is it that they are saying, what exactly is this story of the unicorn that is supposedly on everyone's lips?'

'Well it's a bit like the nursery rhyme sir, except that apparently there really is a unicorn, and it's on its way here. To have a fight. With the lion.'

'And is there a lion?'

'Not rightly sure, sir, but there are theories.'

'Well if it's on its way here, why has the King gone away to look for it?'

'Ah, now you're asking. Maybe he knows more about it than we do.'

Those intellectuals who had never seen a real one could nonetheless speak with assurance about all mythical animals being hybrids – the fruit of men and gods; the animal parts being the god's original creation, but the mixing up of those parts, the fertilizing seed of the idea of that animal and its occult attributes and powers being something that came from the peculiar minds of men, and which was developed and evolved down the ages. Development and evolution having taken place in many different directions rather then a straight line however, the mythic beast, the unicorn in this case, was then prey to gossip and whimsy and caricature until there were many different unicorns, almost as many as there were people's heads because each head held an idea of the unicorn which was subtly different from all the rest, there being by now no absolute archetype against which people's runaway ideas could be checked. The differences were sometimes slight and sometimes great. The commonest differences related to height, to colour and to length of horn, but there were others – some unicorns were very delicate and slender, others were massive drayhorses with shaggy fetlocks. It was true that those few scientifically minded people whose ideas and images stemmed from a close examination of ancient texts as well as palaeontological conjecture found it impossible to hold one version steady in their imagination since they had to deal with lots of differing possibilities, but most ordinary people, by some instinctual process, settled on a unicorn type, a unicorn of certain features and proportions, and kept to it. The very large and muscular ones tended to be the fiercest and the ones that snorted the most. The smallest and daintiest sometimes held a rose in their teeth had beautiful long manes which required a great deal of combing and were quite amenable to giving rides to little girls. The ones with beards tended to be the most frightening and the most magical and often the most unpredictable.

Being as he now was, surrounded by such ideas in everyone

else's thoughts, it was inevitable that a unicorn would creep into
Vangrannicus's head. (In his disturbed state of mind he no longer
had the energy to keep it out.) But which one would it be? Large
and fierce? Magical? Pure white and delicate? At first he was not
at all sure what it was like; he could not quite grasp its essential
nature nor appreciate its finer points, for he had thought too little
about the beast to have formed a proper picture of it; he was unable
to remember having been exposed to any representation of it in
his infancy. All he knew at this stage was that it was very like a
horse, with a sharpened pole in its head. But as to its character
and its origins, as to its purpose, its meaning and its relationship
to sin, to forgiveness, retribution and purification – all this was at
first unknown and remained to be discovered. His was, to begin
with, an ill-formed beast, framed in the dim light of other peoples'
mythology and one which therefore had quite suddenly to find
its own way into the world; as a consequence it was constantly
changing colour and doing different things with its horn and living
one day on nectar and ambrosia and the next on more prosaic
fodder from the manger.

Inevitably Vangrannicus was preoccupied with both the King and
the unicorn as he made his thoughtful way through the corridors
and doors, the stairs and vestibules, through the gates and arches
and across the courtyards and through the gardens which lay
between his office and his grand apartment high up at one end of
the rambling fortifications.

An old woman who was sitting by her window intent on her
knitting, said just as he passed, though without looking up, 'The
King has gone to fight the unicorn. He won't be coming back.'

Vangrannicus ought perhaps to have been alarmed by this but he
thought instead of the words that she spoke as being just another
thirteen tossed onto the mountain of human utterances which had
been piled up since the beginning of speech. He thought of the dead
people, the thousand upon thousand of accents and dialects and
jargon, idiosyncratic pronunciations and turns of phrase and slang
and elocution all heaped up and heard and harkened to and gone
and remembered and then forgotten as the rememberers passed out
of their time and themselves faded away. All the invisible aural
mass of detritus that humanity had generated and would generate

until perhaps the time when all protest became unavailing and there was no longer anything that could be said. He saw the immense gaseous lump silent and solidified, and with each extra irrelevant utterance cast upon it like a stale biscuit.

People said things like, 'Beware the ides of March... give him a four penny one... ne'er cast a clout... room for a little 'un... you're not coming in 'ere with that... as I've always said... it's looking a bit black over Bill's mother's... it's what 'e would have wanted... can I just say... they'll never get away with it... if I had my time over again... you've got to be joking... you can't say fairer than that... I had it out only the other day... could I just have a quick word... well he would, wouldn't he... I wouldn't go there again... have you got a minute... the thing is... you'll never believe this... will you get a move on... the rain it raineth every day...' And none of it need be paid any attention.

It seemed to Vangrannicus, in his current state, that the knitting woman's words had no significance but that the position of those words, their position on the great pile of words might be important. Millions and zillions of words all piled up and then, right on top of the mountain, right on top of the midden heap, those last thirteen. Why should he or anyone pay any attention to these latest thirteen words, other than as the last thirteen?

In any case they were not now the last words, he knew that, for as he entered his apartment and unwound his muffler his wife was saying, 'Don't let it drive you mad, you must not let it drive you mad you know, it could easily drive you mad,' and he stopped still and in his mind's eye he could see the goat in the painting in the office grinning at him.

'*The King has gone to fight the unicorn. He won't be coming back.*'

After supper he went for a walk, wishing for once he had a dog to go with him, and found himself meandering again past the window where the old woman had been clicking her needles. The shutter was closed, there was no light visible. Had it been a real prophecy? Was she an authentic sybil for whom the clouds of uncertainty were regularly parted to reveal the pre-ordained? Or was she just an old woman musing on the gossip she had heard and giving vent to an instinctually morbid inclination?

He genuinely hoped that he was not going mad.

His wife seemed to think he might be, she mentioned it again as she turned off the light, 'Do try not to take leave of your senses, my lord.'

He could not help, however, dreaming of his unicorn, which in the night seemed suddenly to have two heads and was bent on the destruction of the apparatus of government and the murder of all officials. Its victims were cut up and eaten by the beast, whose two horns now seemed to have become a gigantic knife and a gigantic fork. Some relief from the general terror was experienced by the sleeper though when the figures being remorselessly sliced up and gobbled down were un-obliging and red-coated.

Pippa and Willis made their way through the steep and narrow streets of the town which were dark but for the occasional halo of a gas lamp. Neither of them were really quite sure what to think about anything. They both felt that perhaps the strangeness Mr Newsome had written about was trying to invade the town, that it had spread like a clear fog from its origins in the distant countryside and was beginning to creep up these cobbles and upset people's ideas about things. And if that was what was happening was it a bad thing or a good thing? The strangeness would be unsettling, but Mr Newsome said he enjoyed it. The question was, did it interfere with what had always been right and what had always been wrong? Could it be judged as right and wrong or did it bring with it it's own right and wrong which were different from the old ones? Was it a thing to be wished for or to be fought against? And how could you fight a clear creeping fog? Once back in the zoo they did some feeding and some mucking out and some staring into the eyes of certain creatures which tonight seemed more than usually wise – especially the binturong – and then made cocoa, wrapped themselves in woolly jumpers and got down the ludo board.

Such was the mood of the people in the town and the zoo and the castle: they felt caught up in a contest between creeping despondency and high excitement, and it made them not feel quite right. They were all a little mixed up and not knowing quite what to think or just how to think it. Or whom they should love and how well. Whom they should remember, whom they should forget. Whom they should make allowances for and who was beyond the pale.

Far far away two women and an ape, an unhappy zoologist and a disconsolate princess, two German speaking men locked together by their mutual animosity, the lost and troubled monarch himself and a butler far removed from his pantry, all meandered with a shared but different purpose. But beyond these, additional to these people, over and above these there was something else. It was something which did indeed have a horn but which was not at all the sort of thing any of them thought they sought, even though it might be what some of them longed for. And it was coming. It had been coming for a long time, a time unaccountably longer than that which had elapsed since it started out. Nor was it the same thing that it had been in the beginning. It moved with firm and strong and resolute strides and it travelled in one very straight line.

The three different wisdoms which were Jemima, Millicent and Nicodemus, together made a trio which itself now enhanced the oddness of the territory they inhabited. They constituted a triangulation of minds into which an idea might be tossed never to be seen again in its original form. As they sat, three-cornered, about their camp fire their thoughts – inspired and hopeful; alert and clever; unfathomable and potentially savage – charged the night air with relaxed but confident feelings of expectation, which encouraged conjecture, and after a long silence Jemima was moved to look again upon Nicodemus as he appeared through the smoke beyond the flames and to say, 'Its curious that His Majesty never had any apes in his zoo. I wonder why not.'

'Not in his zoo, no I believe he did not,' said Millicent, herself looking through the wood smoke at Jemima, and wondering how much of what she herself had guessed about Nicodemus was true and how much she should tell.

In the silence which then lay about the crackling sticks and the shooting sparks, Jemima's father suddenly rose up and spoke urgently to his daughter, 'Do not turn your back on that animal, never let it get too close to you, look when he yawns, see those huge bone-cracking teeth, never forget that it's a wild animal, it will never be completely tame and its strong enough to kill you with a blow, look how devilish it appears through the fire, its only biding its time, then...'

Jemima thought, 'Oh do be quiet please,' but thankfully it appeared she had not actually said it for Millicent went on with, 'That is not to say he was not interested in apes. Deeply interested. And the zoo is not the only place that animals may be kept, of course.'

Nicodemus grunted and looked through the fire at the other two in turn and thought whatever he thought, which may have been about food, or he may simply have been enjoying the sight of his companions and how they appeared and disappeared through the smoke. But for all anyone could say for certain he might just as well be brooding on revenging himself on the human race.

Millicent had made her decision. She proceeded carefully to lay out for Jemima the evidence and her guesswork which together framed the interpretation she had made of Nicodemus' history as an infant member of the royal family.

Jemima, as was to be expected, asked some searching questions, none of which Millicent could answer and then was silent for a while as she stared at Nicodemus, not as her dead father had stared at him, but as a zoologist with some understanding of animal psychology and some familiarity with the literature on simian assimilation. She had of course no familiarity with the royal family. In the end she said, 'Hmmmm.'

Only just a foot or two beyond the light cast by the camp fire, two eyes watched and two ears listened and tried to make sense of the conversation. The dog Brisk could not help himself it seemed, he could not keep away. His attempt to go off and be a dog, to find a pack and hunt with it, had come to nought and here he was creeping close to a fire in the night, for company and solace. He could not leave alone the ever present question for all domestic dogs – what were people doing, what was the mystery they were trying to solve? and what was a dog's place in it? And as he pricked his ears and tried to pick out any of the few words he might recognise, he realised that not only could he not keep away from people, he was actually now thinking like them. He felt a curious mixture of pride and guilt as he wondered whether they had sausages and distinctly understood the word 'sit' though Millicent was actually talking about a particular 'situation.'

'So, you've no idea how long he was down in the dungeon?'

'No I'm afraid not.'

'Do you still have the infant photograph of him in the window at the wedding – was it a wedding or a coronation? Doesn't matter. Ah good.'

Millicent dug out the newspaper from her pack and handed it over; Jemima brought out her magnifying glass.

As Brisk watched the glass brought to bear on the newspaper and wondered what it was about, he felt a resurgence of his fondness for the puzzling unpredictability which people exhibited and he felt justified in his decision to work his way back. His attempt to shuffle off the domestication that his species had been subject to for so long was at an end. He could perhaps insinuate himself into this little pack of people – they had no sheep, but that did not necessarily matter, people with no sheep often had dogs he'd noticed – he could guard the bicycle, warn of approaching danger, and he could fetch them sticks. The only problem was the odd, hairy and deformed person-like animal who they had with them. Brisk did not think they would get on.

Ignoring the frantic protestations of her dead father, Jemima went over to the ape and examined him as closely as the firelight would permit, but he proved not averse to showing his teeth – as long as Jemima showed hers – and she nodded and muttered something to her human companion.

'Blimey,' thought the dog, 'What's she up to now? Why is she looking at his fangs? Rather her than me.'

Jemima formed an opinion of the age of the ape – an opinion which rather surprised her – but she decided to keep it to herself, having decided that it might be a fact which was capable of proving or disproving something contentious and she thought it wise at this stage to hold the information in reserve. She said, 'Well he certainly looks pretty healthy considering all he's gone through,' and added, as a further diversion, 'Any idea what they were feeding him on?'

'Oh no, just some disgusting slops – it stank, but everything there stank, it really was a vile place.'

Millicent was becoming preoccupied with the looks of her

companions and how the smoke distorted their features and enhanced the range of their potential personalities. Nicodemus drifted from jungle-dark and dangerous to human, childlike and delighted; Jemima was wafted from French film star to high priestess of some pagan woodland cult. Millicent took out her sketch book and in the dim glow of the campfire proceeded to make quick playful outlines, looking from one companion to the other.

Nicodemus did not seem interested in the sketching game tonight, he was yawning again and started desultorily to gather leaves and branches about him in half hearted imitation of the nest building behaviour of his ancestors. He was soon asleep where he lay.

Jemima, however, came and sat nest to Millicent, who drew out a flask of whisky from her bag and they shared nips as a huge variety of unicorns was depicted all over the paper – the artist's bold imaginings continually enhanced by the scientist's anatomical hints and advice. The deceased parent had approved Jemima's indulgence ('Go on girl, you deserve a tot') but one quickly became three and the ritual wiping of the neck of the bottle was forgotten by the time Ms Cake took her fourth little tipple.

It seemed there was an evil genie in the bottle and once uncorked he mischievously conjured the lineaments of Prince Antonio to appear amongst the outlines and the shading of all the horns and hooves, so that Jemima felt a tear forming in the corner of her eye and a desperate need to unburden herself, to speak out about the unfamiliar emotions which had risen up without warning and swamped her in her little tent last night. (Was it only last night?)

However the genie was wrestled to the ground (with some parental help) before she had said very much, indeed, realising, almost before she'd begun, that her confidences were inappropriate she had managed to blot her weeping eye ('oh, the smoke!') and revert to scientific comments (slightly slurred) about graminivores, but it was enough for the very acute Millicent, who cottoned on to things.

Jemima wriggled away into her sleeping bag, suddenly overcome with weariness and humming tired fragments of a less than jaunty air whilst Millicent leaned back against her tree trunk to ruminate, amongst other things, on what might be the precise nature of the great disappointment which haunted her companion. She was looking up through the branches at the black night when she became aware of some very soft movements amongst the grass and dead leaves, and the sensation of a dark shape approaching very close to her side. She heard a gentle panting and looked down into the eyes of a sheep dog which had materialised from the starless ether.

CHAPTER FIFTY

The tantrums of the infant princess Daphne had been a familiar spectacle in the royal household once upon a time, but there was one particular screaming fit which was notable for its volcanic power and the unusual fierceness of the passion that was engendered in one so young. It was not long after the death of her mother, and the little Daphne was demanding in the most forthright tones that the ape Nicodemus be extinguished, preferably by the most gruesome means in the executioner's repertoire. She made it known to her father that if justice were not done she would kill herself and as many of her personal servants as she could persuade to do the honourable thing and die with her. There could be no doubt about her sincerity, though there was no general certainty as to what exactly had occasioned her hatred of the animal – gruesome things were implicit in her rage, but Daphne herself never gave a lucid description of any precise chain of events. Or if she did, people privy to her words saw fit not to remember them. Nevertheless steps were taken to put Nicodemus beyond anyone's reach or ken. Surely the King would never contemplate the death penalty? But he appeared to try to engender, in Daphne at least, the belief that the beast had in fact been put down, and certainly every trace of his existence was removed from the royal apartments.

All the events surrounding the tragic death of Iphigenia of course greatly upset King Freddie, and his own sanity seems to have been preserved (to the extent that it was) only by his being overcome by a selective amnesia and a continual mental reconfiguration of events. By now, for the most part, he had come to believe that Nicodemus was dead, even though he could not be sure how it had come about. Sometimes there were vivid flashes of memory, indeed vivid flashes of different memories, totally incompatible with one another and therefore cancelling one another out. There was a vision of the ape being shot after throttling an equerry; of him failing to grasp a tree branch when leaping from a tower and landing on the Queen who had been taking tea in the garden below; it was even true that for a while the King could not get out of his head the idea that the Queen had actually herself killed Nicodemus – sometimes deliberately, sometimes accidentally. And then perhaps herself. Impossible of course. It had been the influenza hadn't it? Virulent and Spanish.

The details of the different versions his grieving mind had successively invented and presented to him had all blurred together and became lodged in the royal consciousness simply as an ill-defined unpleasantness: an unpleasantness which it was not possible entirely to eradicate, but one which was not to be dwelt on if at all possible.

Yet now, now here in this land of unexpected fountains, this land of Boldoni, this land of mysterious possibilities, it seemed that old stories bubbled up from where they had lain in the mud at the bottom of the royal forgetfulness and were charged with a strong urge to have their old truths crystallised once more. Freddie began to see in his mind's eye the smiling chimpanzee, asking and granting forgiveness. He felt the absent Millicent urging him on and continually solidifying the mirage. Lying under the bright green willow trees he felt he had no choice now, but finally to try to lever open a crack in the carapace of his memory, to squint again at all those vile things that had refused to succumb to the many attempts to eradicate them and lay there still in the dark. If only he could do it with any certainty, if after all this time and subconscious obfuscation he could distinguish fact from myth, erase the detritus of elaboration and extenuation that had over time so obscured events.

As he watched a bee inspecting dandelions, a feeling that he was very close to something astonishing slowly flooded through his body. Even if it was something not conventionally interpreted as benevolent, he knew that there was a blessing in anything that was inevitable, and the astonishing thing in question was assuredly inevitable. He lay down amongst the grass and was himself inspected by the bee. He opened one eye very wide to peer at a toadstool with a bright red cap. He was tempted to take a big bite; he was desperate to hear Millicent's firm voice telling him he must not. He sat up and grasped his ankles and sang his little song, but as the words died away certain things passed again before him in a calm and sedate tableau. Then it was that he saw himself, rising from a grave, pushing away the tombstone; and also there was Nicodemus, arising from his grave, dazed, and looking about, and there, over there, was Iphigenia herself, shaking off the earth and fixing the others with her stern gaze.

It was the unicorn of course. The flesh and blood unicorn was close at hand now and it was the grave and gentle magic pattern made by its wand-like horn which was, with its spell, beginning to expunge anguish and to engender hope, to stir up history and display its forgotten facets. Freddie was ready now, beyond the fountain, at every turn, behind every hedge, over the brow of the next hill, to see, as well as the fabulous quadruped himself, a dark and lovely chimpanzee and – perhaps a little farther off – his much neglected only daughter. It somehow seemed irrelevant that he might be frightened of both of them, for his trepidation was itself beguiling.

Time was passing; even though in this place it felt much less linear than it had in the castle. This was because Freddie had been used to time as a passing sequence of days, one following after the previous and preceding the next, as if it was going somewhere, whereas out here it seemed much easier to recognise that the really salient feature of the mechanism was that the sun which came up in the morning was the very same one that had gone down the previous evening and that everything was slowly revolving and that during the night – though it remained easy to be unaware of it – everything was in fact upside down. He was getting used to the idea that life was to be somersaulted, that it was like going head over heels and occasionally stopping to peer between one's legs at the stars, or, flat on one's back, to sleep in the sunshine, with minor insignificant interruptions of standing in the rain.

At the top of a gentle hill crowned with tall trees he turned and looked back and saw again the fountain, and was reassured. A little further back, he saw two figures making a snake-like and jerky progress through the long grass, the leader's energy and urgency hampered it seemed by being unsure of her way; her companion hopping along on a crutch and anxious to restrain her, yet not having the breath to say anything she would stop to listen to. Freddie wondered who they were. They were not like the usual bystander one encountered here – solitary men, often on distant tractors or else looking blankly over farmyard walls – they were here like him, he thought, for a reason, and not just because this was where they were. They were, without a doubt, looking for something. He decided to watch them for a while, he wanted to see which way they would go and what they might do. He sat down and took off his boots.

CHAPTER FIFTY ONE

Not very far away now from where King Dagobert the Fourth pondered the nature and identities of those meandering about the little valley below him, steady, long legged strides were being taken as something momentous approached over the hill unseen from the other direction. Was it the something whose coming was long desired? Yet it had a savage look about it. It was covered in the skins of other animals; it moved over the grass and between the trees like a prophet returning from the wilderness, larger than life and bearing the symbol of revelations almost too astounding to be taken in by those unprepared for the oblique truths that in the end are destined to up-end all dogma.

Although not all of those present would be able to recognise it, the landscape, subject as it was to subtle changes in the light and the colour of the Northern sky and subject as it was to the shadows of the trees on the hill attaining a certain length and a certain angle, was now, in this instant transformed into an exact replica of the one once depicted by Arturo Boldoni. Millicent, leading her companions on a footpath which now emerged from behind a windmill on the other side of the valley, saw the prospect before her and stopped in an exultation of recognition. It was at last the sublime and mysterious vista in the painting, and there, just over there were the trees which had harboured chitoned maidens, and there just there, beneath that little oak, Boldoni had declared the existence of the glorious unicorn.

Millicent stopped short and caught her breath. Brisk looked up at her sensing that something was either very right or very wrong, Jemima and Nicodemus came up behind and scoured the valley for the unusual thing which had stopped the artist in her tracks. None of them spoke. Jemima felt rather dizzy all of a sudden, she did not know why.

The windmill, which was given a yellowish sheen by the prevailing atmosphere, was a solid and ancient presence which looked firmly shut up but also as if it might harbour something or someone more mysterious than a miller. A little flight of rooks made their noisy way in the sky above it, and Nicodemus and Jemima looked up at them nervously. Millicent was conscious once again of the uncharacteristic dolour which Jemima had betrayed beside the camp fire last night, and once again wondered what could be the cause. She could tell that Nicodemus had also sensed her unhappiness.

Nicodemus was the first to spot Daphne and Trevor but it was unlikely that he could tell from this distance that one of them was his grown-up royal sister. Nonetheless, he peered intently until the others followed his gaze and caught a glimpse of the small figures who continued to make their confused way through the bracken and bushes, but they were soon lost to view.

When Jemima said, 'Oh, and look at the lovely fountain' it was with a distinctly melancholy tinge to her voice. 'How strange...' she trailed off, and Millicent was intensely aware that there was something close at hand which threatened to undermine her companion entirely.

'We've lost them now, there's no point in just rushing round in circles,' Trevor was saying. 'I think I can see the top of the fountain, look, over there, let's go back to the fountain, I think they will come back to it, in fact I'm sure of it, that is why they came here, there's something about the fountain...'

'But I'm sure I saw the top of his black hat just then, over that way, going down there.'

'Look, if we get back to the fountain you can climb the willow tree or stand on the wall of the pond.'

Princess Daphne tacitly agreed and they turned in the direction of the fountain, which meant that they were facing the hill with the windmill on it, but the four personages who had been there looking down had already begun their descent of the narrow path and small trees and undergrowth now prevented either party from having clear sight of the other.

Nonetheless, on the basis of that snatched momentary view Millicent felt able to say, 'It's her, I think, Princess Daphne. She seems to be in the company of Mr Trevor Simpson, an errant zoologist. I am supposed to be looking for him.'

Their appearance at this moment was really a complication and a possible hindrance – Millicent wanted only to reach that corner of the painting where the unicorn had been depicted. People got in the way. And one of them being the Princess added extra complications in the event of Nicodemus recognising her. And the other also added extra complications too, even though, or possibly because, he was the missing husband she was supposed to be looking for.

Then Daphne looked up and saw that the sky was tinged with a strange shade of turquoise and she saw the windmill and its black windows which looked like unseeing eyes, and its sweeps, which were motionless and it was as if everything was waiting for a breath of wind to start the clock again, to begin life again.

And now Freddie, too, noticed the distant dark figure of his erstwhile animal heir, his experimental beast of a son and he felt that he now understood that this was a place of judgement and that he could neither move nor think, but he must accept what was about to be visited upon him; and then Millicent saw the King and was grateful that he lived, but was full, when she looked upon him now, of a sort of foreboding beneath this lurid sky; and Jemima recognised Trevor and thought how strange to see a zooman here and then she remembered why he was here and why she was here. They each and all looked and stared across and into the little valley and tried to remember exactly who these other people were and what they had been doing when last they had seen them, and they all tried to remember what they thought of one another and what they thought of themselves and tried to remember who they supposed themselves to be and then, quite suddenly it seemed, Johnson and the maiden appeared, or became visible – they may have been there all along – and everyone's thoughts were suddenly simplified but still incapable of expression and there was a feeling of gratitude and it was as if the strange couple granted a measure of absolution by their mere visibility. But still everyone knew that something else had to happen; though none of them – except probably Johnson and the beautiful girl – knew what it was.

According to their history as reconstructed by Millicent, Freddie and Daphne and Nicodemus ought to be experiencing the trauma of beholding one another – would they be able to control themselves? Must they be revenged on each other? Would Daphne come to a reckoning with the two responsible (in some way or another) for the death of her mother? Would Nicodemus slaughter the man who had first tried to superimpose humanity upon him and then consigned him to a black hole?

Would Trevor be able to gaze upon Jemima without falling at her feet and resigning utterly from his previous existence? What were Millicent's feelings for the King? Did she now discover that it was only the tragedy he represented which she relished? Was Jemima's detached objectivity to be eclipsed by momentous events, would she continue to try to deny the passion which yearned to overtake her? Or did none of this matter in the face of what now emerged from the trees and made its steady and dignified way toward Johnson and the maiden?

It seemed that none of the feelings that these principals had expected to feel were now felt. A soft breeze had indeed sprung up to begin the very slightest creaking stir of the sails of the windmill, and the stultified pressure in the air was now gently relieved and a sort of swirling happy disappointment arrived on the wind. No one was quite clear at all about the succeeding waves of seemingly contradictory emotions which alternately rose up with the breeze and washed over them and then receded in a warm and not unpleasant way.

Johnson and the maiden stood still beside the fountain but Freddie began to walk down the hill towards his daughter who moved toward him whilst looking over her shoulder up toward Nicodemus and his companions who now walked down the path from the windmill, Brisk leading the way, still unsure of the situation and uttering occasional tentative questioning barks, which sounded strangely hollow in the little valley.

Trevor had only just realised that the other woman with Jemima was his wife, and only then did he notice that the third person with them was in fact a chimpanzee.

The King found that he was glad of the long grass, the little willow trees, the bushes, which interrupted his sight of daughter and ape, even as he moved toward the inevitable encounters he was glad that there was yet a measure of obfuscation to prolong the hiding of one from another right up until this fateful last moment when all his delusions would crumble away. Here present were the other truths, which by now must be truer than his.

Daphne, who had been hoping merely for the clear sight of a man in a bowler hat whose significance she had no real idea of – except that she'd made him the embodiment of all her discontents – was suddenly faced with her past life unexpectedly moving steadily toward her from two different opposing directions. Once upon a time she might have cried out, but this landscape and its fountain would admit no dudgeon or umbrage. She looked from the one to the other as ape and father made their steady approaches, and felt, not as if her own revenge was imminent, but rather as if she herself were guilty of some monstrous forgotten crime.

Johnson and the maiden stood in the almost theatrical green and blue and yellow light that parted the clouds and seemed to bring elements from a different realm to glimmer upon this world and expose wonders never commonly perceived. The pair looked steadily up the hill, into the trees whose sequined and sparkling leaves rustled in a breeze of expectancy and imminent revelation. Suddenly the very tip of a horn was visible. The maiden rose involuntarily onto her toes and Johnson, in a swift and startling movement, took off his bowler hat and held it by his side.

Slowly the straight spiral horn emerged from amongst the leaves and branches of that very tree painted, once upon a time, by Boldoni.

A faint echo of a voice was heard which seemed to come from the sky: *'Und wenn sie nicht gestorben sind, dann leben sie nock haute...'*

More of the horn slowly poked out between the leaves of lime and then a dark shape took a pace forward and stopped. Festooned in the black furs of northern beasts, the tall figure of a black-bearded man was holding the long straight horn which was a narwhal's horn. He surveyed the valley and saw the people in it and the ape, and his look was soft and bore incipient tears of love and relief, and then he looked directly at the maiden and she looked earnestly at him.

The King had turned about and walked backwards as he looked wide-eyed at the figure and the horn; he knew at once that the horn was a narwhal's horn – the horn so often taken for a unicorn relic in days of yore – but remained full of wonder at the strange man, understanding not who or what he could be.

Jemima looked through the beard and upon the face and examined the eyes and even though she was far away she knew what she saw, had known it before she saw it and she gave a little stifled cry. Millicent was alarmed and feared for her companion.

But it was the maiden whom the man approached with stately strides and Johnson stood a little aside as he came nearer. The beautiful girl remained composed but a flood of fateful consummation visibly enhanced the perfection of her demure figure as she looked serenely into the handsome face, the face roughened by gales and lashing seas. She had long been meant to meet him here; she did not know his name or where or how he had lived, such things were beyond her compass and concern.

Jemima knew his name. And Daphne would know his name if she came closer, but though she marvelled she was not yet able to understand that the stone age creature marching into the magic valley had, in the past, dined with her in the most excruciatingly civilised of circumstances.

Millicent did not know him at all, for she had never met the handsome Prince Antonio, the prince who would never more stray upon a croquet ground and was shorn of all the trappings which made life irksome and otiose and for whom 'prince' was become a worthless word he would never hear again.

Miraculously preserved, miraculously surviving, the Venetian Adonis smiled as only a god can smile, whose beams of satisfaction brook no opposition to the imposition of happiness.

As yet, however, Jemima at least was looking wide eyed up at him and feeling many things which did not resemble happiness in any of its usual guises.

For a minute or two, as all eyes were upon the man and the maiden, everyone stopped still.

Brisk could not work out whether it was something about this place which was making the people equally wary and uncertain and simultaneously on the point of elation – as if they were about to be overtaken by something – or whether it was something about the coming together of these particular people which had infected the place itself with doubt and bewilderment and joyful calamity. He prowled from static human to static human rather as if he'd been let out onto a giant chess board, sniffing ankles and peering tentatively up into faces. He was beginning to feel like an abandoned puppy, and was on the point of whimpering when the humans began to move again, silently to question themselves and the unknown powers which beset them all.

Then, 'Oh papa, look, he's here,' said Daphne waving an arm which might have indicated either Nicodemus or the Prince or Mr Johnson.

Freddie tried to say, 'I know,' but nothing came out because he was overcome, and because he did not know. Did not know how the Italian prince had been primitivised, or how the long dead ape had come back to life, nor where the mysterious Mr Johnson had sprung from. Yet, as the sails of the windmill continued to turn steadily now up on the hill, and the clashing and quivering northern lights slowly became more subdued and softer and more restful, for Daphne, Freddie, and perhaps Nicodemus, a general promise of refreshment and resolution continued to filter into the atmosphere and temper the initial anguish that surely must have been generated by the sight of one another.

Trevor watched Daphne ignore the man with the bowler hat and approach the old man who was her father with unexpected equanimity (so it was true then, she was a princess) then he turned to gaze on Jemima who, though she exhibited a different kind of perfection when stripped, as she was, of her serenity, nonetheless it remained perfection and the pain disappeared from his aching leg as he leant against the willow tree and contemplated her.

Millicent, left alone holding Nicodemus' hand, watched him as he watched Daphne and Freddie. She looked for signs of recognition but nothing was certain, he stared at them, but he also looked over at the man in the bearskins with the beard. Daphne and the King were talking to one another but she could not hear the words, nor glean anything of the mood of their encounter – they each, from time to time, looked at the ground or up into the sky rather than at one another, however.

Trevor, just as someone might toss themselves off a cliff hoping for heaven or hell, hopped directly and deliberately into Ms Cake's path as she made her querulous way in the direction of Antonio and cried out her name, 'Jemima!' in a biblical exhortation at least to look upon him, but she did not react.

Antonio had abandoned the power of speech entirely, he and the maiden communicated in some other more direct way, and looked into one another's eyes for a long time before taking one another's hands. Then they embraced and during their embrace a very strange thing happened, for it appeared as if Mr Johnson might have suffered a smile to pass across his face, and it was as if a horse had laid an egg. However he returned the bowler hat to his head, took up the great narwhal tusk and carried it before him with due solemnity stepping carefully with rather balletic strides through the long grass to the King who, after momentarily looking round for Vangrannicus and then remembering where he was, formally and automatically accepted it and held it like a great staff, betraying no disappointment but rather a quiet absent minded acceptance. Then he resumed looking bravely into the eyes of his daughter.

Jemima's acceptance of all that had been ordained was a harder lesson perhaps, but as she came to a despairing halt to watch the godlike couple make their way off into the wilderness, Nicodemus broke away from Millicent's grasp and hurried to her, grappling her in his long hairy arms so that her tears fell upon the hairy shoulders of *pan troglodytes*.

The fountain suddenly leapt high into the air, some new subterranean pulse forcing the myriad diamond droplets up and up to fall in tiny bright glittering prisms like spectral fireworks.

Millicent sat on the ground and waved at her husband and wished she could represent the scene before her but made no attempt to reach for a crayon for she knew it could not be done; she would rather prefer to chalk some magic symbols on a dark wall – and she began to imagine the grey wall upon which she would do it.

The wind became stronger and jostled the trees and grass, lifting unruly wisps of hair on Freddie's head, urging on the grinding of the yellow windmill and spattering Johnson's bowler with drops of water dislodged from the column of the fountain. There came a chill in the air and the splendour of the strange Northern lights receded again somewhat, taking with it a little of the wonder and trepidation that had been visited upon everyone.

Daphne wrapped her coat more tightly about her as she frowned at her father who put both hands on the top of his head and revolved slowly in a bizarre pirouette of agony or despair or simple confusion in the little green clearing which they inhabited.

Trevor slumped to the ground where he found several insects, all of whose names he knew, and began examining them along with his thoughts about life, which latter were undergoing yet another reappraisal.

CHAPTER FIFTY TWO

Freddie paced with the narwhal horn as a long walking stick, having it seemed, for the moment at least, forgotten what it was or what it had suggested or symbolised. The unicorn in his head had fallen into a deep sleep and the question as to whether it would ever be aroused again was one that had no answer.

Curiously, as their talk stuttered and slowed, Daphne found herself revisiting in her mind the look and feel and smells of the places of her childhood, and the generosity and foibles of old servants, friends and dogs (many never to be seen again) and a burgeoning sense of reconciliation began to arise and take possession of the silences. Daphne took her father's paw as they stopped to watch a kingfisher on a low slung bow.

Were they making their way back to the citadel? Nothing had been said as to direction but both of them vaguely thought they might be. Be it the citadel or be it elsewhere, Freddie and his daughter felt the inevitability of there being nowhere now for them to be but together, and they felt this with such a mixture of sadness and relief that the late Queen Iphigenia could easily be imagined gratified on her cloud.

Daphne pictured the riderless horse in the picture in her boudoir and it was suddenly very old and shaggy with something of the look of her father about it.

The King himself stared about him with glazed eyes as if he realised that a miracle had indeed just occurred in this place but it had somehow passed him by. Once upon a time Freddie was used to having broad and ambitious plans, such as building his zoo and investigating the nature of humanity; now he simply wondered whether it might not after all be sufficient simply to decide which way to walk – this little path with brambles and rabbit droppings, or this little path with hawthorn and a rusty horse shoe peeping from the grass? It seemed a more immediate and natural level on which to live. He followed Daphne down the brambly way.

Freddie and Millicent seemed to have slid past each other through the very green and tall bracken below the yellow windmill without there being sufficient of each other made visible to claim the other's attention – though Millicent's rich brown hair had sailed across gaps in the foliage and her strong and becomingly trousered legs had stalked and peeped from behind branches and Freddie's wild blue eye had flashed through the undergrowth. Perhaps they were never to meet again. Millicent had gravitated alone toward the particular tree with which Boldoni had shaded the mythical beast and it was more and more as if she were actually amongst the very brush strokes and could sense the precise mingling of the elements of his palette which had cast the spell, which had revealed the magic, which had lured Millicent here and tempted the horned beast (the real horned beast) out into the open.

Johnson was here too, paying her no attention but smoking again beneath his bowler hat and staring fixedly into the wood. They neither of them had been distracted more than momentarily by the Prince, their faith was undiminished.

A dim face rose up above the sill of the topmost of the little black windows in the mill and looked down on the fountain and the dispersing characters – none of whom was the right one. The rumbling grind of the mill stones and the huge cogs of the machinery was very comforting and Mr Newsome climbed back down the stairs and considered asking the ghostly miller if he might spend the night.

CHAPTER FIFTY THREE

The long forgotten men of the singing dog expedition stood barefoot on the gently rolling deck of their little ship, some bracing themselves with a hand on the top of the large crate which was very securely lashed in its place on the planking amidships. They looked with tired, expectant, bemused and disappointed eyes upon the toy-town dimensions of the little harbour and the castle on the hill which had seemed so important when they left but were now dwarfed by the extravagant sights that had become commonplace during their long and adventurous journeying all across the globe. Home was much diminished and almost laughable. The leader borrowed the telescope of the ship's captain and looked along the deserted quay. Where was the King? Where was Willoughby, surely there must be Willoughby? Some of them had even dreamed of a brass band and bunting.

The prized animal shivered and scratched invisible in its wooden prison. He had known only these dark confines for many a month and when allowed to emerge he would do so into a different time zone, a very different latitude and a very different climate from those into which he had been born. He would never see another singing dog, nor the steamy hills and forests in which he was wont to feed and roam and sing and run. All because he was deemed rare in a country in which his tribe had never set foot and would not care to, this dog's life would dwindle to pining in a straw corner with nothing to do until he finally would forget all about living. Another sad victim of curiosity and collectiblity. Perhaps it should have been no surprise that he had not sung since they'd trapped him, and many of the expedition were worried that medals and rewards might elude them – after all the poor dog looked pretty much like many a mongrel and if it were never to give voice would be indistinguishable to the untrained eye. One or two, the more pessimistic, thought they might be accused of never having been round the world at all.

CHAPTER FIFTY FOUR

For Trevor, all the threads of his life seemed now to have come apart and were fading into invisibility amongst the long grasses, where all his beetle friends waddled and scrabbled much more solidly amongst the dung and the dew, ready to do battle with any headless soldier they might come across. He knew his wife was over there somewhere... and Daphne, the *vrai* Princess Daphne, whose obsession with Mr Johnson was turned off like a switch, and who had suddenly wandered off with an old man, without a word, without so much as a by your leave, he thought randomly, was gone. And Jemima, where was Jemima? Still close at hand he thought but not in a particularly friendly mood. Strange how things and people, especially himself, were so suddenly and so easily irrelevant he thought, poking a wood louse (*porcellio scaber*) with a grass stem.

Did he mind? What was he doing here, was he still looking for the unicorn? If he could just catch up with Johnson – who was only just over there, a moment ago, he can't have gone far – he could have it out with him, find out what he knew. But somehow, now that Daphne had disappeared, it all seemed less important. And why that should be so he could not say, since Daphne did not know who Johnson was, or what he was looking for, and had some peculiar ideas of her own about his identity and significance. Trevor was free now really to get to grips with the unicorn quest but he just felt too tired, bereft of involvement, eclipsed by a wandering hairy prince, altogether more at home on the ground contemplating things whose many sets of legs functioned so well and so precisely. He thought in the circumstances he'd just have a little sleep, and then later see if he could make contact with someone – his wife, or Johnson, or Jemima, he wasn't sure who, it would all be clearer after a bit of a nap. Just as he was nodding off he remembered the ape. Had there really been an ape up by the windmill? Nicodemus strode into Trevor's complicated dream and took part in all sorts of unlikely activities culminating in walking up the aisle of a cathedral in a monkish cowl arm in arm with Jemima, who was in cricket whites carrying a croquet mallet. But when Jemima turned round she had the face of the aepyornis.

CHAPTER FIFTY FIVE

When, many years later, the participants in that bewildering afternoon of refracted grace and stifled excitement, of apparent disappointments which tantalised with new promises, of the unexpected and the inexplicable, of separations and comings together, when the participants expressed the essence of their experience, they for the most part fell back on inadequate attempts to describe the lights in the sky and the moment when the windmill started turning and the strange deep blue shadows in the wood. Though they tried to express the atmospheric galvanism, the piquancy, the steady intoxication, the quiet rapture of the place, they for the most part were shy of mentioning the other people who were there present, nor did they dwell on their failure to make declarations they might have made, nor the compassion which the fountain made available in abundance but which – frustratingly in hindsight – they failed properly to avail themselves of. In truth it had not been easy – the giant expectations and conundrums which inhabited the wilderness obstructed people's views of one another, and all but obliterated any sense of a time to come; the lights made it difficult to be sure what lay in which direction and the possibility of any horizon lying just behind the bright green willows or beyond Boldoni's increasingly majestic trees was lost.

There were times when that little valley, with its fountain and its light green willows and bracken and long grass, resembled, in an odd way, nothing so much as a cemetery. Daphne was fleetingly reminded of the strange dream she'd had at the Black Widow, with all the white shrouded people climbing back into their graves and Freddie had, at times, thought perhaps he actually was dead, but if so, heaven was less splendid and glorified than it was supposed to be, and yet in many ways infinitely more marvellously peculiar – for its unearthliness was very striking but very subtle.

Jemima watched the figures of Antonio and the maiden disappearing into the distance, clasping one another tightly, wrapped in bliss and dreams of the cave, or the little house with the pointed windows, wherein they would dwell for evermore.

Brisk briefly contemplated going with them, but realised they were off to inhabit a future altogether too poetic for a dog and he must try to sniff out something less ethereal.

Nicodemus looked round for Millicent, but she had passed to the other side of the fountain and he could not find her, nor could he find the haversack with all the drawings in it and he mistook the tears in Jemima's eyes for the same sadness he felt, grasping her tightly and obscuring her view of the spot which Antonio and the maiden had now vacated.

And Mr Johnson and Mrs Millicent Simpson remained rooted to the spot for a while, fascinated by the deep dark blue space which inhabited the void between the tree trunks whence Neolithic Antonio had first appeared. They stared at this place, emptied of Antonio, at the leaves and branches which decorated it, and listened to their rustling in the breeze and smelt the air which had been pierced by the esquimaux horn. Millicent licked her lips and breathed deeply, Johnson's large white eyeball grew immense as he bit upon his cigar holder and exhaled dark smoke like a dragon. Independently, but in the same measured rhythm, they started to move toward the wood.

CHAPTER FIFTY SIX

The telescope crammed immeasurable dimensions into its engineered extensions and as a result was itself sufficiently large and long and hefty that it was difficult to hold up and keep still, so that Pippa rested it on the left shoulder of Willis, whom she from time to time ordered to bob, or to stretch up, or to shuffle sideways according to the desired angle of perspective. They were again in the high castle garden surveying the distant land, and this time they had a distinct tiny object in view. Two, in fact and they were bipeds, not sheep. Willis had picked them out first and now Pippa had the eye piece and was trying to focus and keep in view two very tiny foggy grey figures walking through the foggy grey air which was how the magnifier squeezed the light and rendered such remoteness silently intelligible.

'Yes, yes I see them.'

'Can you see them? It's a man and a woman I think.'

'Mmmm, weeell, could be...they're definitely not sheep.'

'Of course they're not sheep... let me have another look.'

'Just a minute... they've stopped and the smaller one is waving its arms and looks like it's stamping its feet.'

'Oh come on, it is my turn.'

Pippa reluctantly relinquished the eye-piece and they changed places.

'Oh yeeees, and the other one has got a stick or a spear, he's waving it about, he's got one hand on the top of his head he might be doing a war dance or something – do you think he's going to kill him?'

'The woman you mean? I agree, the other one is definitely a woman, oh lor, I hope not.'

'Oh no, it's alright, he's sat down, the one with spear is sitting down and the other one is wandering away on her own.'

'Oh good.'

'Wait a minute, she's coming back, she's grabbed the spear, ha ha, she's grabbed the spear and chucked it into the bushes ha ha!'

'I wish we could hear what they're saying, I bet they're shouting, do you think they're shouting? I wonder who they are and what they're doing way over there.'

'Well... who... knows?'

'Except... except that the only people we definitely know to have gone off in that direction are all doing the same thing, aren't they?'

'You mean... oh, he's got up again... looking for the unicorn?'

'Of course.'

'Oh my god, do you think the woman is Jemima?'

Pippa took the telescope as Willis surrendered it in her astonishment, and carefully adjusted the focus.

'No. That's not Jemima, definitely not Jemima. Jemima would never be so... oh she's jumping up and down again!'

Thus were Pippa and Willis distant witnesses to the unpredictable progress of Freddie and Daphne's reappraisal of their family life which, having early on reached a surprising plateau of forgiveness and mutual understanding, was yet prone to violent eruptions of who had done what and to whom. Then after a few very boring minutes for the watchers during which the couple sat apart on the ground and did not appear to look at one another, Willis was suddenly privy to the most remarkable picture of all: they were observed to stand up and come together in a firm and prolonged embrace which elicited an involuntary, enigmatic 'Ahhhhh!' from the observer.

'What?' said Pippa. 'What's happened? What are they doing now? Let me have a look.'

'It's alright, it's alright, they're friends again, have a look.'

And Pippa did have a look and there seemed to be a sudden improvement in the light which shone on the couple as they hugged each other, and a spark of recognition suddenly challenged Pippa to confirm to herself or deny that the man was who he in that instant so strongly resembled.

In obstinate disbelieving silence she looked hard into the little aperture, straightened back up, wide eyed, returned to the telescope ignoring her friend's pleas of, 'What? What?' and, 'Come on let's have a look,' and then she slowly stood upright again, relinquished the instrument as if to declare that no greater wonder could it ever reveal and solemnly uttered the words, 'It's the bloody King!'

Pippa and Willis were not given to vulgar emphasis but an occasion such as this called forth oaths even from them. After a few seconds of silent astonishment there was again much fighting over the eye piece, there were denials, there were affirmations, there was uncertainty, but then, when the object of their frantic surmise happened to adopt a christlike pose with arms outstretched, offering a completely unobstructed full frontal view, there was absolute belief – this was the missing monarch. Suddenly their innocent spying had ceased to be a game and was no longer merely naughty. This was not something that they should be doing – not staring at the King, unawares, not the King, ordinary people were fair game but the monarch's privacy was sacrosanct. And yet it was so exciting, it was the King, he was actually there, over there wandering about in the wilds like some lost shepherd. With a woman. A young woman. The telescope was snapped open again to see if they could make out who she was, but neither of them recognised her.

What should they do? They were in a frantic quandary. Who should they tell? Should they tell anyone? They did of course tell someone, several people in fact. It was not 'something you could keep to yourself,' as Willis put it, nodding slowly as if she were citing a philosophical truth which was profoundly applicable in this momentous circumstance. People got to know – even those who had no idea he'd gone missing – that the King had been spotted far away in the Northern wilderness, and one of the first people to get to know was the artful and mysterious Wilfred.

The artful and mysterious Wilfred, who always knew more than he let on, set about certain preparations. They were secret preparations, even his fiancee was not meant to be privy to this plan. But he could not help betraying, in the sheer intensity of his ever-smiling mask, that he was convinced that the time had come, that a momentous moment in history was imminent and that there was about to be a fundamental shift in the way things were.

Vangrannicus, when they'd found the courage to tell him, amazed everyone by taking the news very calmly, silently retreating to a turret, whither he had previously removed the painting with the goat and the cherub, and locking himself in. Those close to him and who had been privy to his recent ramblings believed he had concluded that the day of the lion was done and the unicorn – in some form or other – was advancing and would take over their little country by stealth or wealth or war. He was resolved to have none of it. The King might be coming back from the wilderness, but it was almost certainly only to collect a few things he had forgotten: he was doubtless being pursued hotly by the usurping creature.

Inevitably, chance and fate combined with the manipulative caprice which derived from the Lanes themselves and also with the vestiges of their own exhausted volition to deliver the King and the Princess to territory that was (if faintly) recognisable as a part of the domain of Dagobert – it was, or pretended to be, a version of the winding road which would bring them to the little bridge at the foot of the hill and thereafter to the little frequented but once opulent steep street of mansions which Millicent and Nicodemus might remember negotiating in their exit from the town. They were by now a damp and bedraggled pair – the sunshine had given way to showers – and Daphne was leaking socks from a hole in her knapsack whilst the last button had slipped off Freddie's Norfolk jacket and rolled into the mud in which it would lie for many hundreds of years, so that he tied about him a piece of string he'd found looped round a gate. The closer they came to the town and the castle (which looked different from here, when you were coming back, and smaller than you remembered as well) the less they spoke and the more miserable they appeared.

Freddie had never felt less like ruling anything. He wondered whether the rich fat courtiers still existed, found it difficult to believe that they could, but then the dread certainty that they did began to well up within him. He wondered whether anyone had been looking after things, would Vangrannicus still be alive? The thought of wearing any of those fur trimmed medieval robes depressed him utterly, as did the very memory of the smell of those fur-trimmed medieval robes. Daphne too was sick at heart and wondering what on Earth might be done finally to rid herself of this genetic disease, this taint, this curse, this royalty, twisting and torturing her since her unfortunate birth. She could not believe that she was returning to the boxed-in world of Helena

Butterworth and people continually asking for her instructions or presenting engagement diaries, or asking what she would eat, or for her endorsement of something or other.

They were coming back, but only because having been away that is what happened to you – you came back. To return to the same place the traveller had started from however seemed impossible. This was always the case, of course, time and dirt and dust and erosion and people dying and strangers being born wreak continual subtle metamorphosis, but as long as a portion of one's mind continues to occupy a particular place there is usually a continuity and a familiarity and such superficial changes are always recognisable for what they are. However sometimes things are more complicated and more peculiar. A place left entirely bereft of the traveller's mind for any space of time ceases to take account of that mind and inevitably ignores it when it attempts repossession. In the worst cases, the returnee often can hardly believe that they've ever been here before. And everything is exacerbated in the case of the Lanes: a mind returning from the Lanes is always such a different mind from that which it had used to be, that coming face to face with somewhere made peculiar by the long absence of the mind it no longer quite is, is an unpredictable experience, especially since any ideas of the way things should be would have been severely interfered with during the sojourn.

More than the simple disorientation of the returning dog men, Freddie and Daphne saw the citadel – as would Jemima, Trevor and Millicent if they ever made the return journey – as if it suddenly presented itself visually in a foreign language: things jarred, walls and towers and gates mumbled incomprehensibly or flatly denied that they'd ever been what they were accused of having been. The architectural syntax followed the wrong rules, streets had changed places and the relative sizes of buildings had swapped about alarmingly; some whole quarters had ceased to exist and the sun now rose through windows which surely had been used only to the cruel caresses of the north wind.

However, for the King and his daughter, who realised that coming back at all had been a huge mistake, or rather perhaps it was some sort of inescapable punishment, these conceptual alterations did not greatly impinge for good or ill since the couple's sadness was too profound. The steep street of villas and mansions which had witnessed Millicent and Nicodemus' flight from civilisation was still there, but it had been all but stripped of any vestige of historical respectability, it seemed as if it had lost its memory and if anyone had whispered to it what it had been, the redolences that it had had, the exquisite atmosphere of faded grandeur which it had exuded, it would not have known what they were talking about. On this day especially it was totally unrecognisable, for it had lost its emptiness, there was no still space for the cheeping of little birds to echo into. This was because the avenue was jammed full of thousands of hideous human beings. It was pulsating with shouting, screaming people jostling one another and heaving this way and heaving that way, breaking out in song, climbing lampposts, throwing flowers and waving flags.

Freddie and Daphne's misery was about to be multiplied tenfold. When they crossed the bridge and turned the corner they were horrified by the huge crowd of people lining both sides of the streets shouting, 'Vivat Rex!' and acclaiming the victor of the historic war with the unicorn whose horn King Dagobert IV carried (triumphantly they thought) like a staff in his right hand.

The shocking noise and the spectacle of so many pink faces – many of them very ugly – all crammed into one street was almost too much for Freddie and Daphne; they would have run away but somehow the bellowing populace imposed its will upon them and they felt they had to begin the ascent of the hill. Indeed, the people pressed in upon them, many of them anxious to touch the 'unicorn horn' and they were in danger of being manhandled or smothered until a ragged phalanx of red coats in the person of Nat and a few of his off duty mates from the Apple Tree arrived, clumsily buttoning their tunics, having heard the noise, and the call of duty being just (but only just) strong enough to drag them from their drink and their dominoes.

The royal pair did not have the presence of mind to be able to think of anything to save themselves. They seemed to have voluntarily mounted their own scaffold. Each knew that this was the last straw, it was difficult enough returning to a place that they barely recognised but neither could contemplate returning to a life which screamed and bayed and waved ridiculous tattered flags, a life which fed on ignorance and hysteria and stupidity and allotted godlike attributes to the two most exhausted, frightened and pathetic people in the country.

But it was about to get worse. Protection of a sort having been afforded by the soldiers who, though few in number, were made boisterous by their beer and playfully zealous in administering hefty buffets to the most hysterically loyal subjects, the pair got to the top of the hill and saw to their horror that there was more, and more frightening, chaos on the other side. Here the crowd was just as thick, but a very different sentiment motivated them. Glory and joy gave way to terror and recrimination for in this quarter of the town had come together all those people who had a very different view of the unicorn. The rumour – and what the King wielded in his right hand was the proof of it – was that the unicorn, the magical and wondrous unicorn which had been coming to save everyone from sin and doom, which was the one true and pure beast in whom all hope resided – had been cruelly slaughtered by the King and now nothing could save the nation from ruin and despair and sickness and death.

This was therefore an even uglier crowd. The gloom and resignation which Freddie and Daphne had experienced coming up the hill was suddenly replaced with immediate and very real fear for their lives once they reached the top and understood the different mood which swayed the crowd here. Indeed they truly thought it was all up with them, and were on the point of surrender. They would have genuinely welcomed the sight of any tumbrel they could climb into which would take them away from all this noise, even if it took them away from everything else as well. They were both ready to make an end.

But then something strange and unforeseen occurred. A gang of strong, sober young men, none of them shouting or screaming, marched quickly out of a garden gate and in a most precise and very firm and disciplined way pushed a hole in the crowd into which Freddie and Daphne were suddenly enclosed and within which they went whirling away as if caught in a maelstrom. Once into a side street the little regiment of strong young men picked up the King and the Princess by the armpits and carried them bodily at the double through a maze of other streets until they had no idea where they were. They found themselves eventually in a little old warehouse by the river, dazed and bemused, and believing in angels.

The sober and earnest young men obviously had instructions not to talk to them, so they all sat there quietly amongst tea chests and sawdust and rope and oil drums until Wilfred himself smartly descended some steps into the room – steps which neither Freddie nor Daphne had previously noticed – and greeted them both with a smile, a flop of his forelock (a nod, not even the vestige of a bow) and brisk handshakes, saying, 'I have made arrangements, this way, there's no time to lose.'

He did not intend to waste time talking, he exuded, as always, an air of knowing what was best, and for their part Freddie and Daphne did not care any more about what happened to them so long as they could get away from the noise and the crowds, so they followed him and were grateful. Wherever he was taking them it must be better than the grim old castle on its cliff, better than the sagging old town on the point of imploding into a civil war engendered by addle-headed interpretations of misunderstood symbols of things. And where half the population were demanding retribution for Freddie's unspeakable crime of monocerosicide. Asylum beckoned, and they would hasten to it sighing with relief no matter what, no matter who offered it to them.

Meanwhile, Jemima, whose exit from the Lanes proved more navigationally vexatious (there was a reluctance to allow her to leave it appeared) had found herself on the bank of a river and was following it in the expectation that it was in fact an upper reach of the great river. Even though its course wound this way and that and often lead her away from the far distant castle which she could just make out in the south, she thought the serpentine but sure progress a better plan than trying to get there by roads. Roads which persisted in playing their frustrating games, continually going back on themselves or fizzling to a cart track and then to nettles and old ruts, and then a crumbling wall or an impenetrable hedge finally blocking the way. Nicodemus was with her of course. In the absence, at the moment anyway, of a unicorn (she had not, and would never, forget those enigmatic tracks beside her camp) she must take responsibility for this lost ape. He must be found a place in the zoo and properly looked after. It was her plan to return here as soon as this was done and after she'd made sure all was well with Pippa and Willis and all the other animals. (It would not be very long, however, before she would have to begin wrestling with a malevolent possibility; she had been infected by the germ of a hypothesis: that there might no longer be a zoo, nor a Pippa nor a Willis.)

Neither could her plan take account of the very tall trees which the tow path now passed beside – an extensive stand of immense trees which appeared as the river flowed round a steep and unexpected hill, trees of a type which Jemima could not put a name to, Latin or otherwise. Great straight trunks rising up and up toward the sky where they finally branched out and made a greeny blue canopy of leaves so very thick that the sun could sparkle only here and there through oscillating holes and intricate interstices. The colossal scale of this arboreal community was intimidating – her neck ached with the effort of trying to see their tops, which were lost in their own camouflage – and Jemima soon began to think of the trees as having animal characteristics; they often seemed to be whispering together.

Then Nicodemus let go her hand and rushed over to the biggest of them all, which, amazingly, he began to climb, even through there were no low branches and the girth of the trunk was such that his outstretched arms barely enclosed a small section. He seemed by some magic able to grip the rough bark with fingers and toes so that he shuffled himself upward at a speed which alarmed Jemima. She was amazed that he could do it at all and terrified that at any moment his strength would fail and he would crash down to Earth. But he continued upward making little grunts of delight and satisfaction until after five minutes or so he gained the relative safety of the first lateral boughs. In another minute or two the only sign of his presence was the rustling and quivering and shaking of distant leaves and the sudden crashing of his leaps from one tree to another. Jemima had to strain to make out where he was as she wandered beneath the great wooden pillars trying to follow his progress.

She had examined Nicodemus minutely, and looked into his mouth, and come to certain incontrovertible conclusions. This was not an ape which could have adorned the royal household twenty years ago, he was simply not old enough. Of course he would have looked old down there in the darkness to Millicent who knew nothing of apes; the way she described that horrible black dungeon, it was inevitable that the situation made her believe he had been incarcerated there for eons, but in fact he was far to young to have been there very long.

The skiff was solid and elegant, with a prow which swept up to mirror the seas with which it longed to contend. At rest on the river, the wood and water nudged and slid across one another like old friends, but old friends who knew rough and dangerous games and were ever ready for one another. With all due respect for the gods who ruled the water and the gods who ruled the winds, the boat had been expertly crafted to grace the river and the sea with the very noblest aspirations. Her builders had toiled precisely and religiously, shaping aged old oak and elm into the planks of a vessel which would always be superior to those who sailed in her and would ever impress upon them her living personality and wisdom. She was called *Swan*, and had something of the imperious character of that bird, but also the concomitant attributes of endurance, fidelity and protectiveness.

There was a little gang plank, and the King stepped upon it with the slow and deliberate tread of one who would never be coming back, a blanket wrapped about him and covering his head. The fog had come down thickly upon all of the place and its doings, and some of Wilfred's myrmidons held flaming torches on the wharf as Daphne now boarded, stowed her lumpy bag and took a place on the thwarts. There were oilskins, a little water barrel and a box of sandwiches in the forward locker – Wilfred was very thorough – but no charts: whilst it was to be hoped they would end up somewhere, they had no destination to reach. Certainly the King felt – if he felt anything – that he was now on the other side of destiny, and this was a feeling which he found gloomy, but comfortable. In fact he found himself believing that the gloom itself would become comfortable. The mist, which no one had expected or forecast, seemed as if it were shrouding the flight of the royals in forgetfulness, just as thunder and lightning might have dramatised such a shift in the history of the realm had god or the climate taken a different view of it.

The King sat carefully in the stern. Daphne lifted the oars one by one and fitted them into their rowlocks, smiling to herself at the ease with which her translation to happiness was to be accomplished. The simple secret had been revealed, by Wilfred: the secret of water, the flowing element of escape but also of evolution – forward and backward.

Just as she prepared to push off with the gleaming wooden blade, a rushing figure pushed its way through the little throng of young men on the wharf, unwrapped something from a paper bag leaned over and thrust it onto Freddie's head. She had some difficulty getting it to stay there and in fact it was awkwardly plonked rather than placed – Freddie did not move. The figure had the mischievous smile and green eyes of Wilfred's fiancee, and the object so unceremoniously deposited on poor Freddie's blanketed pate was the great crown of the realm with all its velvet and gemstones, though the fog smothered their sparkling.

Daphne pushed the boat into the stream and proved herself an accomplished oarswoman as she began to pull away from the stationary little crowd and the commonplace little warehouse – unlikely witnesses of the end of an epoch.

After several minutes, the King, who had remained quite still and never looked back, reached up, grasped the familiar object and without once glancing at it cast it behind him into the great river where it sank gratefully with barely a gurgle. What came into Freddie's mind as he did so was the basilisk. Another mythical beast, surely not one which could really exist, however. It was said to wear a crown, or crown-like crest on the top of its head, for it was the King of all serpents. It was like Medusa, in that its look caused instant horror, which was immediately followed by death. Even the redoubtable Johnson would have difficulty tackling such a quarry. He had a pang of regret that he had not said goodbye to Mr Johnson; of all his subjects who were remotely known to him it was Johnson – the most taciturn, the most unknowable – whose presence he would have found most stabilising in whatever foreign country chance and navigational exigencies should deposit him.

They slid through the muffling fog accompanied only by the slow creak of the oars and the rippling of the waters, passing by the causeway with its immense stone figures which lurked mostly invisible in the steamy vapour except now and then, here and there, when portions of strange anatomies reared up to appear for a moment or two and then fade back into the cloud.

The fog had come down also upon the ship of the singing dog expedition and the two vessels passed one another like ghosts in the night, each unaware of the other's presence. (The dog ship would soon come within earshot of the loyal section of the populace who were still baying for their hero King, and mistake the noise and hurrahs for celebration of their own return, which echoes would render the sight of the empty wharf, when the fog lifted to reveal it to them again, even more eerie. They began to tremble with the thought that some apocalypse had visited the city, and that the voices were no more than the ghosts of the people.)

Ex-King Dagobert IV played the part of his own monumental statue as he sat still in the boat, blanketed in a forlorn sort of serenity, floating steadily towards the obscurity wherein he believed he would find the nugget of happiness which would sustain whatever time he had left.

Daphne meditated and relished the rhythm of her steady efforts, losing herself in the mantra of stroke and breath and creak and ripple, soon attaining a liberating level of consciousness such that she might never stop rowing – only the sudden arising of a new continent could blunt the nirvana of her steady strokes, and the *Swan*'s even progress.

Jemima looked up with anguish into the celestial foliage of the incredibly tall trees, she could not see any sign of Nicodemus, nor hear him. She still believed he was there, somewhere up above probably looking down on her, but even though she called to him continually he would not reveal himself. The light began to fade and she made camp amongst the giant trunks, hoping that her fire and the smell of food might bring him down. Alone again. She stared into the fire and wondered what had become of the spirit of her father, who had not given her the benefit of his opinion for some time. Perhaps he had been promoted to some more remote level of the afterlife. Then she roused herself and half heartedly set up some alarm wires and a camera – she must not forget why she was here – but could think of nothing but what had become of her friend the black ape, and soon sat down again to look into the flames.

For the next few days she stayed in this encampment, spending her time wandering beneath the trees straining her neck in looking up and cupping her hands round her mouth to halloo and call, 'Niiiicooooo.' Several times she was aware of movements in the canopy but she did not see him, and it may only have been squirrels. What was he eating up there? He surely must be starving by now. After a while she began to wonder whether he would follow her if she moved out from under the trees and resumed the river path. But she could not bring herself to do it. Not yet. Just another day.

The multiple sadnesses which accompanied her evening vigils came in a little while to be welcomed as old friends. She thought of Antonio now as a god – marvellous, invisible and unattainable (that strange and beautiful maiden could not have been human) – and it pleased her to know that she had been a witness to his apotheosis. The sadness of the unicorn was almost a comforting sadness, for looking into the night and listening for animal sounds with quiet expectation was a very sustaining emotion; the others might have wandered away but she knew now she would never abandon the quest, not until the unicorn was either found alive or there was proof of its extinction. It was impossible to prove that it had never existed of course, and that was the warmest feeling of all. But the Nicodemus sadness was a very troubling one and there was no relief from it. She threw things onto the fire whose smell he had relished – sausages especially (she imagined herself saying primly to a school biology class, 'apes are not exclusively vegetarian – a common misapprehension', though with the disappearance of her spirit father, she barely recognised herself in that guise now) and watched the smoke as it curled up into the trees accompanied, as it came to be, by a little whispered incantation of entreaty – to the ape himself or to the powers that ruled him – to allow their reunion.

Although the bag with the drawings had been lost, she had a sketch of Nicodemus which Millicent had given to her and she took it out and fixed it to the trunk of one of the tall trees with a thorn. The smoke swirled before it and both obscured and mystified his name and his being and his nature.

Days passed, however, and there was no reappearance of the flesh and blood Nicodemus.

The tigers in the zoo were restless and roared much more than they were wont to do. Perhaps someone had told them that the unicorn was coming and would set them free: free to roam where they pleased, and to eat people if they liked. The other animals, too, were behaving abnormally – some were uncharacteristically static, others were uncharacteristically agitated. Some were meaningfully silent and watchful, others bayed and howled all through the night. The bear, for instance, sat quite still on his little mountain top, his back turned to the castle and civilisation, looking always now toward the wilderness and down the great river.

Pippa and Willis were suddenly nervous of going amongst their charges – animals they had known since they were cubs or pups or chicks had become distant and unpredictable – and sought to delegate feeding and cleaning tasks where they could. In the dark evenings they concentrated hard on the ludo board and tried to ignore the wailings and warnings continually arising from cage and paddock and pen. Yet the sudden blaring of the trumpeting elephants made them jump every time, and they would look anxiously at one another, neither of them knowing what was to be done.

When Wilfred's men finally came, it was just before dawn. Some of them had plundered the castle for suits of armour as protection against the larger carnivores as well as the poisonous, and clanked incongruously amongst their comrades. Others wore thick winter overcoats and balaclavas and the whole jumbled phalanx carried an assortment of sticks and broom handles and nets and hand bells and together they all looked like an assortment of refugees – from an institution perhaps, or, some of them, from time itself. Wilfred having marched them to the furthermost corners of the complex, they began opening cages and encouraging beasts to come out and be driven towards the exit where the massive double doors were chocked open. Some animals there were who, in spite of everything, persisted in hiding in their straw and were only persuaded toward liberty with difficulty, but gradually there accrued an assorted herd of creation to shuffle, ark-like, in a bewildered meander toward the largely forgotten world outside. (Wilfred had confidently predicted that they would forebear from biting one another during their release and nor did they.) They were followed by the motley band of rather hesitant beaters – many of whom appeared to be as unsure of what was happening as the animals themselves – waving staves half heartedly and whose shouts of, 'Hup hup hup!' were mostly muffled by their headgear and lacked any real conviction.

Then Pippa and Willis appeared at the gate, angry and shouting, and berating old Joe the gatekeeper for having let all these people in, and together swinging the double doors to a close. The animals stopped and stood still and then some of them ran backwards and some of them ran sideways and Wilfred's men suddenly fled in all directions when one of the tigers dashed amongst them, but it was only to climb high into a tree.

Sufficiently alarmed and outraged not be in awe of him, Pippa and Willis demanded to know of Wilfred what in heaven's name he thought he was doing. In the ensuing conversation – during which Wilfred puzzled the girls by demanding to know whether any of the animals here present were mythological (the word seemed out of place on his lips, as if he'd read it in a book but never heard it pronounced) – the pair explained that most of the species in the collection would not be able to survive in the local environment if they were simply let out. In addition, many might be dangerous, either to the indigenous fauna, people or innocent farm animals. Wilfred insisted that everything must be free, however, and a complicated discussion ensued in which it was resolved that an expedition of repatriation would be planned and organised. A large and bulky barge was to be commandeered and properly fitted out and all the animals taken back to their countries of origin and released into their natural places.

In the days that followed, the animals seemed to know that something new was afoot, and that on the whole it was a well meant something, and most of them became their old tractable selves again.

How inconceivable would such a thing as the closing down of the zoo have been before the time of the coming of the unicorn? Even though it had been their whole life and *raison d'etre*, Pippa and Willis threw themselves vigorously and zealously now into the zoo's disbandment, like overnight converts to a new religion, and any lingering reluctance was swept away when they understood how important they were to become as the people in charge. Once they began, they found that they especially relished giving orders, and their excitement mounted as they assumed their new roles as captains and commanders and they could not wait to be seafarers and explorers. It is true that at first, when it got dark, they still had to hold hands and encourage one another but it did not take long for the prospect of Jemima Cake suddenly coming round the corner to tell them to stop what they were doing no longer occurred to them. Jemima, it seemed, was not coming back, and everything was different now. They put away the ludo board and spent their evenings sticking flags with animals' names on them into a huge map of the world.

Some weeks later, a very bedraggled Trevor made his limping way through the gates of the zoo – one of which swung on a broken hinge – and stepped slowly amongst the weeds which arose between the flags as he looked from side to side into open and forlorn cages of abandoned straw. As he approached his little brick office he heard a scratching noise made by something just around the corner. The great cassowary had evaded the liberators and lurked alone here, turning his beady eye this way and that beneath the great horny crest on the top of his head which resembled a priestly cap worn at a slightly raffish angle and which dared anyone to make fun of it. Trevor entered in, sat on his chair, took out the little grenadier and stood him on the desk. After a few minutes of staring at the soldier, he got up, went across to the telephone, and began to dial his home number. The cassowary now stood in the doorway. When Trevor stopped dialling, remembering the sight of Millicent striding into the mysterious wood, the cassowary took a step forward across the threshold.

Wilfred climbed the steep wooden ladder high up into the

castle chapel and seated himself at the organ with its banks of keyboards and its myriad pipes and stops. He linked the fingers of his two hands, flexed his knuckles, looked up for a moment at some leprachauns and a mermaid carved into the oak roof beam and launched himself into a colossal toccata and fugue, whilst just beneath him his fiancee pumped the bellows forcefully, staring all the while adoringly with her green eyes at her mysterious beloved's boots as they danced upon the pedalboard. The Bach that thundered from the great reverberating pipes could be heard even in the almost deserted menagerie, where one of Wilfred's men was sweeping out the recently vacated tigers' cage. Odd indigestible remnants of fat courtier were strewn about the place and Wilfred had ordered that they be collected up and burnt. On the whole he was satisfied that this had been the best course, they would only have made trouble, and nobody liked them.

EPILOGIA

Mr Newsome shook a few lumps of coal into the fire in the little range in the back kitchen of what had once been Johnson's cottage, stirred things about with the poker, resumed his chair and his pen, and after sucking the end of it for a moment or two, commenced to set down quickly in an immaculate copperplate hand a long and exquisitely crafted sentence. He was writing his memoirs and his philosophy. After half an hour, he put down his writing board, sat back and called to the very large rabbit for tea and toast. The very large rabbit, however, once again failed to appear, but even in its immateriality provided food for thought, and Mr Newsome frowned a little as he took off his slippers and warmed his feet on the cast iron oven.Outside, a gaunt, long-bearded figure, too morose to be described as forlorn, sat on the ground clutching his knees beside the largest of the neglected apple trees, to which he was securely chained. Culvert Grimes nowadays hardly spoke at all, to anyone, and had certainly resisted all attempts on the part of Mr Newsome to get him to say what he had done with Jolyon Willoughby.

Yet it had only been after he had finished dictating all the stories that he had become mute. There they were, piled up on the dresser, the bound manuscripts carefully written out by Mr Newsome. Grimes had enunciated carefully enough the fictions he and Jolyon had discovered; those starkly shocking tales which the pair had come to believe cryptically encapsulated the elusive truths that lay entwined with history and the unpredictable brutality of daily existence. But now, it seemed, he believed there was nothing more to be said, and neither moaned nor muttered.

For his part, Mr Newsome remained convinced that one day Sir Jolyon would return, shed of his previous shortcomings, and possibly arm in arm with an exceptionally personable lady zoologist. Or possibly an exceptionally personable lady zoologist who was unknowingly heir to a kingdom.

Jemima looked up through the smoke at the totem of Nicodemus's charcoal head pinned to the tree trunk and pondered the myth she'd been caught up in – the tale of the black beast that had slaughtered a Queen. No one knew the whole story and there would, therefore, always be many versions. In time, people would become even more mixed up about it all. The King was sometimes himself a beast, and the beast sometimes a lion. A lion which had sought out its own unicorn just to have a fight with it. Which some said the unicorn won, others the lion; yet others say there was never any battle, and in fact the unicorn materialised in order to save the King from himself. At any rate they both disappeared in the end.

She believed in Nicodemus, but she could not unravel his true part in the story and indeed, she eventually came to understand that there very likely had been more than one Nicodemus. Whereas, hidden somewhere beyond its own riddles and rhymes, she knew there was but one true unicorn, for which she would henceforth ever be lying in wait.

Millicent could feel the eyes of owls upon her as she made her way beneath the dark and silent trees. She could still see Mr Johnson's black bowler hat above the undergrowth as it moved on a track just as abstruse and transcendental as hers, but beginning to diverge somewhat as he began to descend, a few points to the west, whereas her path ascended the incline as many points to the east. She was sure she could hear the faintest tinkling of the strings of a lyre.

Freddie was silently relishing the end of things. Things had never been allowed to come to an end before. He had himself been continuity incarnate, cocooned by perpetuity, born to be a son who was heir only to paternity. But this was now culmination, and with it Freddie came to a sudden understanding of the true shape of things – which was only discernible from the outside. When you came to it, and could see it – could look back at it – the end was flat, satisfyingly flat. There could be no ceremony appropriate to it. It was something plain that came quietly to pass with no proclamation. He was suddenly now undistinguished from those thousands of others who had never been King. What a simple embarkation it had been, and how untrammelled everything would be from here on. At last his imago had broken free, and he was not a purple emperor or anything of the sort, just a dull grey moth flitting happily across the sea toward his own candle.

He stared sternly into the mist over the little waves. The distant noise of baying crowds grew ever fainter until the mewing of gulls extinguished it. There was no exultation, it was at once too fundamental and too ordinary a transfiguration for that. Daphne pulled on the oars with long firm strokes, her tongue extended in concentration, the embodiment of calmness and resolution.

Once they had lost sight of land, and were alone on a grey sea that intermittently hid the horizon as they rose and fell with it, Freddie realised that there had never been such a person as King Dagobert IV at all.

ABOUT
THE AUTHOR

Not much is known about Mr Van Otter. There is a body of opinion in favour of him having been brought up somewhere in the middle of the country, somewhere about the middle of the last century. He has since drifted south, and is often seen staring out to sea from Brighton beach.

He has been a hewer of wood and a drawer of water, has wielded sickle and spade, quill and copier and suchlike, and probably went up to some college or other, once upon a time, and studied something or other.

No one will deny that he has read a lot of books, played the euphonium, taken a lot of photographs, and is happiest on or beside a river. It is indeed, from cruising the backwaters of civilisation that he has found reflected the odd and revealing perspectives of his particular, and unique, brand of fiction.

Also by the author:

THE BOOK
OF OBILOT
David Van Otter

The Book of Obilot is a tale of the adventures and
encounters of a little girl, full of dreams and imaginings.

It is a very strange tale.

The infant Lady Emily Obilot, fleeing from the menace
of the unspeakable Baron Obilot, is searching for her
lost brother, Perceval, who in turn must search for the
Holy Grail. The peculiar and oppressively grim
circumstances of her Cinderalla-like beginnings give
way to equally disconcerting and mysterious territory,
as the narrative is pervaded by resurrected aspects
of the medieval grail romances.

Quaint, freakish and bizarre episodes, as well as the
unsettlingly grotesque, are unfolded in a lively poetic
style, infused with verve and wit, as well as sensitivity
and an oblique, monkish sense of humour.

All aspects of the human predicament are gently paraded
in that subdued and dream-like historical light which seeks
out shades and nuances often invisible under more garish
illumination. It is perhaps a literary allegory to which
Magritte could have subscribed without reservation.

73504455R00240

Made in the USA
Columbia, SC
12 July 2017